Echoes of Glory

Blood on the Stars IV

Jay Allan

system **7**
publishing

Also By Jay Allan

www.jayallanbooks.com

Echoes of Glory

Echoes of Glory is a work of fiction. All names, characters, incidents, and locations are fictitious. Any resemblance to actual persons, living or dead, events or places is entirely coincidental.

Copyright © 2017 Jay Allan Books

ISBN: 978-1-946451-03-3

Chapter One

Excerpt from the Meditations of Tarkus Vennius

I was born a slave, in thrall to those who had conquered my world. I saw my people prostrate before offworld invaders who ruled every aspect of my planet. Yet, my own bondage was short-lived, my memories of servitude few and fleeting. When I was still a child, I saw my parents and their brethren throw off the chains that had bound us for a century, and drive the invaders from our world, cleansing mother Palatia with their blood. The cost was immense in death and suffering, yet no price was too high to reclaim our freedom...and our honor. Those who died in that first epic struggle are memorialized forever on the Wall of Heroes, their sacrifices remembered with almost religious fervor by those who followed.

I came of age amid war and strife, and as a young man I took my place in the battle lines. The task of securing independence had fallen to the generation that preceded me. For mine, the duty was to preserve it, expand it, and to secure vengeance—the blood price of a hundred years of Palatian slavery and misery.

We burst from our homeworld, our fervor unmatched, the cries of millions of murdered ancestors driving us on. We wrought unimaginable devastation on our enemies, killing without mercy. Those who had once called themselves our masters were slaughtered in their multitudes, and the survivors were brought back in their own chains, to spend their lives toiling in the mines and factories to build the Alliance. Their worlds were left silent wastelands, naught but the sound of the wind whipping through the

1

abandoned ruins that had been their cities. Thus was it that the Palatians repaid those who had shamed and humbled us.

I am an old man now, most of my life behind me, a legacy of service and battle. That nascent Alliance, whose new flag I followed to my first wars, is now a powerful nation, spanning thirty systems and fifteen billion human beings. The way we chose— the only way we could have chosen—is hard, not only on our warriors, but even more on the subjugated. For Palatia rules the Alliance, and those defeated in battle are at the mercy of their conquerors. For a people fresh with the memory of murder and slavery, pity is a sparse resource.

Now I look at what we have built, and for the first time I am filled with doubts. The strength that forged the Alliance was wrought in the fires of subjugation, of shame and misery. But Palatia's nightmare will pass from living memory with the last of my generation, and the future will belong to those who have lived their entire lives in strength, in triumph. There is resolution still among us, for we have raised our children and grandchildren to respect our ways. But can lessons and texts and songs sung of the past replace the cold remembrance of a conqueror's lash, of loved ones tortured and killed?

Though I have shared these thoughts with no one, I have begun to fear for the Alliance, to wonder if the iron strength that built and preserved it can endure the loss of our abstemious ways. Can battle waged for plunder and wealth sustain our core as powerfully as combat fought for honor, and for dedication to the state? Will we remain honorable warriors, tough but principled? Or will we become little more than organized pirates, our strength existing only to enrich the coffers of our most powerful families?

Another thought plagues me, one I dare not speak of, nor even allow myself to believe. Did the Alliance I remember ever truly exist? Did the warriors at my side so many years ago serve for honor and country with the selfless purity I'd imagined? Or were the earlier battles I recall fought as much for wealth and material gain as those of today?

Victorum, Alliance Capital City
Palatia, Astara II
Year 61 (310 AC)

Tarkus Vennius was a hard man, a cold man in the eyes of most of those who served him, the very embodiment of the Palatian warrior elite—tireless, pitiless, strong in a way that made granite seem soft as sand. But in the near-darkness of his palatial office, lit only by the dying embers in the gray stone hearth, there sat a grim figure, hunched over. His usual mask of the indefatigable fighter was set aside for a time, exposing the crushing fatigue of an old man, worn by a hard life and too many sorrows.

Vennius was wealthy, and powerful almost beyond imagining. He was respected, feared, lauded as a hero of his people. He had climbed to the very heights of his profession, and the black jacket hanging neatly on the back of his chair bore the platinum starburst, the insignia that identified him as Commander-Maximus, the Alliance's senior military officer and the commander of its fleet.

He knew he was envied, even as he was respected, that untold thousands of warriors dreamed of one day rising to his exalted rank. Yet he felt no joy, no satisfaction in his status, none save a vague and waning sense of accomplishment for the Alliance's decades of victory.

In truth, he felt used up. His wealth, his estates, his many honors…they brought him little joy. The fawning adoration constantly thrust upon him had actually begun to grate on his patience, even the fraction of it he suspected was sincere and not simply pandering by those who sought advancement and favor from him.

He leaned back in his chair, sighing softly, drawing solace from the crackling of the glowing embers. His mind was deep in thought, as it so often was, but this time there was more there than the analysis of fleet strengths and logistics reports. The images in his mind were mostly from the past, and the desire they evoked in him was one he'd never allowed himself to seriously consider before. Giving up his offices, his exalted rank, and retiring to his estates.

It was something he knew was impossible. He'd come too far to escape now. No Alliance officer of his rank had ever left the service, and Vennius knew it was his destiny to die in uniform, one way or another. Yet, there was a worse fate even, one he hoped to escape but knew still stalked him. Tarkus Vennius was one of two or three Palatians whose names had been put forth as candidates to succeed the Imperatrix, when that worthy leader finally succumbed to age.

It was an honor beyond any other, one unthinkable to decline if offered, but Vennius dreaded it above all things. The office was too political to suit his simple soldier's ways, and he knew his grim and cold mannerisms were a poor fit for the job. But he also understood his odds of elevation were high, perhaps an even money bet. And he knew if he was acclaimed, that once again, escape would elude him.

He inhaled deeply, holding the full breath for a few seconds before exhaling. He held a tiny tablet in his hand, no larger than ten or twelve square centimeters. His gaze was fixed upon it, on the image of a woman in her mid-30s, looking out from the screen with a broad smile, one that had been directed at Vennius when the photo had been captured. A sad look found its way onto the old man's face, memories of Katrine Rigellus, from that day and many others, drifting in and out of his thoughts, sapping his usual iron resolve and leaving only a deep sadness in its place.

Kat had been gone for three years now, yet the wound her loss had opened in Vennius's heart hadn't healed. She had been the only child of his best friend, and after Lucius Rigellus's death in battle, Vennius had cared for Kat, coming to look upon her as his own daughter. He'd given her a father's love, and savored a parent's pride in her almost unparalleled series of achievements. She had meant more to him than the offspring of his blood, and he still felt her loss every day.

His own children had been disappointments to him. They had taken their places in the ranks of Palatia's warriors, of course, and their privileged statuses had all but assured them of rapid advancement through the ranks. But they were dissolute, at least by Vennius's hard standards, too distracted by the family's wealth, and by pursuits in areas far afield from the battlefront. He'd been forced to extricate them from scandals and other difficulties too many times, and for all the decorations and accolades they'd received as his sons, neither of them had an achievement of note to call his own.

"You were the ideal, my dear Kat, the perfect Palatian Patrician. Millions look up to you still, follow your example. Your sacrifice has immortalized you, and the echoes of your glory shall never fade." He stared at the image for a few seconds, feeling an unfamiliar sensation, a chink in his icy control, moistness in his eyes. He placed the tablet down on his desk. He wanted to believe all he had just said, to glorify her death, yet there were doubts…and he knew, deep inside, beneath the discipline and indoctrination, that he would trade all Kat's glory, and all of his own, to see her sitting across his desk, staring back at him with that smile. Even just one more time.

He sat, still and silent for a moment, and then he turned toward his screen. He ached to sit and nurse his wounds, to indulge his grief, perhaps drown it in a sea of brandy, but there was no time. The demands were still there, the pressures of his posting. The fleet was back to strength, damaged vessels repaired since the last war, destroyed vessels replaced. The Alliance was as strong as it had ever been—stronger even, at least to outward appearances. But not all was well. There was dissension, talk, in the admiralty and on the Council itself, that the Alliance should have joined the Union attack on the Confederation three years before, that the operation that had cost Kat her life had been too timid, too tentative. That *Invictus*'s defeat should never have been allowed to stay the Alliance's hand.

Such talk was fueled, he knew, by the whispers of Union agents and the spreading of Union coin. It cut at him to think that the Alliance he'd devoted his life to serve, to which his beloved foster daughter had given hers, had fallen so far from its ideals that foreign bribes could steer its policy. He longed to dis-

believe such a possibility, but the evidence had grown too strong
to ignore. He'd sent two Union agents to the scaffold already,
but he had no doubt more were plying their trade, whispering in
the ears of Alliance officers and buying their cooperation with
gold. And, though it pained him deeply to acknowledge it, he
was sure many of those officers were listening. The calls were
growing louder for the Alliance to declare war on the Confederation, to invade and claim its share of the prize, to weaken the
great power that lay closer, and create a buffer against any future
Union aggression.

He'd heard the voices in opposition as well, noble men and
women who could not be bought with foreign treasure, standing by the mandates of the proclamation that had sent Kat and
Invictus on their final mission. The Confederation had proven
its strength, and one of its ships, apparently alone and without
aid, had defeated the Alliance's flagship, and its most decorated
Commander-Princeps. It was now three years into the war, they
declared, and the Union fleets were stopped along the frontiers,
a stalemate that showed no signs of ending soon. Vennius had
added his own voice to theirs, and he was sure the Imperatrix
agreed. The Confeds *appeared* to be weak, even Vennius saw
that in the disarray of their politics and the indiscipline of their
people. But they had a hidden strength that emerged in war.
They had shown it in the previous conflicts against the Union,
and they were displaying it once again, fighting the larger enemy
to a virtual stalemate. No war against them would be short, no
victory easy.

Vennius understood the recent urgency behind the Union
appeals, the desperation to draw the Alliance into the conflict
before the Confederation could bring its superior industry to
bear. Even now, dozens of new ships filled the spacedocks of
the Iron Belt worlds, potentially enough force to shatter the
deadlock and turn the war decisively against the Union. But
Vennius saw no sense in Alliance involvement. The Union was
not to be trusted, and an invasion now only risked another stalemate, one where Alliance fleets diverted the new Confederation
battleships from the Union frontier. The logistics of an invasion

remained difficult, and if the Alliance fleets were bogged down long enough, more Confederation forces would pour out of the shipyards, virtually ensuring a continuing, drawn out conflict.

Still, for all his certainty, it was difficult to make such an argument too aggressively in public. *The way is the way.* How many times had he said it? His people did not avoid wars, they did not fear enemies. Alliance arms were invincible. To even suggest otherwise was the basest treason and cowardice.

No matter how ridiculous it is to claim invincibility, we must continue to do it, to defy rationality in the name of national pride. Kat was our best...and she was defeated. How do they honor her and yet not learn the lesson from her loss?

"Commander-Maximus...Commander-Princeps Horatius and Commander-Honoris Calavius are here to see you." He looked up with a start. The voice was firm, emotionless.

Ah, yes...one of the soldiers...

Vennius looked up with a start. It was late, and he wasn't expecting visitors. He'd sent his staff home hours before. *Except for the guards...*

That was another change as well in recent months, one he did *not* like at all. In all his long decades of service, he'd never felt the need to have bodyguards standing outside his office. That had been Horatius's suggestion. *Insistence, more like it.*

He'd resisted his subordinate's urgings at first, but the more he'd listened to Horatius's reports the more concerned he'd become. Finally, the other officer had gotten him with a blatant call to consider not his own safety, but how valuable a hostage he would be. He still found it unthinkable to imagine Alliance warriors moving against a superior officer, but he also knew things had changed, that the Alliance he'd served as a young man was no more. In the end he'd acquiesced, deciding there was no harm in caution.

"Enter," he said, trying to hide the concern in his voice. The men had not come to his office unannounced at such an hour with good news...he was sure of that. Certainly not both of them. Calavius was one of the two or three officers in the Alliance of rank almost comparable to his own, and a man he'd called friend for half a century. No, this visit in the middle of the night meant trouble.

The door slid open, and the two officers walked in.

"Commander-Maximus…" Horatius snapped to attention.

Calavius stood next to the junior officer, his pose more relaxed, the expression on his face betraying caution, but none of the nervousness of his comrade. It was a less vertical slope he stared up from his rank to Vennius's perch than that looming over his companion. "Good evening, Tarkus," he said, his voice soft, warm, as if speaking not with an exalted officer, but with an old friend. Which he was. The two went back fifty years, to their days as young men, setting out in the hastily-converted freighters and other makeshift craft that had been the first Alliance fleet. "I'd say I was surprised to find you here at this hour, but then this is the first place we looked, so I don't imagine that would be too convincing."

Vennius smiled, briefly and without conviction perhaps, but he managed something, at least, for an old friend. "It is no more burdensome than our battles, my brother, yet I find that the stiffness from my chair wears me down more than our enemies' weapons ever did."

"We are old men, Tarkus. Thus is the field where our battles are fought." He gestured toward the somewhat messy desk. "We have come with news, my old friend. Upsetting news." He turned toward the other officer. "Commander Horatius, please update the Commander-Maximus."

Horatius snapped his arm off his chest and then out toward Calavius, in a textbook example of the Alliance salute. "Sir!" he said sharply. Then he turned toward Vennius. "Commander-Maximus, sir, I have done as you ordered and continued to investigate Union intelligence activity and operations on Palatia…and throughout the Alliance." He paused for a few seconds, clearly uncomfortable about what he had to say.

"Speak freely, Commander." Vennius gestured toward an empty chair in front of his desk. "And please, be seated." Calavius had already taken a seat unbidden, but the more junior officer remained at attention.

"Yes, sir," Horatius said, the nervousness still in his tone. He sat down, though his posture remained as ramrod straight as it had been when he stood.

I was like that once too.

Horatius wasn't a junior officer. He was command rank. But in the presence of the exalted Commander-Maximus, he might as well have been a cadet on his first training cruise.

Such nonsense…yet, I stood there once, no differently than he.

"Now report, Commander. I gave you this assignment because I have faith in your abilities. Whatever you need to say to me, do not hesitate."

The officer sat silently for a few seconds. Then he blurted his response. "There is far more than disaffection fomented by Union agents than we feared, sir. I believe there is an active conspiracy in progress."

The words hit Vennius hard, and he had to fight back the impulse to immediately dispute his subordinate's assertion. "An active conspiracy?" he said simply. "That is a considerable assertion." He'd been worried about trends in the Alliance, but it went against everything he'd believed all his life to even consider that any significant number of his fellow officers could be suborned to treason.

And that's what it would be. Treason.

"Don't discount what he says, Tark." Calavius's voice was grim. "He has assembled considerable evidence. Hear him out."

Vennius looked over at the younger officer and nodded. "Please continue, Commander."

Horatius took a deep breath and launched into a detailed analysis of his investigation, and by the time he was done, Vennius needed a drink.

"Can I offer you a brandy, Commander?" Vennius was looking over at Horatius. He had risen almost immediately after the report concluded and walked to the small bar to the side of his desk. His eyes darted for a moment to Calavius. "I won't even ask you," he said, his tone a failed attempt at humor. "In forty years, you've never said no."

"No, sir," Horatius replied, "Thank you, sir."

Vennius nodded, but then he poured a third glass anyway. He walked back across the room and handed one to each of his companions. Horatius took it without question, as Vennius knew he would do. Would have to do. "To the Alliance," he said, lifting the glass to eye level.

"To the Alliance," the other officers repeated. Horatius took a tentative sip, but Calavius and Vennius drained their glasses in one gulp. It was that kind of night...and the news was *that* bad.

Vennius set his glass down on the desk and sighed softly. "Very well, gentlemen, so how do we move forward?"

Calavius put his empty glass down next to Vennius's. "We need to prepare, to be ready. We need to secure Victorum, for one thing, all the vital installations. The military assets are spread all across the Alliance, of course, but with the fleet at peacetime deployments, much of our strength is here, in the Astara system. Not to mention that the main command centers and logistics nodes are in the capital." He paused for a few seconds. "And the Imperatrix...we need to increase security at the palace as well."

Horatius remained silent, nodding as his superior officer spoke.

Vennius showed no emotion, but that didn't mean he wasn't feeling any. The notion that plotting officers might move against the Imperatrix, whom they had all sworn to serve unto death, was appalling to him, but he didn't let it interfere with his judgment.

"Certainly, all of that, at least." Vennius's expression was hard, like a statue carved from granite. "I want to do more, though. If there are traitors in our midst, we have to root them out. I will see every one of them mount the scaffold for what they have done."

"Of course, Tark...but we need to be ready for anything. With your permission, I will assume personal command over the capital area security forces. I will lock down fleet and army headquarters, and I will make sure all key personnel are protected."

Vennius was nodding, even before his friend finished. "Yes,

Gratian, by all means. I don't think we can afford any carelessness now. I know this is an assignment below your station, but..."

"Not to worry, my old friend. We do what we must in times of crisis...and, of course, no order you elect to give would be too insignificant to obey."

"Thank you. Utilize whatever resources you require, draw what forces you feel are necessary. We must ensure that the Imperatrix is safe, as well as all militarily significant installations. At least until we can determine how deep the treachery runs."

"Consider it done, Tark."

Vennius nodded, and then he sat silently for a moment. Finally, he looked up, his eyes locked on Horatius's. "Commander, I want you to continue your investigations. While Commander Calavius is seeing to our defensive measures, you are going to help me find every disloyal officer and warrior, every Prob and Pleb taking Union coin or conspiring against the rightful government."

"Yes, sir." The officer's tone was sharp, almost feral. Vennius didn't know Horatius as well as he did Calavius, but he'd gotten the impression the Commander-Princeps was old school despite his younger age, dedicated to the principles that built the Alliance. He hoped he was right. Perhaps the worst part of the Union machinations was the distrust it sowed, the way it made him suspect officers, even those like Horatius, who gave no cause.

"I apologize in advance for the lack of sleep you are likely to endure, Commander Horatius...but we are going to rip out this cancer root and branch, and neither of us is going to rest until every traitor faces justice!"

Chapter Two

Grand Hotel
Jade Coast
Planet Oleyus, Iridia III
310 AC

"So, we've discovered one thing for certain on this trip, against all expectations. You actually *can* relax." Andi was lying on her stomach, looking across the bed toward Tyler Barron. She was naked, save for a silk sheet draped over her, positioned strategically enough, she hoped, to interfere with his ability to think about the fleet or the war or even that bloody ship of his. She figured she had a good chance of driving most of it out of his mind, but the battleship always gave her a good run. *Dauntless* was the one thing in Barron's life she wasn't sure she could compete with. And Andromeda Lafarge was always loath to admit there was a rival she couldn't best.

Barron was just through the open glass doors, outside on the terrace, staring out over the crystal blue water. The sea was calm now, the waves just tiny ripples on the white sandy beach. Oleyus's Jade Coast was just about the most breathtaking place she'd ever seen.

Barron turned back toward her and smiled. "I can do a lot of things you probably didn't think I could."

It promised to be a hot day, but it was still early, and the morning breeze coming off the ocean made it as close to perfect as any time she could recall. Save for one thing, a dark shadow looming over paradise. They were leaving in a few hours. Barron had to get back to duty, to his damnable ship, and Andi's crew would be waiting for her as well. Their escape from the universe, from the harsh demands that pulled so relentlessly at each of them, was almost over.

"I know all about the things you can do. But don't try to convince me your mind isn't already back on duty. After these past few months, I think I know you that well, at least."

She had surprised herself with just how much she cared for Barron. She generally disliked government authoritarian types, and she was prone to throw the term "jackboot" around pretty freely. She detested privileged little rich boys and girls who stepped into predestined career paths, courtesy of their names and a roster of accomplished parents and grandparents. Barron was the most famous of them all, his lineage, at least in terms of the navy, the most golden. To the extent she'd ever thought of the famous Tyler Barron before she'd actually met him, it had been with the same derision she directed at all his peers. But he was different, not spoiled, not even a jackboot…or at least not as bad of one as she'd have thought. The more she got to know him, the more she realized that. And the more she liked him. Not to mention the fact that he was easy on the eyes.

She felt like she knew him well, though there were parts of him that were inaccessible, almost impossible to reach. They were very different in many ways, but that was something they had in common. There was an aloofness to both of them, a way they were separate from all those around them.

"It's hard to believe my leave is almost up. Six months seemed like an eternity, but it flew by in an instant." There was a touch of real regret in his voice, she was sure of that. But she could also hear the desire to get back to his ship, his crew. Their extended vacation had come courtesy of the lull in the war, and the long deferred and desperately needed repairs to *Dauntless*. But the quiet at the front wouldn't last forever, and Barron's beloved ship would be ready to return to the fleet soon. For all she liked to think he enjoyed his time with her, she understood that nothing could keep him from the war, not when his comrades would be there, fighting the enemy. He was one of those rare types, sane enough to hate war, yet drawn to it as a calling. She knew he could hardly have been anything else, that his privilege had come with its own burdens, and a reputation he'd been born with, compelled to chase and catch all his life.

"Well, that's not your fault. It was my company, after all, that made the time pass so quickly."

"Yes, it was," he said, more earnestly than she'd expected. His eyes focused on her more intently now, clearly noticing her scant covering, and the curves below. "It's a shame we've got to pack and get down to the spaceport." He paused, clearly forcing himself to look away. "The orbital shuttle leaves in…" He glanced across the room toward a clock on the wall. "…a little over three hours."

Barron could have returned to Dannith on a military transport, of course, but Andi had suggested they take a luxury liner instead, to squeeze out a few last weeks together. It hadn't been easy to find a first-class ship going to a backwater like Dannith, and there wasn't another one scheduled for at least a month, so missing the shuttle wasn't an option.

She stretched her arms out in front of her, sighing softly. "It's too beautiful out to leave," she said, a playful whine in her tone. Lafarge was a hard worker, as deadly serious and diligent in her own pursuits as Barron was in the performance of his duty. But she'd enjoyed the taste of luxury over the past few months, and she didn't relish leaving it—or her companion—behind. Still, it would be good in ways to be back aboard *Pegasus*, back to her own crew. She was a touch envious of the hold Barron's ship had on him, but deep down she realized she wasn't all that different. She longed for *Pegasus* as much as Barron did for *Dauntless*, or close to as much, and though she'd miss him—and paradise—she knew it was time to get back to her own people. Reality had been more patient than usual, but now it was calling.

Her ship was in spacedock alongside Barron's, under repair courtesy of Admiral Striker, his way of thanking her for helping to prevent the Union from obtaining the ancient vessel they had come so close to seizing. The admiral had been generous with her, and though she knew his largesse had been far less than the value of what she had done, it was far more than she had expected. She'd worked the fleet commander a bit, and he'd let her do it, but she'd also known when to quit, to stop pushing and declare victory.

The destruction of the giant warship had likely averted the total dominance of the Union, and she wondered what kind of price could be put on that. Or on the canister of antimatter she'd brought back, that her erstwhile lover had seen fit to take from her. But she was satisfied with what Striker had done, more or less. For all her coldly mercenary ways and her scrapes with the authorities, she was loyal to the Confederation. She knew what the Union was, and what it would mean to live under its rule.

Still, she liked her rewards on the tangible side, cash and other valuables instead of feel good accolades and patriotic satisfaction. For all her acceptances and justifications, she had a hard time shaking the thought of just what price she could have set on a couple hundred kilograms of antimatter. Perhaps that made her seem cold and greedy, but she didn't care what most people thought. *What anybody thinks…*

She realized almost immediately she was lying to herself with that last bit. She liked to view herself as coldblooded, to believe that her uses for people extended just as far as they were helpful to her and not a millimeter farther. That wasn't true, of course, at least not completely. Her loyalty to her crew was genuine, and ferocious as well. She'd fought savagely to protect them on more than one occasion, and she would do it again, if necessary. And she had to admit, she cared what Tyler Barron thought of her…she cared more than she was prepared to acknowledge.

That didn't mean she was apologetic for her ways. Far from it. She clung to her coldness, and her opinion of the universe, and people in general, was pretty dark.

She was fond of Barron—that was as much as she intended to admit to herself, certainly while the war was still raging. There was no place in her life for more than that. She could like Barron, enjoy his company, even indulge in a world-class romp with him as she had just done over the past few months. But that was all she had to give...and, she knew, it was all Barron had to offer as well. There was a spark between them, there was no question about that, a fire that tantalized with "what ifs," but they were set on their paths, and those trails led in different directions.

Besides, as much as she liked Barron, and knew he liked her, he would never be able to understand her, not really. His life had been too different than hers, and she couldn't imagine he would ever relate to her priorities, not until she saw a teenaged Tyler Barron scavenging through piles of garbage in a ghetto's gutter, as she had. She would accede to his sense of honor and duty, buy into the higher-minded things he believed, when *he* had traveled a few kilometers in her shoes, starting that journey with nothing, absolutely nothing. Everything Andromeda Lafarge had ever had, she had gotten for herself...including those proverbial shoes.

Tyler Barron was a good man, far from the spoiled and arrogant types so common among the Confederation's most privileged classes. But, for all his attempted understanding, he could never comprehend what it meant to be utterly destitute, roaming the streets of an industrial slum, a child, alone, looking for something, anything, to eat...or the determination of someone like her to ensure she never ended up in that position again. Barron could discount the importance of wealth, because he'd never known anything else. He could afford high-minded ideals. But Andromeda Lafarge could never forget her poverty.

She looked around the room, at the sunlight brightening the pale-yellow walls, at the breeze blowing the petals of the flower arrangement on the table. She inhaled deeply, savoring the faint saltiness of the sea air. She was sad about leaving the slice of paradise they'd called home for the past several months, but, as pleasant as it had been, it was only a fantasy they'd been living. The war called Barron back to duty, and her own needs and obligations summoned her with no less pull. Admiral Striker had given her a significant reward, more than she'd expected, though it was an infinitesimal fraction of the treasure she'd imagined, fantasizing about selling the antimatter they'd found on the ancient ship...or what they could have realized from the vessel itself and the untold wonders within.

Barron had saved her life, rescued her from the clutches of the Sector Nine, and she was well aware that she would never have managed to retrieve anything at all from the artifact without *Dauntless*'s intervention. But none of that took her mind away from how close she'd come to vast, almost unimaginable wealth. The honorarium the admiral had provided was generous—she tried to look at it that way—but divided up among the crew it was only a good payday...not the retirement score she craved. As much as she wanted to stay, to enjoy the surf and sun and Barron's...pleasant...company, she knew it was time. Time to get back to work. Almost.

She glanced over at Barron, still standing by the patio, and she frowned. He had taken a long glance at her as she lay on the bed, but now he was pretending he wasn't looking at her. His touch of feigned disinterest annoyed her. She scolded herself for her reaction. She'd always prided herself on being cold as ice. She never let people get to her. Never.

Almost never...

She shifted her weight slightly to the side, smiling wickedly as she felt the light silk sheet slide off her and down to the floor. "The shuttle to the spacedock only takes fifteen minutes, you know. And I can pack quickly, Ty." She looked up at him and smiled. "How about you? Didn't they teach you to throw your clothes in a bag on the fly at the Academy?"

Chapter Three

"Things are much worse than we thought, Tark. I've had to relieve a dozen officers in the Capital Area Forces on suspicion of accepting Union bribes. I have no hard evidence, not enough for trials yet, at least, but I felt I had no choice but to replace them. Even a few traitors in key posts could cause immense problems." Calavius had a troubled look on his face. "I don't know, Tark, perhaps I should have…"

"You did the right thing, Gratian." Vennius spoke slowly, a grave tone to his voice. He paused and shook his head. "Whatever else the Union has done, they have us acting like them, imprisoning officers without evidence, without trials. But what else can we do? As you said, it wouldn't take many turncoats in the right positions to cause a series of disasters."

Vennius and his friend walked along the Via Magna. The main boulevard of the Alliance's capital was flanked by massive, blocky buildings, imposing and stark in design. The route ran just over two kilometers, from the Admiralty building at one end to the Council Hall at the other. It was normally busy, with large groups moving about on all sorts of business, but now the everyday traffic was mostly gone. Calavius had imposed a series of curfews and assembly restrictions, and he'd set up a number of checkpoints and roadblocks, predominantly to clear the way for troops movements.

A row of transports moved past the two even then, their heavy treads clanking loudly as they passed. Military personnel and vehicles were hardly an uncommon sight anywhere in the Alliance, but the current traffic levels were far above normal. Vennius had agreed with Calavius's plan to reposition the Capital Area Forces, taking all steps to ensure only loyal units were positioned near the vital facilities.

"What about the palace?" Vennius turned and looked off to the north, to the hulking residence of the Imperator, perched high on a rocky spur jutting out into the sea.

"I have positioned several of my most reliable cohorts to cover all the approaches." He paused, uncomfortably. "I requested permission to deploy some additional forces on the palace grounds to supplement the Imperial Guard, but I was... refused."

Vennius almost laughed. He knew the Imperatrix well, and he could almost hear her telling Calavius to keep his soldiers away from the palace. Vennius had never known a human being as tough and as courageous as the Imperatrix, and he wasn't surprised to hear she had refused additional forces to protect her. She had selected every member of the Imperial Guard personally over the years, and only the most senior of her old veterans were assigned to duty at the palace.

"I am quite sure she did, Gratian. Quite sure." Vennius shook his head. He was worried, more even than he had been a few weeks before, when Calavius and Horatius had first come to propose the enhanced force levels in the capital. "I will speak with her."

"I think that would be wise, Tark. If they can get to the Imperatrix, even a small force could..."

"I know. I know." Vennius nodded, his head moving back to look again at the palace.

"At least she will listen to you."

Vennius *did* laugh this time. "I've known her a long time,

Gratian, but if you think it's a sure thing she will listen to any-one, me included, you're sorely mistaken. She's as likely to send me away with a blast of invective for troubling her with some-thing she already refused to you."

"Well, it's worth a try, anyway. Meanwhile, I'll reinforce the palace area units. We may not be able to deploy additional forces *into* the palace, but we can have them a few minutes away."

"Do it." Vennius turned back, looking down the street as yet another convoy of transports went by. This group had three heavy armored fighting vehicles with them. "AFVs?" he asked, his eyes darting back toward Calavius. "You're really not taking any chances, are you?"

"Just a few, Tark. Think about it. What would happen if a group of dissidents managed to get a few heavy vehicles into the center of the city? They could wreak havoc before we could get our own AFVs in from the outer bases." He paused, as if he was waiting for Vennius to say something. Then he continued, "I just figured it was better to overreact than underreact. Do you think it's too much? Want me to send them back to base?"

Vennius shook his head. "No, you're right. Might be a little hard on the road surface, but what are a few repairs compared to getting caught with our pants down?" He paused for a few seconds. "Is everything in position? Do you feel comfortable about our hold on everything?" Vennius had been fully occu-pied with Horatius over the past few weeks, trying to track down those who had taken Union bribes. They'd made a few arrests, but whoever was running the Union operation was a real pro. None of the prisoners seemed to know much about the others involved...even when Vennius had authorized the use of the enhanced "Red" techniques. The lack of success had sucked him deeper into the operation, and he was glad to have an old comrade like Calavius to handle the capital defenses.

"Do you really think all this is necessary, Tark?" Calavius took a deep breath and sighed hard. "Maybe we are overdoing it."

"No," Vennius replied. "No, I don't think so. There's too much Union money, too much effort on their part for noth-

ing. They're neck deep in the war with the Confederation…
they don't have these kinds of resources to waste on nothing.
There is something going on, and if you ask for my best guess,
it's bigger than anything we're worrying about, and not smaller."
Vennius had been nervous at the first meeting, but now he was
on edge. Something was going on, and his inability to get to the
bottom of it had him worried. It was almost as if the conspirators were getting some kind of warning just in time to cover
their tracks.

"Gratian," he said softly, glancing around to make sure they
were alone. "How sure are you about Horatius?"

Calavius stopped abruptly. "No, Tark…no way. He's solid.
He's one of the most loyal officers I've even met."

Vennius nodded. "Yes…you're right. I know that. It's
just…we're not getting past the low-level types, and none of
them seem to know anything. Even with strong…persuasion. I
was sure we'd be farther along by now."

"At least we've got security under control. With the forces
we've got in position, any attempt at causing trouble is doomed,
at least in the capital and at the vital installations. Even if something happens, we'll have it shut down in an instant, and any
damage will be well-contained."

Vennius looked over at his friend. "Thank you, Gratian.
Your efforts have been above and beyond." He stared out over
the Via Magna, as yet another convoy of troop transports rum-
bled down the wide avenue. "Stay on it for me, my friend. Don't
let anything slip by." There was concern in Vennius's tone, and
he paused for a moment. "I just have a bad feeling, Gratian.
Something is going to happen. Soon. Whatever we're dealing
with, it's well planned. Too well."

Calavius extended his arm, grasping Vennius, hand on forearm, in the Alliance style. "I will stand guard, my old friend,
and I shall let nothing pass. You focus on getting to the root
of this….and bringing the traitors to justice. Together we will
stand watch. We will guard the Alliance. The way is the way."

Vennius gripped his friend's forearm. "The way is the way."
He took a deep breath. "Thank you, my friend. I *will* find them

all, and when I do…"

*   *   *

"Commander…" The officer crouched down, leaning forward on one knee. The quasi-prostration wasn't official Alliance protocol, but Colonel Drusus Lentius occupied a hybrid position in the armed forces. He was the head of Vennius's retainers, which made him half Alliance soldier, and half commander of the Commander-Maximus's private army. The family-bonded soldiers traced their origins back to the earliest days of the insurrections that freed Palatia from its offworld masters, and the greatest families had maintained the tradition, funding private units from the Citizens and Probs on their vast estates.

"Rise, Drusus. By God, you're a Citizen of the Alliance and a decorated officer."

"Sir!" The officer jumped up to his feet. He wore his full-dress uniform, a costume Vennius knew from his own experience was hideously uncomfortable. He didn't feel it was necessary for the retainer to make such a fuss—actually he thought it was ridiculous—though he knew, to Lentius, it was a matter of displaying respect. Vennius was a man who understood loyalty, how to cultivate and maintain it, so he didn't say anything.

He had never cared for the overly submissive trappings of the retainer relationship, most of which had passed out of common usage in the Alliance, but Lentius had always taken it to heart. He had come from a clan of relatively low rank, and he and many of his cousins owed their prosperity to Vennius's sponsorship. The Lentius family, and especially Drusus, took loyalty to almost absurd levels, and despite Vennius's frequent attempts to get the commander of his personal legion to relax, the man still bowed every time he walked into the room.

"What can I do for you, Drusus? You're here for a reason, no doubt?" The family retainers served in the Alliance's wars, but with the current peace, the Vennius Legion had returned home. Most of its soldiers had gone on partial duty and were now pitching in with the work on the estate, especially with the harvest in full swing. Lentius wouldn't be away now, not unless he had a good reason. He was a serious man, and a reliable one. Everything he did had purpose behind it.

"Commander, I am here to request permission to assign one of the cohorts to the capital under my direct command, specifically, to serve as your bodyguard."

Vennius was sitting at his desk, his head lowered, his eyes on a list of dispatches, as he listened to his retainer. But now he looked up, and stared right at Lentius. "Bodyguard? Drusus, have you lost your mind? I have guards all around. There's security in the building at all times, plus the Capital Area Forces positioned all around. In addition, you *have* to have noticed that we've increased force levels everywhere in Victorum. Why would I possibly need more security?" He shook his head. "No, Lentius, I appreciate your concern, but I suspect you can do more for me back on the estates, making sure the harvest goes well. I'm told the grapes this year are particularly plump. I only wish I could spare the time to come home for a few weeks and see it all myself." Vennius took a breath. He'd have thought peace, a rare enough occurrence in the Alliance, would have allowed him some free time, enough at least for a trip home, a few days enjoying the heady smell of the vines, bursting with ripe bunches of fruit. His estates were beautiful, and autumn had always been his favorite season. But it just wasn't possible, not this year, at least.

Lentius interrupted his thoughts. "Commander, I must beg you to reconsider. We have heard rumblings, talk of trouble in the Alliance." He was displaying an uncharacteristic level of resistance, almost defiance, by arguing against Vennius's decision. He hesitated, clearly struggling with the implications of what he was saying. "Can you truly be sure of the loyalty of the forces in the capital, sir? I beg your indulgence in allowing me to take charge of your personal security. The Vennius Legion is one hundred percent trustworthy...I would guarantee that with my life."

Vennius was about to refuse Lentius's request again, but his eyes caught the retainer's. He saw the earnestness, remembered the man's decades of faithful service. Drusus Lentius hadn't come to Victorum, without permission and on his own initiative, on a whim. That didn't mean he was right, but managing loyalty was a complex process. He owed it to Lentius to heed his warnings, or at least appear to give them weight. For an instant, he considered granting the request. But he realized almost immediately he couldn't do it. Rumors of a coup were flying all around, and he could only imagine the reaction to the fleet commander's personal retinue marching into the streets of the capital.

"Drusus, your service, your unswerving loyalty…I cannot overstate how greatly I value these things, or you yourself. You are my comrade in arms, my friend. But I still must refuse your request. Moving my personal forces into the city will only exacerbate things, even point suspicion in my direction. We must be cautious now, and realize that actions can be easily misinterpreted." He paused. "Go back home, my friend. See to the harvest. I have things in hand here." Then he added, "Keep our people ready…but remain in place unless I call for you."

"Commander…"

"My order is final, Colonel." Vennius stood up, walking around the desk toward Lentius. "But know that I trust you without question, and that your loyalty and devotion are among the things I prize most greatly. Now go, Drusus. Go home."

The officer stood still for an instant, his effort to mask his discomfort a dismal failure. Then he looked down as Vennius extended his arm and grasped the retainer's. It was a breach of protocol for the two to exchange such an embrace, but Vennius didn't care.

Lentius hesitated for an instant, but then he took Vennius's lead, and grasped his commander's arm. His face was a mask of conflicting emotions, but he obeyed. He stepped back and saluted crisply, and then he turned and walked through the door.

Vennius watched, seeing worry and doubt in the man's hunched over shoulders and slow, plodding pace. He wished he could have accepted Lentius's proposal, but there was no room for mistakes now. He had to be careful, and see the Alliance through this crisis. And giving anyone reason to believe he was planning a grab for the Imperatrix's chair himself could only make things more difficult and dangerous.

Chapter Four

Sector Nine Headquarters
Liberte City
Planet Montmirail, Ghassara IV,
Union Year 213 (310 AC)

Gaston Villieneuve sat quietly at his desk, reading dispatches. A tall glass rested off to the side, filled halfway with a thick yellowish-green liquid, a sickly-looking concoction made from an assortment of fruits harvested from deep within the jungles of Montmirail's tropical zone. He reached out, picking it up and moving it to his lips. He grimaced as he took a deep drink. It tasted like something that had gone bad a week before—maybe even a month—but the locals swore by the drink as a digestive aid, and Villieneuve's stomach had been bothering him for months now. He was ready to try just about anything that promised relief, and one of the unintended benefits of a government that denied sufficient medical care to most of its oppressed population was the development of a wide variety of home-grown remedies, some of which actually worked.

Including this swill...

It gave him relief from the burning and the almost constant discomfort he otherwise felt, and that was enough to make it worth choking down. He knew his problems weren't the result of any serious conditions—his private doctor had checked him out thoroughly. It was just stress, and the best thing his physician had been able to offer was the rather amusing suggestion that he try to cut down on tension. The doctor would never know how close that comment had gotten him to spending the rest of his life on an asteroid, trying to prolong the lives of miners being slowly eaten away by radiation. The past six months had been a difficult period for the head of the Union's spy agency, and he'd barely survived it. At least he was beginning to hope he'd survived it. Relaxing—never really an option for him—certainly wasn't one now.

Villieneuve had taken a daring gamble...and lost. He'd activated the strategic reserve, without the Presidium's approval, or even its knowledge. He'd committed it to an all-out offensive, just as a smokescreen, a diversion to cover his attempt to retrieve an ancient vessel from the Badlands. He'd planned every aspect of the mission, sent massive forces, pinned down the Confederation fleets. It had been perfectly planned, a sure thing. But still, his gambit had failed. It had failed not because he hadn't sent enough strength, nor because the Confederation had sent too much. Not because he had miscalculated or because his intelligence had been unreliable. No, by all accounts his plan should have succeeded. Save for one thing. Tyler Barron and that damnable battleship of his.

There was no way one ship, especially one as old as *Dauntless*, could have resisted the massive forces he had sent. Not by any rational analysis or understanding of war. But Barron had achieved a stalemate of sorts, destroying the ancient vessel, and with it any chance to reclaim the advanced technology and knowledge of the old empire. Not only destroying it, but doing so and escaping...almost as if to rub dirt on Villieneuve's face. He had almost felt the power in his hands, and word that the ship had been vaporized struck him like a hammer blow.

Things had only gotten worse from there. The analysis of the energy released in the explosion confirmed all too clearly just what he had lost. It was antimatter, that much was certain, more of the precious substance than existed anywhere in the Union—or in the Confederation. Millions of times more. The power he'd lost had not only been that his people could have gleaned from lengthy research and advancement. No, it had been far more immediately tangible than that. Such a quantity of antimatter offered enough power to crush the Confederation, and all the other nations as well. And it had been sitting there for the taking, ready to use in any way he wished. Until Tyler Barron destroyed it. That explosion had cost Villieneuve nothing less than total domination of inhabited space.

He'd been consumed by rage at first, by hatred for Barron and his crew. This was the third time they had interfered with his plans, robbed him of certain victory. It was almost too much to take. But his anger quickly gave way to something far more urgent. Fear. He had lied to the Presidium, forged the orders that had released the strategic reserve, and all for nothing. He had naught to show for his efforts, save for tantalizing images of the ancient vessel, now destroyed…and a shattered fleet, pulled back to the border, incapable of further offensive action. The fact that the Confederation navy had itself been nearly destroyed in the fighting was some solace, but it hadn't gone far to soften the rage of his colleagues when they found out what he had done.

He'd taken what steps he'd had to in order to survive, and on some level, he was still surprised at his success. He had his own foresight to credit, and that of his predecessor. Sector Nine's secret data banks were full of information, including files on every member of the Presidium. Even the Union's supreme governing body was unaware of just what its spy agency actually knew. Corruption, murder, drug addiction, sexual perversions…there had been no shortage of secrets available to Villieneuve for use in bringing the enraged Presidium ministers to heel. His colleagues were men and women who wielded almost absolute power, but they all had enemies, some sitting at that table with them. There was no lack of evidence of egregious thefts or affairs, or in one particularly nasty example, the poisoning of the fifteen-year old son of one of the ministers by a rival.

It had been messy business all around, and he'd won few friends in the process, but that didn't matter to him. Blackmail

and fear were far better guarantors of cooperation than friendship. And for all the anger and bitterness at his unauthorized
actions, one thing was certain. The rest of the Presidium was
more afraid of him now than ever before.

Still, despite his treasure trove of secrets, he hadn't managed to come through the ordeal without bloodshed. Francois
Moldinal had proven to be without corruption—or simply better at hiding it than his colleagues—and he'd been dead set on
bringing Villieneuve down. He'd come close, but, as he had so
often in the past, Villieneuve had his longtime ally, Ricard Lille
to thank for the victory. Killing Moldinal had been a delicate
task, not one he could have assigned to just any assassin. As
much as Villieneuve had wanted to, he couldn't simply have had
the minister gunned down in the street, or even murdered by his
mistress in bed. Killing a member of the Presidium was utterly
forbidden, the one action guaranteed to turn all the others irre-
trievably against him. No, there could be no signs that his rival
had been assassinated. No evidence. Ever.

In the end, Lille had used a poison, a very special one obtained
from his own mysterious sources, unknown in the laboratories
of the Union. It left no trace, none at all, and to even the most
intense medical scans, it appeared that Moldinal had simply died
of heart failure. Villieneuve knew most of the Presidium still
suspected his hand was somehow behind the unexpected death,
but there wasn't the slightest scrap of evidence. With no smok-
ing gun, Moldinal's death was accepted, and amid an avalanche
of hushed threats and outright bribes, Villieneuve moved past
his recent failure and betrayal more or less unscathed, with no
meaningful loss of power or position. Nothing but the pain in
his stomach.

His eyes dropped to the tablet on his desk, and he placed his
thumb over the scanner. The document was highly classified,
linked to his personal ID, and he waited as the AI confirmed his
identity and opened the file.

Lille's words appeared on the screen, the meaningless gib-
berish displayed at first morphing into readable text as the computer decrypted the communique. Lille's reward for eliminating

Moldinal had been another mission, a difficult and dangerous one. The continuation of a previous effort he'd made, one that would have been a success three years before without Tyler Barron's interference.

Villieneuve nodded slightly as he read, and a smile slipped slowly onto his lips, the first burst of genuine satisfaction he'd felt in as long as he could remember. Things were going well, better than he'd expected. Lille was in the Alliance with his people, under cover as spies and provocateurs, not as ambassadors. Villieneuve had never truly given up on the idea of luring the Alliance into the war against the Confederation, and he'd had operatives there since Lille's first expedition, listening, probing for any signs of dissatisfaction in the upper ranks of the Palatian command, seeking weakness wherever it could be found. To his significant surprise, they had found a considerable amount.

Still, his past experiences with the Alliance had left him less than hopeful of success, and the project had remained on a back burner. That is, until the debacle in the Badlands and the massive damage to the fleet left him scrambling for options. The Confed forces were in no better shape than his own right now, but he knew the Union couldn't match the output of the enemy's shipyards and massive industry, not over the long run. Time wasn't an ally, not to the Union. Something had to be done, and the best bet seemed to be luring the Alliance into the fight, whatever it took. And if he couldn't persuade the Alliance to ally with the Union, he needed a new Alliance government, one that would.

He'd known from the start that had not been an easy prospect, nor a cheap one, but as his eyes moved down Lille's report, he began to allow himself to hope it had been a successful one. Ricard Lille was not one to exaggerate his progress, as so many others did, and the list of potential conspirators his people had organized was a long one, with a number of high-ranking names at the top.

Alliance culture was hard, its people raised to be strong. But there was a naivety to it as well, a vulnerability to operators who played the games of espionage and politics as well as those of

Sector Nine did. The more Villieneuve's people probed, the greater the gap they found between the older generations, those who had come of age at the founding of the Alliance or during its early expansion, and those who inherited the wealth and power their parents and grandparents had amassed.

Villieneuve had poured vast amounts of money into the effort, seeking to widen that gulf, to sow dissension and disorder. Assembling the funds, especially after the costs of the first three years of war, was difficult, and he ended up pulling it secretly from hundreds of accounts, repeating the kind of secrecy and deception that had come so close to destroying him months before. But there was no choice, none that he could see. The Presidium would discuss options endlessly while avoiding any definitive action. And he only had a few months before the first new Confederation battleships launched, and perhaps a year before they hit the front in large enough numbers to threaten the deadlock. The time was now. If he was going to turn the war around, win the victory he so desperately needed, there wasn't a moment to waste.

He read the rest of the report. Lille was requesting more coin, an almost unimaginable sum on top of the immense treasure he'd already spent. Villieneuve would have suspected any of his other operatives of graft, but not Lille. His friend was a cold-blooded psychopath, and a man who enjoyed killing above all pursuits, but strangely enough, he wasn't a thief. He tended to demand what he wanted openly, and, if need be, he took it by violence rather than deception. But he accounted for every credit of funding entrusted to him on missions.

Villieneuve extended his hand out toward the comm unit, but he paused before activating it. It would be difficult to obtain the amount of funding Ricard needed while maintaining the secrecy the operation so desperately required. He didn't really trust his people, not even his closest, longest serving operatives…not with something this crucial. He knew the Union's ways too well. Everyone who knew his secrets was a weakness, and Gaston Villieneuve did not put himself at anyone's mercy, not when he could possibly avoid it.

He reached over toward his workstation, punching at the keyboard. He would handle everything himself, directly through his personal AI. He had to rely on Lille, of course, but he had no intention of adding anyone else to that list. Not now. If his plan worked, if his scheme to trigger a coup and replace the Alliance government succeeded and brought that power into the war, there would be time to reshuffle the accounts and cover up what he had done. And even if his machinations were discovered, no one would dare challenge him, not after his efforts had so dramatically shifted the fortunes of the war.

He entered a series of codes, giving his AI access to the Union's central bank. The system would draw what Lille needed, pulling it in increments from millions of individual accounts, covering up the transfers with faked records and arranging for the dispatch of the physical currency Lille needed for his pay-offs. It was as perfect a system as he could conceive, and one he believed—hoped, at least—would cover his tracks for long enough. It helped, of course, that tracing down financial fraud and theft fell within Sector Nine's purview, and as such, within his control.

He glanced back at Lille's dispatch. He'd arranged the funding, and Lille seemed confident he had all the conspirators he needed. There was nothing left to do but issue the final authorization.

He reached out, entering the designated code that only he knew. Then he placed his thumb back on the scanner. He watched as the screen went black, and then a few second later, as a single zero appeared. Confirmation that the signal had been sent. As soon as it reached Lille, the final phase would begin.

Now there was nothing for Villieneuve to do now but wait… and see if Lille could deliver him a new Alliance government, and a new Imperator, ready to repay his debt with an invasion of the Confederation.

Chapter Five

"This is unacceptable, Commander. We have been investigating for weeks now, and still we have nothing to show for it but a few low-level conspirators, none of whom seem to have any useful knowledge on anyone save for other minor players. There have to be more than debtors and disgraced fools in this. The one useful thing we've managed to confirm is that there is—there *must* be—a real plot. There are too many people involved, too much coin. It has to be the Union behind it, and they wouldn't risk something like this unless they had reason to believe they could pull it off." Vennius was shaking his head in disgust as he spoke. His efforts to uncover the details of what he could only assume was a planned coup had grown to consume virtually all of his time, at the expense of other crucial matters. The tension level, the around the clock alerts, the massive troop deployments in and around the capital...it couldn't go on forever. Even without a coup, it was degrading virtually all normal business.

"I have pursued every lead, Commander-Maximum, every scrap of data we possess. To no avail." Horatius stood next to Vennius, almost at attention. The two men were standing along

33

the capital's waterfront, looking northward, toward the Imperial Palace. "I am confident those we have interrogated told us all they knew. They were not particularly admirable specimens, and the means we employed were…thorough."

"Explanations for failure do us no good, Commander. I am aware of the methods employed. I approved them myself. I know you have worked tirelessly, but we must do better. We have only uncovered greater numbers of low-level conspirators. Whatever is coming, it feels near to me. And we cannot be this ignorant when it comes."

"Perhaps the soldiers will be enough to secure the capital and quickly defeat any coup attempt."

Vennius sighed. "You don't believe that, Honorious, no more than I do. That would assume everyone involved in this is a fool. We know that is not the case, if for no other reason than they have eluded our pursuit. The imbeciles we have caught… those at the top have no doubt laughed at our efforts." He looked up again at the massive structure looming over the sea. He'd asked the Imperatrix yet again to allow him to increase the palace garrison, coming close to outright insubordination in his effort, but she'd refused him cold just as she had each of the other times. He suspected she'd have done so in far less genial terms had they not been friends for so many years. The Imperatrix was highly intelligent and her reputation in battle was without compare, but no one had ever called her a patient woman, nor one who tolerated being nagged by subordinates. She expected to be obeyed, and Vennius had seen the results when she was not.

"We can increase the number of inquisitors in the field. Or…"

"No, no…more of what is not working is pointless. We have sufficient resources deployed." He paused. "We are facing something more complex than we've assumed. A Union agent of considerable skill, perhaps a group of agents…and conspirators at a very high level. Dangerously high." He hesitated again, looking right at Horatius. "Whomever they recruited, whatever officers they have suborned, there is no doubt in my mind they

are in positions of power, and far more intelligent and dangerous than the rabble we have rounded up. Perhaps…"

Vennius held his gaze on his companion, and as he did he
felt a tightening in his gut. No matter how he considered it, he
couldn't rationalize the lack of success they'd had. They should
have uncovered something more useful by now. Unless someone
was sabotaging the effort. Someone close to the investigation.

He considered Horatius. The officer had a spotless record,
as Calavius had said earlier, but he hadn't served directly under
Vennius, not until recently. Vennius hated himself for suspecting a well-respected officer, especially one he'd worked with so
closely over the past weeks. But Horatius's involvement in a
coup would explain a lot.

Was it possible? Had his comrade in the investigation been
deliberately steering it away from the truly guilty? His mind
rebelled against the very thought, but despite his attempts to
banish the idea, it remained, and the more he thought about it,
the less certain he felt.

"Sir?" Horatius stood motionless, looking over at Vennius.
"Perhaps what?"

"Nothing, Commander Horatius. I was just thinking out
loud." Vennius tried to behave normally, but he wasn't sure he
managed it. Whatever Horatius was, the officer wasn't stupid.
Vennius found himself twisted into knots by his new suspicions.

No, not Horatius. He is as loyal as they come.

He could see the discomfort in the officer's expression, and
he wondered if Horatius realize what he was thinking. Vennius
felt a wave of guilt. He couldn't imagine a worse disservice than
to suspect a loyal officer of being a traitor. But his duty was to
the Alliance, and that came before everything else. He didn't
want to believe Horatius could be involved in the conspiracy,
but there was no question it would explain his lack of success in
uncovering anything substantive.

"Carry on, Commander Horatius. See to the latest group
of arrests. You may proceed without me." Vennius paused. "I
have…other business requiring my attention."

"Yes, sir." Horatius answered obediently, but there was no

doubt in Vennius's mind the officer knew something was wrong.
And there was something in his voice… Was it dishonor, anger
at the thought of being unfairly suspected? Or was it guilt?

"Report to my office this evening with your report."

"Yes, sir."

Vennius tried to decide if he heard concern in Horatius's
voice. If the officer was guilty, if he'd been part of the plot, he
wouldn't let it show. Vennius was sure of that. Horatius had to
be at least concerned now that Vennius was on to him. If Horatius disappeared, if he fled before tonight, Vennius would know.
He would know that the one man who had worked with him
side by side, who was privy to virtually every action he had taken
over the past month, had been spying on him, misdirecting him.

Making a fool out of him.

"Very well, Commander Horatius. See to it." Vennius spun
around, even as Horatius began a salute, and he walked down
the street, his guards moving into position from where they had
stood a few meters away.

He could hear the soldiers behind him as he walked, and he
saw the shadows moving up as one trotted forward on either
side of him to take point. They were handpicked, every one of
them with a spotless record, but now images of Lentius slipped
into his mind, and he wished on some level that he'd allowed
his loyal retainer to bring troops from the estate. His suspicions
about Horatius had him questioning everything now, worrying
whom he could trust.

Which serves the traitors' purposes even before they make their move…

He hated the whole situation, suspecting his officers, moving through the streets of the capital surrounded by a patrol,
as though he was on a battlefield. He wanted more than ever
before to lay down his stars, resign his offices and return to his
estates. But if that had been inconceivable before, it was utterly
impossible now. He couldn't fail in his duty. Not when the
future of the Alliance was at stake.

He took a deep breath, trying to make sense of his conflicting emotions and suspicions. He had to think clearly now. If he
made a mistake, the results could be disastrous.

No...I can't make any mistakes. Not now...

       *   *   *

The shadowy figure remained in the alley, even as Lille moved closer. He wore a cloak, plain gray with no sign of a uniform or military insignia. There was a hood, draped loosely over his head. He was tucked back in the shadows, and Lille had to hold back a laugh. The officer no doubt thought he was being inconspicuous, but as far as the Sector Nine operative was concerned, his contact might as well have worn a flashing light on his head, fanning the flames of suspicion. Lille knew the best way to hide was in the open, looking like he belonged there, not broadcasting the cloak and dagger nature of the proceedings. It always amazed him how stupid people were.

The Union spy wasn't surprised at the man's skittishness, not really, nor even at his amateurish attempts at stealth. The contact *was* taking an enormous risk meeting him here, even this early in the morning...but Lille had no intention of giving the final go ahead without a face to face encounter. He'd played the games his Alliance contacts had insisted upon, leaving communiques—and sacks of money—in designated places for later pickup, waiting for signals in the middle of the night, and other foolish nonsense. The Alliance wasn't as adept at the ways of espionage as Sector Nine and the Union, but he'd be damned if the bastards weren't every bit as paranoid. It was an odd fit for a supposedly fearless warrior race, but he guessed it had more to do with mistrust of foreigners—him—than anything else.

This time, however, *he'd* set the rules, and he'd held like iron, refusing to back down. He had been compelled to trust his contact, which already had him uncomfortable. At least drawing the man out in the open displayed some level of commitment, of willingness to take a risk. It wasn't much, perhaps, upon which to risk everything, but at least it was *something*.

Lille had done everything he had promised to do. There was a ship in the Victorum spaceport, ostensibly carrying genetically-grown meats and other foodstuffs. In reality, it was packed to the structural supports with money—gold marks, compressed silver bricks, cylinders of pure platinum, an enormous treasure, in virtually every form currency could be physically transferred untraceably.

He hadn't been sure Villieneuve would be able to produce such a sum so quickly, and he suspected his friend and drawn the required metals from just about every place possible, probably even from within the Confederation itself. He found it amusing to think of coin acquired from enemy planets being used to bring about their own ruin. He doubted the Confederation authorities had any true idea of how deeply Sector Nine had penetrated their planets and society. Their own intelligence agency was capable—and Director Holsten was a formidable operative—but the Confeds simply couldn't match a society that spied on every one of its own citizens from birth to death. Spying was bred into the Union's DNA, and the Confederation could never hope to match Sector Nine's effectiveness…or the extreme brutality it so often employed.

The money was the final payment he'd negotiated, and its transfer would signify the start of the operation he'd been working on for months, a project of immense complexity, and one that would change the status of the war. It would begin tonight, and if all went as planned, by this time tomorrow, the Alliance would have a new Imperator. And it would be at war with the Confederation.

"Are your people ready to move?" he said abruptly, stopping just around the corner from his contact.

"Is the final payment here?" the man responded, clearly trying to sound in control. Despite the show of calm, Lille could hear the tension in his voice. He'd heard the same tone in virtually every Alliance official he'd spoken with since he'd begun his operation. For the first month, he'd thought it was fear, that the vaunted courage of the warrior nation's soldiers was a myth, with no more substance than most such claims. But then he'd realized what was truly at play…just how difficult it was for Alliance officers to plot against their own. Almost at once, he came to understand the Palatians, and his handling of the warriors improved dramatically. The culture was simplistic, at least when compared to the manipulative norms he was used to, but there was strength in it, and he realized he had to handle things just right or those he recruited to his purpose would turn on him with an incalculable fury.

"It is. Now, please answer my question. Is everything ready to proceed?" Lille spoke calmly but coldly, projecting as much strength as he could. Dealing with Palatian officers was much like facing off against wild animals. Strength was the only thing they really respected. Or understood.

"Everything is ready. If the funds are delivered, we will begin tonight." The man didn't even try to hide his distaste for Lille, but the Sector Nine operative didn't care. He wasn't looking for friends among his contacts, just for tools he could use. He needed Alliance ships moving down the Dragon's Tail as soon as possible, attacking the Confederation's weak underbelly, taking the pressure off the Union front and drawing off the new battleships that would soon be entering service. He would do whatever it took to see that happen.

He had sought out those he knew were discontented, men and women who were ashamed that the Imperatrix had backed down from confrontation with the Confederation after the destruction of *Invictus*. He played upon that like a maestro, working the sinews of damaged warrior pride, coaxing the embers of dissatisfaction into roaring flames of anger toward those in power. Toward the Imperatrix. She was old, he suggested. Perhaps she had lost her strength, even her competency. Was blind loyalty to a few old men and women in positions of power more important than service to the Alliance itself? Would they follow those without the strength to lead…follow them to ruin?

Lille hesitated, glancing over at the officer, but only for a few seconds. It went against every instinct of his being to trust anyone, especially an asset that was about to turn traitor to his own. *Though, of course, they don't see it that way. They think they're saving the Alliance.* Or at least that's what they told themselves. Not that it mattered. There wasn't any choice. He had to take the gamble.

And he had to do it soon. It had taken longer than expected

to get all the pieces in place…and far more funding. He hadn't expected a stoic race of warriors to be as greedy as they had proven to be. Nor had he anticipated the need to tread quite so carefully with them. The Palatians did not react well to being called liars or unreliable, and the irony of losing their tempers when the man paying them to commit treason suggested they were less than entirely trustworthy seemed utterly lost on them. Of course, they didn't believe they were traitors. He had handled them better than that. They looked up themselves as the patriots, as those rescuing their nation from the clutches of those who would destroy it. The fact that they were also grabbing Lille's coin with both fists and moving to give themselves massive amounts of power was yet another strange inconsistency.

"In the spaceport. A freighter listed as carrying foodstuffs from Pindarus. All in precious metals, as agreed. Plus, a bonus. Ten percent more than the specified amount. For contingencies." *Contingencies…bah. Just an extra bribe, most of which will end up in your pocket.* He knew his contact was the key to the entire operation…and he was just as aware he was creating the wealthiest man in the Alliance, and hopefully in another day, the most powerful.

The man nodded. Then he turned suddenly and looked all around. Lille did the same, but he already knew they were alone. The Alliance was an early-rising culture, but it was insanely predawn now, even for old school warriors. The streets were empty, save for the increased levels of guards, and Lille had been careful to schedule the meeting between patrols. The Palatians were diligent and dedicated, but they were a little straightforward in their approaches to things, and it hadn't seemed to occur to anyone to randomize the times that guards passed various locations.

"All right," the Palatian said. "Assuming what you told me of the…shipment…is correct, we will begin tonight." The man's voice was firm, but there was something else there, a flutter of uncertainty perhaps. It was almost a sin in Alliance culture to show fear, but Lille knew the evening's operation would be difficult for any Palatian officer, and that disgrace and death would be the cost of failure.

A power grab in the Union didn't require quite as much window-dressing and soul-soothing nonsense. The ability to seize a higher position was all that was necessary as justification. But these Alliance fools needed to be convinced the selfish lunge for their own power was really a patriotic act, a sacrifice almost. It was tiresome, and it had made the whole effort far longer and more complex.

"Go then. Verify the contents of the ship…and then see to any last-minute details. Everything must go according to plan."

"There will be no problems. I have arranged everything perfectly. The city is on alert, but I have more than one surprise for those planning the defense."

Lille would have made a face, but years of practice at discipline caught if before it came out.

That's one way the Alliance officers are like our own political masters. They're arrogant as hell…

He nodded, and then he glanced around quickly before setting out down the street. It was time for him to get out of sight. He would be no help in all that had to be done today and tonight. All he could do now was hide, and wait. The day promised to be an auspicious one, and getting himself caught could wreck everything before it even got underway.

Chapter Six

Imperial Palace
Victorum, Alliance Capital City
Planet Palatia, Astara II
Year 61 (310 AC)

"You did not touch your evening meal, Your Supremacy. May I bring you a plate? Perhaps some soup. Or biscuits and fruit?" The valet leaned forward in a bow, his reverential respect for the woman he was addressing utterly clear in both his tone and posture.

"No, Poscuta, nothing. I am not hungry." The woman was old, her skin loose, giving away the full extent of her almost nine decades. Yet the eyes staring back at the servant were still bright, ice blue and crystal clear. Her thick mane of long silver hair was pulled back in a loose braid. There was hardness in her gaze, and wisdom. And, at least for the valet, a man who had served her faithfully for more years than she cared to recall, she suspected there was, just perhaps, the slightest touch of softness detectable in her otherwise firm tone. Age had softened her, dulled the fiery aggression of her youth…and it had taught her to appreciate true loyalty.

"Some tea, perhaps?"

Her impulse was to refuse again, but then she said simply, "Very well, Poscuta. Some tea." It was easier to take something than to continue to refuse.

"Yes, Your Supremacy. At once." The servant bowed lower, holding the position for a few seconds before he sprang up and hurried from the room.

The woman was accustomed to such servitude and deep respect from those around her. Indeed, for much of her long life, Flavia Augustulus Junia Grachus had exercised almost unimaginable power, first as a leader of Palatia's rebellion and then as one of the Alliance's most celebrated admirals...and for the past twenty-one years, as Imperatrix, the head of state of Palatia and all its subject worlds. She had also been a slave once, a lifetime ago, one who had endured immense suffering and abuse as a young woman. Memories of those bitter days still cut through her like a blade and fueled the rage that had driven her through her wars, and still lived inside her to this day, despite the mellowing of a lifetime's weariness.

She stood up, more abruptly than she'd intended, and she stumbled slightly, feeling a flush of bitterness at the lightness in her head and the weakness in her body. She had been a warrior, once, a tireless crusader, and in her prime she had led thousands into battle and laid waste to all who had oppressed her people, bringing death and slavery to those who had been the masters. She feared no enemy, none save time. No warriors had ever bested her, no fleets nor legions of soldiers had defeated her, yet age marched on, and she was powerless before its onslaught. Her mind clung to its usual sharpness, but the body that carried it, and the energy that powered it, were waning.

My time is almost at an end. Soon, I will have to choose one to succeed me...

She walked across the room, toward the great glass doors, swung open and tied back, the ocean winds blowing the light draperies into the room. She pulled the robe she wore tighter against the breeze. The sea air refreshed her, and it made her feel awake, pushing back the fatigue of age, just a bit. That was reason enough to endure a touch of coldness. She'd ordered the doors to remain open, ignoring the ocean chill at this time of year, and also the overwrought warnings of both her doctors and her security teams.

They would lock me in a vault if I allowed it…and in a hospital con-nected to a hundred machines…

Her age had become a liability, she knew, even a danger to the Alliance. The prospect of selecting her successor was a daunting one, with no clear choice extant. Tarkus Vennius was the likeliest candidate, but she'd known the old warrior for decades, and she understood just how much he detested the idea. Vennius was a creature of duty, and she had no doubt he would accept the appointment if it was thrust upon him, but he would never campaign for it, or call upon his friends and allies to support him.

That was unfortunate, especially since Tarkus was the best choice, a true Palatian warrior, in whom lived on the spirit that had built the Alliance. Her people needed such strength and sta-bility, especially now. She knew there was discord spreading, rip-pling waves of disorder that would have been unthinkable even a few years before. She understood the pleas of her guards to take greater precautions, but she, who had fought countless bat-tles, been wounded half a dozen times, struggled against terrible adversaries…she would not, in the twilight of her life, allow fear of some imagined assassin to control her actions.

She stepped through the center door, out onto the stone terrace. It was broad, the floor an interlaced pattern of gray and white granite, quite decorative, at least by the often sterile standards of old Palatia. The rails were a heavy balustrade, and below, the surf crashed hard into the jagged rocks.

The palace stood on the edge of Victorum, in the center of one hundred manicured hectares along the rocky coastline, on the extreme north of the city. It was a large structure, looming boldly over the jagged cliffs and the solid bedrock of its massive foundations, built by her predecessor more as a fortress than a palace. She had tried to resist the trends away from the ascetic ways of the early Alliance, yet she had to admit her resolve had been less than total in that regard. The edifice owed more of its current status to her indulgences than she liked to admit, the glass doors and broad terrace overlooking the sea a prime example. Power wore away at discipline, even as the tides did to the great stone cliffs. Years of conquest had insulated Palatia from the front lines, and the harshness of the stoic structure had gradually given way to more comfortable appointments.

Softness. You decry the waning of the Alliance's warrior spirit, yet here you are, savoring the ocean breeze, staring off into the light of the moon, watching it dance on the rippling waves. Is your heart still that of a warrior? Or are you just an old woman, slipping into dotage?

She was troubled. The weakness she saw in herself was rife throughout the Alliance, and in far greater measure. The Patricians and Citizens were warriors still, raised in accordance with the old dictum. The way is the way. Probs still strove to attain full Citizenship, a goal that almost always required distinguished military service. Adolescent Palatians still completed the Ordeal, enduring torment and suffering to prove their worthiness for a life as warriors. And many still died in the effort, young, not yet men and women, deep in the wilderness…the traditional culling of the weak, even from the ranks of the highest-placed families.

Yet those same young fighters had come of age in a strong Alliance, a victorious one that had conquered system after system, and enjoyed the spoils of those triumphs. They were wealthy, and they knew only success in battle. Defeat seemed an impossibility to them. They had become arrogant and grasping. The Alliance was passing from the control of those who remembered the bitterness of defeat and servitude to a new generation, one that understood only dominance. She wondered if her beloved nation, and its demanding philosophy and culture, could survive the transition.

Or if it should…

It had been three years since she'd sent *Invictus* to probe the Confederation's defenses, and its resolve. Three years since she'd allowed herself to listen to the ambassador from the Union, to his entreaties that the Alliance join in the war against the Confederation. It wasn't the way, to side with other powers, to trust to allies. The Alliance had stood alone, always, viewing all others as potential adversaries. That had been the way, and it had led to six decades of uninterrupted victory.

But that time had come to an end. She'd known that then, when she'd signed the orders that had sent Katrine Rigellus and one thousand of the Alliance's best to their deaths, as she knew it now. Confidence in its warrior ethos, in the power of its arms, had been the core of the Alliance's strength, but it's half century of conquest had finally brought it into contact with larger powers. It was shameful, perhaps, to acknowledge that the Alliance might be unable to defeat either the Confederation or the Union by itself, but that didn't mean it wasn't true. And the prospect of facing both, or one of them gorged fat on the spoils of the other, was a nightmare…one that could destroy the Alliance if she failed to exercise care and steer her people wisely through the current conflict between the two.

She had been weak three years before. She had given in to calls to join the Union's war, accepted the demands to plan an invasion of the Confederation. She'd let herself be persuaded that an Alliance that did not take the chance to seize part of the Confederation was destined for marginalization.

But she had set her own boundaries, decreed that *Invictus* would test the enemy defenses before an invasion could commence, and in the aftermath of that disastrous mission, she had held to her proclamation and turned down the continuing Union entreaties, maintaining Alliance neutrality, even in the face of considerable disagreement among her own officers and people.

She had even expelled the Union ambassadors, convinced they were more spies than diplomats, but she knew the influences were still there. She'd allowed Commander Vennius to execute the pair of operatives he'd found, but she didn't fool herself any more than her venerable fleet commander did. Those who'd been caught were only a tithe of the agents the Union had sent, and she was certain the others were at work even now, plotting, planning, seeking to exploit the dissension her own decisions had caused.

There was Union coin too, so much that it was impossible not to be aware of its presence. She knew such things wore away at the stoicism that lay at the core of Palatian culture, that there was unrest, an unthinkable state of affairs in the early years of the Alliance. Officers in her armed forces were allowing themselves to be tempted by foreign bribes, something she'd have thought inconceivable five years before.

She was angry at the Union interference, but she couldn't imagine it was a true danger, one that threatened the Alliance in any core way. Her belief in her people was too strong, forged through long years of battle and sacrifice. But what would happen to the Alliance in twenty years, when she and the rest of her brethren, those who had built the great nation, were gone? Or in forty years, when Vennius and his peers were all dead as well. Who would replace them? And what would become of the Alliance she had dedicated her life to create and protect?

Her muscles tensed. Her battle reflexes were still sharp, even as the body that carried them slowed. She turned and stepped back through the door, her eyes darting around, moving to the sound. It was Poscuta, of course, back with the tea. She had expected her valet to return, of course, but a lifetime of war left its marks, and she doubted she'd ever be able to truly relax and let her guard down.

She looked over, and she had to suppress the hint of a smile when she saw the servant setting the silver tray down on the table. There was a pot, large enough for a state banquet, and surrounding it there were small plates—cookies, biscuits, even a small pile of tiny sandwiches, anything, she suspected, the valet had imagined he could pass off as a normal accompaniment to tea.

He's determined to get me to eat something…

She had become quite attached to Poscuta over the years, more so than was perhaps proper for the Imperatrix of the Alliance. She had even offered to free him from his bonded service, to set him up in a profession of his own, but he had begged to remain with her. She had acquiesced, perhaps with a touch of relief, as she was a creature of habit and was glad to retain his service. But she had also secured positions for his children in prestigious military units. With any fortune at all, they, the son and daughter of an offworld servant, would one day become Citizens of the Alliance.

"Shall I pour your tea, Your Supremacy?"

"No, Poscuta, that will not be necessary. I will see to it."

The servant paused for an instant, almost as though the idea of letting her pour her own tea was some sort of failure on his part. Finally, he said, "Very well, Your Supremacy. Is there anything else I can do for you?"

"No, I believe I have everything I need. You may retire for the even…"

Her head snapped around suddenly, those combat instincts at work again. There was noise, coming from outside, much louder and more concerning than her valet bringing tea this time.

Airships…

She felt an urge to disregard it. There was always air traffic around the capital. But there was something wrong. There were too many, especially for this hour, and from the sound, they were heavy units. And they were coming from more than one direction.

Those are military, and far more than a standard patrol. I'd know if there were any maneuvers scheduled for right now…

She stepped toward the door again, peering out into the night. There were definitely ships moving. She could see the lights zipping by against the inky night sky. She couldn't understand. There was no way the capital could be under attack. There was no enemy within five jumps of Palatia.

Then she heard the first explosions.

Chapter Seven

Mechcorp Orbital Shipyards
Above Thralia, Chyrus III
310 AC

"I must say, Director Carstairs, your progress has been nothing short of astounding. Mechcorp is months ahead of any of the other shipbuilding concerns. The people of the Confederation owe you and your workers a debt of gratitude. I thank you, and bid you accept my gratitude for your patriotism." Van Striker stood in the center of the room, looking out at the three immense ships enmeshed in a spidery web of structural supports and umbilicals.

"I am humbled by your words, Admiral Striker, and I cannot state emphatically enough the honor you do us by visiting our yards." There was a haughty tone to the man's words, and a bit of the accent Striker had come to realize over the past few days was typical of the Thralian upper classes. Of course, Philodor Carstairs was about as upper class as it got, though Striker knew it had been the man's grandfather and father who had created that reality. If he'd been compelled to guess, he'd have bet Philodor—actually, Philodor III—would prove to be the generation that coasted on the work of his descendants…before his own children began to whittle away the family fortune.

Though Carstairs has certainly held up the family tradition better than might have been expected, even if his brain is a poor copy of his father's . . . or his grandfather's, the real robber baron who built an empire on the backs of a few million Thralians. He's beat more effort out of his bonded workers than any of the other Iron World moguls. Something to be proud of, I suppose.

Striker scolded himself for feeling morally superior. There had been very little—nothing?—he himself hadn't sacrificed to the demands of the war effort, and the oppressed laborers of Thralia were no different. He disapproved of Carstairs's brutal methods, but he was thrilled to have three new battleships so close to commissioning. They were no more than three months from joining his battered fleet, and perhaps beginning the long process of turning the tide of war.

"May I rely on that three-month estimate, Director? I cannot emphasize strongly enough how badly these ships are needed at the front."

"Yes, Admiral, of course. I will even try to shave some time from that, perhaps delivering in ten weeks, or even nine."

Striker felt a pang of guilt at the feral tone in Carstairs's voice. He had some idea of the hell to which his urgency had just consigned Mechcorp's workers. But the pity vanished quickly. The workers would survive their ordeals, at least. It was more than he could say for the spacers who had died—who would die— under his command in battle.

Most of them will, at least. Mechcorp's got a pretty ugly safety record.

"You have your nation's thanks, Director. And mine." He turned and looked back out over the massive shipyard. It stretched kilometers into the distance, its massive frame continuing out as far as Striker could see. The immensity of the complex made the ships appear to be smaller than they were. The new *Repulse*-class battleships were a huge step up in power from most of the Confederation's pre-existing warships. Named for the fleet's martyred flagship, destroyed earlier in the war, the vessels outmassed the old *Repulse* by nearly 500,000 tons. Each mounted a quad particle accelerator as a primary emplacement, replacing the old dual systems, and the rows of secondary batteries lining its sides were more numerous, and half again as powerful to boot. The ships carried ninety fighters, launched from three separate bays, and the whole thing was powered by four massive fusion reactors. The ships would be the most powerful things in space, and they would make a huge difference when they reached the front, even just these first three.

"I would like to invite you to dinner this evening, Admiral, at my estate on the White Coast Archipelago."

Striker felt like he'd been punched in the stomach. Another dinner, more speeches. He almost longed for an alert, some kind of emergency pulling him away. But there was no escape. None at all. "I would be delighted, Director. You have my thanks yet again." *How did you become such a good liar? You were an honest man when you had less metal on your collar...*

"Splendid. My shuttle will leave in half an hour, Admiral. We can enjoy a drink on the trip to the surface—I have a wonderful Megaran Pinot Noir—and share stories. No doubt, yours are far more interesting than mine, though I fancy I can tell an amusing take or two of our efforts in building these ships."

"That would be fine, Director." Striker had seen too many of his people killed in battle to tolerate feeling sorry for himself when the greatest danger he faced was being bored to death, but he still couldn't purge the image from his head of shoving a gun in his mouth. A coward's escape, perhaps, but seductive nevertheless in its own way. "If you'll excuse me, I have to check in with my staff before we depart." *And if I don't get two minutes to myself...*

"Of course, Admiral. Shall we say docking bay two in twenty minutes?"

"Yes, Director...I will be there." *Unless I can figure a way to escape...*

He turned and walked away, sucking in a deep breath as he did. The front had been quiet since the last big Union offensive. Both sides had been too badly hurt to sustain any real action, and a stalemate had taken hold, one Striker suspected would last until one fleet was able to get enough repaired and new ships in the line to launch an attack. Meanwhile, both the Confederation and Union forces were digging in, building bases and fortifying moons and asteroids. When heavy combat did resume, he knew it would be hell. Even if the Confederation was able to get its new ships in the line in greater numbers than the enemy, the clear advantage would be a defensive one, security against another enemy assault. To launch its own offensive, and push to force the war to a conclusion, the fleet would be compelled to drive through a hornet's nest of defensive installations. He didn't even want to think about the cost, or how many more of his people would be killed before this cursed war was over.

He looked around the room, pausing for a few seconds and watching as a group of workers began to pull down the chairs and the makeshift grandstand where he had given his speech and handed Carstairs a medal. He didn't wish for active hostilities to resume, not exactly, but the extended quiet period had made him a sitting duck for duties like this one. He'd been to more than a dozen worlds since the last big battle, and the only weapon he'd wielded was his mouth. Most of those trips had been to receive honors, or to give them out, mostly pointless accolades to those receiving praise more for political influence than any real heroism. It was an open question which of the two he hated most.

"Admiral Striker, sir?" He turned and saw one of his aides walking across the room. He didn't know what the officer wanted…probably someone needed an urgent signoff on fuel consumption reports or something equally vital. Still, it would be cover, at least. He didn't care if one of his aides needed to know how much sugar he wanted in his tea, he was going to make sure it took him the full twenty minutes to consider it.

He felt his stomach tighten as he turned and got a good look at the officer's expression. Whatever it was, it was serious. "I have a communique for you." There was a slight pause, then: "It is Priority Status One, sir." The captain reached out, extending a small tablet. Striker's insides tensed. An enemy offensive? It was impossible, wasn't it? Every intelligence and scouting report had confirmed the Union forces were no more able to advance right now than his own fleet.

The admiral took the device, and he looked around the

room, his eyes searching for a quiet place. He turned and walked toward a corridor off to the side, waving for the aide to follow. He pressed his thumb down on the verification sensor, and a few seconds later, the screen filed with text.

It was from Gary Holsten. As soon as Striker saw the name of the Confederation's intelligence head, he knew for sure something important was happening. His eyes moved quickly down the page, hungry for details. But there were none, just notice that Holsten was approaching the planet, and a request that Striker meet him when he docked in a few hours.

Striker felt an immediate edginess. Holsten hadn't come all the way to Thralia to meet him just to shoot the shit. He was coming for a reason, and whatever that was, good or bad, it was damned sure important.

Who are you kidding? It's almost certainly bad too...

Striker ran his finger across the screen, deleting the message. It hadn't contained anything terribly useful, save for word that the chief of Confederation Intelligence was on his way, but "read and delete" was standard procedure for Priority One messages.

He took a deep breath, his mind racing, wondering what news Holsten was bringing. He had no idea what it could be, but there was one thought pushing forward, a celebratory one pushing its way through, amid all the stress and worry.

This was the perfect excuse to get him out of dinner.

*   *   *

"You look good, Gary. Much better than you did at Grimaldi." Striker smiled as the Confederation's top spy approached, and he extended his hand. He and Holsten had communicated frequently, but he hadn't been in the same room with his friend since just after the fateful battle that had seen both sides' fleet virtually destroyed. "I think the wine, women, and song of Megara agrees with you."

"The song, maybe, though with the war on, there's little but martial music and marches these days. Patriotism has become quite fashionable in the capital." Holsten stepped up and clasped Striker's hand firmly. "The wine and the women are less helpful, at least to my health and stamina. They seem locked in a death match to see which can finish me first."

The two shared a laugh. Striker would have once considered the high-ranking spy an unlikely friend, but as he'd come to know Holsten better, the two had grown close. Holsten's reputation as the pleasure-loving and dissipated scion of one of the Confederation's wealthiest families had, surprisingly, turned out to be far more fiction than reality, a carefully-crafted cover for his more important work. He might be seen frequently with models and actresses on his arm, stumbling around seemingly under the influence of alcohol or more potent substances, but Striker had come to realize that the real Holsten was something entirely different—serious, dedicated…and smart as hell. It was Holsten who had engineered the plan that put Striker into the top command position, replacing the well-meaning but incompetent Arthur Winston, something the spymaster had done at great risk of personal ruin.

"So, your message was cryptic enough," Striker said softly, as the two walked off to a secluded corner. "But I've learned not to discount the importance of your communiques."

Holsten laughed. "Perhaps you could have this time. I may be overreacting, worrying about nothing."

"I doubt that. What is it, Gary?"

"We've been getting disturbing reports for months now."

"From the Union?"

"No…from the Alliance."

Striker felt his stomach tighten. The Confederation had barely escaped a two-front war, courtesy of Tyler Barron's success in defeating an Alliance vessel sent to probe for weaknesses. There had been a period of considerable tension after that, as the Confederation command waited to see if the Alliance would indeed join the Union in its attack. But nothing happened, and the Alliance, which had never officially acknowledged the incursion its ship had made into Confederation space, had even opened limited diplomatic relations with the Megara government. If that situation had changed…

"The Alliance? Have they taken any steps toward…"

"No, not as far as we can see, at least. The Alliance doesn't appear to have made preparations for an invasion." He paused. "The concern is about Union activity in Alliance space. Intelligence operations and the like. There have been signs of unrest. Apparently, a considerable number of Alliance officers believed they should have attacked us three years ago, and even lobbied hard for just that action at the time. From the intel crossing my desk, my best guess is Sector Nine is trying to use that to their advantage."

"How? I can't imagine the Union is looking for trouble with the Alliance, not that they can even get there very easily."

"No, not that. They still want the Alliance fighting us."

"Of course, but you said there are no signs of preparations for war."

"No, none. My sources are confident the Imperatrix is absolutely against any hostilities with the Confederation at this time."

"Then what could the Union…" Striker's words petered out. He wasn't as familiar with the ways of Sector Nine as his friend, but he understood them well enough that Holsten's concern was becoming clear. "They're trying to influence the Alliance government somehow? But they couldn't go to war without the Imperatrix's approval, and that seems unlikely. From what little I've heard, she seems unlikely to yield to persuasion." He shook his head suddenly. "No, wait…they want to replace the Imperatrix. A coup. That's what you're afraid of, isn't it?"

"Exactly. We overlooked such a possibility because of the uniqueness of Alliance culture, but there's no way the Union has committed the resources they have—even just what we know about—unless they thought they had a real chance to pull it off. So, I looked at it from a different point of view. No Alliance officer would sympathize with the Union as a polity. They'd be disgusted by all the backstabbing and political infighting. But I could see them feeling shame for backing down on a war with us. That could be exploited…and no organization in human space is better equipped for that kind of operation than Sector

Nine."

"So, you think a coup is a real possibility? That Sector Nine could succeed in installing a government that will join them in the war against us?"

Holsten nodded. "Can you imagine the impact of that? Not only a two-front war, but one against a fresh combatant. What forces would you deploy to meet a massive Alliance invasion? One that came a month from now, or two?"

Striker shook his head. "I don't even know. It would be a disaster. We'd certainly have to divert every ship coming out of the yards to the Alliance front, and most of the repaired vessels too. That would allow the Union to use its own new construction to gain superiority. We'd likely end up on the defensive on both fronts, hard-pressed everywhere."

"And that assumes the Alliance doesn't strike before you have enough new ships to even mount a defense. All intelligence suggests they can move very quickly when they decide to attack. Remember, their entire culture is based on their military strength. Even when they're at peace, their people are waiting to be called back to war."

Striker let out a long sigh. "So, what do we do?"

"We have to know what is going on, first. We have to be ready to intervene, if the chance arises."

"But we don't have any forces on that front, nothing except a few old patrol ships."

"We'll have to send something. Immediately. Even if it's just a show of force, like last time."

Striker stared down at the floor, silent for a moment. "I can't think of anything that is available. The three ships here are the first of the new construction, but it will be almost three months before they're ready. I can't take anything from the main front. We've barely got enough there to hold the line."

"I realize you can't put together a fleet, at least not for some time. But we need something on that front, one ship, at least, ready in case we need to take some kind of action. Our ships are faster than theirs, don't forget, and that might give us options if we have to try to delay an offensive, conduct harrying actions."

He paused. "Or if an opportunity arises to intervene in some way. Obviously, preventing a coup would be far more advantageous than piecing together a way to meet an attack resulting from a successful one."

"I was under the impression we had a very small intelligence presence in the Alliance."

"Your impression was correct. We don't have the agents or the prep work to materially interfere with whatever the Union is doing, at least not in terms of counter-intelligence. But whatever they are planning, there will likely be resistance, Alliance officers in opposition to the plotters. Perhaps we will get a chance to do something, to help them in some way. In any event, I think we need to have someone in position."

Striker was silent for a few seconds, and then his eyes widened. "You're talking about Tyler Barron."

Holsten hesitated now, and then he simply said, "Yes." A moment later, he continued, "I am hesitant to send him on another desperate mission, but we're not sure this is that at all. He may just sit at Archellia for a few months, and the situation in the Alliance may blow over, or resolve itself." His tone suggested he didn't believe that any more than Striker did.

"*Dauntless* is all the way over at Dannith. Maybe we can find another ship to send, one that's closer." Striker wasn't the type to hold back from demanding the best from his people, but *Dauntless* and her crew had done more than their share in terms of desperate solo missions. It seemed...wrong...to send Barron and his people. Again.

"I'd like to give *Dauntless* some standard fleet duty too, Van, but Tyler is the clear choice for this. He's our only commanding officer with any experience with the Alliance."

"That experience was destroying one of their ships, killing their senior captain. Is that really useful, at least in terms of working with them?"

"For us, no, it wouldn't be. It would be a source of animosity. But Alliance culture is quite different than ours. They respect strength above all things. Defeating one of their best commanders will be considered a sign of strength. They are as likely to respect Barron as to be angry with him for his victory."

"Even so, Gary…" Striker's voice trailed off. He didn't know what to say, or even what to think. He'd had no idea what Holsten's message was about, and he'd have never guessed it was this.

"There is another reason it has to be *Dauntless*, Van." There was grim resignation in Holsten's voice. He didn't sound any happier than Striker about sending Barron and his people into the fire yet again. "He's not only our best captain, he's by far the one with the most experience on independent missions. We're talking about a situation where he might have to make significant decisions on his own, ones that could have tremendous bearing on the outcome of the war. Who else can we send? Who else would you trust to make crucial choices, moves that could avert war with the Alliance…or lead to it."

Striker didn't like it. He didn't like it one bit. But Holsten's argument was flawless. There was no other choice. None at all. "Captain Barron should be on his way back from leave, as well as the rest of his crew. My last report from the shipyards on Dannith indicated that *Dauntless* would be off the line and ready for duty, either by the time he and his people arrived, or within one to two weeks after."

"Archellia is how far from Dannith at maximum speed?"

"Five weeks, maybe four if he really pushes it. *Dauntless's* reactors have been replaced, and the new ones produce forty percent more output. Combined with the engine upgrades, and the new model thrust compensators, that old ship is quite a bit faster than she was before. Tyler will have a number of surprises waiting for him."

"Not the least of which will be orders to proceed back to Archellia."

Striker shook his head. "No, that will certainly not be the least of it. He had quite a struggle out there." He turned toward Holsten, his face a mask of uncertainty. "Let's hope we're not sending him into another one."

Chapter Eight

"Commander-Maximus?" Horatius stood at the open door, peering into Vennius's palatial office.

"Come in, Commander Horatius." Vennius's tone was cold.

Horatius stepped into the room, noting the others standing just inside the door. Calavius was there, and two others, soldiers, wearing what looked like some kind of riot gear.

"Sir?" Horatius said softly, concern slipping into his voice.

"Commander, as you know, we have had little success in penetrating the ranks of the Union-backed conspiracy, despite considerable effort."

"Yes, sir. But…"

"Be silent, Commander." Vennius stood up from his desk and stared across the room at the now clearly uncomfortable Horatius. "I did not want to believe that someone close to me was interfering with the operation, preventing us from finding what we sought. And I certainly did not suspect you…not until there were no other explanations. Still, I hesitated. Finally, I asked Commander Calavius to look into the matter, still hoping my suspicions would be quickly proven wrong. But it was not to be, unfortunately."

"Command…"

"Silence!" Vennius roared, slamming his hands down hard on the desk. "Coin, Horatius? You turned traitor for coin?"

"Sir, I don't understand what you are talking about." Horatius was clearly upset, barely hanging onto his control. "I never took…"

"You deny knowledge of the funds Commander Calavius found in your accounts? Or the recent purchases that seem to exceed your means? The estate in the Northern Provinces?" Vennius turned and spun around the workstation screen on his desk. "Perhaps you'd like to take a look, and refresh your memory."

Horatius stumbled forward, shaking his head as he did. "Commander, I have no idea what…"

There was a loud crack…and Horatius fell to the floor with a dull thud, a spray of blood hanging for an instant in the air where he had stood.

"By God, Gratian, have you lost your mind?" Vennius stared in utter shock at his old comrade, standing perhaps three meters from where Horatius had been standing. The pistol was still in his hand.

"He was guilty, Tarkus. A traitor. There is only one punishment for such a crime." Calavius's voice was frozen, no sign of uncertainty, even of discomfort, over what he had done.

"We didn't know that. Not for sure. He rated a trial, at least. Or at least questioning. And even if he was guilty, we should have interrogated him. He was high-ranked enough that he would have had considerable information. Now we will never know." Vennius turned and extended his hand over his desk.

"Don't, Tarkus." Calavius's voice was cold, menacing.

Vennius turned back, focusing intently on his friend. "What is this, Gratian?"

Calavius shook his head. "I'd have preferred for this to have gone differently, my old friend. But I couldn't take the chance on Horatius. He was too smart, too persuasive. He was likely to convince you of his innocence…which would have been that much easier because he *was* innocent. At least in the context you meant."

"You?" There was anger in Vennius's words, and suddenly realization. Even more, there was utter shock. "You're involved in this?"

"Involved? Oh yes...I am very involved, Tarkus. You might say I'm the mastermind."

Vennius stood silently for a moment, struggling to come to terms with what he was hearing. "So Horatius was..."

"He was as steadfastly loyal to the current regime as they come." Calavius shook his head. "But your suspicion came at an opportune moment. It was simple to plant some money in his account, and fake a few purchase records."

Vennius was fighting to stay alert, his mind racing for options, trying to decide what to do next. Yet, even as he fought that battle, he felt despair trying to take him. He'd as good as murdered Horatius, and he'd blundered into making a gift to the conspirators. He was a damned fool, and all his efforts had been for naught. Worse, he had helped the traitors. "Why?" he asked plaintively.

"Horatius had to die, I'm afraid. He was too dangerous."

"No," Vennius said, his voice becoming darker. "Why?"

"Oh—why did I join the movement?"

A look of disgust came over Vennius's face. "Movement? Is that what we call treason now?"

"Treason is a moving target, old friend. Many of us considered it treason when the Imperatrix cravenly shied away from war with the Confederation, when she allowed herself to be intimidated by the loss of one ship. Did you not feel that, my old friend? Did the warrior's blood coursing through your veins not boil at the shame of it all?"

Vennius's eyes darted around the room, glancing quickly at the two soldiers Calavius had brought with him, ostensibly to arrest Horatius. *What a damned old fool I have been...*

"Don't try it, Tarkus. These soldiers are elite veterans, and they are mine."

Vennius was about to reply when he heard a distant rumble. Then several more, all in rapid succession. *Explosions...*

He turned toward the window, but he stopped short at Cala-vius's command.

"No, Tarkus. Stay where you are. Don't make me do some-thing I don't want to do."

"The explosions…"

"Yes, that is the operation beginning. In a matter of moments, my people will control every vital installation in the capital."

Vennius could feel himself losing the fight against despair. "I did this…I put you in charge of the capital defenses. I opened the door for you."

"Yes, well I can't deny that your delegating the defenses to me made it far easier. Though, if it makes you feel any better, I have no doubt I could have prevailed anyway. It might have taken another week or two to get things in order, but nothing would have changed in the end."

"We have known each other for fifty years…more. I called you friend."

"I am your friend, Tarkus. But this is beyond friendship. This is duty. To the Alliance."

Vennius snorted derisively. "Duty! I am sure that is a pleasant fiction, that you take the Union's coin in the name of duty, that you sell out your people for foreign wealth out of patriotism."

"We could argue the aspects of duty, my old friend, but that would do neither of us any good. Those who forged our Alli-ance took action against the established order, as we do now. And I did not take the steps I did for gold. I was wealthy enough, as you well know."

"Power…you seek power, as if you did not have enough already."

"Power is a tool, my old friend, nothing more. The ability to direct the Alliance the way it should go. The way it must go… that is what is important."

"The Imperatrix…"

"She was a great hero to her people, Tarkus…but she has lived too long. Her strength has drained away, leaving nothing but an empty shell. She should have met her end in battle, years ago. That would have been a fitting end for someone of her achievements."

"You're going to kill her." Vennius turned again, looking toward the window as another series of explosions ripped through the night. There were sounds of closer fighting now, even out in the street in front of the admiralty. He had a sick feeling in his gut. Calavius was no fool. He almost certainly had overwhelming force in place at every key position…which meant those combat sounds were loyal soldiers, holding to their posts, fighting hopeless battles. They were selling their lives to buy useless minutes, sacrifices that would change nothing.

Nothing at all.

"I take no joy in it, Tarkus. But her weakness cannot be allowed to bring the Alliance down. She is old, older than a warrior is meant to become. It is past her time."

"And you're going to make yourself Imperator."

"Yes, Tarkus. It is a heavy burden, but I have no choice. I must see our people to their destiny…and that is not cowering before the Confederation, fleeing like scared children because of the destruction of one ship. It is our future to rule, not to follow. To add the worlds of our enemies to our empire."

Vennius stared in horrified disbelief. Calavius spoke of causes, of saving the Alliance. But this was nothing but a grab for power. He wanted to rule. Vennius wondered how long his friend had nursed such desires, how long treason had festered. Now, the Union had given him the chance. "You miserable traitor. You are nothing but filth. Excrement I wouldn't clean from my boot without a stick." Half a century of friendship had turned to disgust in an instant. To hatred.

"It is not surprising that you cannot see, that you do not understand." There was anger creeping into Calavius's voice as well. "I see now it was foolish to expect otherwise."

"Nonsense. Don't add lies to your treason. Give old friendship that miserable concession, at least." Vennius paused, glaring at Calavius, his eyes defying the hopelessness in his heart. "You're going to kill me as well, of course." Vennius knew he was going to die, but he wasn't going to give his enemy the satisfaction of seeing his fear. He would die as he had lived, as a true Palatian.

"I had hoped not to, my old friend. I allowed myself to imagine, for a few passing moments, that I could convince you of the wisdom of my course, that you would join me, help me on this journey. But, on some level, I always knew you were too stubborn. You will stay with your cause to the last, even when it has veered from its purpose. Even when it leads to destruction."

"You can tell yourself whatever you want, Gratian, but never doubt I see the truth. Make all the farcical claims you wish to duty, to saving the Alliance...but you are nothing but a black traitor, seizing power to appease your own vanity." Vennius had wracked his brain, struggled to come up with any way to inter-fere with the disaster unfolding around him. But there was noth-ing. Nothing except to anger Calavius, and perhaps interfere with his judgment. It was hopeless, almost certainly so, but it was all he had.

"I am truly sorry, Tarkus, that our long association must end this way. But where I must go, where the Alliance must go, you cannot follow." Calavius moved his arm up slowly, bringing the pistol to bear.

Vennius stood, unflinching, staring at his former friend with not a hint of weakness or fear. "You will fail, Gratian. You and every traitor in your service will die in the streets." He took a deep breath. He knew his time was at an end, and despite the outward bravado, he feared deeply that Calavius would prevail.

"I am sorry, Tarkus. I wish there was another..."

There was a loud crash, coming from the outer office, fol-lowed an instant later by gunfire. Calavius turned abruptly, his eyes flashing toward the door as the firing outside intensified.

Vennius saw his chance, not at survival perhaps, but at tak-ing down his old friend. He leapt across the room, his arms extended out in front of him as he did.

Calavius saw him coming, as did the two guards...but both were too late. The soldiers fired, but their shots ripped through the air behind Vennius. The Commander-Maximus was no lon-ger a young man, but his combat reflexes were still with him, and this was a vital moment, one that required all he could muster.

Calavius tried to bring his pistol around, but Vennius reached out, grabbing his opponent's wrist, shaking the weapon free to clang loudly on the floor. The two men grappled, dropping to the ground, as they did.

Vennius knew the soldiers would intervene. They couldn't fire now, not without endangering Calavius, but it would only be a few seconds before they grabbed him and pulled him off his foe. He struggled to get his hands to Calavius's throat, but his adversary resisted, long enough, at least for a pair of hands to grab him from behind and yank him hard. The soldier pulled him off of Calavius, and he ended up on the ground, at the feet of the other guard. The man held a rifle, and now he turned the weapon toward Vennius.

Calavius scrambled up to his hands and knees, breathing hard, spitting a spray of blood from his mouth. "Shoot him! Now!"

Before the man facing Vennius could respond, the door flew open, and more soldiers burst through. A blast of fire took down the menacing trooper, and Vennius spun to the side, moving toward cover behind his desk.

The second of Calavius's soldiers opened fire, taking down one of the newcomers before he was shot twice in the chest and fell over a table on the far side of the room. Calavius dove through the door, into the outer office, where a battle still raged. Vennius was about to follow, when one of the new soldiers ran up to him, dropping to the ground and reaching out to him.

"Are you wounded, sir?"

Vennius was stunned, confused, for just a second. Then familiarity took hold. He recognized the livery—the Vennius Legion. And then the face. "Drusus?"

"Yes, Commander-Maximus." Drusus Lentius pulled away the helmet that had partially obscured his face.

"I sent you home."

"My apologies, Commander-Maximus, but I took it on myself to disobey. I will submit myself for any punishment you impose, and of course I will resign my commission…as soon as we have you to safety. But I just couldn't leave you in danger."

Vennius stared at the retainer, his face still a mask of surprise. "How did you know to come here now?"

Lentius hesitated. "It was Aurelius, Commander-Maximus. When the first shot was fired, he contacted us, just before the room filled with rebel soldiers." Vennius could see his aide standing behind Lentius, his left arm covered in blood. "We came as quickly as possible, but most of the building and the grounds are heavily occupied." He turned and looked back toward the door. "We have to go, sir…we have to get you out of here. We don't have much time."

"Aurelius…you knew about this too?" Vennius began to stand up, Lentius reaching out an arm and assisting.

"My apologies, sir. I will accept my court martial and punishment, but Colonel Lentius was so sure there was a danger…I couldn't allow you to be assassinated. Not even to obey your commands."

Vennius shook his head. "Loyalty is more than blindly following orders." He turned toward Lentius. "You picked a good time to be insubordinate, Drusus. You have my thanks, both of you." Then, suddenly: "Calavius!" He moved toward the door. The outer office was a nightmare, at least a dozen bodies strewn about, including a number of his soldiers wounded. But Calavius and the rest of his people were gone.

"He escaped, sir." Lentius was standing next to Vennius. "Commander, we have to get you away from here. There are enemy soldiers everywhere. They control the city. We can escape through the underground supply tubes, but only if we go now. If we can get out of the city, we can make for home and rally loyal units."

Vennius didn't answer. He turned his head, looking out the window, now shattered, the cool night air pouring in along. The sounds of battle had died down already—the result, he supposed, of the rebels gaining control of their objectives. But there was still combat, in the north. He moved toward the window, staring out at the great structure overlooking the sea. There were flashes of gunfire all around it, and explosions as well.

Of course...I gave Calavius control over the capital garrison...but he wouldn't have been able to infiltrate the Imperial Guards. They would still be loyal...but they will be overwhelmed.

"We need to get every soldier you brought with you, Lentius."

"Commander? We have to get you out..."

"No," he said, his voice like iron. He walked around his desk, reaching down into one of the drawers and pulling out a heavy pistol, old with a battered grip worn smooth from use. He looked up, his eyes cold, resolute, moving from one of the soldiers in the room to another. "We have to get to the palace. Now. We have to save the Imperatrix."

Chapter Nine

Barron watched the small shapes moving around his ship's hull—tenders, freight carriers, even clusters of workers, clad in heavy space suits, completing the final bits of work on the rejuvenated battleship. *Dauntless* had been old when he'd taken command, and more than a little worn by years of service, but that was nothing compared to the punishment his beloved vessel had endured at his hands. She had been battered and patched back together so many times over the past four years, he was stunned that she had endured, that she had continued to give him what he needed...and gotten his people through one desperate situation after another.

She was almost unrecognizable now. After several fits and starts in terms of repairs over three years of war, *Dauntless* had finally gotten her just due. A complete overhaul. The battered and pitted sections of her armored hull had been replaced with shining new sheets of alloy. The burned and melted wreckage where half her secondary batteries had been blown away was replaced by gleaming new guns. The sight of her looking almost new was emotional for him, and he took a deep breath, even as a smile made its way onto his lips.

"She looks great, doesn't she, Captain?" Anya Fritz had walked up behind him, but Barron had been so lost in thought about his ship's rebirth, he hadn't heard a sound.

He turned and glanced at his chief engineer. "She looks magnificent, Fritzie. I still can't understand how you kept her going before, with all the damage and wear. That should be a bit easier now, at least." His smiled slipped just a bit. "I'm hearing rumors that you didn't take any of your shore leave. That you stayed here and worked with the crews."

"I took a week off, sir. Took a tour of Dannith, saw the red crystal beds and the magma river. It was interesting...for about two days." She paused. "You know me, sir. How could I not be there when they stripped *Dauntless* down? They took her apart and put her back together again, better than ever. And I was part of the whole thing." The engineer was smiling, and he could hear the sincerity in her words.

"From what I was told, you tried to run the whole show. I've heard two things from the engineering staff since I've been back. 'Commander Fritz is a technical genius,' and 'Commander Fritz is an unrelenting pain in the ass.'"

Fritz nodded, allowing a little chuckle to escape her lips. "I may have been a bit pushy, sir. But it's my people who will have to keep all this fancy new stuff functioning in battle." She paused. Then she continued, her voice a bit grimmer. "We know what it is like, sir, don't we? What it's really like."

Barron nodded slowly. "We do, Fritzie." He turned and looked at Fritz. "Which is one more reason I wish you'd taken more of a break. We're heading back to the front, and there's no way of knowing when we'll have another leave."

"I'm fine, sir. I feel rested, in my own way. Working in a spacedock with no one shooting at you...it's almost like a vacation. And I have my handprints on everything in there, Captain. When those Union bastards start shooting us up again, there won't be a circuit or a system I don't know like the back of my hand.

"I was going to check with the yard chief, but I suspect I'd be better off asking you. When will she be ready to set out?"

"She's already had a test run, sir. The reactors are fully fueled and operational, and all power systems check out. Almost everything is ready to go." She gestured toward the observation panel, and the flurry of motion beyond. "Most of that is just minor adjustment, and repairs on problems found during the shakedown cruise. They should be done tomorrow, or the day after at the latest. The new fighters are uncrated and waiting in bay twelve. They'll start shipping them over tomorrow. Figure three days to load up the holds with food and other expendables." She paused for a few seconds. "I'd say a week, sir, if everything goes smoothly. A few extra days if last minute problems crop up."

That was sooner than Barron had expected, a fact he owed, no doubt, to Fritz's involvement. He'd been prepared for a month's wait or more, but now the prospect of returning to full duty was on him. He felt strange in a way, after so much time with Andi, but he also knew he was going home. That this was where he belonged.

"Well, Fritzie, I still wish you'd gotten more of a rest, but you have my thanks for taking care of our baby here." Barron took one last look at his ship. Then he turned toward his engineer. "I think I'll see if I can find Atara, and catch up on other business. Make sure everybody else made it back from shore leave in one piece...or if I have to extricate any of the fighter pilots from some base's brig."

*   *   *

"Andi!" Vig Merrick had been walking across the landing bay toward Lafarge, but now he broke into a run. He raced up and threw his arms around her. "It is so good to see you!"

"And you, Vig," she replied, grabbing onto him and returning the hug. She had lost herself on her vacation with Tyler. She'd never been away from her ship or her people for so long, not since they'd first set out together. But *Pegasus* had been laid up in spacedock, and while Admiral Striker had agreed to repair her ship at the navy's expense, she knew the schedule was subject to the needs of the fleet's warships. The work on *Pegasus* should have taken perhaps two months, but she'd known it would be longer, perhaps as much as six. And she'd been right. From all she was told, the final work had been completed just the week before.

"Have you seen her yet?" Merrick pulled back and smiled at her.

"No, I just got back. Have you?"

"Yes...she looks great. They wouldn't let me go aboard, but I saw her from the outside. She looks almost new!"

Lafarge smiled. "That will be interesting to see." *Pegasus* was many things, but in her experience with the vessel, "new" was a word she'd never have used. Her beloved ship had been old when she'd gotten her, at least fifty years, and she'd looked every minute of that. Andi had never been able to piece together a clear picture of what services her ship had performed in its past lives. *Pegasus* had been built as a scout of sorts, intended to explore asteroid fields for areas worth exploiting for mining. But the assortment of systems that had been added over the years, not all of them entirely legal, suggested a more checkered past, even before Lafarge and her pack of adventurers had stepped aboard for the first time.

She returned Merrick's smile. "What do you say we go take a look right now?" Lafarge was acting cool, but the truth was, she couldn't wait to see her ship.

"Let's do it."

"Have you seen any of the others?"

"Dolph is back, and Lyn. I don't think Lex ever left Dannith. As far as I know, he hit the Spacer's District pretty hard." He paused. "I think he's having a little trouble...to be honest, I think most of the crew is. It was...difficult out there, and it's a little hard to shake. I can't say it hasn't gotten to me a little."

Lafarge nodded. "I'm not surprised." She paused. "I'll see if I can find Lex after we get back from *Pegasus*. Maybe talking about it will do him some good." She'd been worried about this sort of thing. Her people were tough, but the last mission had been hard beyond anything they had ever done before. They'd been in danger before, certainly more than once, but this time they'd been dead center in a combat zone, and the theoretical nature of the war with the Union had been replaced by cold reality. They had all come through, no question of that, held it together while they'd had to. If they hadn't gotten back to Dannith and brought back help, Andi knew she and Vig wouldn't have made it, that they would most likely have been tortured to death by Sector Nine.

She had a way of dealing with things, of moving forward from almost anything, without regrets or scars that impacted her abilities. But she knew most people weren't wired in quite the cold-blooded way she was. The fear and stress from something like what they had gone through affected them…and she knew very well, some of her crew—her friends—might struggle to move forward, especially the next time they faced danger.

Though next time won't be like the last time…

I hope.

"I think that would be helpful, Andi. Maybe you can get him to talk, to let it out. I tried, but he was wound up tight. All he told me was, he was fine. But that's bullshit."

The two stood silently for a moment. Finally, Lafarge said, "Well, let's go see what our ship looks like."

"Captain Lafarge?"

She spun around. She'd recognized the voice immediately, but she hadn't really believed it until her eyes confirmed who was standing in front of her.

"Admiral Striker…"

"Have you seen your ship yet?"

"No, sir, I was just heading over there now." Her voice was its usual emotionless calm, but inside she was on edge. She had no idea what Admiral Striker would be doing at Dannith. The planet was the gateway to the Badlands, but it wasn't particularly close to either the battle front or the Core and the Iron Belt systems that formed the heart of the Confederation.

"I think you'll be pleased. I know you're not accustomed to dealing with the navy like this, and no doubt, not all of my colleagues and predecessors would have fully appreciated your true value as an ally, but I pay my debts, Captain."

"Thank you, Admiral. It is greatly appreciated."

"And you weren't kidding about some of the...unorthodox...stuff you've got in that ship. It's probably the first time a fleet admiral has ordered the base crew to overlook a number of, how shall I put it, less than authorized systems in a civilian craft. But again, as I said, I pay my debts. It was a pleasure having you as an ally, Captain. I trust wherever your travels take you, we will remain such?"

Lafarge smiled, despite the tension she still felt. She'd never heard anyone admonish her to stay out of trouble quite so pleasantly and elegantly. "Of course, Admiral." She paused, and her tone became a bit more serious. "I am well aware of the debt I owe you."

"Not at all, Captain. We are even, and I hope friends as well. Perhaps just consider that not all naval personnel are, what did you call us? Jackboots?"

"Yes, sir. I believe that is what I said. Though I would never say that about you." She smiled again.

"That is gratifying."

"I'm surprised to see you on Dannith, Admiral." Lafarge changed the subject abruptly. It was still nagging at her. *Why is he here?*

"Yes, well my duties take me many places. I just wanted to stop and give you my best wishes, Captain. And to thank you again for all your people did to make the operation at Chrysallis a success."

"I am glad we were able to help, Admiral." She almost asked him point blank why he was there, but she knew better than that. *Does it have anything to do with Tyler?* She realized she was making wild suppositions. *But am I? Tyler is the best captain in the fleet...and what else would drag the navy's commander all the way back to Dannith?*

"Best of luck to you, Captain. I sincerely hope we meet again."

Striker's words echoed through the thoughts filling her head. "Oh, yes Admiral, I hope so as well." She hoped she didn't sound as distracted as she felt. "I'm sure we will," she added, more out of politeness than actual expectation.

Striker turned and walked away. Lafarge was watching, but her thoughts were elsewhere. She and Barron had said their goodbyes. They'd both agreed their time together was a passing moment, one that would end when they reached Dannith. He had his duties, and she had her own life and responsibilities. They might meet again, have more time together, but only time would tell on that. It had been painful, more so than she'd been willing to admit to herself, but it was the way things had to be. There was a connection between them, a powerful one, but it didn't change the fact that their lives were heading off on divergent vectors. She considered herself a realist if nothing else, and she would not let herself buy into romantic nonsense that had no place in the real world.

But now she was worried. It was one thing to take off, to fly lightyears away from Barron, knowing he was heading back to war. But somehow the thought of him being sent on another... crazy—she stopped herself before "suicidal" popped into her mind—mission hit her hard. She'd knew Barron could handle being in battle, that his ship and his crew were such a finely tuned instrument, they could handle any normal duty. And some level she knew that was a failure of her normal commitment to realism, though it was one she needed. But now she was filled with dread. Against all her normal logic and cold analytics, suddenly she was overcome by fear, a strange certainty that Tyler Barron would be going into extreme danger. That he would be killed.

"Are you ready, Andi?"

She shook her head as Merrick's words sunk in, trying to clear the thoughts that had begun to consume her. "Yes...of course. Sorry, I just thought of something I have to do. But let's go see the ship first."

Yes, go see Pegasus *now. But after that, you're going to find out what is going on here, why Van Striker is on Dannith...and where he's sending Tyler...*

*   *   *

"Archellia, sir?" Barron looked across the table at the admiral, unable to hold in the surprise at the orders he'd just been given. "But I thought we'd be assigned to the front." He paused. "It's just that...we've been all over the place, Admiral. Except in the line with the fleet." Barron had been stunned when he'd reported for his orders and found that Admiral Striker himself was on Dannith, waiting to brief him. But when the admiral told him where *Dauntless* was going, his jaw had almost hit the floor.

"I understand your frustrations, Captain. Both because you've missed most of the major fleet actions...and also because, quite frankly, your people have been put in even more deadly and dangerous situations time and time again. But I'm afraid there is no alternative this time." It was Striker's turn to hesitate now. "Tyler, we may have a major problem with the Alliance, one with potentially deadly implications."

Barron looked across the table, trying to ignore the pain that was suddenly eating away at his stomach.

"Three years ago, you and your people forestalled disaster with your victory at Santis. Now, we have reason to believe the Union is again attempting to bring the Alliance into the war. We cannot be sure, and I hope this is a false alarm, but we just can't take the chance."

Barron took a deep breath. He didn't know what to say. He couldn't argue with the admiral, but he hated the idea of going back to the Rim. The fight his people had endured out there was the most terrible he'd experienced. The thought of going back was...upsetting. There were a lot of ghosts out at Santis.

"What do you want us to do at Archellia, sir? *Dauntless* is looking great, but it's not like one battleship can take on an entire Alliance invasion fleet. Archellia had almost nothing three years ago...with the intensity of the fighting on the front, I'd be surprised if there was more than a patrol ship or two left there."

"Three," Striker said softly. "There are three small patrol vessels, and the base's fighters, of course...but that's not why you're going. Three years ago, you went to the Rim to prevent an invasion, and you did just that, Tyler. You and your people. Now, we need the same thing from you."

"But, Admiral, I can't believe the Alliance would send another single ship to probe our defenses. If they come again, they'll come with everything they have."

"It's more complicated than that. We think Sector Nine is heavily involved somehow, trying to get engineer a coup, to get the Alliance to ally with them. We need you to stop it."

Barron looked back, stunned. "Stop it? How?"

Striker looked down at the table for a few seconds, then back at Barron. "I don't know, Tyler. You'll have to decide that when you see what is happening."

"From Archellia? Or do you want us to advance? Where? To Santis again? The Dragon's Tail? Into Alliance space?"

"Whatever you feel is necessary and appropriate." Striker put a small box on the table and pushed it across. "You have been named acting military governor for the Rim Sector and beyond the border. We don't know what is going on…all we have are guesses. We need someone up there who can make decisions on the spot…without going up the chain of command."

"Me?" Barron stared back, a mix of shock and horror on his face. "I'm not a flag officer, sir, and I'm certainly not qualified to make decisions like this. What are my guidelines, my boundaries?"

"First, Tyler, you know your promotion to flag rank is as good as done. I only held back on it because I couldn't exactly take you from your people now, not when almost all of them virtually mutinied to resist promotions that would have moved them from *Dauntless*. But, while you may have to wait a touch longer for the star, let's not pretend you're not of flag grade right now."

Barron knew he was a capable officer, but the entire topic made him uncomfortable. He wanted to say something, but it took a few seconds for words to come to his mouth. "Even if that's true, sir…"

"And to answer your other question," Striker interrupted,

"there are no boundaries. You are to go to Archellia. Remain there if you think it the right course of action. Or advance, to the border, beyond into the Tail, or straight into the Alliance. In fact, I think it's likely that is exactly what you will do. If Sector Nine is up to some mischief, we need our own voice in the mix. That's you."

"Then I am *clearly* the wrong choice, Admiral. *Dauntless* destroyed their flagship, killed one of their most distinguished captains. I must be the most hated Confederation officer in the Alliance."

"Certainly, that thought had occurred, but I don't think your analysis is entirely correct. In fact, I think you are likely both the most hated and the most respected. Alliance culture is rather different from ours, as your experiences have no doubt confirmed to you. You showed strength and martial ability at Santis. There may be some bad feelings...but they are also likelier to listen to you than to any other Confederation representative."

Barron leaned back in his chair. He'd come to receive his orders, expecting them to be routine...and he'd been hit with one surprise after another. Finally, he asked, "What are my orders of engagement, Admiral? Am I authorized to fire if fired upon by Alliance vessels?"

"You have no orders of engagement, Captain. You have full viceregal authority outside the borders. You may attack any vessel if you deem it necessary or desirable, whether they have fired upon you first or not. Whether we are at war with the owning power or not. Go to Palatia and bombard if that is what you think you have to do."

Barron felt like a trapped animal, and he had no doubt he looked like one. This was more power, more responsibility that he wanted. "Sir, if I make a mistake...I could cause a war where there wouldn't have been one otherwise."

"That is true, Captain. It is another reason you are the only choice for this mission. No other captain has your experience with independent operations. No one has the same range of unorthodox experiences. You are very likely the only officer equipped to deal with this crisis." Striker paused, looking across the table at Barron. "And, Tyler...there is no one in the navy—in the entire Confederation—I would trust as much with this responsibility as you. Including me."

"Uh...thank you sir, but..."

"Tyler...I need your best on this. The entire Confederation needs it. We can't face an Alliance invasion, not now, not while most of the new construction is still in the yards. If you can't stop a war...you have to find a way to delay it, or blunt its impact somehow."

Striker's voice betrayed the true importance of what he was saying. Barron understood, and he knew there was no way to refuse, no chance to avoid this crushing burden.

"Of course, Admiral. I will do whatever is necessary."

The words echoed inside Barron's head, like some deathly howl. *Whatever is necessary.*

Chapter Ten

Vennius crouched low, ducking under a spot where part of the tunnel's ceiling had fallen on top of a broken structural support. The underground supply tubes crisscrossed all through Victorum, remnants from the days when the city had been called Stanton, named after the offworld commander who had first subjugated Palatia. The real Stanton had been long dead when the enslaved natives rose up and reclaimed their world, but his descendants paid the price for a century's suffering and despair. The records on the numbers of executions performed in the city center by the victorious Palatians were partially lost and inaccurate at best, but no one thought it was less than two million, and many claimed a number several times as great. All agreed, the killings continued for months, turning the streets into nightmarish rivers, washing away Palatia's shame in torrents of blood.

After the Palatians' uprising, the city was renamed and reoccupied, but the population in the early days was a fraction of what it had been. Infrastructure systems like the tubes were abandoned, and by the time the city grew again, the Palatians had constructed alternate transport lines, considering the use of anything built by the occupiers unclean and beneath their dignity.

"The tubes were an excellent idea, Drusus." Vennius paused, waiting with the others who had passed for the rest of his people to get through the choke point. "I might have forgotten about them." *And hopefully Calavius did as well…*

"Yes, sir. Though my thought was to get you out of here. The tubes do not extend all the way to the palace, and the streets all around will be heavily occupied by now. How are we going to get through?"

"This is a coup, Colonel, not an invasion. Calavius will have planned everything as meticulously as possible, but even with control of much of the capital garrison, he still had to move carefully. Anything that caused suspicion would have endangered his plot. He no doubt moved as many officers and troops loyal to him into position as possible, but he could only have done so much so quickly, at least without raising suspicion. That's the fighting we heard earlier. His people had to take out the loyal forces, all those not in on the plan. That would have been relatively easy with the element of surprise, but it still had to be carefully planned.

"Calavius will have troops surrounding the land approaches to the palace, no doubt. But I'm willing to bet he didn't have time to worry about the sea. There are rocky paths all along the cliffs there. I remember discussions about them when I was younger, when concerns about an invasion of Palatia were taken more seriously than they are now. If I can find the path, we may be able to get into the palace…and get the Imperatrix out."

"Yes, Commander." Lentius was too disciplined to show any sign of how crazy he thought the plan was, but Vennius knew his retainer well enough to guess. It didn't matter. If he'd ordered Lentius to set himself on fire, he had no doubt the officer would have obeyed.

"This way should lead to the sea." Vennius spoke with a good deal more assurance than he felt as he pointed down the crumbling masonry of the tube. He looked back one last time as his people continued to squeeze through the partially-collapsed section, then he began to move forward. There wasn't time to wait, nor was there room for all his people in the constrained section of the tube. Lentius had brought an entire cohort with him, four hundred of his veteran soldiers. He knew a lot of them had been lost getting to him at the Admiralty—and getting back out again—but he didn't want to try and figure the actual numbers. There would be time later, and besides, he had to do this, even if it cost him every soldier he had. Even if he ended up dead on the rocks below the palace.

He quickened his pace, pushing forward to the head of the formation. He looked back toward Lentius and Aurelius, both struggling to keep up, slipping on the slick ground. They'd both prefer if he stayed back, no doubt, but he was just as sure they both knew him well enough to keep those thoughts to themselves.

The pistol he'd retrieved from his desk was shoved under his belt, and he held a rifle Lentius had given him in his hands. His eyes darted back and forth in the dark tube, his legs almost knee-deep in the foul, sludgy water, each step kicking up a terrible stench. He still wore his uniform, but it was filthy and torn in half a dozen places. He'd thrown a sack over one shoulder and a makeshift bandolier with extra clips over the other. He was one of the Alliance's highest ranking military officers, a man who had issued orders to millions, but now he felt like a rebel, a partisan skulking in the shadows. He had distant memories of pre-liberation Palatia, but he'd come of age in the early Alliance. Now he felt a flashback to the generation before his, to the men and women who'd crawled through spaces like this, who'd stolen weapons and skulked in the shadows and with their blood and sweat had gained freedom for their people. He had enormous respect for the old Palatian freedom fighters, but it was a long way for him to come in a few hours, from commander of the combined fleet to sneaking through half-flooded tunnels.

He stared forward, trying to make out what lay ahead. The soldiers on either side behind him held battery-powered torches, but the dark, wet concrete absorbed their flickering light more than a few meters out. It was hard to tell in reek of the tubes, but he thought he caught the salty scent of sea air.

He hurried forward, the water splashing all around as he moved at close to a jog. His feet slid a few times on the slick, submerged floor, but he knew time was of the essence. The palace was a strong position, though not so powerful as it had been years earlier. The Imperial Guard was drawn from long service veterans, but over the years it had become more of a ceremonial formation, a place to transfer old soldiers who had served the Imperatrix in her campaigns, often men and women with old injuries and disabilities that rendered them physically unfit for the frontline units. They would fight, Vennius had no doubt of that, to the death if necessary, but he was just as sure Calavius would have committed enough force—more than enough—to overwhelm them. The struggle might go on for a few hours, but it would be over by morning, and the Imperatrix would be dead. Unless his people got there in time.

He felt a strong breeze down the tunnel now, and he was sure it came from the ocean. He continued, another two hundred meters, perhaps one-fifty. Then he stopped suddenly, putting his hand up to signal those behind him. There was a metal grate in front of him, and beyond he could see the moonlight rippling off the waves.

"We're here," he said, his head turning back toward Aurelius and Lentius. The grate was old, twisted and bent in a number of places, but it was still mostly in place, its lock holding firm. He pushed against it, and it gave a bit with a loud clang, but it stayed in place. He took a breath and threw his shoulder into it, but again it held.

"We need some muscle up here." He waved for the troops right behind him to move forward. Three soldiers trotted up, slipping past Vennius and positioning themselves against the grate. "Now," one of them yelled, and they all pushed forward. The metal shrieked and chunks of broken concrete skittered down, but it didn't give way.

"Again," Vennius said.

The soldiers threw themselves against the grate again. One side snapped free and bent forward, but the lock still held.

"Again."

The three troopers pushed one more time, and the lock broke free with a loud snap. The grate fell forward and tumbled down the rocks into a shallow pool below. The soldiers almost fell forward, but they reached out and grabbed the edges of the tunnel to steady themselves—and Vennius himself grabbed the man in front of him.

Vennius slipped past the soldiers and stepped out onto the wet rocks, grabbing where he could to steady himself. He looked up. The tube had taken them closer than he'd dared hope. The palace walls loomed up above, less than fifty meters north. He whipped his head back and forth, scanning as well as he could by moonlight. There was nothing, no soldiers that he could see.

"Cut those torches," he said, turning back to the soldiers crowding in behind him. "We pass messages back and forth up the line. No shouting, nothing that might give us away."

"Yes, sir." Lentius nodded. Then he turned to pass the command down the line.

Vennius moved to the side, hesitating as his boot landed on a narrow bit of rock, slick with wetness and mossy sea growth. He reached above him, finding a jagged place to grab hold, and shuffled across the two meters or so before the flat area expanded into something resembling a true path. He walked a few meters and stopped, waiting for Lentius and Aurelius, and the first few soldiers following them, to get through. Then he continued forward, his gaze rising every few seconds, looking up at the palace above.

Hang on, Your Supremacy…hang on. We're on the way…

*   *   *

"Please, Your Supremacy, stay down, away from the doors." The guard captain stood next to the Imperatrix, very obviously positioning himself between her and the terrace. She knew her soldiers would protect her, that every one of them would die in the effort if need be, but that wasn't how she was made. She had underestimated the threat, failed to take adequate measures to deal with an insurrection she couldn't make herself believe was a possibility. That might yet prove to be a fatal mistake, but if it was, she would meet her death weapon in hand, fighting as she had done for most of her long life.

"Fight your battle, Captain. See to your troops, and leave an old warrior like me to handle herself." The Imperatrix had heeded the pleas of her guards to remain in her quarters, to stay out of sight while they fought to hold the palace. She'd almost refused, and she had gone to her closet and retrieved her side-arm, strapping it on over the old uniform she'd thrown on. She looked out of place, dressed in the faded old fatigues, her silver hair laying down her back. Her guards had been horrified when they'd first seen her, but she silenced them with a single stare.

She had a duty as the Alliance's supreme commander to remain where she was, to avoid the risk that a stray shot would take her down. She realized that, at least after her initial rage had cooled. She hated feeling like a coward, but she understood. Duty came before warrior's pride. But if the defense failed, as she suspected it would, if she was to fall anyway, by God, she would fall in battle, alongside the last of her soldiers. They would never take her alive.

They don't want you alive…

She still couldn't believe she'd been so wrong. She'd been aware of discontent among many of the officers over a number of issues, most seriously her decision to avoid war with the Confederation. But she hadn't imagined so many of her people, the soldiers of the Alliance's legions, would take up arms against her.

Lies…they must have spread lies about me. Told the soldiers what they had to in order to shake their loyalty.

Her face hardened, rage at what was happening, at the treason so easily coaxed from many of her soldiers. She felt a wave of disgust. *People are so willing to believe lies they are told…*

A trio of troopers raced into the room. The Imperatrix spun around, as did the soldiers around her, but the new arrivals were comrades. They were carrying breastplates and helmets, and had heavy weapons strapped across their backs. They stopped and dropped their loads. "From the armory...grab what you need."

The soldiers in the room moved toward the pile of equipment. They'd been wearing their normal duty uniforms, and that meant most had only pistols. Even the rifles a few possessed were light carbines. But the weapons laying on the floor were heavy combat models, rapid-fire electromagnetic rifles that could tear even an armored target in half.

She walked over toward the tiny supply dump, and she reached down, grabbing a piece of the body armor. She strapped it on, realizing that she looked even more absurd with the breastplate over her uniform. *How can I seem so out of place in garb I spent my life wearing?*

She knew age had sapped her fighting strength, that for all her defiance and determination, the first soldier to face her would probably take her down. But inside the weakening shell, there still resided the spirit of a warrior. And she'd be damned if she would meet this challenge with anything less than the last bits of strength that remained to her.

The body armor was heavy, far heavier on her frail frame than she remembered. The last time she'd donned a set had been so many years before. She glanced down at the heavy auto-rifles, and paused. She realized she couldn't manage one of them, not effectively. Defiance was one thing, foolishness another. Her hand moved down to her waist, to the pistol holstered at her side.

Suddenly, a flash lit the room, and a series of heavy explosions erupted outside. She looked out the doorway onto the terrace, but she couldn't see anything. The attack was on the other side of the palace, from the land approach. From the sound of the blasts, it was a far heavier attack than the last one. She listened, trying to identify the weapons in use. *An armored vehicle, certainly...no, at least two.*

The room shook hard, and bits of dust and broken molding fell from the ceiling. Then again, with a blast just as loud. *And artillery. They're shelling us...*

"Captain, they're going to get through this time." She had no solid data to support her conclusion, but she just knew. They'd tried to rush the palace first, using speed and surprise to try for a quick win. But her guards had held, and they'd driven back every attempt since. Now the traitors were serious. They knew they didn't have much time. If Victorum wasn't theirs—and she wasn't dead—by morning, their chances of success dropped sharply. And that meant they were coming now with everything they had.

"Captain, try to reach the other units." She looked at the officer as he worked the small comm unit sitting on the table. Even before he answered, she could hear the static and the heavy interference.

"Sorry, Your Supremacy. Still no contact."

The traitors had done that much right. They were jamming her communications, probably all comm in Victorum except their own designated channels. That probably meant no warnings had gone out, that all the loyal positions in the city had been isolated, and likely taken...all without getting word to any other base, or to any ships in orbit.

Scanners would pick up the energy readings from the fighting, of course, but that could take hours, and a first response would be a scouting party, not a full assault team. It would be hours more, days even, before meaningful help could arrive. And there was no way to be sure what stations had been infiltrated. For all she knew, the first warnings would reach conspirators placed there for just that purpose.

She wasn't the sort to give up hope, but she was a pragmatist too, and things looked grim. The enemy would shell the palace until its outer defenses were breached...and then they would come.

And she would be here waiting for them.

Chapter Eleven

Outside the Imperial Palace
Victorum, Alliance Capital City
Astara II, Palatia
Year 61 (310 AC)

"Commander, this has to be finished. Now." Ricard Lille stood next to Calavius, wearing the uniform of an Alliance Legatus. He'd been all over the city, checking on every aspect of the coup in progress, and he'd been satisfied at every step. Until now.

"I just sent in more troops. I can only use handpicked forces here. Not every Alliance soldier can be trusted to storm the palace. It's one thing to take a bribe or join the rising out of anger at what has happened before…and quite another to attack the palace and kill the Imperatrix. Many of those in our service would abandon us if forced to make that choice." Calavius sounded confident about the status of the operation, but Lille bet himself it was bullshit. He understood the uncertainty about who would actually pull the trigger and kill the Imperatrix when it came to it, but concerns about trustworthy personnel notwithstanding, he'd expected the palace to be taken by now, and he was sure the Palatian had as well.

"There are no excuses, Commander. I have the materials we discussed. Everything is ready to go. In the morning, we will utilize the communications networks you have just seized. We will begin to discredit the Imperatrix and her supporters, to justify what was done as necessary to prevent disaster. But she must be dead by then. If she is still alive, barricaded in her fortress and under fire, many will rally around her."

"I understand that, Mr. Lille." Calavius's answer was brittle, his tension slipping through this time. "But the Imperial Guards are putting up a vicious fight...and as I said, I only have so many troops I can trust with this duty."

"I don't care if you have to go in there yourself, but there can be no failure here." Lille stared right into Calavius's eyes. "It is bad enough you didn't kill Commander Vennius." He paused, noting the surprised reaction. "You didn't know I knew, did you?"

Calavius didn't respond, but the expression on his face gave Lille the answer he needed. "You accomplish nothing by lying to me or withholding information. This entire enterprise would have been impossible without my assistance, Commander, and you are not far enough through it that you can succeed without my further aid. I advise you to remember that. You can be Imperator in a matter of hours, and you can lead your people into a glorious war against the Confederation. In the morning, we will set the stage for the Confeds to take the blame for infiltrating the Alliance government, and for the Imperatrix to be exposed as a puppet of the Megara government. No Palatian will oppose you when that communique goes out." Lille held his gaze, and his tone deepened. "Or you can allow all of this to collapse, and you can die a traitor's death, as you surely will if the Imperatrix survives and maintains control."

Calavius was angry, struggling to hold back his rage. Lille knew he was pushing hard, that no Palatian, not even one as power hungry and enmeshed in Sector Nine's schemes as Calavius, actually liked or trusted Union operatives like himself. But things had gone well past the point of no return, and Lille knew his ally's chances were still heavily dependent on his help.

"I will take the palace...and kill the Imperatrix. Even if I have to blast it to dust."

"Good. Do what you must, Commander…and tomorrow we will rally the entire Alliance behind its new Imperator. You will lead your people to power and glory beyond anything they ever imagined." Lille was frowning inside. He'd always hated giving such inspirational speeches, especially to men like Calavius. But he'd known enough fools to realize such displays almost always worked. It disgusted him how the vast majority of people were so easily manipulated. Greed, lust, and ego were the tools of his trade…along with fear, of course. Fear was his favorite, without question, but he used what the job required.

He could see that Calavius's determination was renewed. "Remain here, Mr. Lille. I am going to direct the final assault. In thirty minutes, I will be the master of the palace, or what is left of it."

He glared at Lille with glittering eyes. "And the Imperatrix will be dead."

Lille just nodded. He'd done all he could. Now he would have to wait, and see if his chosen tool was capable enough to do what had to be done.

"And then I will find Tarkus Vennius, and whoever helped him escape…and I will paint the streets with their blood."

*   *   *

"Move! Odds to the right, evens to the left." Vennius stood at the top of the stairs, waving his arms, urging his soldiers forward. Now that they were out of the tunnels and inside from the dark, rocky path, he could get most of his people in view. He didn't like what he saw. He knew he'd lost a good number of soldiers in the fighting at the admiralty and the desperate race to get to the palace. But now, he guessed he had no more than two hundred left, and perhaps fewer. That meant more than half the cohort was down…and he didn't kid himself. In the current situation, down meant dead. He had no illusions about what the traitors would do to any of his soldiers who fell into their hands.

He knew the palace layout well. The great staircase was one of two, a concession to symmetry, but by far the less utilized of the pair. The rear entrances to the palace saw little use, since they led only to the rocky paths hugging the ocean cliffs.

The paths Calavius neglected to garrison…as I suspected…

Vennius didn't like splitting up his soldiers, but he knew it was the right move now, especially since the sounds in the distance confirmed his fear that the enemy was in the palace already. He had no idea where the attackers were, or how far they had penetrated, and the two hallways arced around and reconnected after perhaps seventy meters. Ideally, he'd have set up a defensive position at the top of the stairs and sent out scouts, but there simply wasn't time. This wasn't about defending the palace or retaking it. He was here to save the Imperatrix, and nothing else mattered. He could lead a tactically brilliant operation…but if he got there after some rebel soldier but a bullet in her head, it was all for nothing.

"Let's go…move. We haven't got time to waste. The Imperatrix is depending on us. We have to save her. We have to save our leader."

Vennius had been quite the aggressive field commander back in his day, but it had been many years since he'd led troops directly into battle. He was surprised how easily it came back, the recollections of tactical command, the ready words to rally the soldiers, even the muscle memory of combat maneuvers. He'd felt like an old man for the past three years, weighed down by grief and a feeling of uselessness. But now there was an energy coursing through his body, one he hadn't experienced in a very long time. One that drove him on, despite despair and fear and blistering rage at a man he'd called his friend. A man he was now determined to kill.

He watched as the last of the soldiers moved forward, his disordered column dividing somewhat sloppily into two sections. Aurelius and Lentius stood next to him. Lentius had his rifle angled up, the butt resting on his hip. He looked the essence of the Palatian warrior, with just the slightest hint of guilt in his eyes. The colonel had saved Vennius's life, and his actions had been crucial to whatever chance remained to defeat the coup, but Vennius knew the officer was torturing himself, expecting—almost wanting—some sort of punishment for disobeying orders.

Aurelius stood next to Lentius, holding a pistol in his good hand, with rather less apparent confidence than Lentius displayed. Aurelius had combat experience, but only the minimum amount Vennius had felt was necessary to justify his grant of Citizenship to his longtime aide. It went against the spirit of Palatian culture to seek to limit exposure to battle, but Aurelius was a genius with numbers, incredibly valuable in his role on Vennius's staff. It was a bit unorthodox, but Vennius had been confident enough that no one would dare challenge him…and no one had.

Aurelius didn't look good, though. Limited battle experience or no, he'd fought like a caged beast in the Admiralty, helping Lentius and his people get through the rebels in time to reach Vennius…and he'd taken a nasty shot to the arm in the process. One side of his shirt was soaked with blood, and his face was pale, slick with sweat. He'd kept up in the tunnels and on the path—somehow—but Vennius knew his aide was close to his limit.

"Drusus, go with the group on the left. I'll take the group on the right. Be as cautious as you can, but remember, time is crucial. We'll meet in the center hallway, right below the stairway to the Imperatrix's apartments."

"Yes, sir." Lentius turned and raced up the stairs after his troopers.

"Stay with me, Aurelius." Vennius reached out, extending a hand. "Come, old friend, hold on to me. We'll get through this together." He was definitely worried about Aurelius. Despite the differences in their stations, he considered the aide a friend. But more importantly right now, if he managed to get the Imperatrix out of here, Aurelius's analytical abilities would be invaluable in developing a strategy to defeat—to survive—the coup.

"I'm okay, Commander. Don't let me slow you down."

"Don't be foolish, Aurelius."

Aurelius looked up at him. "Sir…there's no time. The Imperatrix…"

Vennius swore under his breath. He knew Aurelius was right. He had to leave his friend. "You are to follow, and catch up…do you hear me? That's an order, Aurelius. I know you're hurt, I know you're tired. But I don't care. You have to catch up. You *have* to."

"I will, sir." The aide coughed and struggled for a few seconds to catch his breath. "I'm hurt, Commander…but I'm tougher than you think. I'll be right behind you."

Vennius hesitated, but for just an instant. He hated leaving a comrade behind, but he knew where his duty led him. "Keep moving, Aurelius. Don't you give up. That's an order." He turned and ran down the hallway, chasing after the soldiers. It only took a moment to catch the makeshift column, but it was harder to push his way through the crowd, toward the front. Where he belonged.

He heard the sounds of gunfire up ahead, and as he made his way to the lead position, he saw bodies, three Imperial Guards… no, four. And seven other soldiers. *Traitors.*

He felt a surge of anger, and a slight bit of satisfaction that the guards had given better than they'd gotten. Seven dead traitors…the sight gave him a perverse pleasure. Shock at the coup was giving way…to cold rage.

"Let's go," he shouted. As much as he liked the idea of his enemies being killed, there wasn't much doubt the Imperial Guards had been driven back, toward the stairway leading to the Imperatrix's quarters. The guards had fought well, defended the palace for longer than he'd had a right to hope for. But the fight was almost over.

He moved forward quickly, almost recklessly. They had to get there on time. They *had* to.

He saw something up ahead, and his arms moved, almost on their own, bringing the rifle to bear and firing, even as several of the troopers behind him did the same. He saw an enemy soldier fall, and the shadows of another dropping around the corner and out of direct sight. Then one of his own fell as a burst of return fire ripped down the hallway.

He dropped to one knee and pressed against the wall for

cover, firing the entire time, the heavy rounds tearing apart the fine paneling on the walls.

Damn...we don't have time for a protracted firefight...

"All right, on three we're going to rush the corridor. We can't get pinned down here. We've got to get to the Imperatrix... whatever the cost."

"One..."

"Sir, please stay back...we'll..."

He knew the woman who had spoken. She was a good officer, and loyal. They all were. Vennius would have vouched for every soldier in his legion. They wanted to protect him, convince him to stay behind. But they would obey his orders. "We're all going, Lieutenant. That's final. Two."

"Three." He lunged forward, racing down the corridor so quickly he almost lost his balance. He was shooting as he came on, spraying the enemy position with fire, blasting bits of the wall to dust. His people were all behind him, a surging, shouting mass of warriors, committed to a charge they knew could end only in victory...or death. There would be no retreat. There could be none.

There were nearly a hundred of them, and they came on with an unmatchable fury. One fell, then another, but still they pushed on. A third dropped. A fourth...and then they were there. They spun around the corner, their rifles spitting death on the dozen troopers who'd been taking cover there. Half of the enemy were down in a second or two, and most of the others right after. The last two went down in hand to hand matchups, their midsections sliced open by the Vennius's heavy combat knives.

Vennius could feel a wet warmth on his face from the splattered blood of his enemies. In energized him, filled him with a primal fury, one that only increased in intensity as he heard the sounds of fighting ahead. A moment later he saw Lentius and his troopers rushing down from the far hall.

"Up the stairs, soldiers. Now. Save the Imperatrix. Save the Alliance. And no mercy...no mercy to traitors."

Vennius snapped out the spent clip in his rifle as he shouted his battle cries, and he pulled a new on from his bandolier and rammed it in place.

"No mercy to traitors," he shouted as he raced up the stairs, half a step ahead of his soldiers. And behind him he heard the chants of, "Vennius Legion forever!"

Chapter Twelve

Lafarge walked down the covered street, past the taverns and various sleazy establishments that lined the main avenue of Port Royal City's infamous Spacer's District. Most cities with space-ports had some version or another of the neighborhood, and a similar array of businesses catering to the needs and wants—legal and otherwise—of transient spacers. But Port Royal City was the capital of Dannith, and Dannith lay on the edge of the Confederation, at the edge of the Badlands. Its spacers were even more disreputable than most, rogues and pirates—or near pirates—who scavenged the dead worlds across the border for anything they could sell.

That haunted area of space extended out, far beyond the deepest any explorer's ship had dared to venture in at least three centuries. There was profit to be had scavenging bits and pieces of ancient technology, and legend had it, even fortunes to be made upon occasion. There were stories of chunks of ancient electronics and sections of highly advanced equipment that had earned their discoverers millions. All of that had happened on the black market, of course, outside the notice of the authorities

95

that claimed possession of any old tech found in the ruins of the dead empire.

Lafarge, of course, knew more than any of the denizens of these dimly-lit bars and crooked gambling halls. She had seen not just scraps of old tech, but a great battleship, intact... one that had been constructed for a single purpose. To destroy worlds. She wasn't enough of a physicist to calculate whether the massive antimatter-powered weapons of that vessel could have actually blasted a planet to rubble, or if it was simply capable of destroying all life inhabiting it. Either result could adequately support the decoded designation, "planet-killer." But the ancient wonder was gone now, blasted to sub-atomic particles by the annihilation of an amount of antimatter so vast, it defied the imagination.

She walked into a bar, the fourth...no, the fifth one so far today. She'd come down from the orbital station, looking for someone. Lex Righter was her engineer, and her friend. He'd played a key role in the action out at Chrysallis, but from what she'd heard, it may have been too much for him. He was an intelligent man, one of enormous capability. His engineering skills could have opened doors for him, led him to a comfortable life somewhere far from the rough and tumble frontier of the Badlands. Indeed, they had, until he lost it all. He had his weaknesses as well as strengths, and drinking was one of them.

Righter was strong, in some ways. Lafarge had never seen him lose his cool in a desperate situation, but he was also troubled. He struggled when he wasn't busy, his demons emerging when he had nothing but empty time. His tendency to seek solace in a bottle during such periods had cost him everything—career, family, position. Lafarge had found him a broken man years earlier, and she liked to think the home she'd made for him had saved his life. As his incredible skills in the engine room had saved the entire crew's more than once.

All her people had returned, ready to take their places on *Pegasus* and set out on their next expedition. All except Righter. Vig Merrick had told her Righter had never left Dannith, and she knew that significantly narrowed down the number of places she was likely to find him. She'd searched five already, but that left more than a dozen.

It never ceased to amaze her how spacers, especially those in places like the Badlands, raced back the instant they made a score...and proceeded to spend everything they'd earned as quickly as possible. She was keenly aware of the risks she and her people took, and every credit she'd managed to make had gone into improvements to her ship...or one of the half dozen hiding places where she kept her hard earned, and occasionally ill-gotten, gains.

She'd insisted on paying her way on Oleyus, of course, an unusual extravagance, especially when Barron was more than willing to cover it all, but that had been a matter of pride. She knew Barron was vastly wealthy, but she'd shut him down every time he'd tried to foot the bill. She knew he'd meant well, but she wasn't about to yield her position as an equal in their...relationship...whatever that was. Andi Lafarge had spent her life in the pursuit of wealth, but there were ways she was willing attain that and ways she wasn't. And she'd be damned if she would be some wealthy man's plaything, even if that man was Tyler Barron. No, no way. Hell, Tyler Barron was *her* plaything...at least that was the way she looked at it. And she'd spend her last credit before she would see it any other way.

She cursed herself for thinking of Barron again. They had said their goodbyes, but after her encounter with Admiral Striker, she found herself on edge, concerned about what had brought the navy's commander to Dannith. The more she thought about it, the more certain she was that he'd come to give Barron orders, that *Dauntless* was being sent off on another dangerous mission. She'd tried to ignore those concerns, willed herself to focus on her own business, but finally she'd given in and tried to contact Barron...only to discover that *Dauntless* had left its docking that morning.

She'd tried to find out where the battleship was going, but she'd been told it was classified. Then she'd attempted to contact Barron, only to find out *Dauntless* was on a communications blackout. Something was up, something big. But there was nothing she could do about it. Nothing except trust Barron's abilities. She'd told herself he would be fine, that he would come through whatever mission he'd been sent on, just as he had the others, but she found it all less than convincing. Then she'd decided to just put the whole thing out of her mind, though her current thoughts confirmed that she'd had less than impressive success there as well.

Suddenly, she caught something out of the corner of her eye. Recognition. Not the engineer she'd come to retrieve, but someone else. Someone she'd intended to find eventually...a man with whom she had unfinished business.

She walked slowly, moving to the side, behind the man sitting at a table across the room. The bars in the Spacer's District had a strict no weapons policy, but Lafarge had both an utter disregard for inconvenient rules and a snub-nosed pistol made entirely of high tech polymers, undetectable by any of the equipment the District's establishments employed. Her hand dropped nonchalantly to her side, feeling under her jacket, confirming what she already knew...the weapon was in its place.

She felt a controlled hatred. She'd planned to find this man at the table for a simple reason. She was going to kill him.

She came up right behind him, reaching over and pulling out the chair next to him. "Hello, Rolf," she said, the iciness in her voice practically freezing the bar's stale air.

The man looked up from his drink...and his face went pale. He shifted in his seat, looking as though he might make a run for it, but Lafarge reached out and grabbed his hand. "I'd stay put, Rolf. You know I'm never unarmed...and you also know your chances of reaching the door before I blow your miserable brains out are profoundly shitty."

Rolf Shugart stared back, clearly terrified. "Andi, I don't understand. What are you..."

"Save it, Rolf." She glared at him. The man who had sold her the information about the ancient ship at Chrysallis...and then given the same intelligence to Sector Nine. "I'd ask what you were thinking when you crossed me like you did, but then, you didn't expect me to come back, did you?" She paused.

"You miserable piece of shit. How long did we work together? How many times did I come back here and pay you every credit I'd promised, regardless of how half-assed your data turned out to be or how much the expedition cost me? And you sold me out to the Union."

She glared at the man, seeing that he was growing more panicked by the moment. As she did, her own rage grew. She remembered the treatment she'd received on the Union vessel, the beatings from the Sector Nine operatives…and she knew what she had endured was but a fraction of what had faced her, had it not been for *Dauntless* and Tyler Barron.

"It wasn't like that, Andi, I promise. You've got it all wrong."

"Do you know how many times I've thought about getting to kill you?" Her feral tone dripped menace.

"You have to listen to me, Andi…" He paused, sucking in a deep breath. Then he said, "You can't kill me here. You know that."

"I can't? You think I can't put two bullets in that fat head of yours and be out of here before that sack of meat can stop me?" She gestured with her head toward the bouncer standing next to the bar, the only apparent security in the establishment.

"Andi, please…I didn't…"

"You didn't what? Give us up to die after you took our money? I'm stunned you were stupid enough to stay on Dannith. You had to know by now that I made it back. I thought I'd have to chase you across half the Confederation. I guess I should thank you for making it so easy."

"Andi…I'm begging…"

"Wait…" Lafarge glared at Shugart. "Why *are* you here? You had to know I'd come looking for you, that every member of my crew would be waiting for the moment we could cut your crooked heart out. Something kept you here…something that scared you more than I do."

"No, Andi…I didn't run because I didn't do anything. I don't know what you're talking about." Her eyes moved up and down his figure. He was wearing high end clothes, and jewelry. Expensive jewelry. The man always dressed like a buffoon, but usually a cheap buffoon. She had given him a considerable pay-off before she'd set out for Chrysallis, but she'd known for a fact that most of that had gone to pay gambling debts, just in time to save his ass. The real profit would have come from splitting the gains if she'd returned with any old tech. And yet he looked as though he'd recently come into a large sum of money.

"You're looking prosperous, Rolf. Is this from the bribe you got for selling me out?" Her eyes narrowed, boring into his. "No, that's not it, is it? You're still working for Sector Nine, aren't you? Yes, of course. Your intel on the ship was good, even if it didn't work out for them. They would have come back for more." She paused. "You'e a filthy traitor, Rolf. You'd sell out the Confederation to the Union?"

"You don't understand…I didn't have a choice…"

"Not here." She looked around the room. Their conversation was attracting attention. It was probably nothing, but she had no intention of taking a chance. "You have a choice, Rolf. Come with me, and we'll have a long talk somewhere private. Maybe you can even tell me something I think is so valuable, I'll let you live…though I wouldn't count on it."

"You said I had a choice?"

"Yes. I can put you down right here like the filthy piece of garbage you are, and see if I can beat the bouncer out of here."

He looked around, clearly trying to come up with a way out. But Lafarge was well aware Shugart knew she was a good shot… and he'd be damned sure she wasn't bluffing.

"Okay…let's go talk."

"You first." She stood up, gesturing toward the door. She glanced down at his half-empty glass of some kind of brown liquor—probably expensive from the looks of the accoutrements he seemed to have acquired. She reached into her pocket and tossed a silver coin on the table, enough to pay for any drink. *At least any drink they serve in this dump…*

"This one's on me, Rolf. Let's call it your sendoff…unless you think of some way to dazzle me. She gestured with her hand under her jacket, gripping the undetectable pistol. "Now, let's go. And don't try anything. I want to kill you so bad, I can taste it."

*   *   *

"All stations report condition green. All systems check."
Atara Travis turned and looked back toward the command station. "We're ready, Captain."

Barron sat looking out over the glistening brightness of
Dauntless's refurbished bridge, a little ashamed to be enjoying the
butter-softness of his new chair as much as he was. His ship had
endured a seemingly endless series of repair attempts canceled
and cut short, and she'd begun to show her age, and the terrible
punishment she'd taken over three years of war. Anya Fritz was
a wizard in engineering, and Barron had come close to believing
it was some kind of magic she'd worked in the bowels of his
ship, coaxing the old vessel back from the brink time and time
again. But now, *Dauntless* was reborn, all of Fritz's makeshift
reroutes pulled out and replaced with brand new equipment.
The ship still wasn't new, but she was as close as the full efforts
of Dannith base could make her in six months of round-the-
clock repairs.

Barron looked over at Travis, his first officer…and without
question his best friend. He'd enjoyed himself immensely on
Oleyus, but he was glad to be back to Travis, and the rest of the
crew. They were his family, in very real way, and he hadn't realized just how much he'd missed them until he saw them again.
He felt the loss of Andi, of course, but he was sure that would
fade. Perhaps they would see each other again, another time,
another place. But it was time to get back to work. Duty called
to him, and he was ready to answer, as he always had.

"Commander Travis, set a course for the Vestara transit
point. Thrust at 1g."

"Entering course for Vestara transit point, sir. Acceleration
at 1g." Travis had already calculated the course—to no one's
surprise, Barron was sure—and she moved her hands over the
controls, sending it to *Dauntless*'s AI. "Engaging thrust now."

Barron couldn't feel the thrust at all. It wasn't that 1g was all that much force, but *Dauntless*'s engines had been shut down. The vessel should have been in freefall before the engines fired, operating under zero gravity conditions. But the new compensators, which Fritzie claimed would offset almost twice the 5g of the old ones, also provided simulated gravity when the engines were shut down.

"Well," Barron said, addressing what he suspected all his people were thinking, "she's certainly more comfortable, isn't she?"

"Yes, sir," Travis answered. "I believe we will find a number of areas where performance has been significantly upgraded."

"So I've been told, Commander. I hope we won't need it all, at least for a while." Barron hoped he managed to sound more convincing about that than he felt. "Put me on shipwide comm, Commander."

"Yes, sir." Travis turned back to her board for a few seconds, and then again toward Barron. "On your headset, Captain."

Barron nodded, and he reached down, picking up the comm unit, also new and far nicer than the old one had been. He pulled it over his head and reached for the activation switch, but before he did, it came on by itself. *Oh, right…it's AI-controlled now.*

"All hands, this is Captain Barron. To all crew members returning to duty, I sincerely hope you enjoyed your immensely-deserved leaves. It is my great pleasure to have you back, and to have to opportunity to once more command the greatest crew in the fleet." He paused, glancing around at the bridge staff.

"To those newly assigned to *Dauntless*, I want to welcome you. I like to think you have joined a very special crew…serving on a very special ship." Barron paused, his mind drifting for a moment to all the crew members who'd been lost, out at Chrysallis, and on *Dauntless*'s other missions. He was happy to welcome his new people, but addressing them made him think of loyal spacers—and friends—lost these past three years.

"I had expected our orders to direct us to Base Grimaldi for a fleet assignment on the front lines, but that is not where we are heading." He figured he might as well address *Dauntless*'s destination now, before wild conjecture began working its way around. Vestara was an unlikely route to the front lines, and when his ship took her next jump, to Hawthorne, it would be clear *Dauntless* was *not* heading to join the fleet.

"We are bound for Archellia." The words almost stuck in his throat. "For those who have been onboard for three years, you will remember our last visit, to the Rim…and our fight at Santis. We do not have combat orders yet; however fleet command would not be sending us there without reason. So, I want everybody ready for whatever happens. It's time to shake the remnants of shore leave, and get sharp again, ready to fight. So, now that the welcomes are over, it's time to get back in shape. That means drills…and then more drills. We're going to practice with this new equipment we've got until it feels like an extension of our bodies. And then we're going to practice some more, just for the hell of it. So, since I'm sure you're all extremely well rested, we'll start at 0600 tomorrow, with simulated red alert and all hands battle drills."

Barron could almost hear the moans throughout the ship, though the bridge crew was too disciplined to give any reaction. He wasn't the kind of captain who enjoyed putting his people through pointless exercises, but six months of leave was bound to take the edge off anyone, and he had almost two hundred new crew members to break in. Besides, he was nervous. No, more than nervous…he was downright scared about the situation awaiting them on the Rim. He had no idea what was happening out there, or what he would do to deal with any of it. The only thing he knew was his people had to be ready for anything.

He allowed himself a little smile in spite of his tension. *Anything.*

That's why I'm going to trigger the mock alarm at 0500…

Chapter Thirteen

Imperial Palace
Victorum, Alliance Capital City
Astara II, Palatia
Year 61 (310 AC)

The Imperatrix stood next to the table in the center of the room, her pistol gripped tightly in her hand. She'd been in countless battles, faced mortal danger many times. She had walked across her battlefields, defeated her enemies, and come home to tell the tale. She'd been wounded, many times, and she'd come close to dying once or twice, but always she had prevailed. She had survived.

That was over now, almost certainly. In a few moments, she would die. That was unfortunate, perhaps, but of no real consequence. She'd lived a warrior's life, and now, it seemed fitting that she die in arms. But in death now, she would be vanquished as well. She would think her last thoughts not of victory, of a heroic death, but of ruination and defeat. The Alliance she loved, that she had dedicated her life to building and preserving, would be destroyed. Or it would become something she wouldn't recognize, an abomination to the untold legions who had died to make it great.

She could hear the sounds of battle approaching, and as they moved closer, she knew time grew shorter. Her Imperial

Guards were dead, most of them at least. If they hadn't been, no enemy would be in the halls of the palace, moving even now to her inner sanctum. She mourned for each of them...for their deaths, of course, but also because they had died in defeat, as she would in just a few moments.

"It has been an honor to receive your service," she said to the soldiers standing at her side, her voice steady, showing no signs of fear. "You are honorable warriors, all of you, and you have my gratitude, now and for eternity."

She could see the emotions on the faces of her few remaining guards, hard visages dark with grim resignation. She knew each of them blamed himself or herself in some way. They would view the Imperatrix's death as their ultimate failure, though they would be spared any time to consider that misery. She had no doubt every one of them would die, that not one would choose life even in the unlikely circumstance of the enemy offering it. Even Poscuta had taken up a weapon, though the valet looked absurd trying to wield it. She'd tried to release him from service and told him to hide. It was possible at least, if not likely, that a mere servant *would* be allowed to live. But he wouldn't hear of it, going so far as to refuse her directly. He would die with her, he attested with a level of resolution she hadn't expected, or he would follow, and fall trying to avenge her. Even after a lifetime of war, it still surprised her just how poignant such loyalty could be.

She heard gunfire now, right outside the door. Then it died down, and she knew the last of her people out there were gone. She took a deep breath, and she extended her arm, bringing the pistol to bear on the doorway. They might kill her, but she would not die without cost. They could come, but she and her comrades would extract a price for their lives.

The door blasted open, shards of the heavy wood flying all around the room. Smoke from the explosion filled the air, and she felt the sting in her eyes. She choked on the noxious fumes, but she held firm, squeezing her finger as she caught the first hint of a soldier moving forward. It took all the strength she could muster from her withered arms to hold the gun level, but she managed it, and the first shot took one of the attackers in the head. She fired again, and a third time, each shot dead on, bringing down another enemy.

The rest of her people were firing as well, and she could see the attackers piling up just inside the doorway, dead and dying, even as their comrades poured forth, scaling over their bodies and returning the deadly fire. One of her own dropped, and a few seconds later, Poscuta, her beloved servant, took at least three rounds in the chest and fell with a lifeless thud.

She kept firing, but the smoke had filled the room, and she was having trouble seeing through teary eyes. Her instincts told her to dive for cover, but there was no point. It was over. She had maybe three or four of her people left, and more enemy troopers were pouring into the room.

She kept firing until her pistol was empty, and then she let her arm drop to her side. She'd heard yelling in the outer room, the attackers shouting orders back and forth. Then…

Something else. Shooting, from farther out. Had a few of her guards escaped the initial assault? Were they throwing themselves into the fight at the last second?

Then she felt something. Not pain, at least not at first, but she realized her feet had left the floor. She was moving, almost in slow motion, falling backwards, and she could see the blood pouring out of her chest.

Her field of vision moved, its angle changing…then suddenly, she was looking up at the ceiling. An instant later, the pain came, like a sledgehammer. Her chest hurt like fire, and every tortured breath was a small agony.

This is it…the end.

She gasped for breath, even as she heard the battle sounds intensifying all around her. It didn't make sense. Only a few of her people were left, yet she could hear fire all around. She tried to turn her head and look, but she just didn't have the strength. She wasn't even sure she believed what she heard. After nine decades, at last it was time to face death. Any second now, she knew, one of the soldiers would find her…and he would finish her.

She saw the shadowy shapes, heard orders barked out with increasing urgency, even as she struggled to maintain consciousness. She was determined to meet death head on. She was scared, but she refused to show it.

A shadow loomed over her, the shape of a soldier. It was time. The fight was over, the enemy victorious. *The way is the way*, she thought, repeating the mantra to herself one last time.

"Your Supremacy?" She heard a voice. Familiar. Not an enemy.

A friend? No, not possible…

"Your Supremacy, can you hear me?" The voice was tense, disturbed. Then she realized, the sounds of fighting had stopped.

She felt a hand on her shoulder. "Your Supremacy…it is Tarkus. Tarkus Vennius. Can you hear me?"

"Tarkus?" she said softly, not sure she completely understood what was happening.

"Yes, Your Supremacy. It is me. We've come to get you out of here. But we have to go. Now. There isn't much time."

"Loyal…soldiers?"

"Yes. I have a cohort of my private legion with me, Your Supremacy. We took out the troops that were attacking, but the rebels have control of the city. We'll be overwhelmed if we stay here. We've got to go. Now."

She heard Vennius yelling to other soldiers, then a moment later, hands sliding under her, picking her slowly from the floor. Agony ripped through her, but she held her tongue. She had not lived the life she had to die—or to live, if her rescuers were successful—whimpering in pain.

She felt them lowering her now, something below her. A blanket or a bed covering. Then pressure again as she felt it lifting her from the ground. She could see the soldiers, three on each side, carrying her toward the door. And Vennius's voice, sounding far away now, trying to reassure her.

"We'll get you out of here, Your Supremacy…and when we do, we'll strike back, and line these traitors on spikes along the Via Magna."

*   *   *

"They must have escaped along the sea paths. There is nowhere else." Calavius was yelling to a group of officers, his key conspirators in the coup. There was urgency in his tone… and anger. His soldiers had finally seized control of the palace, hours after he'd expected. The Imperial Guard had been virtually wiped out, a preliminary count of the bodies had confirmed that. But the Imperatrix was nowhere to be found.

"Yes, Commander." The officer in the center of the small group responded, the others standing silently behind. "There is no other place they could have gone." A pause. "Unless the Imperatrix was not in the palace. Is it possible she had warning?"

Calavius hesitated, considering the officer's words. "No," he finally said. "The casualty counts suggest the entire Imperial Guard was here. If the Imperatrix had fled, she would not have done so unprotected." He'd thought at first that she must be hidden somewhere, and his troops had spent the past several hours searching the palace, millimeter by millimeter. But there was nothing.

If she did escape on the sea path, I've given her a headstart…

He felt his fists clench. He was angry—with himself, for not thinking of the sea route earlier, and at his officers as well. Not one of them had suggested sending a patrol there.

But the Imperial Guards are gone…how far can an old woman get on that rugged path in the darkness? That's why you didn't think of it. But it's not too late. You can still get to her.

"I want patrols there at once, both from the palace and from the north to cut off any escape. And I want airships deployed to search the coastline. If she is there, we will find her. Before she eludes us." The terrain north of Victorum was rough, mountainous and heavily wooded. Ideal country to hide form pursuit. He had to get her while she was still on the open path.

"Yes, Commander." The officer saluted. Then he turned, shouting orders to the others standing behind him. The entire group raced down the hill.

Calavius took a deep breath. He needed to control his anger, and truth be told, his fear. He wasn't a coward, certainly not. As any Palatian Patrician of his age and rank, he had seen much battle and danger. He'd been to many worlds, cultures where the privileged and powerful avoided danger, where they sent their minions to fight their wars while they cowered at home in luxury and safety. It had always disgusted him. Palatia's Patricians shared the dangers of those they led. More than that. The casualty rates among the Alliance's young officer class were vastly higher than those of any other group. He'd had many friends when he was young, but most of them were gone now. Fewer than a quarter of the Alliance's elite lived to his age, and close to half the children born into the Patrician class came of age with both parents dead. It was hard, a heavy burden on a people. *The way is the way.*

Calavius's fear wasn't of death, or not entirely, at least. He did find that as he'd aged, his desire to live had become more pronounced, but his worry now was mostly the realization that if he died, if his coup failed, he would be reviled as a base traitor by his people for centuries to come. What he had done, he did to save the Alliance, to retain the martial strength that had made it great. But it would not be remembered that way if he did not succeed.

"Commander!"

Another officer was heading his way, jogging, almost running. Commander-Altum Junia Balventius, a key ally in his coup, and one of the officers he trusted the most.

"Yes, what is it?" He valued Balventius's judgment, but he still couldn't keep the anger at the situation completely out of his voice.

"Sir, I think we have a problem."

Of course…what else would we have? "Yes, Commander?"

"Commander Calavius…there are too many bodies."

"Excuse me, Commander? Too many bodies?" Balventius was a veteran, one with a reputation for being particularly vicious in battle. Was she losing her control, becoming rattled at losses?

"There are more enemy corpses than the roster of Imperial Guards in the palace, sir."

Calavius felt his gut tense up. If the Imperatrix had called for additional forces, she *had* known about the attack. But then why hadn't she called in enough line units to crush his rising? For all his widespread preparation, he'd hardly been able to secure every unit.

"Line units? Off-duty Imperial Guards called back to service?"

Balventius turned and looked behind her. One of her officers was running up the hill, carrying something. A soldier's jacket.

"There are a significant number of bodies clad in these uniforms," Balventius said as she grabbed the coat from her aide and held it up. "We have to identify this livery…it is not familiar to me." She turned back to the junior officer. "Optio, take this to the…"

"That will not be necessary, Commander." There was frustration in Calavius's voice, and resignation. "I know those colors."

His fists clenched again, and he had to fight to hold back the primal scream straining to escape his lungs. He knew the livery well. Very well.

The Vennius Legion.

Damn you, Tarkus…damn you to the Eleven Hells!

Chapter Fourteen

Encrypted Transmission from Originating from Dannith

The transfer has been made, and the operative is in place and has the package. I have tried to eliminate the intermediary as ordered, but I have been unable to locate him. Perhaps he fled from Dannith. I continue to search, and will terminate upon discovery. It is a lapse of security that he lives, but I consider it unlikely to interfere with the operation. The vessel has departed, and is beyond the reach of the intermediary, even if he attempts to undermine the operation.

Abandoned Warehouse
Just Outside the Spacer's District
Port Royal City, Planet Dannith, Ventica III
310 AC

Shugart was sobbing softly, his blood-covered hands down over his knee, clutching at the bloody, gaping wound. Lafarge had started their "discussion" rather abruptly with a bullet right through his kneecap. The bastard was a miserable, treacherous piece of garbage, whose deceit would have seen her and her people dead out at Chrysallis. She was ready to kill him for what he had done, but she had held back. She wanted to know exactly what had happened, and just why her contact had sold her out.

If it was just for money, she'd already decided she was indeed going to kill him. That was why she'd chosen this location. Dannith's economy had long been weak, and the war had only made it worse. The planet had a naval base, but that was about the only sector of its industry that benefited from the ongoing conflict. The rest of its economy was operating at little more than depression levels, and every warehouse and industrial facility in this sector had been shuttered. Not only would she get away with killing the worthless bastard, but his carcass would rot for weeks before anyone found it.

She was convinced Shugart had worked with Union operatives more than once, and that meant he had not only betrayed her, he had planned to do it all along. But it also meant he might have useful information of one sort or another, and she was determined to discover the details. If there was another relic out there, or something similarly valuable, she wanted to know about it…and she wanted to know whether the Union was aware of it or not.

Though she had rather enjoyed it, she hadn't shot her captive frivolously or on a whim. Shugart had never been a brave man, and if he was working with Sector Nine, it was a dead certainty he was scared shitless of them. She knew she wouldn't get anywhere at all, not until he was just as scared of her. Blowing the dirtbag's kneecap off seemed as good a first step toward that as any.

"Well, Rolf, I'll bet that hurts. It hurt when the Sector Nine thugs were giving me beatings too. I have to give it to them, they know their craft." She stared at the terrified, whimpering man with a feral stare. "Fortunately, I know mine as well."

She walked around behind him, smiling as he tried to twist around, to keep his eyes on her. She had to hold back a laugh when he shouted again in pain and turned, looking forward again.

"Yeah…I'd stay still if I were you. It doesn't take much pressure on that blasted kneecap to hurt like a son of a bitch, does it?"

"What do you want, you crazy bitch?"

"I'm impressed, Rolf. I didn't think you had that kind of courage in you. But before you choose your next words, consider the fact that you have another knee." She kicked his leg, and he screamed again, louder this time. He looked up at her with tears streaming down his face, but he didn't say anything.

"That's better. See, people say you're stupid. But I've always defended you. I tell them, 'Rolf isn't stupid. He's just slow.'" She crouched down next to the chair, staring right into his eyes. "Now, why don't you tell me about your deal with Sector Nine?"

"I don't know what you're talking about." His words were forced, and he whimpered and gasped for air as he spoke.

Lafarge held up her hand with the pistol. "Lying to me is a good way to tell me you think that other knee is superfluous... or maybe that there are other things I could think of to shoot off of you." She smiled. "I know you're afraid of Sector Nine, Rolf, but what you need to understand is you should be just as scared of me. More, because I've got you here."

"Andi, please..."

"Oh, we're well past 'Andi, please...' You set me up, Rolf. You sent me out to die, along with all my people. You could have just given your information to Sector Nine, not even told me about it. But you had to try to double dip. I could have gotten past an honest mistake, or even if they'd forced the information from you after you sold it to me. But the Union forces got there right after we did, and they had to come from a lot farther away...which means you gave them the info first."

She paused, rising back to her feet and walking around her terrified prisoner again. "I don't have to kill you, Rolf. All I have to do is turn you in. Selling information to Sector Nine is treason, you know, and the Alliance is at war. Even the ponderous Confederation legal system would get you to the scaffold pretty quickly right now. Losses in the war have been very high, and no one is feeling all that sympathetic about traitors."

She came back around and moved her face right in front of his. "I'd do that, turn you in—it's certainly less risky for me—but to be honest, I think I can do a better job of it myself. So, I guess we have an obvious first question. Do you have anything…interesting…to tell me, any useful info from Sector Nine? Or should I just take you apart one piece at a time?" She brought up her arm with the gun, aiming it toward Shugart's leg. "Starting with this other knee."

"No," he shrieked miserably. "No, please…"

"Listen, Rolf, I'm going to guess you know me well enough to realize you're not going to get out of this by appealing to my sympathy. Not after what you did. So, spare us both the waste of time. Give me useful information…or let's cut the chatter, and I'll get started."

"Okay, okay…" Shugart was broken, that much was clear from his voice. "I'll tell you what I know. Yes…I did give information to Sector Nine. I didn't have a choice. They came to me. I thought it was just another crew like yours. They'd heard I dealt in information about the Badlands." He hesitated.

"Go on," Lafarge said menacingly.

"They paid me. A large sum. I gave them some information, a few rumors about various small finds. But that wasn't enough for them. I'd already promised the Chrysallis find to you, and I knew you'd be straight with me and give me my cut. But they threatened me. They seemed to know I had something else."

"So, you shit yourself and told them everything. And then you sold it to me after that."

"I'd already promised you a prime lead…and you've got a temper. I didn't want to tell you I'd sold your information to someone else."

"You're not even a good liar, Rolf. Do you know that? You sold me the information because you figured the Union would take care of me out there, and you would never have to tell me what you did. But I spoiled the party, didn't I?"

"Andi…"

"Save it, shitbag. All that matters now is if you've got more intel. Something valuable enough to save your life. And you're almost out of time. So, one last time. Have you worked with Sector Nine again since Chrysallis?"

Shugart paused, but the instant she moved the gun he broke

down. "Yes…okay. Yes. They made me help them. They told me they'd kill me if I didn't do it."

"A lot of people want to kill you, Rolf. We may start a club. So, what is it?" Lafarge was disciplined, but her mind started to race. Where there was one ancient ship surviving, there could be another. Or more antimatter. Even one bottle would be enough for her people to buy entire moons of their own. Shugart was garbage, but she knew from experience he had a nose for sniffing out rumors of old tech.

"I have a contact…in the naval base."

Lafarge held back her surprise. This wasn't what she'd expected to hear. What did the naval base have to do with leads on old tech?

"What are you talking about, Rolf?"

"Sector Nine…they wanted me to use my contact."

Lafarge was confused. She almost gave him another kick in the knee, but something held her back.

"They wanted you to use your contact for what?"

Shugart gasped for air. He was spent, broken, his words barely coherent. "They had a transfer…someone they wanted on a ship's roster."

"They wanted your contact to authorize a personnel change? Why?"

"Don't know…not completely. Double agent. Wanted double agent on ship." Shugart was shaking, barely hanging on to his control.

"A double agent? You mean a Confederation spacer who is a Sector Nine operative?"

He nodded his head.

Lafarge was lost. She'd expected a lead on old tech out in the Badlands, not some babbling nonsense about enemy agents in the navy. "Sector Nine hired you to get your contact to make a transfer?"

He nodded again. "Yes," he muttered.

"Did you?"

He hesitated. "Yes…"

Lafarge paused. Shugart was scared, exhausted, terrified.

He'd lost a lot of blood from the leg wound, so much, in fact, she was a little concerned he might die on her before she got the information she wanted. But just what was that? A Union spy in the Confederation navy was a bad thing, to be sure. But it wasn't exactly the kind of thing she traded on.

Get the rest of the information. You can report it anonymously. The sooner the Confederation defeats the Union the better things will be.

She avoided the thought in the back of her mind, that the Confederation could very well *lose* the war, with consequences she didn't care to imagine. If she could help the war effort with a mysterious tip, she would.

"What is the agent there to do? Spy on ship movements? Steal information on tech systems?"

Shugart shook his head.

"Then what?" Lafarge waited a few seconds. Then she pointed the gun at his leg again. "I'm losing patience, Rolf."

"No! Please! The agent is there for…" He paused again.

Lafarge rested the barrel of the gun directly against Shugart's knee.

"Assassin," the hapless creature blurted out.

"Assassin? You mean they sent an agent onto a Confederation ship to kill someone." She felt an icy wave cut through her. "Answer me!" She grabbed his collar and shook hard. "They sent one of their people to kill a Confederation spacer?"

Shugart nodded.

"Who?" she said, losing her own cool now. "Who are they trying to kill?"

Her helpless captive shook his head. "Don't know…"

"Tell me," she almost screamed, bringing her hand across his face in a savage backhand slap. "Tell me!"

"I don't know…they didn't give me a name…"

"The ship. You arranged for a transfer. You must know the name of the ship."

He nodded incoherently.

She slapped him again, harder this time. "Tell me, Rolf! Tell me the name of the ship!"

He was barely conscious. He muttered something

unintelligible.

Lafarge felt as if she was going to vomit. She knew what he was going to say, somehow she knew. But she had to hear it. She *had* to. "Tell me," she said, her voice as cold as death. "Tell me now, Rolf, or I swear to the Eleven Hells I will blow your fucking head to chunks of goo."

He turned his head slightly, trying to look toward her. Finally, he said something. It was quiet, slurred, but this time she heard it.

"*Dauntless.*"

Chapter Fifteen

Old Coast Trail
North of Victorum, Alliance Capital City
Astara II, Palatia
Year 61 (310 AC)

"Get another blanket over her...or a tarp, whatever you can find." Vennius stared down at the Imperatrix, who was in and out of consciousness lying in the makeshift stretcher his people had fashioned. They'd done all they could to bind her wounds and make her as comfortable as possible, but he knew she was still in pain.

It had been a pleasantly cool day, but the night had proven to be cold, a touch of winter in the autumn breezes. The discomfort had been made worse by the rain, misty showers at first, but now a steady downpour. His soldiers were wet, cold, miserable. That meant nothing, of course. They weren't only Palatian soldiers, they were veterans of the Vennius Legion. They would do what was required of them, whatever the discomfort or danger.

He took a breath and looked behind him, his eyes moving down the ragged line. Maybe a third of the cohort was left. The fighting had been brutal, their losses heavy, and all the worse because his soldiers had to wipe out the enemy forces to the last. Leaving live enemies behind to report back on what had happened—and which way his people had gone—would have cost what little advantage in time he had.

He tried to estimate how far his force had come, but he realized years behind his desk had dulled his instincts somewhat. Ten kilometers? Less? The path had widened a bit, north of the city, but it was still rugged, and his exhausted soldiers had to carry the Imperatrix—not to mention the fact that a good percentage of them were walking wounded, stumbling along the best they could with wounds bound up the best they could manage.

He knew he had to get off the path soon. Calavius wasn't a fool. He would figure out how Vennius's forces had eluded him, and it wouldn't take long after that to realize which way they had gone. Vennius was well aware he had perhaps one-hundred fifty tired foot soldiers, while Calavius had aircraft and vehicles and likely thousands of troops available. His people were sitting ducks if they stayed, but if they went inland too soon they'd just get hung up in the mountains to the immediate north of Victorum. There were routes through the rocky terrain, but they were farther north. Another two kilometers, maybe three, and he could get his people off the cliffs and into the forests. That would gain some time, given them ground where they could hide for a while. Calavius and his people would have to secure control of the military establishments all across Palatia… not to mention the fleet in orbit. As important as it was for his treacherous friend to find the Imperatrix, he could not afford to ignore everything else. That might be just enough distraction for Vennius to escape, to think of something.

His stomach ached from hunger, and his throat and lips were parched. Discomfort aside, his people could do without food for a while, but he was going to need to find some fresh water soon. Lentius had been smart enough to disobey his orders and deploy the cohort in the city, but even he hadn't envisioned a march across the countryside. None of the troops had provisions or water bottles.

He trudged forward, ignoring the fatigue and the pain in his old body. There was no time for any of that, and Tarkus Vennius was determined to do whatever he had to do. He might die—all his soldiers might die—but he would not give up. Not while he had a breath left in his lungs.

He was working on a plan, one that extended beyond getting the hell out of the city and hiding. He hadn't gotten very far… in truth, he didn't have much to work with. But he did have a comm unit strong enough to reach orbit.

Calavius had jammed communications all around the city, but Vennius was betting his old friend hadn't had time to arrange for more than local interference, the city limits and not much beyond. If Vennius could get his group far enough north, they just might get into the clear.

Who to contact was another question entirely. His first thought was to send out a general distress call, but that was too risky. Calavius was no fool. *He outsmarted you, maneuvered you into giving him total control of the city's defenses.* He would have co-conspirators in crucial positions throughout Palatia's orbital installations and the fleet. Even if he reached potential allies, his enemies were closer, and they were ready. His command would be wiped out before any help could arrive.

Bellator…

Of course. Commander Egilius's ship.

The Egilii were a minor Patrician clan, poor but of noble origins, and longtime retainers of the Vennii. And Brutus Egilius was loyal. Of all the officers in the army and the fleet, there was no one Vennius trusted more, either to remain true to the Alliance's ideals, or to stay loyal to him personally. Albina Egilius had been a close friend of Vennius's, even an intermittent lover for a time long ago, and when she was killed in battle, he saw to the needs of her son, even more diligently than he would have done for any of the families sworn to fealty. For a passing moment, he had once even wondered if Brutus could be *his* son, but a check of the boy's birthdate and a little math quickly eliminated that possibility.

Yes, he just might be able to locate *Bellator* in its orbital rotation, and if he could, he would send a tight beam communique to his young retainer. There were a lot of ships in orbit around Palatia, not to mention satellites, fortresses, and listening posts.

He knew even the tightest beam was likely to be picked up, but with any luck at all it would be flagged as routine, and it would take some time to work its way to eyes that saw anything out of the ordinary in it.

If he could get his people to *Bellator* it would buy time. He knew he could only evade Calavius's search so long in these woods, and that was likely a period measured in hours, not days. And the battleship's sickbay would offer the medical care the Imperatrix desperately needed. He looked back toward the cluster of troopers carrying her. She looked even worse than she had earlier. Vennius was no doctor, but he knew the Imperatrix's wounds were bad, and that his makeshift first aid had only been of limited benefit. He had to get her better help, and he had to do it soon. Or she would die in that improvised stretcher.

Bellator was the answer. If they could get clear of the jamming in time.

*   *   *

Centurion Caelina Herminius rushed back through the woods. Path would have been a charitable description for the tiny, overgrown trail she'd been following. Commander Vennius had entrusted her to hold the rear, to position small combat teams in the likeliest places pursuers would pass. Their orders were clear. To hold as long as possible, to buy time for the main column to move farther north. She knew what "as long as possible" meant. Her people positioned away from the approach of the enemy might survive to return, but any of her teams that were engaged by the pursuing forces were expected to fight to the death. Vennius hadn't given such orders expressly, but then he didn't have to.

Herminius had six groups deployed, four troopers in each. That was twenty-five total, including herself, nearly one fifth of the cohort's remaining strength. Some of them would survive, with luck, though she'd placed herself along the approach she considered most likely. If she was right, her skill and intuition had likely signed her death warrant. Her orders were vague with

regard to her personal actions, but given the choice of fleeing while her people fought to the end…and standing at their
sides…she knew what she would do. The only thing she could
do.

The way is the way…

Her head spun around. She'd heard something. It could
have been a deer or another animal. In fact, that was probably
what it was. But she wasn't taking any chances.

She stopped and crouched low, looking around through the
dense forest. The leaves would be down in a few weeks, but
now the visibility was still poor. That was an advantage to the
column, and to her small defensive parties, but it was still frustrating to stare off through the woods and not be sure what she
was seeing.

There was nothing now. But she was sure she'd heard something. She almost stood up to head back toward the troopers
she'd deployed fifty meters down the path, but something kept
her where she was. She knew patience could be crucial, that two
enemies could face each other, and the first to move would be
dead.

Then she saw it. Movement in the brush, a shadowy figure.
No, three. Moving in her general direction, but off at an angle.

Scouts.

She didn't move. She barely breathed. No doubt her adversaries had thought they'd heard something too, and she wasn't
going to give cause to reignite their suspicions.

Her rifle was in her hand, and now she started to bring it
up, slowly, almost imperceptibly. The troopers were moving up
off to her right. In another minute, they'd come close to giving her a flank. She could take down one, she was sure of that.
Probably a second one too. But three seemed unlikely, at least
before her target could drop down. Then they'd be shooting
at each other in deep cover, and that meant they'd be wasting a
lot of ammo for nothing. Her four troopers would hear the firing, almost certainly, and they would come. The enemy soldier's
chance of survival was poor, but that wasn't what concerned
her. He didn't need to live to hurt her people. He just needed

to get a message back to whatever force was almost certainly close behind.

Herminius didn't have comm, at least none worth using. Her people were at the edge of the area of effect for the jamming. She might get a staticky message through, and she might not, but the chance of managing a clear communication was too small to give away her location. Whatever she started here, she was on her own, at least, at first.

She thought about pulling back, trying to get a warning to Commander Vennius. But she wasn't out here to scout out enemy forces. Vennius already knew they were being pursued. She was here to delay the enemy, and taking down their scouts, forcing whatever forces were approaching to slow down and shake out into combat formation, seemed the best way to do that.

Crack.

She was a veteran, and not one to delay when she'd come to a decision. Her shot had been perfect, dead on target, and one of the enemy troopers dropped to the ground.

She could see the others reacting even as she adjusted, bringing her rifle around, aiming for the second enemy. The soldier was moving quickly, but it was clear he was unsure what direction the attack had come from. That was enough to seal his fate.

Crack.

Two down. Her eyes scanned the forest, searching for the other soldier, for any signs that gave him away, but there was nothing. Her gut tightened, and suddenly she realized, she was no longer the only one hunting.

Crack.

The shot rang out from out in the forest, somewhere. It came close, too close. She dived down, taking cover behind a fallen tree. She knew about where her enemy was—he couldn't be far from where he'd been when she opened fire—but whoever was out there, he was a solid veteran.

Another shot blasted into the large tree trunk in front of her, showering her with splinters.

Whoever he is, he knows just where I am...

She looked cautiously over the tree, her eyes scanning the dense woods. She'd gotten an idea from that last shot, and she was sure she had the general spot. But close wasn't good enough. They were both in cover, and she knew this duel could be a long one. But time was on her enemy's side. She didn't have a doubt in her mind the soldier out there had sent an alarm, that the enemy's comm could cut through their jamming. That meant more enemy forces were on the way, that they would probably be there in a matter of minutes.

Her job was to delay the main enemy force, not fence with one trooper in the forest. She had her adversary pinned down, but he had her suppressed as well.

She heard sounds off to the side. Her closest group, moving toward the sounds of combat. Her people were veterans. They would move cautiously...but they were heading right toward the enemy soldier. She had a sickening feeling in her gut as she realized at least one of her troopers was going to die. She had no comm, no way to warn them. All she could do was make sure it wasn't for naught.

She gripped her rifle tightly, staring out at her enemy's location, waiting. Then it happened. She saw the movement, and even as she was reacting, she heard the shot. She felt a surge of rage—she didn't know for sure the enemy had hit one of her people, but the trooper out there was good, and she knew it was unlikely he'd missed.

Her finger tightened, and her own rifle cracked loudly. She'd caught a hint of movement. It wasn't much...but it was enough. She watched the leaves rustling as her target fell to the ground. She was up in an instant, rushing as quickly as she could through the dense undergrowth, rifle out in front of her. She was pretty sure she'd managed a killing shot, but training and experience had taught her never to take something like that for granted. That was how soldiers got killed.

She leapt up, over the cluster of rocks her opponent had been using as cover, and as she did, she fired three times, riddling her enemy's body. But her frantic charge had not been necessary. Her first shot had taken off the top of the soldier's head.

"Centurion…are you okay?"

She spun around, signaling to her troopers to stop. There were only three of them. Her instincts had been correct, but none of that mattered now. There was no time to think about the dead. Her people had a mission, and that was to delay whatever was coming this way.

"Spread out, and grab some decent cover. We've got enemies coming this way, probably a lot of enemies. And our orders are clear." Her voice was grim. "Hold them as long as possible. Buy time for Commander Vennius to get the Imperatrix out of here."

*   *   *

Brutus Egilius listened to the words on the headset, trying to understand what was going on. The voice was a match, but he had to be sure it was really Tarkus Vennius speaking to him.

He was the only one hearing the transmission, but his tone and his responses had been enough to silence the bridge. He could feel the edginess of the crew as they listened to him speaking to someone who claimed to be the Commander-Maximus, the highest-ranking officer in the Alliance fleet.

"You say you have the Imperatrix with you?" His tone was cautious. He had nothing but respect for Vennius, but he was far from certain he was actually speaking with his mentor. He'd been getting communiques for hours now, strange warnings from up the chain of command. There was some kind of security breach on the surface…and that made him all the more suspicious. Was this some attempt to trick him? Or was the situation on the surface serious enough that the Commander-Maximus—and the Imperatrix—were in trouble? It seemed far-fetched to him.

"Yes, the Imperatrix is with me," the voice replied. "Brutus, there is no time to waste. I will transmit our coordinates to you. I need you to send down a flight of shuttles and bring us up to *Bellator*. Immediately."

Egilius felt his head shaking back and forth, a subconscious expression of his doubt. "I'm sorry, sir, but I need to confirm your identity before I can obey an order like that." Regardless of how unlikely the whole story seemed, he was torn. It seemed probable this was some kind of trick, particularly in light of whatever was going in Victorum. But the thought of refusing Tarkus Vennius, the real Vennius…not only would it be gross insubordination to disregard the orders of the fleet commander, it would be a shameful failure to acknowledge his family's— his own—debts to the Vennius patriarch, a man to whom he'd sworn personal loyalty unto death.

"I don't have my AI, Brutus, or my secure comm. I can't access my…" There was a short silence. Then: "Sliver Lake."

Egilius froze in place.

"It was her favorite place, Brutus. Your mother went up there every chance she got. She especially liked the upper neck, near the Three Waterfalls. I had promised her a stretch of land up there, to build a house…when she retired." There was a sadness in Vennius's voice, one *Bellator*'s captain understood perfectly. Albina Egilius had never retired, nor would she ever. Instead, she had died in the mud and blood outside the capital city of Tarkath, shot down leading one section of the final assault.

Egilius felt a rush of emotion, of old memories. He had been young when his mother was killed, two years from the age of the Ordeal. But he remembered Sliver Lake clearly. She had taken him there every time she'd come home on leave. He'd never seen her so happy as she was when they'd hiked the lake's pristine shores and swum its cold, deep waters. But he'd never spoken of it to anyone, and that could mean only one thing…

"Commander, it really *is* you. What is happening, sir?"

"Yes, Brutus, it is me, but there is no time to explain. I need you to listen carefully. Send down a flight of shuttles, at least three, as quickly as possible. I'm sending coordinates now. And don't tell anyone else, not fleet command, not orbital control… no one. Do you understand?"

"Yes, sir." He was still confused, but he was convinced he

was speaking to the Commander-Maximus, and he was ready to do anything Vennius commanded. He turned and gestured toward his first officer. "Now, Optiomagis. I want four shuttles launched at once to the surface coordinates coming in now." An extra ship couldn't hurt. "And send a decurius of stormtropers in each. Fully armed and armored."

"Yes, Commander."

"Shuttles are preparing to launch now, sir."

"Very good, Brutus. And remember, not a word of this to anyone. Trust no one you're not absolutely sure about."

Egilius spun around again, back toward his exec. "External comm off, Optiomagis. Now!" Then, back into the comm unit. "Understood, sir." He paused for an instant. Then he added, "Is there anything else I can do, Commander?"

The line was quiet for a moment, nothing more than faint background static. Then Vennius spoke again. "Yes, Drusus. One thing." Another pause. "You can bring *Bellator* to battlestations."

Chapter Sixteen

Lafarge sat in her chair on *Pegasus*'s cramped bridge. It was shiny and clean, far cleaner than she'd ever remembered it, old, worn panels and chairs replaced with pristine new ones. Admiral Striker was nothing if not a man of his word. He'd agreed to fix her ship, and he'd done a first-class job of it.

It felt like home to be back where she was, and she longed to feel settled, at peace, at least to whatever extent she ever did. But now she was leaning forward in her chair, tense, almost like a great cat ready to spring on a moment's notice. Her stomach was tight, and her hands were intermittently clenching around sweaty palms. She'd thought her time with Tyler Barron was done, at least until fate threw them into each other's paths again. She'd nursed a thought or two about one day giving pure destiny an assist, but not for some time still. Barron had a war to fight, and she had a job to do as well. But now none of that mattered to her. Rolf Shugart's words had been utterly unexpected, but the instant she'd heard them, she knew what she had to do.

She'd rounded up her crew and blasted off, barely asking for clearance before she did. She knew rationally that *Daunt-*

less would be gone before she could catch her, but she had to try. She had no idea where Barron's ship was heading, and her hurried but thorough attempts to find out had achieved little success. She knew *Dauntless* had departed for the Vestara transit point, but that was all. Either her contacts—and her contacts' contacts—really knew nothing about the battleship's ultimate destination, or they were maintaining ironclad secrecy.

Vestara seemed an odd choice for a vessel heading back to the front lines, and the transfer of a ship back to the main fleet didn't seem a secret important enough to shut down all her intelligence sources. Every failed attempt to learn where Barron was going only increased her concern. She *had* to reach him. She had to tell him what she'd learned from Shugart.

"*Dauntless* isn't here, Andi. We've searched everywhere. There are no publicly-accessible records of her transiting, but she must have gone through the Vestara point." Merrick maintain his usual professional tone, perhaps with a touch of softness thrown in. Lafarge's crew all knew about her relationship with Barron—she wasn't sure how, as she hadn't told anyone. But they had a way of finding things out, and thinking back, she realized she probably hadn't hidden her interest well.

"I have to find him." She spoke softly, her words meant only for herself, but *Pegasus*'s bridge was a small place, and she suspected Vig had heard her. Whether he did or not, her friend didn't react.

"Set a course back to Dannith, Vig. I'm sorry, I know we were all set to head back into the Badlands, but I've got something I have to do. I can't ask any of you to come, but I'll return here when I'm done, and, if you're all still around, we can go on our next expedition."

"You have to chase Tyler Barron and *Dauntless*, that much is obvious. I don't know why, since you've been as tight-lipped as I've ever seen you. But you're not hiding the worry as well as you think. You have to give us credit, Andi. We know you well, perhaps better than you think."

She looked over at her first officer—her best friend. She was surprised for an instant…until she suddenly realized she wasn't. She knew her people, and she was underestimating them in assuming they were any less perceptive than she. "I'm sorry, Vig. I'm not trying to hide anything. I'm just…" Her voice drifted off. She wasn't sure what to say. She was an intensely private person in most ways, even around those she trusted, like her crew. But more than that, she was wrestling with her feelings for Barron. She had no place in her life for such attachments, and she'd made her peace with that. But if what Shugart had told her was true…well, she couldn't leave Barron in danger, not without doing everything she could to warn him.

"You're all tied up in knots, Andi. It's more obvious than you think. At least to us. And the fact that you've got Rolf Shugart tied up and locked in the cargo hold seems like a significant clue." Merrick paused. "We know you have to try to find *Dauntless*. Whatever it is, I can see it's important, to you at least. And that makes it important to us. The Badlands will still be there, Andi…in a month, in a year. You've got to do what you feel you have to." He stared across the meter and a half from his station to hers. "But if you think I'm going to let you do it alone, if you think any of us are going to let you go by yourself…then you don't understand us as well as I thought you did."

She looked back at Merrick, but it was some time before she managed to force words through her mouth. She was dedicated to her crew, and she knew they were to her. But she'd always had trouble with loyalty. She could give it, at least to those few she felt deserved it, but she couldn't expect it, not really. She could understand her crew's affections, in an abstract way, at least, but somewhere deep inside her, she considered her problems hers. She'd never learned to ask anyone for help.

"Vig, I don't even know where I'm going to go. *Dauntless* was sent somewhere…somewhere likely very dangerous. I have no idea where to even look. Or how long it could take."

"None of that matters, Andi."

"I appreciate your loyalty, Vig, but I can't drag the entire crew into danger when there's no gain to had. That's not what they signed on for."

Merrick chuckled briefly. "Andi, I've already talked to the

crew. They're staying, every one of them. Wherever you go, however long it takes."

"But..."

"No buts. You can tell us what's so important, or you can stay tight-lipped about it. But we're with you either way. To the end."

Lafarge considered herself a cold fish, but she felt a surge of emotion at the display of friendship and loyalty her first officer was displaying, for himself and on behalf of the others. "Thank you, Vig," she said softly. "I don't know what to say..."

"Well, you can start by issuing some orders. Every minute we sit here, *Dauntless* gets farther away."

She took a deep breath. She had no idea where to look for *Dauntless*. But she knew someone who would know exactly where the battleship was headed. Admiral Striker. He might even listen to her and pay heed to her words. The problem was, he was gone from Dannith too. She could only guess at where he went, but at least she had a clear first choice in his case. Fleet Base Grimaldi.

"Vig, plot a course to the Killian transit point. I've got to find Admiral Striker, and Grimaldi is the likeliest place he'll be."

"Yes, Andi." There was no hesitation in his tone, but she heard a bit of nervousness. She understood completely. Base Grimaldi—and the whole Krakus system—was embargoed to all but crucial military traffic. If she could reach Striker, get a message through quickly enough, she was confident he'd hear what she had to say. But *Pegasus* would never be allowed through the outer pickets...and it would take ages to work her way through the chain of command, assuming she could ever get to the admiral.

Unless she blew past the checkpoints and drove *Pegasus* toward the base, close enough to get a message through, one that had a chance of reaching Striker right away. It was a dangerous plan, one that carried more than a little likelihood of getting her ship blasted to atoms. But it was the only way.

"Vig..." She hesitated for a moment. Her crew had stuck with her, but now she was going to lead them right into the most heavily defended place in the Confederation, without clearance. That was *definitely* not what any of them had signed up for.

"Course set, Andi. Ready to engage."

She reached down and flipped on her comm unit. "Lex, how are the engines holding up?" *And how are you?*

"They're in great shape. The repair crews retuned the energy allocation system. We're faster than we were before, Andi. I'm not sure how much exactly, not yet, but at least a third."

She'd been worried about the engineer. He'd gone on a world class bender, by all accounts, and she'd been looking for him when she'd stumbled on Shugart. But Lex Righter had apparently pulled himself together, and he'd shown up sober and ready for action. She was still concerned about the engineer, about how he was handling all that had happened out at Chrysallis, but that was tomorrow's problem. Right now, he was at his engines and ready to do what had to be done.

"Well, Lex…let's see what they can do. We've got to get to Fleet Base Grimaldi. And every minute counts."

"No problem, Andi. Just make sure everybody's strapped in. The old girl's got a lot more kick than she had before."

"Whenever you're ready, Lex."

She leaned back in her chair. She still had doubts about bringing her people with her. Regardless of their loyalty, it felt wrong to her to put them in danger over something that had nothing to do with them.

"Lex reports full thrust in twenty seconds, Andi." Vig turned and looked over at her. Almost as if he'd read her mind, he added, "We're in this all the way, Andi. For you—and that would be enough. But Captain Barron and his people saved me too, and they treated us fairly. Whatever this is all about, if you think it is important, that's enough for us."

She took a deep breath as the thrusters kicked in. For a second, she felt the increased power of the engines, but then most of the pressure seemed to vanish. The upgraded compensators *really* made a difference. Another sign of just how extensively Striker's people had upgraded her old ship.

She returned Merrick's gaze. He was willing to follow her

anywhere, on her word alone that it was important. All her people were. The hell into which Andi Lafarge had been born, out of which she'd crawled by wits and determination, had prepared her for many things, but not the unconditional loyalty and affection of her crew. She wasn't sure how to handle it. But she knew one thing. She had to trust them in return. And they had a right to know why they were risking their lives.

"It's Sector Nine, Vig," she said abruptly. "They snuck an agent onto *Dauntless*, one of the replacements for her crew."

She stared at her friend, blue eyes cold, as she struggled to keep the fear out of her voice.

"They have an assassin on *Dauntless*."

Chapter Seventeen

Internal Transmission Within Alliance Fleet Command

AS *Bellator* has failed to respond to multiple attempts at scheduled communications, presumably due to mechanical failure. However, the vessel has now launched several unauthorized craft, which appear to be on a course to land on the surface of Palatia. Request further orders. Should we send a fleet command shuttle to dock with *Bellator* and determine her status?

Viridi Forest
North of Victorum, Alliance Capital City
Astara II, Palatia
Year 61 (310 AC)

"Single shots! Aim before you fire." Centurion Caelina Herminius crouched behind a fallen tree, looking out at the advancing enemy forces in the pale light of early morning. A blast of automatic fire would have been an ideal defensive tactic, but her people simply didn't have the ammunition. They were running low, and when they ran out completely, they were as good as finished.

She'd managed to recall most of her scattered scouts, and they had formed something that resembled a defensive line. She had no hope of holding the troopers heading toward her tiny force. She'd known success would be measured in time. Minutes, perhaps even an hour, however long her people could hold the line and buy time for Commander Vennius. And so it had been, for perhaps the last forty-five minutes.

Vennius had sent up orders for her to fall back slowly, not to sacrifice herself and all her soldiers to a suicidal fixed defense, but she knew the best way to delay the enemy was to pick the most defensible spot, and stay right there. She'd set down every field of fire herself, positioned every one of her people with care, and she'd seen the payoff in three enemy advances pushed back.

Now, half her people were down, and the mass of troopers approaching would run over the rest of them, regardless of what she did. Worse, she'd gotten word from her flankers. The enemy was coming around both ends of her lines. She was a Palatian to the core, a warrior above all else. She was willing to die, to see all of her people die, but not for nothing. Throwing away the rest of her command wouldn't buy more than a few seconds, and that was pointless waste. She could achieve more by harassing the attackers than by dying for no gain.

"We're going to fall back now. I want odds to drop back three hundred meters. Evens cover the move, then follow while odds provide support. Pass it down, make sure the troopers on the flanks are in the loop." She was shouting so loudly, she was probably telling the enemy advance forces what she was doing. But there was no choice. Her position was right on the edge of the jamming radius around Victorum, and she had to be sure her people got her orders.

"Odds…go. Evens, covering fire." She stayed in place, even though her position made her an odd. She wasn't going back, not until every one of her people still alive had pulled back.

That was twelve, besides her, exactly half the strength she'd started with. Fifty percent casualties were heavy by any measure, but she'd expected them all to die. Anybody she brought back now was a bonus. Or anybody who made it back even if she didn't.

She saw movement, and she fired. Then again. She thought

she saw a figure fall, but she couldn't be sure. It didn't matter. Her primary concern wasn't scoring kills. There were too many troops approaching. No number of hits was going to alter the situation. But if her people could keep up the pressure, force the attackers to be cautious, slow the enemy advance enough, then they could make a difference.

Assuming Commander Vennius has a more detailed plan than fleeing into the woods...

She didn't doubt Vennius's skill, and her loyalty was rock solid. Her family had served his since the earliest days of the Alliance, as her own children would continue to do, even if she failed to return home.

If there still is an Alliance...

She had no clue what was happening, but the idea that her people were fighting other Palatians to save the Commander-Maximus and the Imperatrix still seemed unreal. She'd faced enemies before, but they had always been offworlders, foreigners. Enemies. Now she had killed her brethren, and lost troopers to Palatian fire. She tried not to let herself dwell on it...the thought made her sick to her stomach, and just distracted her from the fight at hand. She would do her duty, but in her gut, she knew her nation—her home—would never be the same.

"Evens, pull back." She'd looked behind her, but the woods were too dense. Visibility was far less than three hundred meters, at least for picking out her people who'd gone to cover. But she could hear the sounds of fire, picked shots. And the attackers were close now. It was time to pull back.

She turned and ran, crouching low and trying to keep as much cover as possible as she ran. The forest floor was treacherous, covered with roots and branches, and rocks half-buried in the dense black soil. Tripping now, breaking a leg or an ankle, would be a death sentence.

She could hear sounds from above, the roar of airship engines. *Again.* Whatever rogue group was chasing them, they not only had significant resources, they appeared to have air superiority around the capital. *What is happening?*

She saw the line of odds up ahead. The evens were going

to move another three hundred meters, past the odds, but Herminius intended to stop with her forward line. She had perhaps thirty meters to go. Then, suddenly, she was down. She hadn't felt the shot, and she didn't remember falling. But now she was lying on the mossy ground, staring up at the green canopy above.

Pain came, but only for a moment. She tried to move her head, to look down at her body, to see where she was wounded. But she couldn't. She managed move her arm, putting her hand on her chest. She felt the wet warmth, and she knew, even before she pulled it away and saw the blood covering it. The shot had entered her back and come out through her chest, and as she struggled for air, coughing to clear the bloody fluid filling her lungs, she understood. She'd fought on a dozen battlefields, but this would be her last. She felt a rush of emotion, sorrow because she would never see her children again. Concern for her soldiers, and for Vennius and the Imperatrix. Fear... of death, of the unknown. But there was relief of a sort too, beneath the pain and loss, almost a gratefulness that she would not have to see what was to become of her people.

She took one last breath, labored but deep, and then she was gone.

*   *   *

"They're coming, sir. Centurion Herminius is dead. Four of her people made it back. They say there are at least five hundred enemy troopers on their tail."

"Very well, Drusus. Do what you can to set up a defensive perimeter." Vennius shook his head as he looked out of the woods, into the large clearing beyond. There was no point in running further. There was nowhere to go. Escape would come here, or it would not come at all. Vennius trusted Brutus Egilius completely. He had no doubt the officer would send the shuttles he'd requested. The question was, would they get through...and if they did, would it be in time?

"Yes, sir." Lentius turned and began to head deeper into

woods. The defensive line Vennius had ordered was already in place. His order had really been for the commander of his legion to take his place and direct the fighting that would begin any moment.

"Drusus, wait…" Vennius took a few steps from the heavy tree line, out into the waist-high grass. "Do you hear that?"

Lentius followed, cupping a hand to his ear. "Yes, sir," he replied, a burst of energy in his voice. "The shuttles?"

"Let's hope." Vennius turned back toward the woods. "And let's also hope they're not too late." The shuttles would be vulnerable on the ground. If the pursuing forces burst out of the woods while his people were boarding, it would be a massacre.

"We've got to hold them back, Drusus. We need time."

"I'll take a picked force forward. We'll get you the time you need."

"No." Vennius knew Lentius was suggesting a last stand, one from which he wouldn't return. The Commander-Maximus had sent many valued officers on such missions before, but now something stopped him. Something beyond the fact that he'd known Lentius for decades and he liked the officer immensely. It wasn't even emotional. It was cold in a way that troubled him, but it was there and he understood the wisdom of it. "Send the picked force, but I don't want you to lead them." He paused then, fearing Lentius would take the order as a lack of faith in him, he added, "I need you here, Drusus." His words were meant to reassure the officer, but they were nothing but the truth. Vennius had no idea what was happening out there, how many officers Calavius had suborned to his treason or what lies he'd used to gain the support of others. He *did* need Lentius. And Aurelius and Egilius. They were all he *knew* he had, members of a tiny elite. Those he knew he could trust.

Lentius still had a troubled look on his face. Vennius understood. It was hard to be ordered to mount a self-sacrificial defense, but to send his soldiers and not be allowed to join them? That was hell to an officer like Drusus Lentius.

"Now, Drusus. There is no time…and send as few as possible. We need what strength we can save. Come back here immediately after you've set up the line." *I know this hurts you, my friend, but it is where your duty lies.*

"Yes, sir." Lentius turned and headed off, but Vennius could see the pain in his hunched shoulders.

He turned back around, looking up, just as he saw the first shuttles move into view. They were coming in fast, at sharp angles. *Egilius sent his best pilots...*

"Let's move," he shouted toward the cluster of troops standing behind him. "Get the Imperatrix up. We move her on the first shuttle. She is our first—our only—priority." He watched for a few seconds as the soldiers reached down and pulled their ruler up from the pile of leaves they'd used as an improvised bed for her. Then he looked back, watching as the shuttles swooped down...just as fire erupted all around the makeshift camp's perimeter. The pursuers had caught his small group.

"Faster...let's go," he yelled. The soldiers carrying the Imperatrix moved up next to him, pausing for a moment as the first two shuttles landed. Then Vennius waved his arm, and they ran out into the open grassland. Vennius himself turned around, sliding his rifle from his shoulder. "I want every one of you to stand firm until the Imperatrix is on one of those shuttles and off the ground," he shouted to the soldiers around him. He could see Lentius's forlorn hope forming up in the distance. They were fighting hard, but Vennius knew they wouldn't hold for more than a few minutes. There were just too many troops attacking...and these weren't outworld conscripts, they were Alliance soldiers.

He looked back. The soldiers carrying the Imperatrix were about halfway to the closest shuttle, moving as quickly as they could with the rough stretcher. He did a quick calculation in his head. They weren't going to make it. The enemy forces would be through his defenders in a few more seconds, and if they caught his people in the open grassland it would be over.

He'd come all this way to be a few minutes late. Maybe one of the shuttles could escape, at least. He wanted to think of his efforts as a success if he got the Imperatrix out, but he knew it would be futile if he didn't escape too. She was badly wounded, in no shape to rally loyalist forces. He knew he should go now too, that he had to be on that shuttle when it took off, but he couldn't force himself to move. He'd sent thousands to their deaths in his career, but he'd never run away and left a command behind.

Then he saw movement, first from the perimeter, as a line of enemy troopers began to burst past his forlorn hope. And an instant later, out in the grasslands, as soldiers began pouring out of the shuttles. They were clad in full body armor, and they carried heavy autoguns.

He understood immediately. Egilius had shown more fore-sight that he had. He'd dispatched the shuttles, but he'd sent stormtroopers as well…and they were far more heavily armed than Vennius's people. Or their pursuers.

"Pull back, now," he shouted to his forces. "Fall back on the shuttles." He turned and ran out into the open meadow, waving to the new arrivals. "This way," he shouted. Set up a line just inside the woods."

The soldiers ran forward, reaching Vennius's position. An officer stopped and walked over to him, shouting as he did for the rest of the troopers to continue on.

"Commander-Maximus, I am Centurion Sintius. Com-mander-Princeps Egilius sends his best wishes. If you will move to the shuttles, sir, my troopers and I will hold back your enemies."

"My thanks, Centurion, to you and your commander." Ven-nius watched as his troopers raced out of the woods, moving toward the waiting shuttles. He looked back into the forest, just as Sintius's advancing line opened up. The heavy fire tore into the woods, ripping apart brush and trees and sending chunks of shattered wood flying all around.

The attacking forces stopped cold and went to ground, as several dozen of their number were torn apart in just a few sec-onds by the intense fire.

"Commander-Maximus, please sir…you must come now. My orders are to see to your rescue as well as the Imperatrix's." Vennius looked back at the centurion, then out at the field. Half his people had already boarded the shuttles, and the rest were moving swiftly toward three of the vessels. The fourth, the one carrying the Imperatrix, had already closed its hatches. Just as Vennius's eyes moved across the sleek vessel, its engines blasted, and a few seconds later it lifted off, rising perhaps twenty meters on its underjets, before the main thrusters fired, and it zipped off, disappearing quickly into the predawn sky.

"Please, sir," the centurion said again, clearly caught between respect for Vennius and his need to safeguard the Commander-Maximus.

"Of course." He took a few steps then looked back. "Begin pulling your people back, Centurion. We're not lifting off until everyone is onboard." He knew he was being foolish, but he didn't care. The Imperatrix was already on her way. That part of his mission was accomplished. He'd lost enough of his people this terrible night, at the Admiralty and in the palace…and along the whole nightmarish route of retreat through the woods. He'd done what had to be done, and he wouldn't second-guess himself. But he wasn't leaving anybody else behind.

"I mean it, Centurion. We're not lifting off, not a meter off the ground, until everybody is secured." *I don't know the extent of what is happening, but I feel sure of one thing. I can't spare one loyal soldier. Not a single one.*

Chapter Eighteen

Free Trader Pegasus
Bootis System
Approaching Krakus Transwarp Point
310 AC

"Unidentified vessel, you are decelerate at once and transmit your ID beacon. You are in proscribed space. If you do not obey at once, we will be forced to take immediate action."

Immediate action. Lafarge didn't like the sound of that. She didn't like it at all. It was one of the things she hated about the way government—military or otherwise—operated. Why didn't they just say what they meant? *Answer us at once or we will open fire...we will destroy you.* Of course, she wasn't sure they'd *destroy Pegasus.* For all she disliked authority, she was willing to bet the Confederation fleet would go to considerable lengths to avoid blasting a small civilian ship that, as far as they were concerned, was most likely lost and possibly suffering from a comm failure.

Good. Think that.

She knew she'd never get close to Grimaldi, but she had to at least get into the Krakus system. Then she could blast out her message to Striker at full power and hope, somehow, that it made it to him before some escort ship blasted her newly repaired engines to scrap. Still, the idea of playing chicken, of rushing the transit point and hoping whoever was in charge of the picket line wasn't a trigger-happy jackboot, seemed like a terrible plan. *Too bad it's the only one I have…*

"Stay on course, Vig."

"You got it, Andi." Merrick sounded a little nervous, but for the most part he seemed to be holding it together. Andi had been touched by her crew's willingness to stay with her. *No, not willingness…insistence.* But now she wished she had left them behind as she'd initially intended. It was bad enough she was risking her life to try to save a lover whom only a week ago she'd never expected to see again, but the idea of getting Vig and the others killed too was over the top. She felt an urge to order Merrick to cut the thrusters, to yield to inspection and attempt to get her message to Striker through normal channels. She wasn't even sure the admiral was at Grimaldi. She could take be taking the risk to get through to Krakus only to be destroyed when her transmission didn't reach an absent Striker.

She didn't move, though, didn't say a word. She couldn't stop, not even to save her crew. She had to try to reach Striker, to warn him about the assassin on *Dauntless.* She didn't know anything about Sector Nine's specific plan, but what else could it be except to assassinate the Confederation's most famous captain? She was pretty sure Shugart didn't know either, that he'd simply been a conduit between Sector Nine and the naval back office that got the assassin on Barron's crew. She'd given him a good working over, and she was almost certain she'd beaten all he knew out of him.

And if he is still lying to me…if he is holding back…I will throw him out the airlock myself…

Unless Tyler…no, you won't let that happen…

But if it does, Rolf Shugart will die a death he can't even imagine…

"Unidentified vessel, this is your last warning. Reverse thrust and transmit your beacon, or we will open fire."

Better…a clear threat, at least. Was that so hard?

"Vig, transmit the beacon. We've been in a Confederation military shipyard for months. We might be in the database, and if we are, they might be less likely to shoot at us. Maybe they'll figure we're a Confederation Intelligence ship or some kind of courier with a comm failure." She knew her best bet was to plant doubt in the mind of whatever commander was making the decisions out there. She was a lot more comfortable depending on doubt, on the concern of some officer that he might open fire on a vessel that turned out to be legitimate than she was on moral hesitancy to blast an unknown vessel. She didn't think much of the character of most people, but she knew fear and worry were strong motivators.

"Transmitting."

"And be ready on the engines. I want full blast on a direct course to the transit point…as soon as I give the word."

"We're ready, Andi. Lex is down in the engine room, just in case." Lafarge wasn't the only one who didn't trust outsiders. Every system appeared to be in top condition after the refit, but Vig and Lex were still clearly cautious.

She looked up at the bridge's small screen, watching as several ships moved toward *Pegasus*. Still no shots, not even a warning blast. *That's right…try to figure out why* Pegasus *shows up in your roster sheets as just serviced at Dannith. I only need a minute or two…*

"Vessel *Pegasus*, you are not listed on our manifest. You do not have clearance to transit to Krakus. Repeat, you do not have clearance to transit."

No threat of shooting us…that's good…

"Almost ready, Vig…" She leaned forward in her chair, eyes on the display, counting slowly under her breath. She couldn't depend on the pickets waiting indefinitely. They were confused now, and that was buying time. But they would move at least one of their ships to the transit gate, where it would be in position to destroy *Pegasus* before she could jump. She had to get there first.

There wasn't much doubt that blasting at full toward the gate would provoke a hostile response. *Pegasus* was faster than she looked, than the Confeds out there would expect her to be, all the more so after the upgrades Striker had installed, and that was an edge she planned to use to the fullest. She would have surprise, for a time, at least. Everything depended on perfect timing…making the move before the Confeds lost patience, but before it was too late.

"Almost…"

She was frozen in place, watching as *Pegasus* moved closer to the transit point. She wasn't going to get there before the ships moving to intercept. Not at current acceleration. *You guys probably think this is all we've got…*

She waited, more seconds passing, her eyes darting toward the chronometer. It seemed almost impossible, but less than a minute had passed since she'd last looked. Each instant seemed to last an eternity.

"Vessel *Pegasus*, this is Captain Roland James, of the CFS Mustang. I order you to…"

"Now, Vig."

Merrick didn't respond. He just turned and hit a single button on his workstation. Everything was already prepared, the course laid in, the engines charged and ready for full output.

Lafarge felt the thrust slam into her, pushing her back against the plush cushioning of her chair. The seat was new, courtesy of the refit. She felt her stomach rolling, the result of the rapid sequencing of engine thrust, changes in output from maximum thrust to ranges within five percent of max. The evasive maneuvers were a precaution, in case Captain James had the guts to open fire. It was too easy to hit a vessel moving at fixed acceleration, so Lafarge had mixed it up, giving James's targeting people something to think about.

"Forty seconds to transit." Vig struggled to get the words out under the crushing force.

Lafarge could hear Captain James on the comm. The change in his tone was clear. He interpreted her actions as a threat. A ship might move at a fixed velocity and fail to answer because of a comm failure, but a desperate blast toward the jump point, and an acceleration capacity far beyond what he could have expected from a tramp freighter…it was too much.

She saw flashes on the display. The patrol ships firing at *Pegasus*. The sudden acceleration had provoked an immediate response.

Good for you, Captain James. She didn't like her ship being fired upon, but she couldn't help but respect the officer's willingness to take decisive action. *Hopefully, there are no master marksman in this "behind the lines" patrol group.*

"Keep cycling through those random thrust mods, Vig. That frigate out there might not be much in a fleet action, but she'll do a job on us if she hits. And I'm not ready to scratch the new paint. Not yet."

The humor was as much for herself as for her companion. She was afraid, of course, as she knew Vig was. But there was nothing to be gained by acknowledging it.

"Ten more seconds, Andi…"

She held her breath, even as another ship opened fire and *Pegasus* shook hard from a near miss. She was counting down in her head…*five, four, three…*

Almost there…but it will be even worse on the other side…

She felt the strange queasy feeling she always did as *Pegasus* slipped into the transwarp tube. Time was hard to track in the bizarre alternate space that allowed travel at speeds effectively faster than that of light, but she knew the jump was only three lightyears. That would take half a lifetime at even the fastest speeds her ship had ever hit, but in the tube, it would be less than fifteen seconds.

It was hard to think clearly, but she tried to focus. She had to be ready to send her transmission immediately, and hope it got to Striker quickly. Then she would have to shut down her ship and surrender. At once. Unless she wanted to fight half the Confederation fleet.

She felt a hard lurch as *Pegasus* emerged into normal space. She turned and glared over at her number two. "All right, Vig, point this beam right at the station, and put every watt of power you can scrape up onto it."

"Ready, Andi…on your channel."

She could already hear the messages coming in, stern warnings to heave to, and prepare to be boarded. The whole idea of yielding was uncomfortable for her, but this time there was no choice. She flipped the switch on her comm unit.

"Attention, Admiral Striker. To any party intercepting this

communication...it must be delivered to Admiral Striker at once. Admiral, this is Andromeda Lafarge on *Pegasus*. I have vital information regarding Union activity. Please, Admiral...I must speak with you at once. It is a matter of life and death. Please respond to this communique."

She recoiled at the pleading sound in her voice, but that was exactly what she was doing. It was more than her ship at stake, more than the freedom of her crew. It was Tyler's life too. If Striker didn't get the message right away, if she got trapped in some bureaucratic hell with a bunch of lower level functionaries...there wouldn't be time to save Barron. *There might not even be time now...*

"Unidentified vessel, you are ordered to cut all thrust and reduce energy output to minimal life support levels. This is the last warning you will receive."

She flipped the channel on her headset and took a deep breath. "Confederation patrol vessel, this is *Pegasus*..." The word almost stuck in her throat. "...yielding as ordered." She ran her hand across her throat, a gesture to Vig to cut the engines and the reactor. He turned immediately and did just that.

She felt the thrust vanish almost immediately. Her body expected freefall, but instead she felt near Megara-normal gravity. She'd almost forgotten the upgraded compensators Striker had included in the repair package he'd gifted her.

"Attention Confederation patrol vessel, we have cut all thrust and reduced power output to minimal levels. Awaiting further orders."

She sighed softly, wondering how long it would take for some underling to kick her message far enough up that it got to Striker. If Striker was even at Grimaldi.

"You will remain at zero thrust and low power output and prepare to be boarded. Any deviation from these orders will result in immediate..."

"There is no need for that, Commander Belloch. Captain Lafarge is a friend of mine."

She stared straight ahead, shocked and relieved at what she was hearing. It was Striker! He'd gotten the message.

"Ah…yes, Admiral. Certainly, sir." A short pause. "What do you want us to do, sir?"

"Andi, this is Van Striker. Is something wrong?" The admiral ignored the picket commander, directing his words right to Lafarge."

"Yes, Admiral. I'm so glad you got the message. I have something to tell you…but not over the open comm."

"Is it important?"

"Yes, Admiral. It's life and death…"

"Come in then. Immediately." A short pause and the sound of Striker speaking to someone in the background. "Andi, dock at bay Gamma-3. I'll have someone there to meet you and bring you to me." Then, a second later: "Commander, it is extremely urgent that Captain Lafarge gets to the base as quickly as possible. You are to allow her to proceed at maximum thrust, and you will clear all traffic from her path. Is that understood?"

"Ummm…yes, of course, sir." Lafarge knew just how much Striker was breaking the normal rules for her. Even through the fear driving her, a small smile found its way onto her face. Against all odds, she really liked Van Striker. *Maybe all authority figures aren't so bad.*

"Thank you, Admiral. I will be there shortly." She turned back toward Merrick. "You heard the man, Vig. Let's get those engines back up at full. Course…directly for Grimaldi station." She'd made it…she'd made it to Striker. But she knew Barron was still in danger. She knew she might still fail to reach him in time.

She leaned back, taking one last easy breath before the force of acceleration hit her again.

Chapter Nineteen

"Well done, Brutus. You have my thanks and my gratitude."
Vennius walked onto *Bellator*'s bridge, flanked by Aurelius and
Lentius. He was disheveled, his uniform covered in mud and
blood and torn in several places. He looked like anything but
the top military officer of the Alliance, though that was what he
remained, at least on *Bellator*. He was less sure what he was now
outside the confines of Egilius's battleship, how far Calavius had
gotten in stripping him of his rank and distinctions and brand-
ing him a traitor. Whatever his current status, he knew time was
not his ally.

Brutus Egilius leapt up from his chair and walked across
toward his mentor. The bridge officers present sat utterly still
and watched, their faces wearing one version or another of curi-
osity or tension. Vennius understood. He'd never experienced
anything like the past twelve hours, and he tried to imagine
how it would have seemed to him watching something like this
unfold when he was a junior officer. For all the danger and
responsibility he faced now, he far preferred it to the helplessness of an optio or optiomagis sitting and watching, waiting for
orders and trying to decide if their immediate commander was

149

on the right side.

"Commander-Maximus, I am gratified you made it here safely," Egilius said. A short pause, then: "Sir…what is happening?"

"Treason, Brutus. Treason. A coup, backed by Union gold." Vennius reached out and grasped Egilius's arm in the standard Alliance greeting. It wasn't technically proper between two warriors of such different rank, but after the past night, Vennius didn't give a shit. He suspected in the days to come, loyalty and friendship would matter more than rank. "I'll explain more later, but there's no time now. We have no way of knowing how far this conspiracy extends, though I suspect it reaches even into the ranks of fleet command."

"That is shocking, Commander, almost beyond belief. I find it difficult to accept."

"I did as well, until I found out who is leading it. Commander-Honoris Calavius." Vennius had trouble speaking his old friend's name, and he almost choked on bitterness and anger. Though he'd seen it all with his own eyes, he was still finding it hard to accept that a man he had known for most of his life, at whose side he had served countless times, had become a traitor. *No, Calavius controls Palatia. He controls the media outlets. You are the traitor, or at least that is what the people will be told…*

"Commander Calavius?" Egilius looked utterly shocked, and he was silent for a few seconds. "Are you sure, sir?" he finally managed to ask.

"Yes, Brutus. I am absolutely sure. He told me himself, and then he tried to kill me. If Legatus Lentius had not intervened with a cohort of my personal legion, I would be dead now, lying on the floor in front of my own desk." *Like Commander Horatius. I am sorry I doubted you, Valen. You deserved better. You were loyal, and the first casualty of this war. I pray I have the strength to avenge you.*

"If Commander Calavius is involved, who could not be?" Egilius was clearly shaken.

"Us, Brutus. You, me. Lentius and Aurelius, your people on *Bellator*, and the survivors among my soldiers. That is who we can be sure of." In truth, Vennius was less than certain that

every member of *Bellator*'s crew could be trusted, but he was
running short of allies, and he chose to place his face in Egilius's
leadership. "And the Imperatrix, of course. Have her wounds
been tended to?"

"She is in sickbay now, sir. She is very badly wounded, but
she is being treated." He hesitated. "But if we don't know who
we can trust, what can we do?"

"We get out of here, Commander. Now. Set a course for
the Centaurus jump point. It is closest, and it leads to a nexus
of six transwarp tubes. With any luck, we will be able to escape
pursuit."

"Escape? And leave Palatia to the traitors?"

"Palatia is already controlled by the traitors, Brutus, and if
I know Calavius, he has people throughout the fleet as well. I
could stay here, challenge whatever lies Calavius had spread, and
fight to the death. But that would be self-centered. We have the
Imperatrix, and our duty is clear. We must keep her safe, for she
is the legitimate head of state of the Alliance, and the symbol
around which we must gather resistance."

Egilius turned toward his executive officer. "Optiomagis,
set a course for the Centaurus transit point. Maximum acceleration." He turned back toward Vennius. "What do we do if
anyone tries to stop us, sir?"

Vennius looked around the bridge, at the nervous faces staring directly at him. The bridge was cast in the red glow of the
battlestations lamps, the signal that *Bellator*'s weapon stations
were manned and armed. Egilius's ship was ready for battle.

"No one stops us, Commander. No one. If anyone tries...
we open fire. We destroy them."

*   *   *

"That ship is full of traitors! I want it pursued and destroyed,
at once!" Calavius stood in the spot where it had all begun
twelve hours before, the office that had, until recently, belonged
to Commander-Maximus Vennius.

"Yes, Commander, at once. I will have to be careful. I can

select ships with reliable commanders, but I will have to do something to deal with the rest of the fleet. We will be inundated with alarms and officers calling in for explanations." A pause. "We did not expect to have to deal with the Commander-Maximus escaping Palatia."

The voice on the comm rang with obedience, but also with concern. Commander-Altum Rotan Otius was a full-fledged member of Calavius's conspiracy, one of the first senior officers to come onboard. Otius had been a profligate spender all his life, and he had squandered most of his family fortune, making him an ideal target to be tempted by foreign coin. He had also been passed over several times for promotion, and he blamed Tarkus Vennius for that misfortune. Otius was fully committed to the coup, Calavius was sure of that, but the commander's control over the fleet units at Palatia was tenuous at best. Many officers who had taken bribes were far less certain, and others were being controlled only by lies and propaganda. Otius had expected days, weeks even, to consolidate control over the fleet. He'd anticipated having to deal with captains and ships resisting the transfer of power eventually, but not less than a day into the coup.

"I did not expect Vennius to escape either, Commander. But that changes nothing. He is your responsibility now. As you have known from the beginning, we cannot be sure exactly what steps will be necessary, and we do what we must. I understand the difficulties of securing the fleet, but nothing takes priority over destroying the traitors. Is that understood?"

"Yes, Commander. Understood."

Calavius cut the transmission. *Damn.* Much had gone well the previous night, and reports had come in from all around Victorum and other key locations planet-wide. For the most part, his forces now occupied everything vital—military bases, media outlets, key industrial and transit hubs. For all intents and purposes, Palatia was under his control. The orbital bases and the fleet were somewhat less secure, though everything there was moving according to plan as well. Given another two days, perhaps three, his people would have everything locked down.

The way would be clear...for his elevation to Imperator, and for the long-awaited invasion of the Confederation.

So close, so much executed perfectly. And yet...

He looked all around, kicking a small pile of debris next to his foot. The room was a shambles, as was most of the building. The Admiralty had been the site of some of the heaviest fighting of the night, both during the initial storming and later, when Vennius's retainers appeared and managed to reclaim it for a few moments.

They hadn't been able to hold the building, of course, but it was impossible to overstate the damage that had been done. They had saved Vennius, and he'd later managed to get to the palace to rescue the Imperatrix. And the disasters did not end there. Vennius and his cursed band of soldiers had now somehow managed to take the Imperatrix north, getting out of the jamming radius and summoning help from one of the orbiting battleships.

Bellator. *Of course.*

Calavius raged, at his co-conspirators, at Ricard Lille, at anyone but himself. He had planned everything perfectly. He should have been warned that one of Vennius's creatures commanded a battleship in the Home Fleet.

It was bad that his people hadn't managed to eliminate Vennius and the Imperatrix, but their deaths were the only two objectives not achieved. Chasing them now, facing morning without everything as neatly wrapped up as he'd intended—none of that was good. But allowing them to get away entirely, that was out of the question. If Vennius and his band were still loose on Palatia, they could cause trouble, no doubt, but his people could have run them down eventually. But the thought of the Commander-Maximus and the Alliance's head of state escaping Palatia, even fleeing the Astara system...it was a potential disaster.

It would leave Calavius in total control of Palatia, of course, and free to begin his propaganda campaign in earnest. But a shadow hung over it all, the prospect of the survivors spreading their own messages, rallying forces to their cause. Calavius had known Vennius for a long time, and while the two were enemies now, he had not lost enough perspective to underestimate his old friend. Vennius was a dangerous adversary, and the fact that both he and the Imperatrix were out there remained an enormous hazard.

Bellator had to be destroyed. Anything else posed too big a risk.

But fighting between fleet units this early will be bad. It will put too much pressure on the commanding officers and their crews.

He shook his head. It was dangerous, but there was no choice.

Damn you, Vennius. Damn your stubborn carcass to the Eleven Hells!

*   *   *

"The fleet movements are strange, sir. They are definitely responding to our maneuver, but it seems inefficient. There are ships better positioned that are just sitting, while vessels from farther away are moving to interdict." Egilius turned and looked across *Bellator*'s bridge. He'd offered his chair—and tactical command—to Vennius three times, but the Commander-Maximus had refused each time. Vennius understood leadership, and also that Egilius was a skilled commander and one of the few officers he could trust now. Showing confidence was crucial, and besides, he doubted his rusty ship maneuvering skills could outdo Egilius's. *Bellator*'s commander knew his ship and his crew, and Vennius was an old enough veteran to appreciate the value of that.

"Calavius cannot respond in accordance with normal tactics. He doesn't dare order most of the ships out there to attack one of their own, not this early. Given time, he will spread lies, invent crimes and scandals and a justification for his seizure of power. But for now, he must rely upon those officers who are deep in his conspiracy, and that limits the ships available to send after us." He paused. "It gives us our chance to escape."

"None of the fleet units closest appear to be responding in any way, sir. And most of the others are too far away. Of the responding ships, only *Vexillium* will definitely cut us off. *Gladia* will be close…they will probably get into firing range, but not for long." He hesitated. "Unless our engines or reactors take a hit, of course."

Vennius nodded. "*Vexillium* is a good ship. Commander Pilius's vessel. He is skilled, capable…but unimaginative. We can outfight him, Brutus, I am sure of that. Still, he is strong-willed. He will be aggressive."

"He will launch fighters, Commander. If we counter, we will not have time to recover the squadrons."

Vennius stood silently for a few seconds. He'd made decisions like this before, sent brave warriors on one way missions. But this time he wouldn't do it. He wanted to think it was a moral decision, but the fact was far colder. He would need those fighters later.

"Hold the squadrons, Drusus." Vennius turned and looked at the display. *Vexillium* was coming on an angle, one that would position it between *Bellator* and the jump point. "Change course, Commander," he said suddenly. "Take us directly at *Vexillium*. Maximum acceleration. Bring us down their throats."

Egilius seemed surprised for a few seconds, but then a look of understanding came over his face. "Yes, sir," he replied sharply, turning toward his tactical officer and repeating the command. He looked back at Vennius and gestured toward an open workstation. "I suggest you strap in, sir. Unless you wish to take command?"

Vennius shook his head. *Four times.* "No, Commander. Fight your ship." He walked across the bridge, sitting down and pulling the harness across his body.

He sat quietly, closing his eyes for a moment as the force from *Bellator*'s engines slammed into him. His people had killed Alliance soldiers the night before, hundreds of them, but that had been in self-defense, fighting to survive. It was no different now, not really, but sitting on the bridge, issuing orders, it some-how seemed more premeditated. Vennius had moved from crisis to crisis, making snap decisions to keep his people alive. Now he considered the staggering dimensions of what he truly faced. The chance to quickly defeat Calavius's coup had passed. Even if *Bellator* could get past *Vexillium* and escape, that was just what it would be. All it would be. Escape. He would leave the traitors behind, in control of Palatia.

It was necessary, of course, the only way to continue the fight. *Bellator*'s destruction here would herald the total success of Calavius's treason. Vennius would be grateful for death if that happened. He had no desire to outlive the Alliance he had served his whole life. But he wasn't ready to give up, not yet. Not while the slightest strength remained in his body.

His thoughts drifted from the pending battle, to what would follow escape. Cut off from most of the fleet, almost without resources. There was no quick victory to be had, no way to go forward, save to resist Calavius at every turn. With his death, Vennius would have bequeathed to his people a dishonorable leader and the pointless war and destruction he would bring them. Worse, he suspected Calavius would lack the strength to resist the encroachments of his benefactors, that, most likely, the Alliance would fall to eventual dominance by the Union.

But with his survival, he would bring them a horror no less stark and terrible, one he'd hardly have imagined just weeks earlier, a nightmare of epic proportions.

He would bring them civil war.

Chapter Twenty

Excerpt from the Chronicles of Calavius I, Imperator

I stand here, newly named Imperator of the Alliance, ruler of my people. What I have done, I have done to save Palatia and the Alliance. The actions I have taken were motivated not by personal ambition nor the desire to rule, but by the calling to restore vitality and glory to our great Alliance. As a warrior, I have sought only to serve, to seek honor and glory in battle for my nation and my family.

We had lost our way, the way that has governed our actions since the days our people cast off their chains and as a people swore, 'never again.' We shall now reclaim our honor, and purify our world. Along that path there is a test, one that will shake us to our warrior's souls. There are those among us who are not committed to the way. Those who resist the call of the warrior. Those who would have peace at the expense of honor, of glory. Among this group are those I once called friends. It grieves me deeply, and yet still I must answer this call. We must not allow weakness to stay our hand, nor personal affections interfere with our sacred duty. We must do what is necessary, and spill what blood is required to wash away our sins.

Mother Palatia calls to each of us. I cry out for all to root out these traitors, to hunt them down, and, be they friend or comrade, brother or sister, do what must be done. For as I now swear to bring one who I once called brother to the scaffold, so Palatia calls on each of you to do the same.

Together we will cleanse our world, and no price will be too great to pay. Stand with me, Palatians. Meet the future and be true to your warrior heritage.

The way is the way.

AS Bellator
Astara System
Approaching Centaurus Transit Point
Year 61 (310 AC)

"Hold…"

Vennius sat silently, watching as Egilius issued orders. He'd aided the officer his career, driven by partly by a clannish sense of loyalty, but also by genuine respect for the younger man's abilities. Now, watching his young protégé direct *Bellator* in its duel with *Vexillium*, a struggle of momentous importance, he knew his support had been justified.

Vennius had seen few officers of Egilius's rank who could maintain such a level of focused calm facing not only his own death—and that of his crew—but the very future of the Alliance itself. Vennius knew crises like the current one gave the most capable the chance to shine, to live up to their potential, even as they were thrown into the crucible and tested. He hoped Egilius would be up to the task, that his ability would be enough to endure the great weight so suddenly thrust upon his shoulders. Vennius had fought more than a few battles himself, and right now he put the odds at roughly fifty-fifty of *Bellator* getting through the transit point, and rather less of making good a true escape with its systems still intact. It was a terrible gamble for a warrior to take with his own life, but with the magnitude of all that was at stake now, it was gut wrenching.

"Hold…"

Vexillium was just beginning to launch its fighters. *Sloppy… very sloppy.* Vennius frowned, even as he realized the opposing ship's missteps increased the chances of escape. *Bellator*'s change of course, its aggressive run right for its adversary, seemed to have taken Commander Pilius by surprise. His reaction time was clearly slow, his moves clumsy. Vennius was grateful now, of course, but he couldn't help but think to himself, in other circumstances, he'd have relieved Pilius for allowing *Bellator* to seize the initiative. He wondered how Calavius would deal with such things. *Not well*, he answered himself. His old friend had always been a bit harsh in his dealings with subordinates, and now Calavius fancied himself Imperator. That could only exacerbate his weaknesses.

Remember, you know Calavius better than almost anyone. That knowledge is a weapon, one of your tools to destroy him...

Bellator's fighter squadrons were on alert, sitting in their ships in the launch bays, ready to go on a moment's notice. They wouldn't be given the order, however, not unless there was no choice. Vennius knew escaping from the Astara system was only the first small step toward survival. Toward fighting back. He had no idea what would happen when they encountered other Alliance vessels, or how effectively Calavius would be able to convince the fleet's officers that Vennius was the real traitor. But he was sure of one thing...he'd need every bit of force he could get his hands on, and that included the forty-eight fighters sitting down in *Bellator*'s bays.

"I want all laser batteries armed and ready, Optiomagis," Egilius said. He sounded calm, cool, almost like a block of ice. Vennius suspected, from his own memories if nothing else, that the truth was rather different. In all of his battles, amid the glory he'd gained and the victories he won, he never remembered going into battle and not being scared. Scared shitless. He'd hid it as well as he suspected Egilius was doing right now, but he remembered it all these years later. And even now it was still there, that icy vice grip in his gut, watching to see whether Egilius and his veteran crew would prevail.

"All batteries are fully-charged and locked on, sir. Awaiting your command to fire." The tactical officer sounded strong, confident. Vennius never ceased to be amazed at the contagion of demeanor in battle. A leader like Egilius stood firm, and his people fed off his strength. *Fear too, spreads...even more quickly.*

Vennius watched, his eyes darting to the display then back to

Egilius. They were already in range, close enough to open fire. But still, Egilius held the command.

Vennius knew what *Bellator*'s commander was doing, and his estimation of the younger officer grew yet again. *Vexillium* was launching fighters. That was the tactically correct move, at least it was when *Bellator* was heading right for the transit point. But fighter operations made it difficult—almost impossible—to effectively fire batteries en masse. And Egilius was using that time to get closer, maneuvering for a devastating volley before *Vexillium* could fire its own broadside.

Vennius knew the tactic was bold, and success depended, as much as anything, on timing. And guts. Egilius proved himself to have plenty of the latter as he passed the point where Vennius decided *he* would have fired if he'd been sitting in the command chair.

"All batteries ready…I want one hundred ten percent power on all guns."

"Yes, sir. One hundred ten on all batteries."

Vennius was impressed again. Overpowering the guns was risky too, but every watt of power poured into *Vexillium* increased the chance of *Bellator* getting out of the system, without suffering crippling damage itself. Chances were pretty good Egilius would lose a few batteries, mostly to burnouts in the overloaded systems. But that would be easy to repair on the fly, and nothing was as important as getting the first shot and making it count.

Vennius's eyes darted to the display, counting the enemy fighters. They were all out now, and shaking down into attack formations. *Vexillium* would be ready to fire any time now. But Egilius was still playing for time. *Bellator* had been on alert for several hours, and its people were prepared for the fight. *Vexillium* had been thrown into combat on far less notice, and any kind of battle occurring in Astara had to be a shock to its officers and crew. Egilius had several advantages, each of them small individually, perhaps, but together maybe just enough. And *Bellator*'s commander was playing them for everything they were worth.

Come on, Brutus…you're out of time…

If Egilius waited too long, if *Vexillium* got off the first volley, and was able to follow it up with virtually unopposed fighter attack, it would all be over. Egilius was pushing it to the limit, and he was taking a terrible gamble to do it.

Vennius leaned forward, feeling the order to fire trying to force its way from his throat. He struggled to hold it back, to trust his officer. But as he looked at the display, in his mind he saw the great laser blasts from the opposing ship, ripping into *Bellator*. It was his imagination, but he knew it would be reality, in only seconds now.

"All batteries…open fire!"

He heard Egilius's voice, so loud it echoed off the walls of the bridge. And an instant later, he felt the vibration, heard the distant whining sounds of every gun on *Bellator* firing.

Vennius watched the display, feeling a wave of excitement as the AI reported hit after hit. Egilius had picked his time well, and he'd taken advantage of the fact that *Vexillium*'s launch operations had limited its evasive maneuvers. *And he's drilled his gunners well too…*

His eyes were locked on the screen, waiting as *Bellator*'s scanners evaluated the hits and the AI completed damage assessments. But before anything appeared on the display, Egilius's voice ripped across the bridge again. "Revise course, heading alpha-2," he said. "Maximum thrust…and I do mean maximum, Optiomagis. Disengage all safeties. I want the engines at one hundred fifteen percent."

Vennius was surprised. He'd given Egilius freedom to run the ship, and now the commander was banking on the damage inflicted in his initial broadside to buy enough time to make a run for it. Vennius would have held his course, exchanged volleys until *Vexillium* was crippled. But that would have taken time, and *Bellator* would have been damaged too. Bolting for the transit point was no less of a gamble, but perhaps one with a better chance of success. *My faith in Egilius was not misplaced.*

The surprise of the maneuver had another advantage, one that became apparent as the scanners displayed *Vexillium*'s return shot. It was ragged, no more than half the battleship's guns...and it was a clean miss, *Bellator*'s change in thrust upsetting the enemy's targeting.

Vennius struggled to move his body in the seat, trying to get as comfortable as possible—or more accurately, to minimize the terrible discomfort. Full thrust was hard enough to endure, but with Egilius overpowering *Bellator*'s engines, the pressure was almost unbearable.

He sucked in a shallow breath, feeling as though the g forces would break his ribs as he did. But his eyes were still fixed on the display as the damage assessments confirmed what the enemy volley had suggested. *Bellator*'s broadside had hit *Vexillium* hard. At least three batteries had been destroyed outright, and the AI projection suggested several others had been silenced by damage to electronics and power transmission systems. One of the battleship's engines had sustained a hit as well, though it was somewhat indeterminant as to how bad it was. Still, anything was helpful. *Bellator* had gained a jump on its opponent with the suddenness of its maneuver, and if *Vexillium* was at less than full thrust, she would never get close enough to stop the escape.

Bellator shook hard. *Vexillium*'s second volley hit, at least with some of its shots. Vennius could hear Egilius on the comm with his engineer. There was damage, some of it serious, but nothing that would interfere with the ship's flight. The engines were unaffected, and the reactors were still pouring energy in well beyond the maximum rated limits.

Vennius knew Egilius had given his opponent a choice. Cease fire and try to match vector and velocity to pursue *Bellator*...or stay on the current course and maintain fire, with the range increasing and the fire arc decaying with every shot. He waited to see what *Vexillium*'s commander would choose, and the absence of further attacks answered the question. *Vexillium* had taken the bait...she was pursuing *Bellator*. Vennius knew immediately that Egilius had won the battle of wits. The pursuing battleship was too far back, too late in its reaction, and its damaged engines had to chance of matching *Bellator*'s thrust. And Pilius had sacrificed his last shots, the final chance to stop

Bellator, for the hopeless pursuit.

There were no other ships close enough to intercept. They were going to make it, at least through the jump. Under normal conditions, they'd have a whole squadron right on their tails, but Vennius knew it was more complicated than that. The fleet was in disarray, and there would be confusion, questions to ask and answer. Many officers would accept the lies Calavius told them, but others would be skeptical. Some might even resist. If *Bellator* could get out of Astara, and get a jump on any pursuit, they could buy some time.

Vennius sat still, trying to ignore the pain the g forces were inflicting on him. His mind was elsewhere, even as he watched the transit point looming just up ahead on the scanner. *Vexillium* was still pursuing, but she was falling behind. *Bellator* was going to make it.

Vennius felt strange, excited for the impending success of the escape, but cold too, somber at the thought of characterizing an ignominious flight from his home world as a victory. There was a long road ahead, and a difficult one. But the shameful retreat kept his cause alive. Calavius had tricked him, gained the upper hand, but Vennius swore one thing to himself. It wasn't over, not yet. He would fight, and he would steal a page from his foe, and do whatever was necessary to achieve victory. *Whatever is necessary.*

He forced as deep a breath as he could manage into his lungs as the ship slid into the transit point. Calavius had been his friend for half a century, but now there was nothing left of that affection, nothing but cold determination. And hatred for an enemy.

No, this is not an end. It is a beginning. And before it is over, I shall look into your cold, dead eyes, my old friend.

Chapter Twenty-One

"We're being challenged, sir." The tactical officer ran his eyes past Vennius as he turned toward Egilius. The Commander-Maximus had not interfered with one of Egilius's decisions, not in the initial escape from Astara, and not in the series of running fights against pursuing vessels sent to stop *Bellator*'s desperate flight, but his presence was still a distraction to the ship's bridge crew.

Reaching Sentinel-2 had not come without cost. *Bellator*'s battle honors now included not only the destruction of foreign enemies in past wars, but now also of two Alliance ships. One of the Alliance vessels had been a battleship with a crew of nearly one thousand. That fight had been a difficult one, despite the fact that the attacking vessel had been old and outclassed. The cost of the nascent civil war now included fifty of Egilius's own people among the dead.

"I will take that, Commander." It was the first time Vennius had stepped in. Commanding *Bellator* in battle would under-mine Egilius's authority and confuse the crew, but dealing with the base commander was something clearly requiring Vennius's stature. Assuming he had any stature remaining. Sentinel-2 was too far out for word to have reached it about the coup. *Bellator* had traveled there about as quickly as possible, foreclosing the possibility that the traitors had been able to send word ahead of the ship's arrival. But that didn't mean the plot didn't extend out this far. Gaius Cassius commanded Sentinel-2. Cassius was an officer with a spotless record, and one Vennius called a friend. But he was still cautious. Calavius had been his friend as well.

"This is Tarkus Vennius Maximus. I will speak with Commander-Altum Cassius immediately." His spoke with all the authority, almost arrogance, that would be expected of his position. Now was not the time to display weakness.

"Yes, Commander-Maximus. At once." The officer's response seemed genuine. *Of course, that could just mean he's a good actor.*

A few seconds later: "Commander Vennius?" Gaius Cassius had a low, gravelly voice, almost unmistakable. "How can I be of service, sir?" Again, the respect and sincerity he'd expected were there in the response. Cassius was an intelligent man, but in all the years Vennius had known him, he'd seen not the slightest indication of a talent for deceit. But he still wasn't sure, and as much as he felt the urge to tell Cassius everything, he held back. He had to be sure, and even if his old colleague was loyal, it was highly likely there were at least some conspirators in his command. Sentinel-2 was too close to Palatia for the plotters to have ignored it entirely in their plans.

"Commander, I wish to discuss some important matters with you. You are to board a shuttle at once and come to *Bellator*." It was somewhat of an odd request. Typically, a newly-arrived battleship would dock with the base. But Vennius was an officer of extremely high rank, and he knew it wouldn't look all that out of the ordinary for him to summon his subordinate to him.

"Yes, Commander. At once."

Vennius cut the line. He looked over at Egilius. "Commander, I want a detachment of fully-armed stormtroopers near the bay when Cassius's ship lands." Vennius was hopeful the base commander was still loyal, but there was no harm in being sure. Cassius's willingness to come aboard was a good sign, but he still couldn't rule out the chance that the shuttle would be packed with armed troops, hoping to get a chance to gain control of *Bellator* by surprise.

I allowed myself to be deceived once, and I swear that I shall remain vigilant henceforth. I was a fool once, but never again.

"Yes, Commander Vennius."

"And Brutus," he added, "keep them out of sight. I want them ready in case they are needed, but if Commander Cassius is loyal, as I suspect, there is no need to insult him." He paused. "We have few enough ready allies…and we must preserve those who would stand with us."

*   *   *

"It is difficult to believe, Commander." Cassius sat opposite Vennius in *Bellator*'s cramped meeting room. Alliance ships were rather more spartan affairs than their Confederation counterparts, and such luxuries as large conference facilities and comfortable wardrooms were mostly absent. The two men were alone.

"I lived through it, my old comrade, and I still have trouble accepting it. Nevertheless, it is true. Every word of it." Vennius was certain now of Cassius's loyalty, at least as much as he could be. He'd allowed Calvinius to deceive him, but he was trying to maintain some level of trust in his judgment of people.

Cassius shook his head. "It's hard enough to believe we have a high-ranking traitor, even one. But hundreds? Thousands? Not in the Alliance. Not our fellow Palatians." It was clear the officer wasn't disputing what he'd been told, simply despairing of a reality he didn't want to accept. Cassius had reacted first with shock and disbelief, but Vennius could see it turning now to anger. He took a deep breath. He felt the same rage as the base commander, of course, but he also knew his cause needed cold rationality and not wild emotion.

"They are traitors, Gaius. To you, to me…to any who stand with us. But to view them only as traitors is to think of them as lesser, and many of those involved are fine warriors. They do not consider what they are doing treason. We must remember that. They view the Imperatrix's decision regarding the Confederation to be an abandonment of all that makes us what we are. In their own eyes, they are cleansing the Alliance... saving it." Vennius paused for a few seconds, allowing what he had said to sink in. "I despise them for what they have done, Gaius, and I am sworn to destroy them ...but I would be lying if I said I couldn't understand, at least on some level, what drives them. Calavius is vermin, he has fallen from what he once was, and is now driven by personal lust for power. But most of those who follow him no doubt believe they are taking desperate actions to save the Alliance." Vennius couldn't understand how an officer could accept foreign bribes and yet still maintain the attitude that he or she is driven by loyalty, but he had seen it enough to know that it was often true.

"I, too, questioned whether we should have taken the opportunity to invade the Alliance. Yet that is no excuse for failing in our obedience. It is not for the Palatian warrior to question the Imperatrix's wisdom." Cassius's voice was softer, a bit of the stridency he had displayed moments before gone.

"And yet, is there not always a point at which a warrior *must* do just that? Not over the events of the past three years, certainly, but can you say there is *no* order you would not follow, no course of action you could not accept?"

Cassius sat still and silent for a moment. Finally, he nodded slightly. "Perhaps..."

"I say this not to defend the actions of those we now face, for they are traitors who must be destroyed. But we must remember, the warriors we battle feel they are serving a cause as well. Most of them, at least, and certainly those of lower ranks...those who will do most of the fighting. They are battling to preserve what they feel the Alliance must be. Indeed, it is the Imperatrix who dared to imagine change, who saw that our ways must adapt, for showing caution in testing the Confederation, and in choosing not to go to war. We now face not the Unaligned Systems or the petty principalities we have battled before. We have grown powerful on our victories, yet perhaps arrogant as well. We have not faced an enemy as strong as the Alliance, not since the early wars, my days sitting at a weapons console and taking orders." Memories flooded back to Vennius, the feeling of being outnumbered and outmatched in combat. He had almost forgotten what it was to truly doubt victory in a pending battle. *You are about to feel that again, old man…*

"The Confederation and the Union dwarf us in size and resources. An Alliance warrior fears no enemy, but can he best five adversaries? Ten? Is it bravery to make empty boasts one knows cannot be fulfilled? We must add wisdom to courage and strength as we move forward…and many of our people will struggle with that. Our enemies will have much support, even among those not directly involved in their coup. Many will believe the lies and propaganda they hear, and despise us for traitors. Never let yourself think otherwise, or become overconfident."

Cassius sat quietly for a moment. Then he said, simply, "I understand, sir." A few seconds later: "I am with you, Commander-Maximus…you and the Imperatrix. To the end, be that victory…" He paused again. "Or be it death and the loss of all we hold dear."

Vennius extended his hand, reaching across the table to grasp Cassius's arm. As before, the difference in their ranks made gesture unorthodox, if not outright improper. But that didn't matter anymore. Victory or defeat, life or death, Vennius understood that all he knew was about to change. Had already changed.

Cassius froze for an instant, but then he clasped Vennius's arm, returning the handshake. He looked right at Vennius. "So, what do we do, sir? How do we begin the fight?"

"We must secure the squadron stationed here. You have three battleships and a number of escorts, correct?"

"Yes, Commander. *Draconis*, *Impetus*, and *Aquila*. Supported by five frigates and five light escorts."

Vennius had known the order of battle, of course, but fatigue and tension had driven it from easy recollection. *Draconis* and *Impetus* were fairly modern, moderately heavy, battleships. They would be welcome in the line in the battle in the fights that no doubt lay ahead. *Aquila* was an older ship, one that traced its history back almost as far as he himself did. Still, she had a history as a lucky ship, and even the twenty-four fighters in her small bays would be helpful.

Four battleships…to take on the rest of the fleet? No, we must have more strength, much more…

"We must rally more of the fleet to our cause, get our own message out, counter the lies and propaganda our enemies are spreading. The escorts…we must send them out at once, Commander. To every base and outpost we can reach. I will record a message, a call to the warriors of the fleet to join us." Vennius was filled with doubts. He'd given Calavius too much time, and he feared his appeal would be viewed by many as the lies of a traitor on the run. But there was no choice.

"Yes, Commander, of course. We should prepare a list of destinations. The longer we wait, the likelier the traitors will arrive here and blockade us in."

"That is true, Gaius. But there is something we must do first. Something difficult and upsetting."

"Sir?"

"We must be sure of the officers we send out. Certain of their loyalty. It is good that we got here before any courier from Calavius's regime, yet that is far from surety. It is likely the plotters attempted to secure allies in every major base or fleet formation, and just as possible that there are those in your command who will sympathize with the…others." He'd almost said traitors, but he stopped himself. It was tempting to voice his anger in every characterization of his adversaries, but he knew he faced a fight, most likely the hardest of his life. They might be traitors to his way of thinking, but they were Alliance warriors, and he knew just how savagely they would fight.

"How? I know some of the officers well enough to vouch for them. But that is not nearly all of them, even of the ship commanders."

"Even those you would vouch for deserve scrutiny. I would

have stood up and shouted my support of Calavius…before he came to my office and tried to kill me."

"So, what then? We have no time for extensive investigations, nor, I suspect, will an inquisition do much for morale."

"No, nothing public. Nor anything time consuming. We must simply do our best. You, Egilius, Aurelius, Lentius, and I. The five of us are beyond question." That wasn't entirely true. Vennius was almost certain about Cassius, but nothing would be served by acknowledging whatever minor doubts he harbored. He needed the base commander, and for all the crackling of his enhanced suspicions, he knew he had to trust his judgment. There were no certainties in this game, only good bets. And he'd put his money on Cassius.

"We will interview the commanders of each ship, and I will direct *Bellator*'s AI to review the base records—every communication, every action undertaken by any officer in the squadron over the past half year. Only those who pass both of these tests, the computer's dispassionate review and the gut feel of one of us in person, will remain in command."

Cassius had a worried look on his face.

"You are concerned, Cassius, that we will relieve loyal officers. Correct?"

"Yes, sir. A rushed investigation of the sort you propose can only achieve one of two things. Either it will allow some of the guilty to slip through, or it will create many false positives. We may cause grievous insult to loyal officers. Perhaps even drive them to the other side."

"All you say is true, my friend. Yet what alternative is there? We must get ships underway, within a day, if not hours, and we must do all we can to assure the reliability of those we send. All we can do is seek to make amends to those wrongfully relieved." He paused. "But they will not go to the other side, not if they are truly loyal. What Palatian would sell his allegiance because he feels slighted? No one we want on our side."

"Very well, Commander." Cassius sounded somewhat convinced, if not entirely. Vennius understood. It wasn't danger that was the hardest part of the way, nor of loss of those close to one. It was not arduous labors or pain or exhaustion. No, the true test of a Palatian's heart was the willingness to do that one found repugnant when such was necessary, when the alternative was even more unthinkable. Vennius knew he would ask much of the warriors who supported his cause. Death of course, for many of them at least, but more than that. He wondered if, even with victory, any of them would ever be the same again.

"Let us get started, Commander. I trust you can arrange for maximum discretion. I'd like to withhold knowledge of the coup from all but a select group, at least until we've had a chance to screen the ship commanders and the key base personnel. Assuming we get that much time before Calavius's forces get here."

"I agree, sir. We must have as much in place as possible before any traitorous forces arrive."

"Do your best to place those you most trust in security positions, also, Gaius." The more Vennius considered it, the more convinced he became that the plotters had personnel in place, waiting for word the coup had succeeded. It was crucial to maintain control of the fortress against internal attack or sabotage.

"I will, sir. I'll do that first. I have a few stormtrooper officers I am sure are loyal. I will ensure that they are on duty...and I will have the armories locked down under my access codes."

"Very good, Commander. We'd best get started."

"Yes, sir." Cassius stood and saluted. Then he turned back toward the door.

"Gaius?"

"Sir?" The officer turned back.

"Do you have one ship commander you trust completely? One you can vouch for here and now?"

Cassius hesitated, a sign Vennius took to suggest he'd gotten through to the officer, convinced him of the need for grave caution. "Yes, sir. Two, perhaps three."

"Choose one. Whomever you trust the most. I have a mission of enormous importance...and I need a ship ready to leave within the hour. A fast ship."

"Arias Corpus. He commands *Hastam*, a newer frigate, one

of the fastest ships in the fleet."

"I would have Commander Corpus deliver a message for me."

"A message?"

"Yes." Vennius paused. "A request for aid."

"Aid?"

"Yes, Gaius…" Vennius hesitated. He knew what he intended was not the way of the Alliance. But there was no alternative. Calavius was too far ahead. The Imperatrix was in *Bellator*'s sickbay, gravely wounded and unconscious. Without her voice added to his, he would struggle to counter his enemy's lies. He was without resources, cut off from even his own family fortune, while Calavius had immense piles of Union coin. He would fight, alone if need be, but even with the ships he could reasonably hope to rally to his side, he knew in his heart he would lose. If he had to change to prevail, he would do just that. If the way had to evolve, then so be it. Sixty years of Alliance history would be for nothing if Calavius won…and led the Palatians into Union servitude, a threat his old friend was too foolish to see through his lust for power.

Vennius looked right at his ally. "Commander Corpus will take my message to Archellia. Calavius has the support of the Union, and warrior's pride is not enough to overcome that. We need our own ally." He paused, feeling almost as though he would choke on his words. Images of Kat slipped into his mind, thoughts of her dead at the hands of the Confederation.

Yes, they killed her…she was the best the Alliance had, and one of their ships defeated her. We must have that strength on our side.

It was a test of his own will, to look past the rage he felt for the loss of someone he considered a daughter. But she had been a warrior as well, and her vessel had been the invader. The Confederation captain who had killed her had been doing his duty, and no more.

She would be the first to agree. There is no choice. We must have help.

"We must seek help from the Confederation, Gaius. It is the only way we can prevail. The only way to save the Alliance."

Chapter Twenty-Two

CFS Dauntless
Approaching Archellia, Cassiopolis III
310 AC

"Archellia Base Command, this is CFS *Dauntless*, requesting permission to approach and dock."

Barron sat in his seat quietly, listening as Travis went through the formal procedure of requesting clearance. He knew she remembered as well as he did how meticulously the base personnel had taken their identification and security precautions last time *Dauntless* had been there.

"*Dauntless*, this is Archellia Base Control. Welcome back. You are cleared to dock at portal three."

Barron almost laughed at the new informality. He likely *would* have laughed had he not been so tense about the mission…or if his thoughts hadn't been on the desperate combat his people had fought the last time they'd been out on the Rim. They'd been in battles since, terrible ones, but the struggle at Santis had been his first, and it had been a holocaust. He knew he would never forget it. It had changed him, in ways that had developed him as a commanding officer, and in others he regretted. And now he was back.

"Acknowledged, Archellia Base Command." He could hear the faint amusement in Travis's voice as well. Three years of war had changed many things, even in a backwater far from the bat-

173

tle lines, and the prickly attention to pointless details appeared to have given way to more practical process.

"A little easier this time, sir." Travis did allow a tiny smile to slip onto her lips.

"No doubt they've had exhausted and wounded personnel rotated in from the front...and some of the second-tier rookies have likely seen tours on the battlelines." The war had affected the whole Confederation, and Barron doubted there was anyone who hadn't been shaken by how close the Union had come to breaking through. "Anyway, let's take advantage of it, shall we, before they ask for timestamped orders in triplicate. Bring us in, Commander."

"Yes, sir," Travis replied sharply.

Barron leaned back in his chair, his thoughts slipping again to the mission, and the frustrating lack of any details or concrete information. He understood why Striker had sent him—though he wasn't sure he was totally convinced he was the one most likely to get somewhere with Alliance counterparts. He knew the Alliance had a culture that was...different...from the Confederation's, but he had defeated Commander Rigellus and destroyed her vessel. He'd learned a bit more about Rigellus from the Confederation's sparse intelligence files after *Dauntless* had returned to Archellia, and what he'd read had only confirmed the favorable impression he'd gotten of his doomed adversary. He felt as though they could have been friends if they'd encountered each other in different circumstances. She had been an enormously respected and popular officer. He imagined the Alliance sending the commander who had killed *him* and destroyed *Dauntless* to negotiate with Admiral Striker.

"Captain, we're getting a flash transmission. Admiral Lowery would like to see both of us in his office as soon as we dock."

Barron glanced back, a surprised look on his face. "Old Lowery is still here, eh?" He'd known that already, of course. He'd just blurted it out to cover his own surprise at the admiral's summons. Lowery was a bit of a stuffed shirt, as he recalled, so maybe it was just pointless formality. But his gut told him otherwise.

"Advise the admiral we will be there promptly, Commander."
Was it possible something had happened? If Sector Nine was
really at work in the Alliance, anything was possible. His stomach tightened. Maybe Lowery had word of Alliance forces moving toward Confederation space…or even crossing the border.

Barron hadn't known what to expect, but Admiral Striker
wouldn't have sent him if he hadn't been worried about Union
activity in the Alliance. *What do I do if we're too late, if the Alliance
is already set to invade? Buy time, that's what the admiral said. But what
can I do with one ship against the entire Alliance fleet?*

"Bring us in as quickly as possible, Commander."

"Yes, sir."

"And hold all shore leaves for the present. I want all personnel aboard and ready for action until further notice." That one
would get some groans, he knew, but he didn't much care, not
now. His whole crew had just had an extended leave…and if
he needed them on short notice, missing out on a few days of
Archellia's mundane spacer's haven would be the least of their
problems.

*　　　　*　　　　*

"Captain Barron, Commander Travis…thank you for coming so promptly." Lowery stood outside the door to the conference room.

"Of course, Admiral." Barron snapped off a salute, followed immediately by Travis. He remembered Lowery as a
rather more officious officer, one who certainly would never
have thanked a subordinate for following his orders, regardless
of their difference in fame and stature. *He's scared of something…*

"Your communique made it seem important, sir." Barron
added the last bit as an afterthought.

"It is, Captain. Extremely so." A short pause. "I am glad
you are here. You can probably…handle…the situation better
than I. I think it is more in line with your experiences."

"May I ask what it is, sir?"

"I will show you. If you will both follow me…" He turned

and put his hand over a sensor on the wall. The door slid open to the side, revealing a large meeting room with a table long enough for at least a dozen people. There was one man sitting quietly at the far end. He was wearing a uniform, one Barron couldn't place. Then it occurred to him. He was looking across the room at an Alliance officer.

He turned toward Lowery. "Sir…"

"Captain Barron, I want to introduce you to Commander-Princeps Arias Corpus of the Alliance navy." Lowery turned toward his guest. "Commander Corpus, this is Captain Tyler Barron and Commander Atara Travis. As you may or may not know, I believe the rank of commander is somewhat different in our service than in yours. Commander Travis is the captain's first officer on *Dauntless*."

"It is an honor to meet you, Captain Barron." Corpus rose as he spoke. "Your exploits are known even in the Alliance. And your ship, of course." Barron could hear true respect in the officer's voice, and something else, a harder edge. Barron hadn't been *completely* sure his name was attached in the Alliance to the battle with *Invictus*…at least until now.

"An honor for us as well, Commander-Princeps." Barron had studied up on his Alliance history and doctrine, at least from the meager data available. A commander-princeps was the equivalent of a Confederation captain. "It is a surprise to find you here." He glanced over at Lowery. "I assume something significant is behind your visit."

"I think it is best if Commander Corpus explains to you, Captain. I have received orders to assist you in any way. Despite our…differences…in rank, you have been granted final authority over all matters involving the Alliance."

Ah…that explains why he seems so…subdued…

"Please, Commander…" Barron gestured for the Alliance officer to sit again. He flashed a look at Travis, and the two sat down, facing Corpus. "Now, what brings you to Archellia?"

"I will not waste your time with diplomatic niceties, Captain. It is not our way." Corpus's tone was polite, but there was a hardness behind it. Barron had an idea how uncomfortable the

Alliance officer was…being in the Confederation, and, he suspected, about to ask for some kind of help.

"Please, Commander. I welcome your directness."

"There was a coup in the Alliance. Traitors recruited and funded by the Union have seized control of Palatia. They control most central government functions as well as an undetermined, but significant, percentage of the fleet."

The Corpus's presence meant something important had happened, but Barron still found himself stunned. He'd asked for directness, and that was just what he'd gotten.

"I trust there is ongoing opposition? You wouldn't be here if there wasn't."

"There is, Captain. Commander-Maximus Tarkus Vennius escaped Palatia, with the Imperatrix and a small force." He paused, glancing down at the table for a few seconds. "I am afraid Her Supremacy is severely wounded. She was in a coma when I left."

"Left where?"

Corpus paused again, a little uncomfortably this time. "Commander Vennius has established a base where he is rallying support. I came from there."

Barron understood that Corpus wasn't ready to tell him just where the base was located. He wasn't offended—rather, his respect for the officer's caution and judgment grew. "What is Commander Vennius's tactical situation?"

"He has rallied some forces, but…" Another pause. Barron could see the Palatian had difficulty speaking of weaknesses to a foreigner. Not helpful in the current circumstances, but again, understandable.

"Commander, I appreciate your caution. No doubt I would feel much the same in your shoes. But you came here, obviously seeking something from us. I respectfully suggest you tell me the entire situation. Nothing we speak of will leave this room."

"Admiral Lowery advises me you will make the decision on how to respond to my requests?"

Barron glanced over at the admiral and then back to the Alliance officer. He sighed softly, trying to hide it as well as he could. The authority Striker and Holsten had given him was perhaps the last thing he wanted. But that didn't matter. He had his orders…and the responsibility that went with them.

"Yes, Commander. I will make any decisions regarding the Confederation's response. And I must know everything before I decide how to proceed."

The officer paused again, and Barron could feel the man's eyes moving over him, assessing. Finally, he nodded. "Very well, Captain Barron. Commander Vennius is cut off from headquarters, from the Admiralty, and from the Alliance's main transportation and communications hubs." He hesitated again, looking even more uncomfortable than he had before. "The Alliance has a very centralized system of command and supply, Captain. When the commander lost Palatia, he lost easy access to the rest of the fleet and to supplies. We can only guess how successful the traitors have been at suborning ships and legions to their cause. They have total control of the media and of communications, so it is likely that even loyal warriors will be deceived into supporting them."

"The situation sounds grave, Commander. What would you have me do?"

"I am here to request Confederation intervention. To ask that you send ships and soldiers to assist us in the war against these traitors."

Barron knew the Alliance culture was a blunt one, but he was still surprised by the straightforward way the officer had just asked him to involve the Confederation in another war.

"Commander…I sympathize with your situation, but we are already at war. Our resources are stretched as it is."

"I have a recorded message from Admiral Vennius, Captain." The officer reached into a pocket and pulled out a small tablet. "May I play it?"

"Yes," Barron replied, looking briefly back at Travis, who gave him an "I don't know any more about this than you" look.

The officer touched the small screen.

"To whatever officer or leader of the Confederation is listening to this message, I am Tarkus Vennius, Commander-Maximus of the Alliance…and now leader of the resistance forces. The Alliance has been subverted by a coup executed by a group of disloyal officers, but planned and funded by the Union."

Barron listened to the voice. The speaker was old, he could tell that much. And tired. No, exhausted. But he could hear strength there too. He scolded himself for thinking he could tell anything meaningful about this man by listening to a taped message…but he believed it nevertheless. Whatever else the speaker might be, he was clearly a leader, and for all the fatigue in his hoarse tone, Barron was willing to bet he wasn't beaten yet.

"I ask now for your aid, for active Confederation military intervention, for supplies and logistical support. I know this is an audacious request. I acknowledge now what we have refused to admit previously, that our vessel *Invictus* was sent to probe your defenses three years ago. We have had little contact, and by no reasonable standard can we claim to have been your friends. Still, I ask for your help, and I urge you to grant my request for a single reason. Because our needs align. We face the same dangers, the same enemy."

Barron could feel his stomach tightening. He'd already come to the conclusion he knew Vennius was approaching. He dreaded the position it would put him in, and his mind raced for an escape. But there was none.

"The Union has instigated this coup for a single reason, to gain effective control over the Alliance and to bring it into the war against the Confederation. If our resistance fails, if the traitorous forces are able to establish and stabilize control over the Alliance and its armed forces, there is no doubt the Confederation will face all-out invasion. For me, and for those who follow me, the price of failure will be death, for we will never yield. For the Confederation, the consequences will be no less severe, a two-front war I can only assume will leave you hard-pressed to hold your enemies back on either frontier."

Barron couldn't believe what he was hearing, all the more because it was exactly what he'd expected. He wanted to react, to rub his hands on his temples, to shake his head…to scream out loud. But he sat like a statue, listening.

"I urge you, therefore, to send what forces you can to Alliance space, to come to our aid while there is still time. As Commander-Maximus and acting leader while the Imperatrix is wounded, I make this offer. Help us defeat the traitors, and regain control of Palatia and the Alliance...and when that is done, we will stand by you in return. We will declare war on the Union, provide forces to aid in your ultimate victory, and when that war is won, the Confederation and the Alliance will remain allies."

Barron could tell how difficult it was for the speaker to ask for help, and he was even more certain the words he was hearing were sincere.

"This is not our way, to ask for help and to promise treaties. We have always stood alone, fought alone, and it is unthinkable to acknowledge that we cannot prevail on our own. Yet, times change, and so must we. If you do not aid us, we will fight. We will rally every ship and every warrior we can, and we will struggle to our last breaths. And we will lose. Then you shall bear the assault alone, trapped between two Union claws. You must decide...shall we fight together, and prevail, or fight alone...and fall. I speak for the true government of the Alliance. My words are my warrior's bond, and I shall die before I fail to keep any promise I have made."

Corpus pushed the tablet across the table. "Commander-Maximus Tarkus directed me to play this message for you and then to give you the tablet so you may review it and the information it contains." Corpus paused, clearly uncomfortable again. "There are detailed files, a complete order of battle of the Alliance military, as well as the forces controlled by Commander Maximus and those known to be under the control of the traitors."

Barron was truly surprised at the openness and trust Vennius was showing. *That had to be difficult, especially for an Alliance officer.* He could see that Corpus disagreed with his commander's action, though he suspected the officer would refuse to admit it under any level of duress. Loyalty came first for Alliance warriors...Barron knew that much about the culture.

He turned toward Travis, his eyes locking on hers. She was still for a moment, her face unreadable. Then she just nodded.

Barron looked down the table at the Alliance officer. "Commander Corpus…I am afraid our ability to effectively intervene at this time is severely limited." He could see the officer shifting in his seat, ready to continue his argument. But Barron held up his hand. "However, I believe your words. I believe Commander Vennius."

He took a single deep breath, pushing back against the turmoil rising up inside him. He'd been horrified when Admiral Striker had sent him to Archellia and given him the tremendous power he had…but the reality was far worse than he'd imagined.

"What help we can provide, we will, Commander. I will dispatch a request for more forces to be deployed to the Alliance frontier, and if it is acceptable to you, *Dauntless* will go back with you now."

"One battleship?" Barron could hear the disappointment in the man's voice.

"For now, I'm afraid one is all we have near the Alliance border, Commander. I hope there will be reinforcements available in the near future." The words came out of his mouth, but Barron had no idea where such forces would be found. He knew he was putting his people into a nearly hopeless fight, but the alternative was to wait for the inevitable invasion that would follow Vennius's defeat. Once again, there was no good choice.

Corpus stood up and nodded. "I thank you, Commander Barron. Your aid is welcome…whatever it may be." It was clear in his voice he viewed his mission as a failure, the aid of one ship woefully inadequate.

"We face a difficult time, there is no doubt," Barron said, a strange little smile slipping onto his lips. "We may only have one ship available now, Commander, but it is not just any ship. It is *Dauntless*…and this will not be our first hopeless battle. We have faced impossible situations before, and we are still here."

Barron's eyes narrowed and bored into the Alliance officer's. "And I do not intend for this to be the one we lose."

Chapter Twenty-Three

Fortress Sentinel-2
Orbiting Planet Varena, Cilian System
Year 61 (310 AC)

"Six battleships, Commander-Maximus. *Gravitas, Electi*, and four identities still unconfirmed." Cassius stood in front of the large display in Sentinel-2's main control room. The screen was centered on an area around the transit point from which the invading fleet had just emerged. "Eight escorts, sir, two frigates and the rest lighter craft."

Vennius sat in the makeshift station Cassius had ordered built for him. It was adjacent to the base commander's, about two meters away. "Very well, Commander." *Less than I'd feared. Calavius must be having more trouble than he'd expected consolidating control. Word must have spread that the Imperatrix is still alive.*

Vennius guarded against optimism. He and his small force had been left alone longer than he'd dared to hope, yet even that time had amounted to relatively little. He had no idea how many of the escorts he'd sent out had been destroyed—or defected to the other side—and how many were still seeking forces to try to rally to the cause, but none had sent back reinforcements. Not yet, at least.

Still, he had four battleships plus the base, not a hopeless matchup by any means. He'd expected a more decisive assault once Calavius had located him, one overwhelming blow to end his resistance before it even began. The fact that his nemesis could not spare a larger force—and he had no doubt, if Calavius had been able to send more, he would have—was a good sign. Vennius was disciplined, and he took it as nothing more than a sign of a slower than expected consolidation. Still, anything that took time had to increase the strain between Calavius and his Union allies. *His Union masters…*

Vennius stared at the four small circles that represented his battleships, drawn up exactly where he'd ordered. He'd positioned them carefully. When the enemy engaged his line, they would find themselves in range of the station's heavier guns, but their own batteries would be too far out to strike at the fortress.

His eyes caught the cluster of smaller icons, the eight enemy escorts. His forces would feel the loss of their own small craft he had detached. The enemy's frigates and other craft would have none of their counterparts to face off against them, and they would be able to come around and attack the flanks of the battleships. It was a danger, especially if the fight went on for too long. The fortresses squadrons erased the enemy's fighter superiority, but Vennius knew he'd have to send some of his wings after the frigates, which would give the enemy back its edge along the main line.

"They're coming straight on, sir. One large formation."

Unimaginative. Clumsy. "Let them come, Commander Cassius. Our forces are to remain in position."

"Yes, sir."

"All ships, and the base…scramble fighters."

"Yes, sir." A second later: "Fleet order, all squadrons to the launch bays."

"Commander, when the enemy enters range, I want every heavy battery on this station to open up…and to maintain fire at the maximum rate. Every minute until we destroy the attackers, or compel them to retreat, is that much more damage to our own ships." That was Vennius's real concern. The battle would be a close match, but he'd never let that trouble him. However, Calavius would have more ships to send as he consolidated his control over the fleet, and Vennius knew he had very little capacity to repair his four battleships if they were too badly hit. An outright win would end the war for Calavius in a single stroke, but even if Vennius defeated the enemy it could be part of an attritional victory for the usurpers. Vennius hoped he had reinforcements coming, but he couldn't count on it. Nor could he be at all sure the Confederation would heed his call for aid. *Invictus* had invaded their space, after all, and killed their people. He'd considered how he would react in their shoes, but he put it out of his mind. It was too demoralizing.

"Commander-Maximus, Commander Egilius is on the comm." The communications officer stared across the control room, clearly ill at ease with having such a high-ranking officer there.

"On my comm, Optiomagis." Vennius put his head to the headset. "Brutus?"

"Yes, sir. The battle line is ready. What are your directives?"

A hundred thoughts burst into Vennius's head, but he held them back. He was an old enough warrior to know he had to pick his commanders and then let them do their jobs. Sitting on the fortress, micromanaging the battle would do more harm than good. And for all his decorations and his illustrious record of battle, he had spent the last two decades sitting in his chair, far back from the front.

"Keep the force together, and watch the escorts trying to get around your flank...and other than that, fight your battle, Commander. You have my utmost faith and confidence." He knew Egilius was good, very good. That was why he'd named his protégé tactical commander of the fleet. He'd been hesitant, afraid the other commanders might resent being placed under the new arrival, but he'd gotten a break there. Egilius was the most senior of the four, and that gave Vennius the cover he needed.

"Yes, sir." Egilius sounded pleased...and a bit edgy. "Thank you, sir."

"Victory ride with you, Commander." Vennius cut the line. He'd given instructions and he'd wished Egilius the best. Droning on longer could only distract the officer from his task at hand.

He glanced at the other circles, the ships flanking *Bellator*. All the battleship commanders had proven to be loyal, or at least that was the consensus opinion. If he and Cassius had made a mistake on that, they would soon know, with potentially devastating consequences. If one of the supposedly loyal battleships turned on them, it would be over.

Vennius had relieved three of the escort commanders on suspicion of colluding with the traitors. One of those had already been released, with Vennius's apologies and his sincere hopes he hadn't created an enemy where there had not been one before. The other two were Calavius's creatures, he was sure in one case and almost sure in the other. They would face firing squads as soon as the battle was over. Vennius didn't know if he could win this struggle, but he was certain of one thing. It would be the most brutal fight he'd ever experienced. There was no room for mercy, for forgiveness.

"Commander, all fighter squadrons report ready for launch."

Vennius nodded. He stared down at the floor and closed his eyes for a moment. This would not be the first Palatian blood drawn at his command, and unless his forces faced defeat and destruction here, it would not be the last. But it still tore at him. He had been through countless terrors in his long career, but he'd never faced a nightmare like this. *How many of those warriors have I known? I've commanded them all, praised them, decorated them. Now I must kill them…and in their thousands if I am to save the Alliance.*

"Launch all fighters," he said, his voice like iron.

*   *   *

Bellator shook hard, a shower of sparks raining down on her bridge. Egilius felt the sting on his neck, a tiny bit of still hot metal hitting him before falling to the deck. He didn't move, didn't even acknowledge the pain. His ship—no, his fleet, was fighting for its life. No pain could distract him now, no wound.

If he lived, this was where he would stay, until the battle was won, or until it was lost. And it would only be lost when he and every warrior serving with him was dead.

"More power to the forward guns," he yelled, his eyes dropping to the monitors on his workstation. One of his ship's reactors had been damaged. It was still functioning, barely, but there wasn't just enough energy to charge all of *Bellator*'s systems.

"Cut thrust to minimum necessary for evasive maneuvers. We have to maintain maximum fire."

"Yes, Commander." Orin Metus was Egilius's operations officer, and his second-in-command. The two had served together for several years, and their effectiveness as a team was one reason *Bellator* was one of the highest-rated ships in the fleet.

Egilius looked at the main display, his eyes focusing on the swirling mass of tiny dots in between the two battle lines. The dogfight had pulled in one squadron after another until almost every fighter in the battle that survived was there, waging a desperate struggle for local superiority. He was sure his forces would have prevailed by now, save for the fact that he'd been compelled to send three of his squadrons to engage the escort ships, to keep them off his flank.

He'd done what he'd decided was necessary, but now he questioned himself. Fighting eight frigates and other escorts was a tall order for three squadrons, and their absence in the center had put that vital battle into question.

Bellator shook again, and this time the bridge lights flickered. Egilius glanced down at his screen to check the damage report, but even before his eyes focused on the words, he knew the battered reactor was completely out now.

Damn. His ships were pounding the enemy as well. Several of their ships were severely wounded, and one seemed to be completely crippled. But his mandate was more than simply to win. A victory that left his four vessels too badly damaged to be quickly repaired would be little better than an outright defeat.

"Commander, *Draconis* and *Aquila* are to concentrate all available batteries on *Electi*."

"Yes, sir."

Egilius eyed the reports coming in from his scanners, and from the flights of drones he'd launched to deliver assessments of damage to the enemy ships. *Electi* was bleeding atmosphere and fluids, and one by one her guns had fallen silent, until just one turret was still firing. It was hard to tell whether a ship's damage was spread out and superficial, or whether it reached deeply into the vessel, threatening total destruction. But Egilius's gut told him *Electi* was close, that a few moments of concentrated fire would finish the battleship once and for all.

He'd felt strange when the fight began, as he had in Astara when he'd opened fire on *Vexillium*. But his four ships had over three hundred casualties already, and fifteen percent of his fighters had been destroyed. The flow of blood had been enough, finally, to wash away his old allegiances. He'd fought alongside many of the warriors on the opposing fleet, but he doubted his actions no longer. They were traitors, foul and black-hearted, and the blood of all who had died, who would die, was on their hands. They were worse than any outside enemy. They had come here, and they had killed his people, their fellow Palatians. And now he would send them straight to the Eleven Hells without so much as a second's pity.

"Our guns too…all batteries with an arc on *Electi* are to fire. Divert all available power to those guns."

"Yes, sir."

"Cut all non-vital power output. Lighting and life support to minimums."

A slight pause this time. Then, "Yes, sir." A few seconds later the bridge lights dimmed, and the background noise of the air vents went silent.

Egilius felt his hands tightening into fists, his jaw clenched. *Bellator* shook yet again, her reduced thrust weakening her evasive maneuvers, making her an easier target. He worried for his ship, felt the pain of the damage she was suffering…but he needed every watt he could get for his guns. He had to end this battle—win it—as quickly as possible. And he knew only one way to do that.

He saw small white plumes on the screen, all along the icon representing *Electi*, impacts from the laser cannons targeting the wounded ship. The vessel's engines appeared to be completely inactive, leaving the ship moving on a predictable and unchanging course. Now, Egilius truly smelled blood.

One shot after another slammed into the dying battleship. Egilius almost ordered his people to switch targets. *Electi* was no threat, nor could she escape. But he held back the command. Battles were about more than a tally of hits and misses. The destruction of one of their battleships would hit the attackers hard, and Egilius knew that was the way to end this fight, to repulse the attackers before his own flotilla was battered to scrap.

He could hear the distant whine of *Bellator*'s laser cannons, firing again and again…and then, suddenly, the screen lit up, the symbol representing *Electi* vanishing with a flash. He knew out there, fifty thousand kilometers away, the battleship had vanished in the fury of uncontrolled nuclear fusion. Nearly one thousand warriors, men and women he had called comrades, had just died…at his hands. He suspected it would hit him later, not only what he'd just done, but the realization that it was only the beginning. But there was no time. He had more former comrades to kill.

"All vessels, target the nearest enemy ship. Maintain fire."

*   *   *

Vennius watched the battle rage, and even as it turned in his favor, his thoughts moved to the future. His people would repel this first attack, he was almost sure of that now. Brutus Egilius had proven himself to be as capable commanding a fleet as he had been his own ship. But Egilius had been facing fellow Alliance warriors, not the draftees of some neighboring world. There were no easy victories in such a conflict, no side breaking and fleeing early in the encounter. The victory here was vital, but by the time it was fully won, Vennius knew the cost would be high.

He'd watched on the screen as *Electi* was destroyed. It was a crucially important development in the battle, but all he'd felt was a coldness inside. He didn't waver...he would kill a million former comrades, a billion if need be, before he would yield his Alliance to what it was like to become under Calavius, and his would be masters from the Union. But there was no joy either, no wave of satisfaction, as he had felt so long ago in his own battles.

He gazed at the row of screens, watching as the AI updated the data as vessels maneuvered, fired, and were hit. He was struck by the sanitized feeling of it all. The fortress was firing its longest-ranged guns, and of course its fighters were out there in the maelstrom of the great dogfight. But no enemy ship had gotten close enough to bombard the station, not even a fighter or bomber making a desperate run. Vennius felt almost as though he was at his desk in the Admiralty, sipping tea as he read dispatches, reports of what had already occurred. But what he was seeing now was live, happening even as he sat and watched.

He knew what was truly taking place was anything but sanitized. He could visualize the meaning of those symbols on the screen, the sweat and blood and death out there, under the guns of the enemy. He could see it in his mind with total clarity... because he'd been there before. It had been decades since he'd seen his ship being blasted to scrap all around him. Half a lifetime, it seemed, since he'd felt the pain of wounds, seen his fellow spacers broken and burned and dying. Those bright flashes, the AI's way of showing hits scored on a vessel, also meant his great battleships were being twisted slowly into wreckage. Each of those neat little indications meant men and women sucked into space, crushed by falling debris, incinerated in the great explosions that rocked the ships.

When he was younger, even as he endured all of that up close, he'd only craved more. Glory, victory in battle, conquest...they drove his warrior's heart in those days, pushing him onward. But the old man who was all that was left of that dynamic young fighter saw the cost more than the glory. He felt the void in his life where Katrine Rigellus had once been…and her father, Lucius, his oldest friend, more than a brother. Lucius had been gone so long, Vennius's memories of him had begun to fade, his visions of his old comrade's face blurring with each recollection.

He sighed softly, even as he heard excited cries begin to spread across the control room. The attackers were retreating, pulling back toward the transit point. He knew his people had won a victory, though having lost Palatia and most of the fleet, he was hard-pressed to consider it anything but a minor reprieve. Still, he owed it to his people to encourage them, to allow them to bolster their morale and celebrate their success.

"Commander-Maximus…Commander Egilius is requesting permission to pursue the retreating force." Vennius could hear the edge in Cassius's voice. He could feel it in the feral eyes of those staring at him from all around the control room. They ached to release Egilius, to send him in pursuit of the beaten enemy. But Vennius's eyes were on the displays, and the damage reports from his ships. Not one of his four battleships had made it through the fight without damage. *Aquila* was the worst. The old ship would limp back to base on half power at best, and his people would patch her together the best they could. But the other three vessels had also suffered, and *Bellator* had numerous systems failures. No, there could be no pursuit. Even fleeing enemy ships would return fire, and his small fleet couldn't endure another shot. Not if there was to be a chance of having his ships ready in time for the next battle. The one he knew would be coming.

"Negative, Commander. The fleet is to fall back on the station and commence full damage control operations."

"Yes, sir."

Vennius could hear the disappointment in Cassius's voice. He could feel it all around him. But he didn't care. He had a war to win. Glory was meaningless, and vengeance, even, was of no importance. Only the future of the Alliance, and the legacy of sixty years of battle and sacrifice, mattered still.

Victory was all that mattered. Destroying the enemy. Killing Calavius.

Chapter Twenty-Four

CFS Dauntless
Polis System, Near the Etruria Transit Point
310 AC

Barron stared at the display, his eyes cold. He'd come through the Rim and out of Confederation space, down the series of sparsely inhabited and unaligned systems known as the Dragon's Tail. Now *Dauntless* sat almost at a standstill, in front of the transit point that would take her into Alliance space.

The trip had been a hard one, especially the journey through the Krillus system. Barron wasn't a superstitious man, but he'd felt the ghosts there, the hundreds of his people who had died in that monumental struggle. His people had fought seemingly endless battles since then, and many more had died, but that fight at Santis, under the light of the yellow sun Krillus, occupied a dominant place in his nightmares. He wasn't sure if he felt as he did because Santis had truly been his worst fight, or if it was because the struggle had been his first. But though he was a hardened veteran now, and a decorated officer on the verge of assuming flag rank, he had been shaken by the trip through Santis's system.

He'd struggled to put it out of his mind when *Dauntless* finally transited out, and even the dark unknown beyond the far borders of the Confederation had been a relief. But this was another kind of stress. The situation in the Alliance was uncertain, subject to the vicissitudes of war since Commander Corpus and *Hastam* had left to begin his journey to Archellia. Assuming, of course, Barron believed everything Corpus had told him…and he wasn't there, not yet. Though his impression of the Alliance officer was a positive one, his doubts still held a place near the forefront of his thoughts. Jumping into the Etruria system could be an act of war against the Alliance, depending, of course, on who was in control.

Barron had the authority, even if he knew his actions would lead to war. Striker had left no doubt about that, given him no wiggle room to hide behind the need to request permission. Tyler Barron had the power of a king out here beyond the Rim. Any decision he made would automatically have the power of law. It was authority he didn't want, but having accepted it, he knew his duty was to exercise it.

"Commander, set a course through the transit point. We're moving forward."

"Yes, Captain." Travis sounded concerned, but there wasn't a doubt in Barron's mind she agreed with his decision. His first officer was not one to be deterred by danger or consequences. She was as aggressive as he was, more so, even.

"Advise Commander Corpus in *Hastam* that we are transiting." The Alliance ship had followed *Dauntless*. Barron appreciated its presence. At least one of the warring factions in the Alliance would be deterred if he ran into their ships.

"Commander Hastam acknowledges, sir."

Barron nodded. He leaned back for a moment, his eyes still fixed on the display. As far as he knew, no Confederation ship had ever entered the Alliance. There was a trickle of trade between the two nations, but it passed through intermediaries, mostly those of the Unaligned Systems still independent of Alliance rule. Barron had scoffed at Striker's assertion that he was the Confederation officer with the greatest understanding of Alliance culture, but then he realized it was true. He knew very little, but his colleagues knew even less. Even Gary Holsten's intelligence files on the Alliance had proven to be disappointing in terms of any real insights.

Barron was about to give the order to move forward, but he paused. "Commander, bring us to battlestations." He looked over toward her workstation. "We don't know what is there, but the Alliance is not the type of culture to leave their border entirely unprotected."

"Yes, Captain." He heard the seriousness in Travis's tone, and he knew she understood his words, the meaning behind the order. Barron would try to talk his way out of trouble, of course. But if they ran into an enemy that wouldn't let them pass, he was not going to back down. If Alliance forces tried to bar *Dauntless*'s way or turn her back, Barron was ready to fight. He couldn't turn around now. The prospect of a hostile Alliance fleet allied to the Union was too daunting. If he had to open fire on an Alliance vessel to reach Vennius, he was prepared to do just that.

He heard the klaxons blaring, saw the red light of the battlestations lamps, and he looked straight ahead. "Engage engines, Commander. Bring us into Etruria."

*   *   *

Joseph Ventnor stood in *Dauntless*'s forward galley, working with the other stewards to lock down the cupboards and batten everything down for transit. He was new to the ship, one of the recent batch of replacements for casualties. He'd never been in battle before, and the prospect of it terrified him.

Service staff had no real role in battle, save for what he and his comrades were doing now. At least on most of the ships of the fleet. But he'd heard enough conversation to realize that *Dauntless*'s stewards did much more. They helped carry wounded to sickbay, assisted the engineers with damage control…anything to contribute to the ship's combat power. He'd heard all about Tyler Barron's famous ship, but he'd never expected to serve on it, not until the last-minute transfer that had sent him there.

Ventnor had been relatively aloof, and in the weeks since he'd come aboard, he had hardly said a word to any of his comrades. He suspected the others thought of him as an introvert, and for the most part, aside from where their duties crossed, they'd ignored him.

He *was* shy by nature, but that wasn't the cause of his stand-offish behavior. Ventnor was different from all of them, in ways not one of his colleagues knew…could ever know. They were here to serve the Confederation, to fight its war and follow the orders of their officers. But Ventnor had different priorities. He was here to do a job, and it was not the same one the rest of *Dauntless*'s crewmembers were doing.

He'd watched Captain Barron, at least as closely as he could without raising suspicion. *Dauntless*'s commander spent an astonishing amount of time on the ship's bridge, or in the small office located just behind. He slept *maybe* four hours a day, and he usually ate his sparse and rushed meals with Commander Travis…and sometimes, alone in his quarters.

That was it…his quarters. Barron usually ordered something simple, especially when he ate alone. A sandwich or soup and a salad. And when he did, a single steward delivered it. There was a guard outside the captain's quarters, but no one else inside. Yes, that was how he'd do it.

There was one problem with that plan. He turned and looked over at Lars Cole. Cole was the senior steward, and he took Captain Barron's meals to his quarters. Always. Even when Cole was off duty, he was called if the captain ordered something.

Cole had welcomed him aboard and shown him around the ship when he'd first reported for duty. Ventnor liked his colleague, at least as far as he knew him, but that was of no importance. He was here because he had no choice, because he'd gotten himself in trouble, and this was the only way out. He'd taken Sector Nine's money, paid off those he'd owed…people who shouldn't be crossed. Too late, he'd realized he'd traded one group of ruthless thugs for one far worse. If he completed his mission, they'd promised him enough additional money to leave the service for a quiet retirement somewhere. And if he failed, they had been very clear. They would kill him…but first they would cut his wife and daughter to bloody chunks.

He might like Cole, but he had to get rid of the steward, or he'd never get to Barron. How could he do it and not get caught? He had the vial his contact had given him, but it was only enough for the captain. If he was going to kill Cole, he'd have to do it some other way. And he had to manage it without getting caught. He needed a distraction, but what?

His head snapped around suddenly, looking toward the source of the red light glowing in the galley, the reason he and his comrades were securing the galley. Battlestations! Of course.

The prospect of battle scared the hell out of him. He wasn't sure why *Dauntless* had been sent out so far past the Rim, but he knew it had to be dangerous. Tyler Barron was the most celebrated captain in the fleet. If he was sent out here, there was a damned good reason for it, and that very likely meant extreme danger.

But perhaps opportunity as well. His eyes moved to the lamps again. *A fight…if there is a fight. I can stay close to Cole during the battle. I may get the chance I need.*

                              *   *   *

"Commander Ephisius…Commander Vennius is still the fleet's senior officer, and he serves the Imperatrix and the Alliance. I carry his blanket authorization to issue commands in his name. You are ordered to disengage your weapons systems and allow us to pass."

Barron sat and listened to Corpus communicating with the commander of the Alliance battleship. As he'd suspected, the border was not unguarded. The vessel out there, less than one million kilometers from the transwarp point, was a capital ship. It was lighter than *Invictus* had been, perhaps seven hundred thousand tons smaller than *Dauntless*. But that didn't mean it wasn't powerful, or that engaging it wouldn't be costly and dangerous. Tyler Barron did not underestimate enemies, and after his encounter with Katrine Rigellus, certainly not ones from the Alliance.

He hoped to avoid battle, at least this far out, away from

Vennius's stronghold. He'd agreed completely when Corpus had suggested he made the entreaty, but it didn't take too much analysis to realize the exchange was not going well.

"The Imperatrix is dead, Commander Corpus...murdered on the orders of Tarkus Vennius. The traitor has been stripped of his offices and ranks, and he and his followers have been trapped. The Imperator has sent forces to destroy Vennius and his band of traitors."

"Imperator! There is no Imperator. And no one killed the Imperatrix. She is alive, and under the protection of Commander Vennius. You must listen to me!"

"I have been warned that Vennius adherents might attempt to suborn me. Do you have any proof of what you say? No, none. You simply offer your word, even as you enter Alliance space alongside a Confederation battleship. I was told Vennius had conspired with the Confederation, that he had killed the Imperatrix at their behest, but I could not believe it. Yet, here you are, along with a foreign warship, championing his cause. You are a traitor, Corpus, and your death will be a cleansing." The line went dead.

Barron didn't wait for Corpus's communication. The effort to avoid conflict had failed. There was nothing left now but to win it. "Launch all fighters."

"Yes, sir." Travis turned back to her station. "Control, launch all fighters."

"Acknowledged, Commander." Barron could hear Stara Sinclair's voice blaring through Travis's speaker. Sinclair had been the heart and soul of *Dauntless*'s launch control section for as long as he'd been captain, but he'd finally made it official, along with the launch director's title and a lieutenant commander's insignia. *Dauntless* had the best fighter squadrons in the fleet, but it was easy to focus on the hotshot pilots and ignore the vital support staff that helped make them the deadly force they were in battle.

"Engines at fifty percent...5g acceleration. Full evasive maneuvers." He was far outside any plausible firing range, but he wasn't about to take any chances. His battle with *Invictus* hadn't revealed any Alliance weapons as long-ranged as *Dauntless*'s primaries, but that was hardly conclusive. Better to be cautious, even if it meant a rougher ride into the fight.

"Engines ready, Captain...prepared to engage on your command."

Barron sat quietly for a few seconds. *Six months in paradise, a taste of a life of peace...and now I'm back here, staring into the burning eyes of death once again.*

"Engage engines, Commander. Take us in."

*   *   *

Stockton climbed into his cockpit, his leg freezing in place for a second before he forced it down. Jake "Raptor" Stockton was the fleet's leading ace, widely regarded as the deadliest pilot ever to have launched into combat. It was almost as if he'd been born in a fighter, and he'd never felt quite as comfortable anywhere else as he always had in his sleek, deadly machine. But that had all been before.

Before his ship had crashed. Before the flames had engulfed his body. He could remember the agony, the astonishing torment of the fire. Stockton had always been the ultimate survivor, one who thought he would fight to the last and never surrender, but writhing in the twisted, half-melted wreckage of his ship, all he'd wanted was death. Anything to end the pain.

He hadn't died. Against all odds, he'd survived. Stu Weldon, *Dauntless*'s chief surgeon, had saved him. Somehow. The procedure had been impossible outside a class one medical facility at a base, certainly nothing that could have been done on a ship in battle in the middle of the Badlands. But Weldon had indeed done the impossible, and despite the pain, and the long convalescence, Stockton had to admit he was fully recovered. At least physically.

He leaned back in his seat, reaching out for the fighter's controls. His eyes were focused on his shaking hands as he willed with all he had—unsuccessfully—to steady them. Stockton had a reputation for fanatical bravery, and his exploits were spo-

ken of on every ship of the fleet. But since the day he'd been
cleared to return to duty, he couldn't even walk into the launch
bay without a pit of fear yawning in his gut.

He flipped the switches on the control panel, feeding power
to his engines, readying for launch. He remembered past missions, sitting, waiting for the order to go…the excitement, the
anticipation. Now there was nothing but cold fear. All he
wanted was to pop the cockpit and climb out, run back to his
quarters. The thoughts disgusted him, and he hated himself. But
he couldn't force them away.

"Blue squadron, you are cleared to launch." It was Stara's
voice, solid, confident…and far more to him. At least it had
been more. Since he'd been released from the hospital he'd been
moody, grim, closed off. He knew that, and he'd sworn he'd
get a grip on himself, but he just didn't know how. He couldn't
understand why she still put up with him, how she countered
his callous indifference with continued compassion and understanding. He was more amazed by her than he'd ever been, and
less able to show it.

He grabbed the throttle and then he hesitated. He'd been
shaky enough in training runs and patrols, but this was the first
time he was going into battle since the crash. The cool, deadly
fighter he'd been was gone. In its place was a sweating, scared
wreck of a man, his veneer of invincibility shattered by what
had happened almost nine months before.

"Blue squadron," Stara's voice repeated, "you are clear to
launch."

All Stockton had to do was pull back on the throttle and
blast his ship's thrusters. The rest of the squadron would key
off his moves and follow him. But that simple act, something
he had done hundreds of times, now seemed insurmountable.
Slowly, steadily, he steeled himself to the task. Then, with one
burst of determination, he did it.

He was slammed back in his chair, the g forces pressing
against him. He tried to focus, to reconnect with what had once
made him the deadliest pilot in the war. He cursed the self-
indulgence of his recent behavior, and he warred with himself

to get back to where he'd once been. It was bad enough to sulk around the ship, answer Stara's affection with anger, ignore his closest friends...but if he didn't pull it together out here, he would get people killed. His people.

His hand tightened on the controls, and he brought the fighter around, moving toward the cluster of enemy ships on his screen. *Dauntless* had the edge in this fight, outmassing its opponent, and likely outclassing it too, though Stockton remembered enough from Santis not to underestimate Alliance adversaries. *Don't treat these people like Union pilots...they will be much better. Much more dangerous.*

His fingers moved over the comm controls. He knew his people had to be worried about him. He'd tried to hide his fear, and for a time, he'd convinced himself he had. But now, he began to see things more clearly. His people knew him well, and they were perceptive. He remembered a dozen recent moments, seemingly chance encounters in the corridors, and he realized they had been probing him, trying to reach him, to help him. *How blind could I be?*

Enough. You are Jake Stockton. Raptor. This fighter is your arms, your legs, part of you.

He willed with all he could muster to regain his old focus. It worked, to a point, but still, in the background were the flames, the searing hot, vicious chemical fire that had charred his flesh. The pain, indescribable, so much so that he knew his recollections fell woefully short.

"Blue squadron, form up on me. It's time to get back to work." He tried to keep his voice as calm, as steady as it had always been. He came closer than he had in the last few weeks, but he could tell the difference...and he knew his veteran pilots could too.

He knew also, that as good as they were, if he was less than he had been, more of them would die. He fed on that, tried to bolster himself. But he knew "Raptor" Stockton was gone... and that he wouldn't return. Not until the flames were banished from his mind.

Chapter Twenty-Five

Excerpt from the Inaugural Speech of Imperator Etticus Gratian Calavius Altudis ("The Pretender")

It was with heavy heart that I moved to do what was done, and nothing short of the sacred call to save the Alliance could have forced me to such action. Tarkus Vennius was my dearest friend, yet even friendship cannot stay the hand of the loyal Palatian in the face of treason. I received my decorations and my final military rank from the hand of the Imperatrix, and at the time my heart swelled with pride. Yet, she too, in age and dotage, abandoned her people. She left no choice to those of us who would preserve the nation our fathers and mothers forged from the chains of their bondage.

I call upon you now, all those who overcame the pain and did what had to be done. Raise your hands high, hold your heads like Palatian warriors, and fight—against those among us who chose treason, and against all foreign powers. I, for my part, promise to lead, to sacrifice whatever I must to ensure that our children—and their children—inherit an Alliance as strong and proud as we did. The Alliance forever.

And let us never forget the simple maxim, the words handed to us, so simple, yet so deep in meaning. *The way is the way...*

Imperial Palace
Victorum, Alliance Capital City
Astara II, Palatia
Year 61 (310 AC)

"You did the right thing…Your Supremacy." Ricard was an accomplished spy, an assassin without equal, but even his iron control almost failed him. He'd urged Calavius to move forward with the proclamation naming him Imperator, despite his own doubts about proceeding while the Imperatrix and Vennius were still at large, but he was still uncomfortable with the whole thing. The consolidation of power was still shaky, and he suspected many in the Alliance fleet and army were paying lip service only to the new regime. He'd done all he could, his staff bribing and blackmailing as many officers of note as they could manage, but the whole plan had been based on the lack of viable opposition. And Vennius, sitting at Sentinel-2, certainly qualified as opposition. If he was still too weak to be considered "viable," that could change at any moment.

"I did," Calavius replied. His arrogance that seemed to have increased exponentially after the Council, with armed soldiers standing along the walls of the Great Hall, officially deposed the Imperatrix and named him the Alliance's new ruler. Ricard contrasted the man in front of him with a panicked Calavius, overwrought over news that the first expedition he'd sent had been repulsed by Vennius's forces. He'd had to talk Calavius into proceeding with the coronation, and now the newly-official ruler walked around the room like history's greatest conqueror.

The Union spy had decided moving forward was the best option, or more specifically, the likeliest to result in the outcome he desired. Destroying Vennius would have been ideal, of course, but failing that, a war against the Confederation declared by the new Imperator would suffice. Those unwilling to blindly follow Calavius, or to raise their weapons against Vennius, would find it far more difficult to remain on the sidelines when a foreign war beckoned. When the Alliance forces moved against the

Confeds, Vennius and his small fleet would become irrelevant. More than irrelevant. Forcing Vennius to operate against Alliance forces engaged in a war with the Confederation would turn other officers and spacers against him, men and women who might otherwise support his cause.

Ricard's thoughts drifted to Calavius and the now-deposed Commander-Maximus. He had always suspected Vennius was far the superior of the two men, much more capable than his now-estranged friend. Now, of course, after the events of the past few weeks, he was sure of that. But none of it mattered. Tarkus Vennius had been a brutal warrior during his career, but nevertheless, he was that rarest of mythical beasts…an honest man. No amount of urging or bribery could have turned him against the Imperatrix, nor convinced him to support the Union. So, there had been no real choice. Ricard had been compelled to choose the lesser of the two…and turn him into a winner.

He had hoped at first, for a brief instant, that Vennius might be open to his appeal. The Alliance's fleet commander been close to Katrine Rigellus, very close, and Tyler Barron had defeated her. Killed her. Revenge, rage, resentment…they were powerful tools, and ones Ricard was an expert in wielding. But then he'd come to truly understand the Alliance's bizarre culture. Yes, Vennius hated Barron for killing his friend, almost his daughter…but he respected the captain for the very same reason. *Dauntless*'s victory over *Invictus* made Vennius *less* likely to oppose the Confederation, not more, and for all his personal pain at the loss of Rigellus, Barron's victory had increased Vennius's esteem for *Dauntless*, and for her captain.

"We must discuss next steps…Your Supremacy."

"Next steps…there is but one step before all others. That traitor Vennius must be killed."

"Yes, of course, but we must also move against the Confederation while the time is ripe, before they are able to deploy newly-built ships to the border."

"I will honor my promises to you, Mr. Ricard. After Tarkus Vennius is dead."

Ricard noted Calavius had ceased to include the Imperatrix

in his demands for Vennius's death. He didn't fool himself that there was anything substantive to that. Calavius needed the Imperatrix—the former Imperatrix, Ricard reminded himself— killed, perhaps even more than Vennius. But having taken the scepter himself, he seemed to have developed a distaste for the subject of regicide.

Ricard held back a sigh. He had planned the entire coup. It was his tactical capability, not Calavius's that had led to the Imperator's palace. And yet, here he was, arguing to be heard, to be listened to. *I could take this all away from you, Calavius, and I will do just that if you double cross me...*

Ricard had only come to the Alliance because Villieneuve had asked him to, because the Union was in danger of falling onto the defensive in the face of massive Confederation production. But it was only after he'd arrived that he realized how important his mission truly was. Alliance culture had been based on a sort of tunnel-vision, a reaction to their history of subjugation and enslavement that bordered on the fanatical. The early Alliance had faced mostly independent planets and small, loose federations, none of which had been able to stand up to the zeal and energy of the liberated Palatians and the warrior culture they had created. But now, the Alliance was on the verge of coming into contact with larger entities, such as the Confederation and the Union.

Their hard-edged creed led to an insistence that they could face any enemy, and any who suggested otherwise were in danger of being called cowards or traitors. Yet, Ricard could see there were those in the Alliance's upper echelons who had begun to understand that its future must include allies and cooperation. The Imperatrix had been cautious about committing to his proposals three years before, and he suspected Vennius, too, saw the need for the Alliance's intractable ways to change. He could even see the Commander-Maximus bringing the Alliance closer to the Confederation. Another reason why Vennius needed to die. Soon.

"I will continue to supply the resources you need, Your Supremacy..." *Remind him he is still dependent on your funding. He may have officers hesitantly taking his orders, but he is far from having control of the full revenues of the Alliance government.* "There is another vessel on its way with more coin." *Which I wasn't entirely sure Gaston could procure.* He was impressed, and more than a little surprised, at the truly staggering amount of money his commander and friend had managed to deliver. Neither he nor Villieneuve had been prepared for just how much subverting the Alliance government would cost. *They may be warriors, but the asceticism of their fathers and mothers is long gone.* Hardly an officer he had suborned had not negotiated and renegotiated, walking away with two or three times what Ricard had thought would do the deed.

Ricard looked at Calavius, and he allowed a bit more forcefulness into his voice. "But I have superiors to whom I must answer. We have provided an extraordinary amount of funding and aid, and I must have something to show for all of that."

"You have the word of the Imperator of the Alliance, Mr. Ricard. That should be sufficient to satisfy your masters."

Ricard noted the imperious tone, and the disrespect implicit in replacing his word, 'superiors' with 'masters,' but his discipline held, and he didn't react. "Of course, your word is of tremendous value, Your Supremacy. But there is more than trust at play here. There is timing. There is urgency. We have extended our hand in friendship, helped you in eliminating the traitors from your government. Now, we need your promised aid. If the Confederation is able to survive the war, even secure a favorable peace, there can be little doubt they will next look in your direction." Ricard knew his words were pure fiction. The last thing the undisciplined, spoiled masses in the Confederation would tolerate was an offensive war, one waged for conquest instead of defense. But he was betting that Calavius's Alliance training would make it impossible for him to imagine any nation not exploiting an advantage against a neighbor.

"You say that your people cannot fight their war without our assistance. And, as I have promised, we will aid you. We will invade the Confederation, and we shall destroy their fleets. We will avenge *Invictus*, and we will seize their worlds. Their people will serve the Alliance."

Ricard didn't reply at first. Even before the Union had gone to war with the Confederation, he'd expected the Confederation to be a tough enemy, though he'd held his tongue. Yet, even his own caution had proven inadequate. The Confederation forces fought with great courage and ferocity. He suspected Calavius would learn the lesson he'd failed to absorb from *Invictus*'s defeat...that the Confederation was far more dangerous than it appeared.

He kept his discipline, held back the smile he felt pushing its way out. That would be perfect, of course, Alliance fleets, arrogant from decades of victory against lesser opponents, running right into brand new Confederation battleships. The Palatians would get a chance to test their courage and their image of themselves as warriors, and when all was finished, the Confederation would be destroyed by a two-front war, and the Union forces would then advance...and they would crush a weakened Alliance fleet. A war between the Alliance and the Confederation was likely to be a holocaust, and Calavius would rule over a nation riddled with the scars of dissension remaining from the coup. When both nations had fallen, the Union would be supreme, and the rest of the cluster would fall like overripe fruit.

Calavius glared at Ricard. "We will do all we promised, Mr. Ricard...but first we will destroy Tarkus Vennius and the traitors who follow him."

Ricard almost continued the argument, but he stopped himself. There was no point. Calavius was so angry with Vennius— or, truth be told, scared of his old friend—that he could think of nothing else but the commander's destruction. And if that had to be done before the attack on the Confederation, it had to be soon. The Confederation shipyards would start to launch new battleships in a matter of months, and the Alliance had to strike before they reached the line. If they waited too long, even an outnumbered Confederation would be able to feed new ships into a defensive effort, creating a long, bloody stalemate instead of a decisive breakthrough.

Ricard looked at his creation, his creature. The Imperator of the Alliance. As was so often the case, ego and too much power had sapped the strength of a competent soldier. Calavius wasn't going to defeat Vennius, not quickly. Not alone. Ricard would have to help every step of the way, devise a strategy to take Sentinel-2…to kill Tarkus Vennius and the deposed Imperatrix. And damn the cost.

Chapter Twenty-Six

"Primaries recharging, Captain."

Barron was looking down at his workstation's small screen, reviewing the damage reports. *Dauntless* had taken two hits, bombers that had managed to get through the defensive fighter patrol to firing range. It reminded Barron that he was facing the Alliance again, and not poorly-trained Union draftees. They were true warriors, and they were good. At least as good as most Confederation squadrons, though Barron thought of his own wings as the best in space.

His squadrons had handily defeated the enemy fighters, and his own bombers had scored three hits themselves. That, coupled with the direct hit his gunners had managed on first shot with the primaries, had hit the Alliance ship hard. Barron could see its captain's skill—the ship's well-executed maneuvers that caused *Dauntless*'s next two shots to miss entirely. He was facing a talented opponent, though the difference between this fight and his memories of the duel against Commander Rigellus was stark. He'd been pressed to the limit of his abilities in the battle three years before, and he'd tasted true desperation in Santis. Here, he respected his opponent, but he didn't doubt his people could win. His concern was more on minimizing the losses and damage suffered in the process.

"This is probably our last shot before the enemy's main guns come into range, Commander. Advise the gunners, I'm expecting their very best here."

"Yes, Captain."

Barron knew such encouragements weren't really necessary, not with his crew. Still, even the hardest veteran could lose focus. He'd seen veteran pilots, victors of dozens of combats, inexplicably killed by opponents they should have easily vanquished. His gunners, the deadliest in the fleet by far, who had hit uncounted times from extreme range, had all occasionally missed crucial point blank shots. It was a lesson Barron took to heart, one of the few military maxims his grandfather had passed on to him. Ego, overconfidence…they were the deadliest enemies one could face.

"Twenty seconds to full charge."

Barron looked up, his eyes darting to the small screen that displayed the primaries' charging status. The bar was almost entirely lit up in red, just a sliver of white background remaining.

His stomach had twisted into knots when the enemy fighters had first scored their hits. The Confederation's particle accelerators were the highest-tech weapons deployed since the fall of the empire, a huge tactical advantage against an enemy like the Alliance. They were longer-ranged than anything their adversary possessed, allowing Confederation battleships to open fire before their opponents could respond in kind. But that benefit was attained at a price. The highly-complex systems had always been enormously subject to breakdown, and even a few moderate hits had been able to knock them out or cut off the extensive power systems that fed them. But *Dauntless*'s new weapons were the latest versions, even more powerful than those they replaced, and perhaps more crucially, a lot more durable. The battleship had taken two solid hits from the bombers. Systems were damaged, crew members were killed and wounded. But the primaries were still online. Between the deadly, long-ranged weapons and the hits scored by his own wings, Barron knew the final close-up duel would be a lopsided affair.

He saw a wave of text scrolling up his workstation screen, reports from engineering. Fritzie had lost none of her drive or ability, that much was clear. The ruptured power conduits along the starboard side had been rerouted, and the compromised compartments sealed or cut off. *Dauntless* was damaged, but for all practical purposes, she was still fully-operational.

"Primaries charged, Captain."

"Fire." The familiar whine rattled across the bridge a few seconds later, and the lights dimmed as the weapons unleashed an enormous burst of power into a destructive blast. A few seconds later, Barron was surprised by the report. A clean miss.

Damn. Were his people rusty after their long rest? Did he have to do something to hone them back into the razors they were before *Dauntless* went into spacedock for six months? *No*, he reminded himself. *It isn't my people. These are not Union enemies. These are Alliance warriors.* This war would be different. And a war it would be. His crossing the border and engaging this vessel meant the Confederation was now effectively at war with the Alliance—at least, part of the Alliance.

The Union had won the battles it had with numerical superiority, with a willingness to send vast numbers of ships to destruction and crews to their deaths. But the Alliance could match the Confederation in a fight at much closer to even numbers. They could perhaps even overcome the technical deficit between the two fleets. No doubt, *they* believed they were the superiors. And perhaps, overall, they were. Theirs was a culture entirely built on war, where there was no other honorable profession. Young children studied tactics and war, and the elite subjected their adolescents to an endurance test in which between one and two percent died. Barron understood he couldn't treat these enemies as Union conscripts, and he intended to make sure his people understood that too.

"Primaries recharging again, sir."

Barron just nodded. His thoughts were on what he had started here. Striker had given him the authority, but he hadn't intended to use it, not most of it, at least. *And now you barged across the border and got into a fight with the first ship you found...*

He knew there was no choice. Commander Corpus's arrival at Archellia and the news he had brought with him left little doubt. War with the Alliance was a certainty, whether he reacted or not. And Tyler Barron was not one to bury his head in the sand and wait for events to unfold. Perhaps his action would forestall disaster, or diminish its severity.

"We're coming into their range now, sir."

"Full damage protocols, Commander. Evasive maneuvers, program Alpha-3. Continue charging primaries."

Travis responded to each order, her replies as rapid and sharp as his own commands. He'd enjoyed his leave, and part of him longed to be back there without the stress of duty and combat. But he felt he was back at home now, he and Atara working seamlessly together. He knew his first officer deserved her own command, that she should be on the bridge of her own ship, even now. But she had refused the promotion...and for all he was aware she deserved to advance, he was relieved she had stayed. He knew he'd have to move on too, one day soon. His partnership with Atara, and the perfect crew they'd put together, was just a fleeting moment in his life...but he was grateful to keep it all for just a little longer. Whatever hell they had to push through together.

"Thirty seconds to full charge on primaries."

Barron might have switched to his secondary batteries before, afraid the enemy's opening volley would knock out the fragile main weapons. But he was betting on the new equipment, on Fritzie's confidence in it.

Dauntless shook, a hit Barron could tell immediately had been a glancing blow. Then again, a few seconds, later, harder this time. He looked down at the damage control, his gut tight, waiting to see if some power line or secondary system had been hit, knocking out the primaries. But they still showed green. And the status monitor read full power.

"Primaries charged, Captain."

"Fire," he said, a smile slipping onto his face. *I guess you were right, Fritzie...they've toughened the things up!*

*   *   *

"All right, bombers back to *Dauntless*, now. Everybody else, on me. It's time to pursue and finish off these enemy birds." Kyle Jamison was already bringing his fighter around as he ordered *Dauntless*'s squadrons to do the same.

"Yes, Thunder."

"Acknowledged."

"Yes, sir."

"Acknowledged."

Last again.

Jamison shook his head as the responses came in from his squadron commanders. It was the final one that troubled him, coming in seconds after all the others, the voice deadpan, lifeless. "Raptor" Stockton had always been the first to respond, and his answers had crackled with energy. Stockton in a battle had always seemed like a creature in its natural habitat, a predator loping across the savannah, the king of his domain. Now, he seemed lost, out of place.

And he's going to get himself killed if he doesn't get past this…him and a lot of his pilots…

"Scarlett Eagles and Reds, take point. Yellow cover the left flank, Green the right." He paused. "Blues in reserve."

He knew the Blues belonged up front, leading the entire strike force, and he also realized putting them in reserve was telling every pilot out there that he was worried about Stockton. He'd almost sent Blue squadron forward, as he normally would, but something stopped him. He couldn't get the image of Stockton out of his head, his old focus and instinct gone, blundering into the laser blasts of an otherwise doomed Alliance fighter. He didn't enjoy disrespecting his best friend, but he liked the idea of speaking about Stockton's exploits at a memorial service even less.

The Alliance pilots were too good for any of his people to give less than one hundred percent. Had the enemy been facing a normal Confederation ship, they would have put up a good fight, perhaps even won. But *Dauntless*'s strikeforce was not only elite, she had a larger complement as well, courtesy of the strays they'd picked up at Arcturon…*my God, was that more than two years ago?* Outnumbered and outclassed, even the skilled and courageous Alliance squadrons had suffered heavily and pulled back. *Not quite broken,* Jamison realized, but they had retreated, seeking to defend their mother ship with what they had left.

Jamison didn't think the battle would go on long enough for *Dauntless*'s bombers to rearm and launch another strike, but just in case, he was going to make sure there wasn't a fighter left to intercept them if they did.

Besides, these Alliance pilots are all crazy…if their mother ship goes, they'll all be making suicide runs, screaming oaths to their ancestors about honor. He shook his head. His own people were slightly less crazy, perhaps…but only slightly.

"Full thrusters…we should have just enough fuel reserves to catch them before they get inside their base ship's defensive envelope." Jamison knew that didn't matter much. The enemy ship was heavily engaged with *Dauntless*. It wasn't likely she had enough power or focus to spare mounting an anti-fighter defense right now. But he wanted those birds destroyed, and he'd give his people any push to get it done.

He felt the pressure slam into him as he blasted his own engines at full. A quick glance at the scanner showed his wings doing the same, the whole line of ships lurching forward, accelerating toward the enemy.

Jamison stared at the screen and shook his head. Blue squadron was last, again, his elite force looking as sluggish as a group of trainees. *C'mon, Raptor…pull it together, man…*

He didn't think less of his friend for the troubles he was having. Beyond the agony of his injuries and the long and torturous recovery, he understood Stockton better than anyone else, save perhaps Stata Sinclair. Stockton's insane courage and the razor focus he'd used to such deadly effect had been driven by a sense of invulnerability…and now that was gone, burned away in the flames that had come so close to killing him. It remained to be seen if Jake Stockton could make it back, rediscover what he had been. And Jamison was very worried his friend would fail that challenge. If he did, there wasn't a doubt in his mind Stockton would die out in space, in one of these battles, and probably sooner rather than later.

C'mon, Jake, you can do this... But he felt the emptiness of his own words, and he realized there was nothing he could do, no way to reach the man he considered a brother. Nothing he hadn't tried and failed with already.

There was no time for any of it now, though. The retreating enemy fighters were turning. They knew they couldn't get away, and he wasn't surprised the Alliance pilots preferred a hopeless fight to being picked off as they ran.

His people had more work to do, and although they had the advantage, he was certain the win would be costly.

*   *   *

Barron pulled off his jacket and tossed it onto one of the large chairs against the wall. He stretched his neck, rolling it around on his shoulders. He got very tense in battle, and afterwards he always felt it in aching muscles and stiff joints.

He looked around his quarters. They were new, yet almost identical in layout and appearance to what they had been before the refit. Admiral Striker's touch, he imagined, probably one of his own idiosyncrasies he'd projected onto Barron, assuming the captain wouldn't want anything different. That was common in the service, ranging from a general preference in some officers to an outright obsession in others. He wondered which it was for Striker.

Whatever it was, it was one trait Barron didn't share. Actually, he'd have welcomed a different look, a change of pace. But he didn't care that much.

He sat down, extending his legs and resting them on the small table in front of his chair. It was probably a breach of etiquette, especially with his boots still on, but Barron didn't care. These were his quarters...and besides, he'd always found it difficult to worry about superficial nonsense when his people were dying around him. Or had just died, in this case.

The battle was over, the enemy ship destroyed. He'd stayed on the bridge until the last of the damage was under control and all of his pilots were back aboard, including the four who'd ditched their damaged fighters and been picked up by the rescue boats.

The fight had gone better than he'd had any right to hope, but there was still a shadow following him. He'd started a war. A second war, a second front. He knew there hadn't been a choice, but he felt the weight of responsibility heavy on his shoulders.

Was it like this for you, Grandfather? How did you carry your burdens? Commanding a ship…it's difficult, and every man or woman killed is like a knife through your heart, but this? It's too much. How many thousands will die because of what I've done here? Millions?

"Captain, the steward is here with your food." It was the guard at his door, the voice on the comm unit pulling him from his thoughts. He'd long thought the custom of posting a sentinel outside his quarters was a foolish waste of a Marine, but it was tradition, and his attempts to abolish the whole thing were met with loud and strenuous complaints, and he'd relented. His Marines took his safety as their sacred duty, and in the end, he just hadn't cared enough to take the duty from them.

"Send him in." He smiled. He hadn't ordered food. *Atara…* His first officer was his comrade and his best friend, but occasionally she tried to step in for his mother as well.

"Put it on the table, Lars…" He turned, and his words drifted off. "Excuse me…Spacer Ventnor, isn't it?" Barron always made an effort to memorize the new members of the crew, but there had been a lot of them this time, and he only gave himself a coin toss on this one.

"Yes, sir." Ventnor moved toward the table and set down the tray.

"Spacer Cole serves my meals…where is he?"

Ventnor paused, shifting his weight back and forth. "I'm sorry, Captain, I thought you knew."

"Knew?" Barron stood up.

"Spacer Cole was killed during the battle, sir."

Barron was shocked at the man's words. He'd seen the casualty reports, but he'd only focused on the totals, intending to review it all in greater depth later...when he wrote the dispatches to the families of those killed in battle.

He'd lost seventeen of his people in the fight just concluded, a light toll for a fight such as the one just concluded, though every one of them hurt, as they always did. Most of the dead and seriously wounded had been gunners and scanner technicians and others posted near the ship's exterior when hits had impacted, or engineers caught close to the reactors or the high-energy transmission lines when they were damaged. And fighter pilots, of course, probably most of all.

It had been an extraordinarily bad stroke of luck for a steward like Cole to be among the dead. Lars Cole had been Barron's steward since the day he'd set foot on *Dauntless*. The steward and his wife had split up years before, but Cole had two grown children back home, Barron thought he recalled.

Ventnor stepped back from the tray. "I'm sorry, sir. From what I've heard in the galley, Spacer Cole was well liked." A pause, then: "Can I serve you, Captain? You really should eat something."

Barron shook his head. "I'm fine, Spacer Ventnor. Dismissed." That last part came out more abruptly than he'd intended, and he followed it up with, "Thank you, Spacer. I will eat something."

Ventnor saluted and turned, walking back to the door and out into the hallway.

Barron stood where he was for a moment, indulging a few thoughts of Cole before he put the dead steward in the place he kept all his lost crew members. Then he walked over to the table and looked down at the tray. *Definitely Atara*, he thought with a weak smile. There was enough to feed a small army, and most of his favorites were there. He knew she was trying to keep his strength up, that left to himself, he would go hours, even days after a battle without eating anything. Unless she forced the issue.

He reached down, grabbing the large teapot and pouring a

cup. *Fine, Atara, I'll have something.* He reached out and grabbed half a sandwich in one hand while he raised the cup to his lips with the other.

The tea was good, hot and fairly sweet the way he liked it. The warmth felt soothing as it slid down his throat, and he realized just how hungry he was.

He took a bite of the sandwich and then, after he swallowed, another deep drink of the tea.

Chapter Twenty-Seven

Free Trader Pegasus
Etruria System
310 AC

Lafarge's eyes were fixed on *Pegasus*'s forward display, watching the data her scanners were feeding her as quickly as they could survey the system. There was nothing yet. She was sure *Dauntless* had come this way. She and her crew were not navy, but they had their own sets of skills honed during years of searching for the slightest hints of old tech. There were ways to track a ship, things to look for, even in the vastness of interplanetary space—residue from fuel burns, radioactive exhaust from reactors, even routine waste dumps. It wasn't easy to find, not over such enormous distances, but there were ways to narrow the focus. *Pegasus* and her crew had tracked a ship this way, a big one. She couldn't be sure it was *Dauntless*, but neither could she think of any other vessel so large that would be out here, beyond the Rim.

Striker had told her he'd sent Barron to Archellia, that there was trouble in the Alliance, and he'd wanted someone he could trust at the edge of the Rim, just in case. *Just in case*, his exact words, almost as though Barron and his newly repaired battleship and its veteran crew had been sent to a backwater on the off chance something happened. She wasn't sure if Striker had been trying to maintain the shattered remnants of security after

217

he'd told her as much as he had, or if he had downplayed the situation to minimize her worries, but either way, she didn't believe a bit of it. If Barron had been sent to Archellia, the situation was downright critical.

Still, she'd hoped she would find *Dauntless* docked at Archellia base, Barron finding any excuse to hide aboard, chafing at the constant tide of fawning attention from the provincials on the planet. Even more, she'd wanted to find him whole and healthy, and not dead at some assassin's hand. That was why she was here, why she had followed *Dauntless*. Why she would follow him right through the Alliance and beyond the Far Rim, into the deepest darks of endless space if she had to.

But Barron hadn't been at Archellia. *Dauntless* had left there, and Admiral Lowery had proven to be far less willing to share information with her than Striker had been. She'd wasted days on Archellia, lost time while *Dauntless* moved farther away. Time during which an assassin could choose his moment...and strike. Finally, she'd gotten to Lowery, using the credentials Striker had given her. Archellia's commander still had difficulty with the idea of telling a civilian, a freebooter and petty adventurer to his way of thinking, where Barron had gone. Perhaps worse, at least from Lafarge's perspective, Lowery hadn't really known. All he'd been able to tell her was *Dauntless* had set out for the Rim with an Alliance vessel.

It didn't make much sense to her, but it had given her a direction, and she'd managed to follow *Dauntless*'s trail—at least she thought it was *Dauntless*'s trail—ever since. Right through the Rim and into unaligned space...and over the border into the Alliance. The eeriness of the empty systems beyond the Confederation that troubled so many was lost on her. She and her people had ventured deep into the Badlands, and the haunted, dead planets there preyed on the soul more than any backwater out here. Still, her nerves had awakened as she neared the Alliance, and they'd practically caught fire as her ship crossed over into that mysterious nation.

She didn't have the status of military governor that Striker had given Barron, nor virtual viceregal authorities to cross borders and risk international incidents. But she didn't give a shit, either. She had to get to *Dauntless*, and she'd blaze a trail across the Alliance, the Union, and half the old empire to do it if she had to. She suspected Striker had known that when he'd told her all that he had, that he'd been sure no one he could send to warn Barron would have moved faster or with greater determination than she.

"Andi, we're getting some readings." Vig's words hit her just as she noticed the blips on the screen. At first, she thought it might be a particularly large waste dump, but there was too much mass. The radiation levels were high, too, very high. And there were large bits, much bigger than anything blasted out of a refuse port.

"Something happened here, Vig," she said nervously. "And my gut tells me it was some kind of fight." She didn't continue with the other thoughts in her mind. The fears.

They hadn't scanned enough debris yet to account for something as large as *Dauntless*, but then she knew they wouldn't have. Not yet. And what she was looking at now seemed very much like a portion of the remains of a capital ship.

"Lex, you've got to get more power to the scanners. I don't care how you do it." She knew she was letting her fear show, but she couldn't help it. She had to know if these chunks of radioactive metal were all that was left of *Dauntless*.

"I'm on it, Andi," came the reply. The sympathy in the engineer's voice was discernible. Clearly, he too was concerned that they had found *Dauntless*'s remains.

But how? Shugart told me it was an assassin. Could it have been a saboteur instead?

She looked back at the screen. Or did *Dauntless* run into Alliance vessels?

She shook her head. *Dauntless* was newly refit, and crewed by the best of the Confederation navy. They had already defeated the best the Alliance had three years before, and if anything, Barron and his ship were stronger now than they had been then. If Alliance forces had taken them down, there would be more wreckage. Tyler Barron wasn't invincible, she knew that. But she was sure of one thing…if he'd gone down, he wouldn't have gone alone.

"What do you think, Vig? Could this be the wreckage of two or three battleships?"

Her second-in-command shook his head. "I don't know what we'll find deeper in, Andi, but it doesn't look like it to me. My gut says we're picking up the wreckage of a capital ship, but only one."

Merrick's tone was somber, but Andi felt a rush of hope. She couldn't imagine Barron being destroyed without taking some of the enemy with him, no matter what the odds. She'd seen him get the better of five Union battleships at Chrysallis.

"This isn't *Dauntless*," she said, in a tone that was half confidence and half hope. "They came this way…and perhaps they fought an Alliance ship here." A short pause. "But this isn't them."

She shook her head. She suspected Vig was worrying about her, about whether she was losing her objectivity. She understood such a concern, and she *was* worried about Barron, more worried than she'd ever remembered being, but Andromeda Lafarge never lost her judgment—not over a mission, or a lover, or any danger she faced. She was sure that wasn't *Dauntless* out there, as sure as she could be.

"Keep the scanners at full power. Record and catalog everything we find…and try to determine which way the victor of this encounter went." There wasn't a doubt in her mind now that victor had been *Dauntless*. Barron and his people had faced an Alliance ship here, and they had destroyed it. The more she thought about it, the more she became convinced. "We need to keep moving. We need to catch them, as quickly as possible."

"Yes, Andi." Merrick still sounded less than totally convinced, but it was clear her confidence was at least somewhat contagious.

She felt better, but only for a moment. *What the hell was Tyler thinking, invading the Alliance alone, firing on at least one of their ships. Destroying one of their ships.*

It seemed insane. Admiral Striker had told her he'd sent

Barron to Archellia, to be ready to deal with the fallout from suspected Union meddling in the Alliance. Striker had also told her he'd given Barron almost limitless authority to do whatever he thought was necessary. But leaving Archellia almost immediately and plunging across the border? Fighting Alliance forces in their own territory? It didn't sound like Tyler Barron.

She felt a sudden panic. Was he being controlled somehow? Was the "assassin" really an operative, somehow compelling Barron to do things he otherwise wouldn't? It all seemed very cloak and dagger, hard to believe. *But what else could be going on?*

"We're picking up more debris now, Andi. Almost definitely wreckage from a spacecraft, but the mass still suggests only one vessel." Merrick's tone was guarded. It was clear he wasn't as sure as she was that the vessel in question was not *Dauntless*.

Andi just nodded. It was an Alliance ship, she was almost certain of that now. But she was no less anxious, her mind racing, wondering what could have caused Barron to take his ship right into Alliance space and provoke a war. It didn't make sense.

And worse, even if *Dauntless* had survived whatever battle had occurred here. it didn't do much to increase *her* survival prospects. Barron didn't have an invasion fleet with him. His ship was alone, moving deeper into Alliance—now enemy—space. He would end up facing more than one ship. Eventually, he'd be hunted down by whole fleets, and *Dauntless* would be surrounded and overwhelmed. Assuming whatever agent Sector Nine had managed to get aboard his ship didn't just kill him first.

Hasn't killed him already…

"Vig, any progress on tracking where the survivor went?"

Merrick's head was bent over his workstation. He turned and look across the tight space to Lafarge. "I think so, Andi. I can't be sure…if you want certainty, it will take hours, maybe even days."

"We don't have hours, Vig, and we certainly don't have days. Let's go with what you've got."

"My best guess is the Sovanna transit point. We're picking

up heavy ion trails leading that way. It's far from proof, but I'd say a capital ship went that way."

"Then we're going to follow it." She took a deep breath and exhaled. "Full thrust, Vig. We don't have any more time to lose."

"Yes, Andi…right away."

She heard the worry in her friend's voice, and she knew it was for her. She could feel herself losing it in a way she never had before. She tried to cling to hope that she would be on time to save Barron, but it was becoming more difficult. Had *Dauntless* escaped the battle in this system? Had the Sector Nine assassin aboard failed, or not yet struck? If even one of those things went wrong, Tyler Barron was dead.

She wanted to believe he would be okay. She *had* to believe it. But it was getting harder.

"Engines ready, Andi."

She took a deep breath. "Let's go," she said. "Full power."

Chapter Twenty-Eight

CFS Dauntless
Entering Planet Cilian System
Deep in the Alliance
Year 310 AC

"Captain?" The voice sounded concerned, distant. It took Barron a few seconds to realize Travis was speaking to him.

"Commander?" Barron's mind was foggy, unfocused. He shook his head as he spoke, trying to clear his thoughts.

"We're picking up Alliance ships, sir. So far, everything is as Commander Corpus said it would be."

"Very well, Commander." Barron paused. He tried to take a deep breath, but his chest was heavy, and he had to gasp to suck in the air. He wrote it off to the g forces of acceleration...until he remembered *Dauntless*'s engines were only firing at 1g.

"Captain, are you okay?"

He looked up, seeing Travis standing halfway between her station and his.

"I'm fine, Commander," he answered, suspecting his tone was entirely unconvincing. "I'm just tired...I had trouble sleeping last night." Again, he realized that wasn't going to go far, especially with Travis. She'd seen just how long he could go without sleep, staying at maximum focus during combat conditions.

He didn't know what was wrong with him. Contrary to

what he'd just said, he had actually slept well during his last rest period. His stomach had been a little unsettled when he'd gotten up, and he hadn't eaten anything since the night before... but he doubted something as simple as a skipped breakfast was causing his uneasy feeling.

"Captain, I think you should go to sickbay, and let Dr. Weldon have a look at you."

Barron shook his head. "Absolutely not, Commander. We just entered this system. In a few moments, we will find out exactly what is happening in the Alliance."

Travis stood where she was. "Captain..."

"I'm fine, Commander," he said, knowing he was lying. He looked up at Travis, and she was blurry, even though she was less than three meters away. It didn't matter. He could *not* be sick now. There just wasn't time.

"Let me call Dr. Weldon to the bridge, sir." She took a few steps forward, moving right next to him. "Please, sir," she said softly. "We need you at your best. Maybe Dr. Weldon can give you a light stim or something."

Barron didn't like the idea of making a spectacle of himself by having the ship's chief surgeon come to the bridge to tell him he had a virus or some other minor illness. But he turned his head, and nearly lost the contents of his almost empty stomach.

"Very well, Commander. If that will satisfy you." In any other situation, he'd have quietly gone down to sickbay and had Doc Weldon give him a stimulant and an anti-viral shot. But not now. Not while *Dauntless* was approaching a massive Alliance base and the line of battleships deployed next to it.

Travis went back to her station, and she ordered Weldon to the bridge. A moment later, she turned back toward Barron. "Captain, Commander Corpus advises he is contacting the base. He requests we hold position and maintain communications silence until he advises otherwise."

"Very well...Commander." Barron felt dizzy again. He'd always been self-sufficient, and he was rarely sick. But now he was glad Doc Weldon was on the way. *I could use a shot or something...just to clear my head.*

Barron looked at the display, trying to keep his eyes focused. He was seeing double now, and it took significant concentration to zero in on just how many symbols were there. *Six capital ships*, he thought to himself. Is that all?

If there was truly a schism in the Alliance, it was beginning to look very much like his side—the one that favored the Confederation—was the weaker, possibly by a considerable margin.

What am I going to do now? How can one battleship make a difference...and what will happen to the Confederation when this faction is defeated? He knew his nation would fight to the finish, but he was just as sure, deep down, that they could not win such a conflict, not against the Union and the Alliance at the same time. He had to find a way to help these Alliance forces, to keep the pro-Union faction from winning a quick victory.

But how?

*   *   *

"She looks terrible, Doctor. Whatever you've been doing, you need to do better." Vennius stood next to a sickbay cot, looking down at the emaciated old woman lying there.

"Commander-Maximus, we have done all we can do, as did the medical staff on *Bellator*. It's a testament to the treatment she received there that she is even alive now." Commander-Princeps Nadia Tectus was Sentinel-2's senior medical officer, one of the few of the Palatian Citizen class who had chosen a non-combat career and still attained great respect for her achievements. Vennius knew the Imperatrix was in the best hands possible, but he couldn't get past the frustration, and the fear, that he'd brought her all this way only to watch her die.

"I have great respect for your skills, Dr. Tectus, but we must do more. We must ensure that the Imperatrix survives her wounds."

"I'm afraid that is quite impossible, Commander." Tectus glanced down at the woman in the cot. "Everything possible has been done for her. Her wounds have been treated as well as they could be, enough for her to survive, but..."

"But? We have no place for 'buts' now, Doctor."

"I'm afraid we have no choice. The 'but' that matters here is her age. The Imperatrix is old, Commander, and the stress from her wounds, and from the flight from the palace, may have been too much for her." Tectus paused. "We have done all we can, Commander. All that remains is to wait, and see what happens."

"Wait and see what happens? This is the supreme ruler of the Alliance! And we are in the midst of a crisis that makes her survival necessary."

"Mortality does not respect rank or title, Commander. The Imperatrix is a very strong woman. If she wasn't, she'd have died back on Palatia." She paused again, and her voice become grimmer. "For all her strength, she was very near the end of her life anyway. I doubt she had more than two or three years remaining, Commander. And with the stress all of this placed on her body…"

"You must save her, Commander Tectus. She is my friend, but that is not why. She deserves to live out her days and die in her own time, but that is not why either. The reality is a colder one, but real nevertheless. She has lived a life of duty, risen from chains to lead her people. And that duty is not over. She must live to see the Alliance through this crisis."

Tectus stared back at Vennius, a conflicted look on her face. "Commander-Maximus, you have my loyalty and support in this fight. I believe you are the rightful fleet commander and that those who have usurped that power are traitors. But, I respect you too much to tell you other than the truth. So, I say now, as a doctor, and an Alliance officer…the Imperatrix deserves her rest. If she lives, it will not be for long, nor will it be a life worth living, especially for a woman who was so vital and who led such a dynamic existence. I will treat her wounds, I will aid her if she begins to recover on her own strength. But I will not use extraordinary measures that will prolong only her pain. I will not turn her into a zombie, to be paraded around as a symbol. I respect *her* too much for that."

Vennius felt a surge of anger at the doctor's defiance…or was it defiance? He stood where he was, stone still, and in his mind a conflict began to rage. He was worn, exhausted, driven to the edge of his wits in trying to keep the resistance alive. One side of him argued Dr. Tectus was right, that her words were honorable and wise. The other side was weighed down by the responsibilities that threatened to crush him—and overwhelmed with hatred and fury toward Calavius. He had become obsessed with destroying the man who had once been his friend, and though he knew his rage threatened his judgment, even his sanity, he still could not control it.

"Just do what you can, Doctor," he said, his words tight, clipped. It was a compromise of sorts between the two sides of his mind, and it was the best he could manage.

"Tarkus…" The voice was frail, weak, barely audible. Vennius almost didn't hear it…almost.

His eyes darted down, and then he dropped to one knee next to the bed. "Your Supremacy," he said, glancing quickly up to the doctor and then back.

"Tarkus…no titles. We are…old friends? You called me… Flavia once…did you not?"

"That was many years ago, Your Supremacy, when we fought together."

"Please…"

Vennius looked around, then back to Tectus. She nodded, the movement barely perceptible, but he knew she was urging him to grant the Imperatrix's request. Still, he paused. It was improper. It went against all he'd been taught. But then his eyes connected with those of the old woman lying in front of him. He'd seen almost indescribable strength in those eyes, a force that had inspired him more times than he could easily recall. But that power was gone now, and all that was left was the frailty and weakness of an old friend. One he knew was dying.

"Very well…Flavia." He extended his arm, putting his hand over hers. "We are at Sentinel-2, Your…Flavia. You are receiving the best care possible. You will be up and around soon."

"I don't think so, Tarkus…and I would have no lies between us now. I am dying, am I not?"

Vennius bit back on the emotion he felt welling up inside.

Finally, he choked out a few words. "I don't know."

"Thank you, Tarkus...no falsehoods, not now. Promise?"

"I promise."

She smiled for a few seconds, and then she closed her eyes. For an instant, he was afraid she was gone, but then he realized she was sleeping.

He stood up and turned toward Tectus. "See she is comfortable, Doctor. And do what you can for her. She is my friend. She saved my life once." He paused and took a deep breath. "I fear I will prove unequal to repaying the deed."

"I will contact you at once if there is any change, Commander."

"Thank you, Doctor. I am sorry if I was...difficult earlier."

"Not at all, Commander."

"I will..."

"Commander Vennius, *Hastam* has returned." Aurelius came rushing into the room. "Commander Corpus has contacted the base...and he brought a Confederation battleship back with him."

Vennius's head spun around. He pushed aside the part of him that was Flavia's friend, grieving for her injuries. He needed to be Commander Vennius now, the leader of the resistance. He waved his arm. "To the control room, Aurelius. Now. We must speak with Commander Corpus...and the captain of this Confederation ship. At once!"

"Yes, sir." The aide turned and headed back the way he had come, Vennius following right behind.

He paused at the door, looking back for a few seconds. "Keep her comfortable, Doctor...she deserves that, at least... no matter what."

Tectus nodded, and then Vennius was out the door.

*   *   *

"Captain Barron? *Dauntless*?" It was clear the officer on the comm was trying to keep shock from coming through in his words, and just as obvious he was failing utterly. Barron had suspected his name would be known in the Alliance, and he'd told as much to Striker. But there was more here, not just anger at the defeat of an Alliance battleship. This was *personal*.

"Yes, Commander Vennius. I am Captain Tyler Barron, commanding CFS *Dauntless*." Barron knew there was no point in trying to avoid the topic, so he decided to do the reverse, and to out and out own it. "My duty compelled me to face your vessel *Invictus* in battle three years ago. Captain Rigellus was an extraordinary adversary, one I honor to this day." He knew enough about Alliance culture to realize shrinking away from what had happened would only make things worse.

"She was an extraordinary officer, Captain Barron…and a woman worthy of your honor." Barron could hear the anger in Vennius's voice, but also the pain. *He knew her.*

Barron flinched as Doc Weldon slipped the cold metal of the med-probe down his neck. It was beyond annoying to be poked and probed while addressing a foreign leader—*one who probably wants your head for killing Commander Rigellus*—but at least Weldon had already taken pity on him and given him a shot. It hadn't been quite the syringe full of energy he'd been hoping for, but it had cleared his head a bit.

"I regret that I could not meet her as an ally, rather than an…" He almost said "enemy." "…opponent."

"Indeed, Captain." The voice had changed a bit, a slight move toward the conciliatory. "That entire incident was unfortunate. Its origins have their seeds in the machinations of your enemies, the Union…as does the current situation."

"I have come at the request of Commander Corpus. He advises me that the Alliance is divided, that your forces now battle each other." Again, Barron's instincts told him directness would serve best in this encounter.

"That is the case, Captain. There is no time for posturing, nor for half-truths. I was deceived, Captain Barron, by a man I long considered a friend. My blindness to his schemes allowed him to seize control of our home world, and, I believe, most of the fleet. We have repulsed one attack, but I expect another at any time." Vennius hesitated for a few seconds, and then he continued. "Now, I will sacrifice all that remains of my pride, of my honor. I request aid, Captain, from you, who slew my beloved Katrine...and from the Confederation, against whom we conspired with the Union. The loss of *Invictus* was just punishment, for we should never have invaded your space at their behest. Now, we are brought low, and your people and mine share common cause."

Barron's armed jerked forward as Weldon shoved a probe into the flesh of his shoulder. "Commander Vennius, I have come to aid you any way I can. Whatever happened between our people, you are correct that we have an enemy in common. The Union must not be allowed to prevail, for they defeat us, you will certainly be next. And life under their rule would be as repugnant for your people as for mine."

"I thank you, Captain." Barron could feel how difficult Vennius's words were for the commander. 'Beloved Katrine'... the words were still stuck in his mind, along with the pain in the voice that had uttered them. "What force can you bring to bear?"

"I'm afraid *Dauntless* is the only battleship I have to offer you at present. If you will allow it, I will send Commander Corpus's ship back with several of my officers and an urgent request for reinforcements." Barron put his hand up to his head. He'd felt better after Weldon had given him the injection, but now he felt weak again, almost as if he was about to faint.

He forced his attention back to Vennius. "I will not lie to you, Commander. Our fleet is fully deployed on our border with the Union. There are no forces available anywhere near the Rim. It will likely be months before anything can be sent to your aid, perhaps even a year. *Dauntless* will have to do, I'm afraid... for quite some time."

"We thank you for coming, Captain, and for what force you have to offer." He could hear the discouragement in Vennius's tone. The Alliance officer clearly didn't think *Dauntless* would be enough. *But then, he doesn't know* Dauntless...*or her crew.*

"We will fight at your side, Commander, if it is necess..." Barron stopped abruptly. He could hear the sounds of sirens and warning bells coming through the comm. Then, Travis spun around.

"Captain, we're picking up forces transiting into the system. Three battleships, so far. No, four."

"Battlestations, Commander. All squadrons report to launch bays."

"Yes, sir."

The klaxons rang out, and once again, *Dauntless*'s crew prepared the great battleship for war.

"Five ships, Captain. Six."

It was a major attack, that was apparent…the one Vennius had said he expected. *Dauntless* had arrived just in time…to save Vennius's cause, or to fall alongside the Alliance commander. Barron didn't know which, not yet."

"Seven ships. Eight."

Chapter Twenty-Nine

CFS Dauntless
Cilian System
Deep in the Alliance
Year 310 AC

"Captain…you have to come down to sickbay with me at once." Weldon reached down and picked up a small comm unit from his bag. "I will call for a stretcher."

Barron's head spun around to face the doctor—and he almost fell out of his chair from the resulting wave of dizziness. "Are you insane, Doc? We've got enemy forces transiting into the system. We're going into battle. Whatever it is, a virus, something bacterial, you'll just have to give me a shot and be done with it. I promise I'll come down to sickbay after the battle and…"

"It's not a virus, Tyler." Weldon's voice was deadly serious. "You are sick, very sick…and I have no idea what's causing it."

"Very sick…Doc, you're too dramatic. I'm just a little dizzy, probably overtired. Just…"

"You're more than a little dizzy, Tyler. Your heartbeat is extremely irregular, and your blood ox levels are dangerously low. I have to get you down to sickbay now, or…"

Barron looked at his doctor, aware that the entire bridge crew was staring at the two of them in undisguised horror.

"You must have made a mistake, Doc...I'm in perfect health. You poked and probed me for hours when I got back from leave. I'm just feeling a little under the weather."

"Listen to me, Tyler...I need to get you to sickbay right now, and I have to do a full workup.

Barron felt a pit in his stomach as the full reality of what Weldon was saying hit him. He didn't understand...none of it made any sense. But it was clear Weldon was serious.

"Doc, listen to me. We're going into battle. I don't care what's wrong with me, or what you have to do to keep me alert and functioning until that combat is concluded...but I will not be moved from here. Not while this vessel is in danger."

"Captain, this is serious. We have to go. Now." Weldon was his friend, and Barron could hear real worry in his voice.

"I will not be moved." Barron's words were like iron. He saw Atara Travis jumping out of her seat, heading his way, trying to hide the stunned expression on her face. "Back to your station, Commander Travis. Now." He turned and looked around the bridge. "All of you, listen very carefully. I will not leave the bridge while we face imminent combat. Now, back to work. We're at red alert, and I know you all have duties to occupy you. Stay focused on the enemy, and do your jobs, or by the Eleven Hells, you will all answer to me."

He looked up at Weldon. "Whatever you gave me before made me feel better, Doc, at least for a while. Can you give me a higher dosage? Or whatever else you have to keep me right here and commanding this ship."

"Tyler...anything I give you now could kill you."

"Will it kill me immediately?"

Weldon didn't answer.

"Do it, Doc. That's an order."

"Tyler..."

"Do it. Now."

Weldon hesitated, but then he reached down and pulled out a syringe. He held it for a few seconds, his eyes pleading with Barron. But the captain's gaze was hard and relentless. "Do it, Doc. Right now. Or I will take that thing from you and use it myself."

Weldon still hesitated…but then he extended his arm, giving Barron the injection. He turned without a word and leaned over, putting the syringe back into his bag.

"Keep that out, Doc…in case I need more." Barron felt better than he had a few seconds before, but the shot had worn off quickly the first time, and he intended to take another injection if he needed it to get through the battle, and another…and another. As much as it took to get him through…

*   *   *

"Billings, what's the problem? Six months of rest and you're not up for a little work?" Anya Fritz had shoved her head in the narrow tube, and she was looking up to where Walt Billings was wedged, trying to replace an energy flow control unit. She knew the engineer was doing his best, and Billings was number one on her crew, but she just didn't know how to turn it down. She spent every battle racing from one problem spot to another, driving her people mercilessly. She knew they had names for her, that they talked about her when she wasn't around, complained about the brutality they felt she showed them. She also knew her intensity had saved them more than once, along with *Dauntless*. She and her people had an odd relationship, one where controlled animosity was somehow juxtaposed with loyalty and devotion.

They know they're the best, and they realized there's a price to pay for that kind of performance…

"I'm almost done, Commander. The bracket was twisted. I had to force the thing back in place with the power-wrench."

"I knew you'd have a good reason, Lieutenant. But if it isn't too much trouble, as soon as you manage to finish here, I need you at reactor A. The shielding is buckling, and we've got to backstop it or we're going to have to scrag the thing to prevent radiation leakage." Losing the output of a reactor in the middle of the battle was not good. As hard as Fritz was on her engineers, Captain Barron was no less intense, and the last thing she wanted to do was tell *Dauntless*'s skipper that he'd lost a huge chunk of his power.

"I'll be there in five minutes, Commander." A pause. "Is it true there's something wrong with the captain?"

Fritz sighed hard. She'd heard the same rumors. Even in the middle of battle they were flying around the ship. Captain Barron was sick...he was wounded. She didn't know any more than Billings did, and she was no less worried about it. But she knew it would do no damned good for *Dauntless*'s crew to be worrying about their captain when they had a battle to fight.

"No, Billings, I just talked to him," she lied. "He's fine."

Actually, Fritz hadn't heard from Barron at all, and that more than anything had her worried. *Dauntless*'s captain was on the comm with her constantly in battles, checking in after every hit, asking for status updates...and, she suspected, doing the same thing she did to her people, feeling that the relentless pressure enhanced productivity. But not this time. And with every moment her comm unit stayed silent, her concern grew.

Come on, Cap...call me, harass me about the reactors. Something...

But the unit remained silent.

*   *   *

Vennius watched the battle unfolding all around Sentinel-2. Calavius had sent a bigger fleet this time, but Vennius had been reinforced since the last encounter. The escorts he had sent out as heralds had at last scored some successes. The battleship *Fulgur* took its place at the end of his line, its thirty-six fighters more than replacing his small fleet's losses from the first engagement. Five of his original escort ships were back, along with another seven they had found and rallied to the cause. Most important, perhaps, was the success Commander Corpus had achieved. Tyler Barron and *Dauntless* had joined his force, ready to fight.

It was a bittersweet triumph, and he raged inside, images of Kat flashing through his mind. But he knew imagining thoughts of vengeance on Barron were beneath him, and beneath

Katrine's dignity. Barron had won their battle fairly, and honor would have required Vennius to accept his new ally, even if bitter necessity hadn't. He'd wished for a moment that Corpus had found another ship, a different captain, to bring back. But then he realized that was a foolish, shallow thought. Tyler Barron was the best the Confederation had, as was *Dauntless*. He'd hoped for a larger force, more ships to aid him in his fight. But if one battleship was all he could have, he knew he couldn't have wished for a better one.

This man and his ship bested Katrine…and if they did that, they must live up to their reputation…

"Commander, the fighters are attacking."

Vennius nodded at the report, angling his head so he could see the display. The squadrons from the base had joined up with those from his battleships. He had escort ships covering his flanks this time, and that relieved him of the need to detach squadrons from the main force, increasing his striking power. But Calavius's forces had more fighters now too. It looked very much like a replay of the last battle, with one giant, inconclusive dogfight between the two lines. Save for one thing.

His eyes moved to the side, to the cloud of tiny dots representing *Dauntless*'s squadrons. His intelligence reports had suggested the Confederation vessel carried sixty fighters, an impressive enough complement. But there were more ships on the screen, nearly seventy, and one look told him the Confederation birds had greater thrust capacity than his own. *Dauntless*'s fighters had an awesome reputation, and their exploits in the war against the Union had reached even the eyes and ears of interested parties in the Alliance.

Some of those pilots out there fought against Kat's squadrons…

Vennius had selected *Invictus*'s crew himself, and he knew that every fighter pilot Kat had taken with her had been one of the best the Alliance had. He looked at *Dauntless*'s squadrons shaking into battle formation, and he could see their skill at work. He knew they had seen three years of constant combat, of brutal battles against an enemy that outnumbered them. Many who had survived the battle with *Invictus* had no doubt fallen in those

fights, but some remained. That was almost certain. And now
that skill was deployed on his side, to save the Alliance. It was a
strange turn of events, one he could never have predicted.

He sat still, silent, watching as his fighters engaged the enemy
squadrons...and then, a few minutes later, as *Dauntless*'s wings
slammed into the flank of the confused, swirling battle. They
hit Calavius's fighters hard, driving into them with a ferocity that
would have made any Alliance warrior proud.

Vennius watched, and as he did, he began to understand how
Invictus had lost her fight. And he knew these squadrons, this
ship, this crew—and their captain—deserved their reputations.
He was glad they were on his side.

*   *   *

"Raptor, you've got one on your tail!" Talon's voice was
urgent on the comm, her worry clearly on display. Corinne
Steele was one of Blue squadron's oldest veterans, a pilot who'd
been flying with Stockton since the Battle of Santis.

"I'm fine, Talon," he replied, suspecting his voice conveyed
no more conviction than he felt. He'd been trying to evade
the Alliance pilot behind him, but his moves had been sluggish,
every attempt to break the pursuit too late or too slow. He'd
have lost the average Union pilot by now, he was sure of that.
But the Alliance flyers were a damned sight more dangerous.

"I'm on my way, Raptor," Steele said, her voice brittle with
tension. "But I'm twenty thousand kilometers from your positon, so you've got to hang on."

"I said I'm fine, Talon. I can handle this." Stockton was
scared, so scared his body was drenched in sweat, despite the
climate control of his cockpit. But he was also frustrated, and
determined to break out of the funk that had been dragging him
down. He wouldn't be what he had become...he would be what
he had been, or he would die in the effort. And he'd be damned
if he needed one of his pilots to bail him out from one enemy
in pursuit.

He swung the throttle around, a sharper move than he had

managed up to then, if still slower and clumsier than what his old self would have managed. He thought for an instant he'd surprised the pursuing Alliance pilot, that he'd broken free. But then he saw the movement, the fighter still there, in his blind spot.

For all he'd told Talon he didn't need help, he felt a hint of relief when his eyes moved to the display, and he saw that she had disregarded his orders. She was still coming on, but it would be almost two minutes before she got there. And two minutes was an eternity.

He watched on the display as the enemy's laser blasts zipped by, one so close it almost grazed his ship. That one caused a few burnouts in electrical systems, and it warned him of his mortality.

He remembered a hundred times he'd watched rookies, talking them through crises, their first encounters with the enemy. He'd been successful sometimes...and not some others. The numbers in fighter combats were daunting, and the hard truth was, few in his profession survived for very long. The high command was almost devoid of fighter pilots, mostly because there were so few old pilots to promote to flag rank. Stockton had never even considered the odds before, and now it was all he could think of.

He swung his fighter hard to the starboard, blasting at full thrust for a few seconds, and then letting his engine power drop off. It was abrupt, unpredictable, the closest he'd come to something his old self would have done. But the enemy was still on him, still firing. He'd recaptured a flash of his former capability, but now he felt coldness and fear again.

"Enough of this...you're Raptor, not some wet behind the ears trainee. Pull it together, man." He put all of his will into an effort to focus. He tried to let go, almost to become part of his fighter, as he'd always done before. But he couldn't quite get there. His moves were solid, but they were all delayed. He thought about each one, where before it had been almost pure instinct. He managed to stay one step ahead of his pursuer, but he knew before he would have broken free of the pursuit, even managed to come about and destroy the fighter chasing him.

He was better than he had been these past few weeks, but beyond the fear, all he felt was frustration. After what he had been, he couldn't accept being just a solid pilot. He was Raptor…and he would be again. Or he would die trying.

"Just a few more seconds, Raptor." It was Talon's voice. He could see her ship on the tactical screen now. She was coming on hard, right for the bird on his tail. Even as his eyes focused on the small icon, his ship shook hard and went into a wild spin. He'd taken a hit. Not a direct hit…if it had been that, he'd be dead. But his screen was going wild. His ship was definitely damaged.

"Got him, Raptor!" He felt relief at Talon's words. He wouldn't have lasted thirty seconds longer in his damaged ship.

"Thanks, Talon…appreciate it." He knew she'd just saved his life. He was grateful, but his mind was full of shame and self-loathing. *He* was the one who came to the aid of his people. *He* saved *them*, not the other way around. He felt fear inside, the stark terror that had plagued him since that day in the launch bay, and he hated himself for it.

"Raptor…my scanners show your ship is pretty banged up." It was Kyle Jamison, and Stockton could hear the concern in his friend's voice.

He looked at his scanners. His fighter was damaged, but it was still functional. He'd lost his top engine, but his reactor and weapons were still operational. He would never have left the battle before, not while his ship had fuel vapors and even one half-power laser left.

He knew Jamison was giving him an out, an excuse to go back to the ship. It filled him with self-loathing, and part of him screamed out to refuse, to stand with his squadron and plunge back into the fight. But then he said, "Roger that, Thunder. Returning to *Dauntless*."

He shook his head, even as he angled his thrusters and blasted off toward the battleship.

There's no need to fear death anymore. Raptor Stockton is already dead. And life as a shaking, useless coward is no life at all…

Chapter Thirty

CFS Dauntless
Cilian System
Deep in the Alliance
Year 310 AC

"Give me another shot, Doc." Barron was staring straight ahead, his eyes fixed on the display as he pointed toward his arm.

"Captain..." Doc Weldon was standing right behind Barron's chair, holding on as the battleship shook with each evasive maneuver.

"No arguments, Doc. We're in the middle of a fight...and I have to stay sharp."

"Tyler...I need to get you to sickbay. These stims I'm giving you are only making things worse. Please."

"Captain, I can handle the bridge...you know that. Go with Doc." Travis had turned in her chair, for about the hundredth time in the last hour, to look over and check on him.

Barron knew both of them were concerned about him. Truth be told, he was scared himself. He'd never felt like he did, and he was beginning to believe Doc that something was seriously wrong. But none of that mattered, not fear, not illness, not the worry of his crew. Not while the battle still raged. The enemy was pushing toward Sentinel-2. Barron hadn't had much time to evaluate the overall tactical and strategic situations, but it was a damned good bet that without the base, Vennius's cause would be lost. And the Confederation would have hostile Alliance fleets racing toward its soft underbelly. No, there was no way he could leave now. Not until the fight was won.

"Both of you, listen to me…" He paused, gasping for breath. "I will not be moved from this spot, not while we are in battle. He turned his head back toward Weldon, trying, without success, he suspected, to hide the dizziness he felt. "Now give me that shot, Doc. That's an order."

Dauntless shook hard, almost as if to stress Barron's point. His eyes darted to the display. There were two enemy battleships approaching. Barron's ship had been facing off against another of the Alliance vessels, but that ship was silent now, hit half a dozen times by *Dauntless*'s great primary batteries. It was clear the power of her main guns had caught the notice of whoever was in command of the attacking fleet.

Barron snapped his head around toward Weldon. The doctor had fallen to one knee, barely hanging onto the Barron's chair until the ship stabilized. He looked like he was going to continue to argue, but then he just reached down and grabbed the syringe. He hesitated, just for a moment, and then he gave Barron another injection.

Barron felt the drug's effect almost immediately, but it was weaker than it had been before. "More, Doc…I need a larger dose."

"Captain…"

"Do it," Barron snapped, surprising himself with the anger in his voice. He turned, noting the status bar on the primaries. Almost charged. "Commander, target the closest approaching ship. We need to stop at least one of them before they get their own batteries into close range." The hit from a moment before hadn't done any major damage. The Alliance main guns had a shorter range that *Dauntless*'s primary batteries, and their power dropped off sharply as distance increased. But Barron knew from his memories of Santis…those weapons could rake his ship at close range and do horrific damage. *Dauntless* was stronger than the Alliance ships, none of which seemed to be as large and powerful as *Invictus* had been. But he reminded himself again that these were not Union conscript crews. The Alliance spacers had been raised since birth to be warriors. They were enemies to be respected. Feared.

"Now, Doctor," he repeated, holding back the anger this time. It was frustration, at how miserable he felt, at the timing, at the crushing responsibility of knowing he had involved the Confederation in yet another war. None of it was really targeted at Weldon, and certainly not at Atara Travis. He knew their resistance was driven by concern for him, even if they were in the path of his growing rage.

"Primaries locked on and fully charged, Captain."

"Fire," Barron commanded, wincing slightly as Doc jabbed the needle into his arm again.

*   *   *

Stockton sat for an instant in his fighter after it came to a stop, gritting his teeth and resisting the urge to climb out as quickly as possible. His mind was racing with thoughts of fire, of the agony of his flesh burning off his body. He'd always considered himself tough, able to take whatever came at him. But he'd been stripped of that illusion. He had suffered more than he'd thought possible, and he knew he would do anything to prevent that from happening again. He had been broken, like a prisoner who tortured beyond the bounds of endurance. But it had been no enemy inquisitor who had defeated him, it had been the fire.

And he didn't know how to find his way back.

He could feel his body shaking. This was the hardest, sitting in his ship in the bay. This was where it had happened, that day he'd lost control of his shattered fighter and crashed hard into the bulkhead. He'd tried to escape from the cockpit then, but the auto-eject system had failed, and the manual latch had been twisted and inoperable. He'd banged on the clear hyperpolycarbonate of the cockpit, even as he felt the flames rising up, the indescribable pain of the fire.

He slammed his fist against the release control, and the hatch opened. He'd stayed as long as he could manage, but now he scrambled out of the fighter, climbing quickly down the ladder to the deck. His eyes moved to the rear of his ship, to the half-melted remains of his number one engine. He knew fighter combat well enough to realize he'd survived that shot by a measure of scant centimeters.

At least in space, the vacuum would kill the fire.

He turned and moved toward the bank of lifts along the edge of the bay. He'd spent endless hours in this space, enjoying the near-silence when *Dauntless* wasn't on alert. Just being around the sleek craft, lined up and ready for the moment action called…it had been his life, his calling. But now, he just wanted to get back to his quarters.

"Jake?" He heard the voice, and he froze.

"Stara…shouldn't you be in fighter control?" The words weren't the most personal he could have spoken to a woman he loved, but they were the best he could manage. He already hated himself, and Stara, for all her herculean efforts to reach him, only made it worse. His shame was magnified in front of her, and her compassion mocked him.

"Lieutenant Winters is filling in for me. The squadrons are engaged. There's nothing for us to do now but watch, and I wanted to check and see if you were okay."

"I'm fine," he snapped, regretting the anger in his voice almost immediately. "I've got to go, Stara," he said, turning back toward the open lift in front of him. "You'd better get back to your station." He didn't look at her. He had an image of her face in his mind, hurt, confused by his aloofness. He didn't want to see the real thing. Not now.

He lurched forward, into the car, and reached out to the control panel, counting the seconds until the doors closed, leaving her behind in the bay. Then he stood there, enduring a fresh wave of self-loathing.

*   *   *

Egilius was standing on *Bellator*'s bridge, firing off commands. He was holding on to the back of his chair to steady himself, as he snapped his head back and forth, from one station to another.

"Damage control, I want those starboard batteries back online...now!"

"Optiomagis Metus, increase the cycling on the evasive maneuvers. We're too close now...we can't give them any easy shots."

"Gunnery, all batteries target *Arguere*."

A flurry of acknowledgements came back to him, from his comm and from all around the bridge. Egilius had been surprised when Vennius had given him tactical command of the fleet. He'd felt out of his depth, unready for such a responsibility. But he'd quickly adapted, overcome his hesitancy. Vennius needed him...the Alliance needed him. Nothing more needed to be said. He had to give not just his best, but whatever else he had buried deeply in himself. He had to prevail. Vennius had to prevail. Whatever the cost. *The way is the way.*

He turned back toward Metus. "Contact *Draconis*. Commander Hephesus is to come around and target *Arguere* from the flank."

"Yes, sir."

The battle was raging, undecided. Either side could still win, and Egilius knew he had to push, to hurt the enemy enough to make them fall back. He focused mostly on tactical matters—his place was to defeat these enemy ships, here and now—but he understood the strategic situation facing Vennius, and he also knew that the longer the Commander-Maximus could hold out, the more difficult it would be for Calavius and his traitorous followers to gain total control of the Alliance. Simply surviving would be a victory for Vennius, at least one of a sort. But that survival had to extend past just this battle. The resistance needed to maintain a fleet in being, the ability to stay in the fight. And that meant Egilius not only had to win, he had to defeat the enemy while keeping his own ships from being battered to scrap.

"Commander Hephesus acknowledges, sir."

Egilius turned his head, his eyes settling on the main display. *Draconis* was already adjusting course, altering its vector toward the target. As in the earlier fight, Egilius was banking on the likelihood that the outright destruction of vessels would break the enemy's will faster than spreading damage across the whole fleet. It was far from a certainty the enemy would break off if they lost a couple ships, but his gut told him Calavius couldn't risk all the vessels he controlled. Not while so much of the fleet seemed to be uncommitted.

He looked off to the side, to the enemy flank, where the Confederation battleship was moving in from its entry transit point. *Dauntless* had arrived at an opportune moment, just before the traitors attacked. Egilius didn't like to admit his forces needed help, but they were outnumbered and still carrying damage from the previous battle. He wasn't ready to jump right to acknowledging a *need*, but he was damned glad to have the help.

He turned toward the smaller screen on his own station. *Arguere* was being battered by three of his ships. The vessel was trying to pull back, but its velocity and vector were far from optimal for such a maneuver, and though the damage assessments were incomplete, it was clear the ship's engines had been hit pretty badly.

"Match *Arguere*'s movements. All ships, maintain close range and continue to fire."

"Yes, sir."

Egilius felt a strange combination of feelings. Excitement, the cry of the warrior aching for the kill he could feel coming. It was tempered, though, by discomfort, by a queasy hesitancy. Weeks before, he'd have called *Arguere*'s crew his comrades. He'd have fought at their sides. He knew the vessel's captain. Savilla Danelus was a good officer. And though she was more of an acquaintance than a friend, Egilius knew her well enough to bet that she was here not because she had plotted with the perpetrators of the coup, but because she believed the foul lies

Calavius and his people had spread.

An honest Palatian warrior who believes we are the traitors, who acts on her honor, as she sees it, to save the Alliance. And now I have to kill her.

"Increase power to batteries. One hundred ten percent. And tell engineering I want the reactors pushed to the limit." Egilius regretted what he had to do…but he was still going to do it. Danelus had chosen the wrong side, and for that, honest mistake that he believed it was, she had to die. There could be no half measures, no hesitation to do what was necessary. Not when the future of the Alliance was at stake.

"Commander, *Castellum* has been destroyed by the Confederation battleship."

Egilius's head snapped around. He hadn't been paying attention to *Dauntless*'s sector of the battle. The Confederation vessel wasn't even in range yet.

Wasn't in our range yet…

He ran his hands across his workstation screen, replaying the sequence of events leading up to Castellum's demise. *Dauntless* had been moving forward. Suddenly her thrust dropped, her engines switching over to evasive maneuvers only. Then she opened fire.

The range was beyond that of any Alliance weapon. Egilius knew of the Confederation's particle accelerators, but only in abstract terms. Now, he watched their deadly effectiveness, as *Dauntless*'s primaries tore into *Castellum.*

The besieged vessel blasted its engines, attempting to close the range, but by the time it opened fire, half its batteries were destroyed. The duel between the two ships continued, and two other battleships rushed to *Castellum*'s aid. But they were too late. As *Dauntless* continued its fire, one of its bomber squadrons attacked, coming in from the flank and putting four plasma torpedoes into *Castellum*'s guts. The battleship hung in space for perhaps a minute, atmosphere and fluids spewing out of great rents in her hull, flash-freezing as they hit the frigid cold of space. Then, the Alliance vessel lost containment in her reactor, and where she had been a second before there was nothing but a small sun—massive heat and radiation that gradually dissipated, leaving nothing but a cloud of intense radiation behind.

Egilius had followed Vennius out of personal loyalty, and also because he was dedicated to the Imperatrix. Even so, he'd harbored his own concerns when the Imperatrix had shied away from war with the Confederation three years before, uncomfortable with the faint scent of dishonor in shrinking from a fight. But now, he understood why the Alliance's ruler had done as she had, why she had given so much respect to the Confederation as a potential enemy. It was difficult for an unbeaten warrior race to accept that there were those who could stand against them. But, watching *Dauntless* in action, Egilius felt that comprehension coming to him.

"Commander! *Arguere*."

Egilius jerked his head around, eyes focusing on the main display. *Arguere* was there, but her velocity and vector were fixed, her engines completely dead. Her batteries were silent, and energy readings were minimal. Her reactors had apparently scragged, denying her attackers the thermonuclear display of an end like *Castellum*'s. But the ship was dead nevertheless, or close to it.

Egilius felt a moment of confusion, and he wondered if he had just killed Commander Danelus. But his hesitancy was brief. He was a Palatian warrior, and there was no time for uncertainty or concern about enemy dead. It was unfortunate that Danelus had allowed herself to be persuaded by traitors, but she had, and if she had died for that mistake, so be it.

"Commander, we're picking up thrust profiles across the enemy line. It looks like they are attempting to withdraw."

Egilius was already watching. It was true. Every ship with functional engines was blasting at full thrust. Many of them were still moving toward his line—it would take time for them to overcome their velocities and reverse course. Egilius knew he wouldn't be allowed to pursue, that Vennius would once again hold his ships back to minimize the damage they sustained. But he could damned sure blast them as hard as he could while they were decelerating and still in range.

"All ships, hold positon and maintain maximum fire until the enemy is out of range."

"Yes, sir."

Egilius moved around his chair, sitting down. He pulled his headset on and flashed a glance at Metus. "Get me the Commander-Maximus, Optiomagis." It was time to report that the enemy was running.

*   *   *

"All squadrons are to pursue." Barron was leaning to the side, struggling to force the words from his throat. He was tired, weak, and though he was trying to hide it, his vision was so blurry he was functionally blind. "I want those remaining enemy fighters destroyed."

His thoughts were fuzzy, but he was straining to stay focused. He knew the danger posed by fighters abandoned by retreating mother ships, and he wasn't about to let his guard down. *Dauntless* had endured suicide attacks before, and suffered greatly. And these were Alliance pilots. None of them would surrender. When they realized they were trapped, they would all try to score a final hit, a suicide run they would feel gave them an honorable death. He would not allow it. The battle was won, but he had no doubt there were more to come. He couldn't afford any damage he could avoid.

"I want all point defense batteries on alert. None of those enemy birds get through. Understood?"

"Yes, Captain." Travis had been trying to hide the worry in her tone, but now she was failing utterly. She repeated his command to the anti-fighter turrets, and then she stood up and turned around. "Captain…"

"I will turn the ship over to you, Commander, just as soon as the enemy ships transit out of the system and the last of those fighters are rounded up." Barron glanced back at Weldon. The doctor was sitting at one of the spare workstations, monitoring the situation in sickbay. Barron thought he might escape his shadow for a while, that Weldon would be compelled to return to sickbay to treat the wounded, but aside from a few hits early on, *Dauntless* had escaped any major damage. Casualties were blissfully light, for a change. He was grateful for that, but he wouldn't have minded a few minutes without Doc staring at him. He'd almost outright ordered the chief medical officer back to sickbay, but he'd held back. That was a fuzzy area of regulations, and knowing Doc as he did, he wasn't sure his friend wouldn't have pulled out one reg or another allowing him to declare his concern for the captain's health and disregard orders. Or even relieve him.

"Commander Jamison reports the enemy stragglers are contained. He is confident his people can chase them all down before they pose a threat to *Dauntless* or any of the allied Alliance ships." Travis was staring at him with the same expression Doc had worn through the battle.

"Very well, Commander," he said, ignoring the concern in her voice. *We're going to have to come up with some way to designate the friendly Alliance ships from the forces of the coup.* Allied Alliance ships seemed clumsy and unclear.

"Enemy ships are beginning to transit, sir." The retreat of the attacking vessels signaled a victory, and, for *Dauntless*, at least, a fairly bloodless one. Vennius's forces had taken it worse, lacking *Dauntless*'s ability to engage from farther out. *Aquila* had been destroyed, and several of the others had been badly damaged. The enemy had gotten close enough this time to attack the base, but damage there was moderate, and from what Barron had picked up from Alliance communications, it was all under control.

It was a triumph, one that rated a substantial celebration. But *Dauntless*'s bridge was almost silent, not a cheer, not even quiet congratulations from one officer to another. Nothing but the sound of the instruments…and eyes staring from all around, locked on the captain they all loved, and about whom they were all terribly concerned.

Barron took another breath, and he stood up, wobbling slightly as he did. He turned looked around the bridge. "I've never heard it so quiet here," he said softly. Then, he felt a sharp pain, in his chest…and he was on the deck, lost in darkness.

Chapter Thirty-One

CFS Dauntless
Cilian System
Deep in the Alliance
Year 310 AC

Dauntless's bridge crew stood at their stations, staring in stunned, horrified silence. They had just won another battle, defeated the enemy forces with a minimum of damage and casualties. But there no celebration, no joy. Their eyes were fixed, all of them, on the motionless form of their captain.

Barron had clearly been sick during the battle, and the tense presence of the ship's chief medical officer at his side through the hours the fight had lasted had told them something was very wrong. But nothing had prepared them for what had happened next. Tyler Barron had just dropped to the ground, fallen hard, and he hadn't moved since. The man who had led them away from certain death time and time again.

Atara Travis rushed to his side, her hand on his face, even as Doc Weldon grabbed his bag and joined her. She put her fingers to Barron's neck and, after a few seconds, she looked at Weldon, her face a mask of total helplessness. "I can't feel a pulse," she said, the fear in her voice clear for all to hear.

She reached out and took Barron's hand, holding it as Weldon pulled equipment from his bag, placing a portable scanner

251

against Barron's skin. Travis waited, her eyes fixed on Weldon. She was in a near panic, something none of those around her had ever seen. She knew her invincible shield had failed her. She had faced death with this crew more than once, stood at Barron's side as they stared down one threat after another, and through it all she had been a block of granite, at least for public display. But seeing Barron so helpless, it was too much. She was as close to losing it as she'd ever been.

She had considered the possibility that Barron could be killed, of course. It was her duty as first officer to think such things, to be ready to take command. But not like this. Barron had been fine. Then, as the battle was about to begin he took his post looking...sickly. He'd claimed it was a virus of some sort, and she'd accepted that, at first. She'd tried to get him to leave the bridge, to turn command over to her, but she'd known before the words left her lips that would never happen. Tyler Barron would never leave the bridge when his ship was threatened. She was as sure of that as she was of anything.

"Doc?" She'd tried to wait, to give Weldon a chance to examine Barron before bombarding him with questions. But her patience was gone. She *had* to know what was happening.

The doctor ignored her, and he pulled out his comm unit. "Sickbay, this is Weldon. I need a medpod with full life support gear and a trauma team on the bridge. Now!" The last word was said with such emphasis, Travis knew the situation was as critical as she feared.

"Doc, what is it?"

Weldon reached back to his bag, pulling out another syringe, larger and longer than the one he'd used before. He held it above Barron and jammed it into the captain's chest, right through the cloth of his uniform. He held his scanner back in position, swearing under his breath as he read the small screen.

"He's dead, Commander," Weldon said grimly, "and he'll stay that way if they don't get that medpod up here in the next few minutes."

"Dead?" Travis had feared the worst, but the words coming from Weldon's mouth hit her like a massive fist to the gut.

"No pulse, no respiration. His heart's stopped. It looks like complete cardiac failure."

"How is that possible?" Travis asked, still grasping to comprehend what Weldon had told her. "He checked out in all his physicals. He is...was...in perfect health."

"I don't know, Atara." Weldon was focused on his patient, but Travis could tell from the doctor's words he was as close to the edge as she was. "If this had happened somewhere else... in the street on Dannith or while he was on shore leave, he'd be finished. But if I can get him into cryo-stasis quickly enough I may be able to revive him." Weldon's voice deepened, became grimmer. "If I can figure out what caused this."

"Can you?"

Weldon didn't reply...and his silence was as clear an answer as any words could have been.

Travis looked up, seeing the faces of the bridge crew staring at Barron's...body. "Back to your stations," she yelled. "We're in an Alliance system, and we just fought a battle. This ship is still at red alert." She understood their concern, and she knew how much they loved Barron. But she was in command now, and as scared as she was for her friend and captain, she knew her duty to him.

She stood up. "I said back to your stations. You are Confederation officers, and we're in a war zone. Pull yourselves together, or I'll throw you in the brig...if not out the airlock." She felt bad about coming down so hard on them, but she couldn't let *Dauntless's* crew lose it now. They had fighter squadrons to land, and there was no way to be sure the battle was truly over.

The lift doors opened, and a group of techs pushed out a med pod. It looked like a coffin to Travis, but she knew it was the only thing that could save Barron right now.

The bridge crew had all returned to their stations, but they were glancing back and forth from their consoles to the cluster of people around Barron and then back again.

Travis paused for just a second, squeezing her hand around Barron's before she let go and walked back to her seat. She knew she should be in the command chair, but she couldn't bring herself to sit there, not while Barron was still lying on the deck. "I need updated damage control reports," she snapped sharply. "And anti-fighter batteries are to remain on full alert in case anything slips through."

"Ummm…yes, Commander," came the first tentative reply.

She looked back as Weldon as his people lifted Barron from the deck and put him into the med pod. They set him down and sliced his uniform open, attaching a series of electrodes to his chest and neck. A few seconds later, she heard the sound of the pod's top section closing, and a whoosh as the normal air was flushed out, replaced by the combination of gasses that would help generate a state of cryostasis.

"Let's go…down to sickbay. Now." Weldon stood behind his techs as they pushed the pod into the lift. He turned once, just for an instant, taking pity on Travis and the others on the bridge. "I'll call you as soon as I know anything, Commander."

Travis just nodded, words failing her, and she stared across the length of *Dauntless*'s bridge as Weldon slipped into the lift and the doors closed.

*   *   *

"I need updated casualty reports, and I want damage assessments from every ship. That means now, Optiomagis." Vennius was storming around the control room, snapping out orders directly to the staff. He'd been trying to act through Cassius as much as possible, but now Sentinel-2's commander was down in the fighter bay. The enemy had gotten close enough to get a few shots at the fortress, and it had been blind luck that directed a plasma torpedo right into one of the base's two bays. The fire was out of control and threatening to spread, and Vennius was taking no chances. He'd sent Cassius to direct his people on the scene.

Sentinel-2 wasn't just a station or a fortress, a tactical asset to be used in battle. Right now, it was the center of resistance to the coup, the effective capital of the Alliance's government in exile, and losing it would be a disaster on multiple levels. Those fires *had* to be contained, and Vennius couldn't take the chance a supporter of the coup had slipped through the screenings. A saboteur could turn significant damage into a catastrophe, and he would not allow that to happen.

"Base damage control summary on your screen, Commander-Maximus. Updated reports coming in from fleet vessels."

"Very well." He turned his head toward the main display, his eyes zeroing in on *Dauntless*. The Confederation battleship had acquitted itself well, destroying one enemy battleship almost singlehandedly, and dealing out considerable damage to several others. Vennius had read the intelligence reports on the Confederation's primary batteries, but seeing the awesome weapons in action was something else again. He began to appreciate what Katrine had faced, both in terms of technology, and also in tactical skill. Captain Barron had directed his vessel brilliantly, using his primaries and his fighter squadrons to deadly effect.

Vennius knew he had to send a communique to *Dauntless*. He had to congratulate and thank his new ally. Normally, he wouldn't hesitate to contact a fellow warrior—and whatever else he was, Tyler Barron was certainly that—but he knew this would be difficult for him. He respected Barron, and his rational mind told him *Dauntless* had done nothing more than defend Confederation space in the fight against *Invictus*. And yet, this man, this ship...they had killed her.

"Get me *Dauntless*," he said grimly, gesturing to the communications officer. "On my headset." He walked back to his chair and sat down hard, grabbing the unit and pulling it over his head.

"I have *Dauntless*, Commander-Maximus."

"Captain Barron?"

"No, Commander Vennius, this is Commander Atara Travis. I am *Dauntless*'s first officer, temporarily in command."

Vennius hesitated. This was unexpected. There was something about the voice on the comm, something in its strength, its firmness, that reminded him of Kat. But that wasn't all he gleaned. Something was wrong.

"Commander Travis," he finally responded, "has Captain

Barron been wounded? I trust it is not serious."

"The captain has been…incapacitated, Commander. But I assure you I can assist you in any way you require."

Vennius listened to the woman's voice. There was strength there, that was unmistakable, and pain too. Something *was* terribly wrong on *Dauntless*. She was trying to disguise it, but Vennius had led warriors for more than four decades, and his ears were skilled at sensing pain and duress.

"Is there any way we can assist, Commander?"

"Your offer is greatly appreciated, Commander Vennius, but I believe we have everything under control."

Vennius shook his head. *That was a lie.*

"I was going to invite Captain Barron to come to the base to discuss the situation, and our options moving forward. I suspect you know some, but not all, of what has happened in the Alliance."

"Allow us some time to recover our fighters and get our damage control efforts in hand, and then if the captain is not able to accept your invitation, with your permission, I will come in his stead."

"That would be perfectly satisfactory, Commander Travis. You will contact me when you are ready?"

"Yes, Commander. As soon as possible."

"Thank you, Commander Travis. I look forward to meeting you in person." Vennius cut the line.

She's hiding something. But what? They fought on our side, holding back nothing…and if Barron was wounded, why wouldn't she just say so?

Unless…was it possible Barron had been killed in the battle? That didn't seem likely. *Dauntless* didn't appear to have taken enough damage to seriously threaten an area as secure as the bridge. But anything was possible…a hit in just the right place, a blowout in a system located near the captain's position…

No, it has to be something else. His thoughts were wild, undisciplined. Part of him rejoiced at the thought of the man who had killed Kat being dead himself. But that was foolish self-indulgence. He needed an ally as capable as Barron, especially if the only help he could expect in the near future was one battleship. Barron was an honorable warrior, a man who deserved his respect. He had dreaded meeting the officer, plagued by his thoughts of Kat. But now his thinking had changed…and he found himself hoping he *would* get the chance…to meet Tyler Barron, and to fight at his side.

*   *   *

Travis was angry with herself. *You should have been more prepared for that communication. You should have handled yourself better.*

She was struggling to regain her concentration. Her duty, both to the Confederation and to Barron, was clear. She had to command *Dauntless*, and she had to do it with all the skill and dedication Tyler Barron would have. That seemed an impossible task, though she'd done it before. But now wasn't before. Despite her greatest efforts at discipline, her mind kept drifting back to sickbay, wondering what was happening down there. She'd almost contacted Doc three or four times, but he'd told her he would call with any news. All she could do was distract him from his work.

Her communication with Commander Vennius caused something else to hit home. She had to stand in for Barron not only as *Dauntless*'s captain, but also as the Confederation's envoy to the Alliance. Though she lacked the formal viceregal authority Barron had been granted, she knew she had to step into his shoes, do what she imagined he would have done.

"Get me launch control."

"On your line, Commander." Lieutenant Darrow typically moved from his place at the communications console to cover her station when she was in command. But she was planted in her usual seat, barely able to even look at the captain's chair. She would command, but she would do it from where she sat.

"Commander Sinclair, I want you to keep a close eye on the squadrons. I want those enemy survivors hunted down, but Commander Jamison is to head back before fuel status becomes critical."

"Yes, Commander." Sinclair sounded shaken, something

Travis had never heard from the launch control officer before.

"And I want Green squadron switched over from bomber kits to interceptor. Just in case we need to launch a patrol before the others return." Travis's efforts to force her mind to *Dauntless*'s needs were partially successful. She still wanted to double over and vomit from the stress and worry, but she was holding it together. And all things considered, that was a good result.

"Yes, Commander. We can have them ready in forty minutes. Perhaps thirty." A pause, then: "Commander, is it true about the captain?"

Word spreads quickly, even on a ship this size...

"Captain Barron is in sickbay, Commander." She paused, not sure what else to say. "Dr. Weldon is with him." Her tone discouraged further questions.

"Yes, Commander. Thank you."

Travis cut the line. She looked down at the comm unit, as if she could use her eyes to will a message from Weldon. But there was nothing. Nothing but silence...and the yawning pit in her stomach.

Chapter Thirty-Two

"I want to thank you for your openness, Commander Vennius. That could not have been easy." Travis sat at the small round table in a room Vennius had apparently been using as an office. The Palatian had clearly been concerned when she'd told him again that Captain Barron wasn't available, but he'd invited her to the base and given her a complete recounting of the coup and events since—withholding nothing, from the sound of it.

What little she knew about Alliance culture was enough to give her an idea of the flagellation Vennius was probably inflicting on himself, and the humiliation it caused him to speak of his flight from his home world, especially to an outworlder.

"I asked for your aid, and you have come. To be less than honest would be an affront to honor." A pause. "Your people fight like warriors, and they should be treated as such."

"Thank you again, Commander. I am only sorry we do not have more force with us. We requested reinforcements, but I'm afraid there is nothing else close to the Rim, and little to spare elsewhere. We may be on our own for quite some time, and from what you've told me, with no way for us to materially force the issue outside of this system, Commander Calavius will likely

be able to consolidate the rest of the Alliance fleet, or a significant portion of it. When that happens, he will come here, with
overwhelming strength. Ultimately, your continued presence
here is an intolerable threat to him, even as he tightens his grip
on Palatia."

"You are correct, Commander, in every particular. Your
understanding of the Alliance is impressive, and somewhat surprising." He paused. "May I ask a question that has nothing to
do with the current situation?"

Travis was a little nervous at the change in subject, but she
said, simply, "Certainly."

"Were you on *Dauntless* three years ago?" Vennius sat still
and looked at her intently.

"When the vessel was last on the Rim? When we battled
Invictus?" She returned his gaze, but she wasn't really expecting
answers to her questions. She knew what Vennius meant. "Yes,
Commander. I was first officer then, just as I am now. Much of
the crew is the same, though we suffered considerable casualties
at that battle, and in other battles since."

The two sat quietly for a few seconds. Travis was uncomfortable, unsure where Vennius was going with the inquiry. But
he just looked back at her. She thought she caught a hint of
emotion, of pain, but then he changed the subject abruptly.

"As you noted, I have told you everything about the situation
in the Alliance. I hope that offers you a basis to begin to trust
me. Now, I would ask the same from you. We are alone, and
you have my word as a Palatian warrior that there are no listening devices active in this room. I ask you now, and I give you
my oath that what you tell me will remain between us." A pause.
"What is happening with Captain Barron?"

Travis took a deep breath and exhaled slowly. She didn't
want to tell Vennius…she didn't even want to talk about it. But
she wasn't just *Dauntless*'s first officer and acting commander.
She was the Confederation's diplomat on the scene, the liaison
to the Alliance. To the Alliance *resistance*.

"The captain is ill, Commander," she said softly, trying to
keep her voice as even as possible. "I would tell you more, truly,

but we do not know what it is."

"Is it serious? Life threatening?"

Travis hesitated, feeling another urge to shut up, to keep Barron's condition a secret. But she knew her duty, to the Confederation, to the ship and its crew...and to Barron himself, in whose place she stood.

"It is very serious, Commander Vennius. The captain is in a medpod in partial cryostasis. It was the only way to keep him alive."

"He was wounded in the battle, then?"

"No. As I said, we don't know what happened to him. He seemed to be ill as the battle was beginning, and it got steadily worse. Almost immediately after the enemy forces retreated, he simply collapsed. That is when we put him in the medpod. He has not regained consciousness since." *His heart has not beat since, not on its own. He would be long dead if the pod wasn't breathing for him and pumping his blood.* But she held that part back.

Vennius had a grim look on his face. "My sympathies, Commander. That is no way for a warrior like Captain Barron to die."

"He's not dead, not yet," Travis replied, the sharpness in her tone apparent to her almost as soon as she spoke.

"I meant no disrespect, Commander. I, of course, offer my fervent hopes Captain Barron will recover from whatever... malady...has afflicted him."

"I apologize, Commander Vennius. I have served with Captain Barron for quite some time. It is difficult enough to deal with the fact that he is gravely ill, but to have no idea of the cause..."

"It is always preferable to know one's enemy, to face your adversary across a clear and open field."

Travis could see the difference in their two cultures, but she knew Vennius was sincerely offering his best wishes. There was something else there, too, something she couldn't place. At first, she'd thought it was some animosity toward Barron, but now she was less sure. Vennius seemed to genuinely respect the captain. She was usually extremely intuitive, but Vennius was a bit of a mystery. Still, she had to admit she liked the Palatian. She wasn't sure how quickly that would extend to real trust, but her gut was telling her he was a good man, at least of a sort.

"I will keep you apprised of the captain's condition, Commander. Meanwhile, we will continue damage control on *Dauntless* while you do the same here. We have no way of knowing when the enemy will return...and we must be ready."

Vennius nodded. "We will be ready, Commander."

The two sat quietly again, for perhaps a minute. Then, Travis asked, "Have you considered sending another group of escort vessels out? To attempt to reach and recruit more fleet units... and to scout the nearby systems? We seem to know very little of Calavius's status. It is even possible others are resisting him, cut off and separate from us here."

"I have been reluctant to risk too much of our remaining strength. We were compelled to fight our first defense without any small craft. The enemy was almost able to outflank our line." He looked down at the table. "Still, we cannot sit here with no knowledge of what is happening. I will dispatch the lightest escorts on this mission, holding the frigates back with the rest of the fleet."

"That is exactly what I would do, Commander. The light escorts are of limited power in the battle line, and they're fast, maneuverable. They will have the best chance of evading hostile vessels."

"I will see it done at once, Commander."

"I'd better get back to *Dauntless*." She stood up, facing Vennius. She wasn't sure exactly what to do. His rank was vastly higher than hers, and they were allies. Yet, *Dauntless* was not in the Palatian's chain of command. Even more confusing, she was not officially an ambassador, but she was acting as one. She didn't give a shit about any of that, of course, but she wanted to show Vennius appropriate respect. Finally, she simply extended her arm in the Alliance fashion.

Vennius stood up, a hint of a smile on his lips as he reached out and clasped his hand on her arm. "You are familiar with our greetings, Commander. I am impressed."

"The guest should respect the host's customs; do you not agree?" She knew he did agree. That phrase, and the handshake itself, constituted most of her specific knowledge of the Alliance's culture, at least outside pure military facts. But if Vennius wanted to believe she knew more, she was content to let him do so.

"I will keep you apprised on the captain's condition."

"Please do, Commander." Vennius reached down to the table and pressed a button. Two stormtroopers in dress uniforms hurried in. "Centurion, you are to escort Commander Travis to her shuttle."

"Yes, Commander."

Travis was impressed with the discipline of the troopers. She knew Alliance stormtroopers were proud and well-drilled, but she also remembered Santis, and the fact that Bryan Rogan's Marines and the survivors of the garrison had bested twice their number. The Alliance officers weren't the only ones proud of their people's strength. "I thank you, Commander Vennius." She paused for just a few seconds, and then she turned and walked out the door.

*   *   *

"I don't know what it is, Commander. I've run every test, every procedure. I've had the AI review everything. As far as I can tell, it's just heart failure."

"That's not possible, Doc, and you know that. At Tyler's age, with his medical history? You examined him yourself not that long ago. No signs of anything. His heart scan showed perfect health. He was in top physical condition. Can heart disease naturally progress as such a rate?"

"No, of course not. But there is nothing else. I can't explain it."

"Radiation? Could he have picked up some kind of contamination?"

"One that didn't affect anyone else onboard?" He shook his head. "No, I don't see how that is possible...but I still screened him for every known form of radiation. Also, every known toxin, virus, bacteria, fungus…everything. I have the AI doing an intense DNA scan now. Perhaps he has some genetic anomaly that was missed in earlier examinations."

"His family is not exactly obscure, Doc. If there was some kind of deadly genetic issue in their history, don't you think it would be known by now?"

"I don't know, Atara," Weldon blurted out, his frustration showing clearly. "I just don't know. I have no idea what to do. I'm watching him in that med pod, hovering somewhere between life and death. I can keep him revivable for a while longer, Commander, but not indefinitely. And the longer this goes on the less chance there is of bringing him back."

"I'm sorry, Doc…I know you're doing your best." Travis tried to keep her tone soothing. She was almost overcome by her own fear and helplessness, but she knew Weldon was as devoted to Barron as she was, and that he had been working around the clock for days now. "Is there anything I can get you, anything you need?"

Weldon shook his head. "I wish there was. I'm out of ideas, Commander. Apart from waiting for the DNA scan, I'm basically just trying to keep him alive…close to alive…for a few more days." He paused. "I'm going to have to replace his blood and bodily fluids soon…and that's going to cut the chances of a successful revival. Every hour that goes by reduces our chances, even if we're able to figure out what is at play here."

"Barring some previously undiscovered genetic malady in the Barron genes, this had to be something external, right? I mean, there is no way this was normal degradation of his heart function. Something had to cause it. Maybe some kind of virus you haven't found yet."

"I can't conceive of any known form of heart disease that appears so suddenly and progresses to total failure in a matter of hours, no. But I've done every search possible for viral and bacteriological agents…and for biochemical signs of their presence. I've even checked against the database of known weaponized diseases from the old empire. Nothing."

"You have to keep trying, Doc. We've got to find out what this is. We have to save him."

"I know, Atara...but I have no idea what to do. None at all."

Travis sat there, holding back the urge to push harder, to order Weldon back into his lab. That would be pointless. Weldon had been Barron's friend longer than she had, and she was sure he would throw himself into the reactor to save the captain. He would do anything possible, even without her pressuring him further. And she saw no reason to increase the pain he was already feeling over his failure to diagnose the problem.

If Tyler dies, he will suffer no less than you...even more, because he will blame himself for not saving him...

"Do whatever you can for him, Doc. He couldn't be in better hands, not even if he was in the Prime Medical Center on Megara." She got up and moved around the table, putting her hand on his shoulder. "Tyler is lucky to have you. Whatever chance he has, you gave him."

Travis knew her duty to *Dauntless*, its crew, and its captain whom she loved like a brother. She had to take his place, to fill those massive shoes, not just in battle, but in situations like this. Her people were in pain, and they needed her—they needed to see her strength, to draw their own from it. She'd filled in for Barron before, of course, commanded *Dauntless* in his absence. But it had never been like this before, and she felt the responsibility with a weight far greater than ever before. She understood, more even that she had before, the stunning pressure Barron endured.

So many times...he sat there like a pillar, giving his strength to all of us. He was always there for us to lean on...but there was never anyone like that for him. I understood command before, the responsibility, stress, duty. But now I see the incredible loneliness it brings.

She felt a surge of determination bolster her shaking spirits. She would fill in for Barron. She would not let him down. She would not let the crew down. Whatever it took.

Whatever it cost her.

"Commander Travis?" Darrow's voice drew her attention back from her thoughts. She reached down and grabbed the small comm unit on her belt.

"Yes, Lieutenant?"

"We're picking up energy readings from the transit point."

Her gut tightened. "The enemy fleet returning?"

"Negative, Commander. The readings are from our entry point. From behind us."

Reinforcements? But her thought was fleeting, and an instant later realism intervened. *No, not possible.* But if the enemy had other forces, if they were coming in from behind *Dauntless* now...

"Bring us to battlestations, Lieutenant. Advise Commander Sinclair I need Green squadron ready to go as soon as possible." She nodded to Weldon and bolted out of the room, heading toward the bank of lifts. "And get me Commander Vennius, now. Patch him through to my comm."

"Yes, Commander."

If the enemy had another fleet ready to attack so soon, and from a completely different direction, that was bad news. It would mean Calavius had managed to rally a lot more of the Alliance fleet than she—or Vennius—had hoped.

"Commander Travis?" It was Vennius.

"Yes, Commander-Maximus. We may have a problem."

Chapter Thirty-Three

CFS Dauntless
Cilian System
Deep in the Alliance
Year 310 AC

"A vessel is emerging, Commander. Energy readings do not match the mass of a major warship. It looks smaller than an escort, even."

Travis moved across *Dauntless*'s bridge, passing by the captain's chair without stopping, or even looking at it. She just wasn't ready...and she could command from her own station as well as from Barron's.

She shook her head. Energy readings from a transit point were hard to analyze, and ship size estimates were educated guesses at best. Besides, if there were ten or twenty smaller ships coming through one after another, that could be just as big a threat.

"Launch Bl...Scarlet Eagle squadron, Lieutenant." Her reflex was to send out the Blues, as Barron would normally have done. But she was worried about Jake Stockton.

"Launch control acknowledges, Commander."

"Weapons status?"

"All stations at red alert. Primaries and secondaries report ready for action. Commander Fritz advises all reactors are at full power."

"Very well." She looked ahead, toward the main display. *Dauntless* was as ready as she could be for whatever was about to burst into the system.

"One contact, Commander. Inbound at high velocity. Detailed readings coming. Looks small, mass lower than even a light escort. A scout of some kind, maybe?"

Travis turned back toward Darrow. "Full power to scanners, Lieutenant." She cursed herself for not deploying scanner buoys around the tranwarp point. Barron hadn't done so either, which was unlike him. He tended to be overly cautious about such things. But she knew they were both affected by the situation, by the discomfort of being in Alliance space. Barron had no doubt decided to forego his normal procedure because he was treading softly in the presence of Alliance forces that still floated somewhere between old enemies and new allies. Travis would have liked to write off her own failure with the same logic, but the truth was, she'd been so occupied with Barron, and with meeting Vennius, she just hadn't thought about it. *How many times have you told a spacer, carelessness gets people killed?* "Lieutenant Timmons is to scout forward. We need positive ID on that ship…and on anything that follows it."

"Yes, Commander." A brief pause. "We're not picking up any additional readings. That ship may be alone."

"It may, Lieutenant, but we're not going to assume that. It could be a scout positioned ahead of an incoming fleet."

"Commander, we're receiving a signal. They're trying to contact us."

"On my channel, Lieutenant," Travis snapped, pulling her headset on as she did.

"*Dauntless…Dauntless*, this is *Pegasus*. Andromeda Lafarge, calling for Captain Barron. Please respond." Travis was stunned at what she was hearing. It made no sense. *What would Pegasus be doing all the way out here?* But those concerns were pushed aside almost immediately. Lafarge was a courageous, capable woman. Travis had come to respect her during the operation out at Chrysallis. But right now, the voice on the comm seemed on the verge of panic.

"Captain Lafarge? Andi?" Travis was very aware that every eye on the bridge was on her. "Is that really you?"

"…Atara? Yes. I need to talk to Tyler. Now."

Travis hesitated, not sure what to say.

"It's urgent, Atara. A matter of life and death."

"Tyler isn't on the bridge, Andi. He's…" She didn't finish.

"No…" The anguished cry came through the comm unit, loud in Travis's ears. It was clear her tone had told Lafarge all she needed to know. "I'm too late."

"Too late? What is this about?"

"Is he dead, Atara? Please, I have to know."

Travis was confused. "No, he's still alive…" That was a question whose answer was far more complex and uncertain than it seemed. Was Barron alive? Or dead but still revivable? There was no point in confusing things further now. "How do you know?" Travis felt the tension hitting her again. There was a wave of angry suspicion, but it passed almost immediately. *Andi couldn't be involved in this. She wouldn't hurt Barron.* Travis was sure of that. *But how could she know?*

"Did you catch the assassin? Did he fail? Is Tyler okay?" Her questions were rapid-fire, the tension—no, the outright fear—she felt clearly on display.

"Assassin? What are you talking about?" But even as she asked, a cold feeling gripped her.

"There's an assassin on *Dauntless*. Sector Nine got him assigned with your last group of replacements."

The coldness in Travis gut turned frigid. "Lieutenant," she yelled, turning toward Darrow. "Get Captain Rogan. I want his Marines on full alert. They are to garrison all vital stations…and I want twenty, fully armed, in sickbay. Now! No, ten minutes ago!" The last words were spoken so forcefully, they seemed to hit Darrow almost with kinetic force.

"Yes, Commander."

Travis turned back to her comm unit. "Andi, how do you know about all this?"

"One of my contacts. It took a little…persuasion…to get

him to spill it all, but he did. He has contacts in the naval office
on Dannith. He helped Sector Nine assign their man to *Dauntless*. As soon as I found out, I tried to catch you before you
left, but I was too late. So, I went to Grimaldi Base and found
Admiral Striker…and he told me he sent you out to the Rim. I
tracked you here." A pause. "You guys are a little careless with
your ion discharges."

Travis was impressed…no, amazed. She'd liked Lafarge
since the two had met, and she had thought well of the rogue
captain's abilities, but this story was almost too much to believe.
Her thoughts moved back to Barron, and to the idea that there
was an operative loose on *Dauntless*. She felt the coldness in her
turn to fiery rage as she thought about it. Sector Nine could
never have gotten one of their own agents onto *Dauntless*. Whoever it was…it had to be a Confederation spacer turned traitor.
It had to be. Working with the enemy…to kill Captain Barron.
When she found him…

"Andi, what else did you find out?"

"The assassin has a poison…it's apparently completely
undetectable in any med scans."

Understanding hit Travis like a thunderbolt. *That explains
it…*

She slapped her hand on the comm unit again. "Doc, please
respond."

A few seconds passed. "Commander, there is still no change.
And what is with the Marines down here? I've got them all over
the place, in the…"

"Doc, it's poison. Tyler was poisoned."

"I scanned him for every known toxin. More, I searched for
any chemical changes in his body. There was nothing."

"It's something undetectable, at least by normal means. And
those Marines are going to stay right where they are. We have
a Sector Nine assassin onboard, and until he's in custody, every
vital area of this ship is on lockdown."

"What do we know about this supposed toxin?"

"Nothing but what I told you, Doc."

"I need something to go on. Any information will help."

"I'm sorry, Doc, I don't have any info on the poison, just that it exists."

"Atara?" It was Lafarge, Travis's line to her still open.

"Hold on, Andi..."

"But I have some of the poison."

"What?" Travis had been about to tell Lafarge she would contact her again shortly, but now her undivided attention was back on *Pegasus*'s captain. "You have the poison?"

"Sector Nine gave my contact the poison to deliver to the assassin. My contact is a greedy and untrustworthy man, and he apparently kept some and only delivered a portion of what he'd been given. Evidently, he thought he could produce more to sell. When I bea...convinced him to cooperate, he told me about it. I have it with me."

"Andi, you have to get that here. It could save Tyler's life, but we need it now."

"We're on the way, Atara. Just clear us to dock, and I'll have it to you in less than half an hour." Travis's eyes caught the display, and the arrow and small numbers next to *Pegasus*'s icon that showed the vessel's thrust firing at what had to be full power.

"Andi...one more thing."

"Yes?" Lafarge's voice was pinched, forced. It was clear *Pegasus* was indeed at full thrust, and the resulting g forces were evident in her tone.

"Do you have a name? The assassin. We had over two hundred replacements reporting for duty at Dannith."

"Yes, of course." A pause. "I'm sorry, I should have told you that right away." Travis listened as Lafarge gasped for a breath. "Ventnor," she said. "Joseph Ventnor."

Travis hesitated. For a few seconds the name didn't mean anything, but then a spark of familiarity emerged. *Ventnor...a steward.*

Then she remembered. Spacer Cole had been killed in the battle. Barron's longtime steward was dead, suddenly, and then...

"Andi, you're cleared to dock. Get here as soon as you can." She closed the line, her fingers moving over the controls, acti-

vating a direct channel to Captain Rogan. "Bryan, I need you
to find a member of the crew. Spacer Ventnor, from steward
services. He is a new transfer...and he is a Sector Nine assassin
suspected of attempting to kill Captain Barron."

"Yes, Commander." She could hear the grim determination
in his voice, and the seething anger he was barely holding in.
She knew the Marines loved the captain, and she was sure they
considered the attempt on his life as their own failure. That
wasn't fair, of course, but it was certainly useful in terms of
motivation.

"Bryan, he may be dangerous."

"That is of no concern, Commander."

It was of concern to her. She wasn't looking to add dead
Marines to the cost of this unfortunate incident.

"Still, be careful...and take him alive. We need him for questioning. For all we know there are more enemy agents onboard."

"Yes, Commander. We will bring him to you alive."

Travis could almost hear the unspoken, "barely" before
"alive."

"Go, Captain. Get it done."

She closed the line and leaned back in her chair. She was a
suspicious person by nature, one who tended to think the worst
of any situation. But she'd always felt safe on *Dauntless*, among
the crew. Until now.

One more thing the enemy had stolen. One more reason to
despise them.

*   *   *

"Sergeant, take your squad down the left corridor. I want
you to search sector 11B, and I mean every millimeter. Do you
understand?" Bryan Rogan was always firm and deadly serious
in a combat situation, but his words now almost clanged, like a
hammer on an anvil. There was an assassin loose on their ship,
one who had almost killed the captain. Or had killed the captain...it was far from certain that Barron would survive. Rogan
was going to find the miserable piece of shit, if his people had

to take *Dauntless* apart bit by bit.

"Yes, sir," snapped the sergeant, turning almost immediately and waving to the line of fully-armored Marines behind him. "Let's move it."

Rogan lurched forward, gesturing for rest of the Marines in the corridor to follow. He'd sent teams to Ventnor's quarters and to his duty station. They'd found nothing, even after widening the search to surrounding areas. Rogan had gone first to sickbay, to inspect the Marines on duty there. He blamed himself for what had happened to the captain, and he was determined to make sure no other threat would get anywhere near Barron. There were Marines next to the medpod, and more in the rooms leading to it. He had patrols outside sickbay and sweeping the corridors all around. If that miserable traitor, Ventnor—or anyone else—tried to get to Barron, he'd have to fight through thirty Marines, every one of them anxious to avenge what had happened to their captain.

His people had been searching for hours now, every Marine on the ship, all 202 of them, engaged in the hunt. And not one of them would stop until they found the fugitive.

He stopped just short of the next door, and waved to the two Marines at the front of the line. They jogged up around him and positioned themselves in front of the hatch, turning and nodding their readiness to Rogan. The Marine captain reached out and slid the access card into the slot.

Nothing.

He pulled it out and tried again, but still the door remained shut. He looked at the card. Commander Travis had authorized full access. That meant it should open every door on *Dauntless*. He stared intently at the lock and tried to open it again, without success.

"Commander Travis," he said into his com, tightening his grip on his rifle as he did. "We're at hatch 79032, and my access card is not working. Request you open from your location."

"Hold on, Captain." There was a short pause. "Captain… the hatch is not responding. It appears to have been tampered with onsite."

"Understood," Rogan snapped, gesturing to the rest of his Marines to be ready. "Request permission to blow the door, Commander."

"Permission granted, Captain. Do what you have to do." A short pause. "And remember, if you find him, I need him alive." Rogan could hear the regret in Travis's voice, and he understood how much she wanted to order his people to gun down the piece of shit the instant they found him. His desire for the same was no less intense, but he knew why she needed him alive.

He would follow his orders, as he always did...no matter how much his hands were shaking with rage, with the almost irresistible urge to kill the man he hoped was hiding in the compartment in front of him.

"Corporal Joven...get up here with one of those charges. We're going to blow this door."

Chapter Thirty-Four

CFS Dauntless
Cilian System
Deep in the Alliance
Year 310 AC

"This is an extraordinary substance, Commander." Weldon's face was pressed down against the large scope. "I've never seen anything remotely like it. It can't be natural, but I'm not even sure how this was synthesized."

Weldon and Travis were in the main sickbay lab, alone. She could hear sounds in the distance, the doctors and technicians going about their business, most of them working on some form of analysis on the strange toxin that had brought the captain to the brink of death. Weldon had every member of his staff on duty, a red alert of sorts affecting *Dauntless*'s health team. It was all hands on deck to solve the mystery...before Tyler Barron died.

"Does that mean you can create an antidote...or are you trying to tell me having this sample isn't going to help?" Travis stood behind Weldon, her body stiff with stress. She'd met Andi at the docking port and the two had rushed the small vial to the lab. Weldon had been working on it for the past several hours, and Travis had forced herself to stay away as long as she could. But her endurance had reached its end, and she'd come for…something, an update at least.

"I don't know." Weldon looked up from the instrument and turned toward Travis. "It's incredibly complex. It binds to the victim's DNA in some way, and causes chromosomal changes. And in the process, it leaves no trace of itself. It creates a genetic heart defect where there was none before…but that's an incredible oversimplification."

"I don't question the complexity, but all that matters is saving the captain."

"Don't you think I know that, Commander?" Weldon's voice was raw, not quite anger, but exasperation.

The two of them glared at each other for a few seconds. Then Travis said, "I'm sorry, Doc. It's not your fault. It's just… this is our last chance to save the captain."

"I know that, Atara…believe me. If I can reverse the genetic modifications, I can repair the physical damage to his heart. It's tricky surgery, but I'll see it done. But it won't accomplish a thing unless I can reverse what was done to his chromosomes."

Travis sighed softly, shaking her head. "Is there anything you need, Doc? Anything at all?"

"Thanks, Atara…but there's nothing. Just some quiet while I try to figure this out."

Travis nodded. "Call me, Doc…if there is anything I can do."

"Of course," Weldon replied. Then he turned back and put his face against the scope. Travis stood there for a moment, and then she slipped out the door, leaving *Dauntless*'s chief medical officer—and one of Tyler Barron's oldest friends—to his work.

*   *   *

Bryan Rogan stood against the wall, watching as Travis and Lafarge questioned the prisoner. The Marine had delivered the fugitive alive, as ordered, and Travis suspected it had taken all the discipline and control Rogan possessed not to kill the bastard.

"Are you going to deny again that you poisoned Captain Barron?" Travis stared coldly at the terrified captive. "Or that you murdered Spacer Cole?"

Ventnor sat still, avoiding her gaze, utterly silent.

"Because you can forget about that right now. I had the AI review all security footage. Lars Cole was not killed in the battle—at least, not by enemy action. You murdered him in cold blood, and you did it so you could gain access to the captain."

Ventnor didn't respond, he didn't even look up.

Travis stood where she was, glancing back at Lafarge before she hauled off and punched the prisoner in the face. It was a violation of regulations to rough up a captive, but she'd had the cameras deactivated, and she figured someone would have to flay Bryan Rogan alive to get him to rat her out. And Andi Lafarge was barely containing her own rage. She suspected if she left *Pegasus*'s captain alone with the man who had poisoned—who may have killed—Tyler Barron, he'd have to endure a lot worse than a punch in the jaw.

Ventnor looked up now, a stream of blood dripping from his mouth. "I didn't…" He started what sounded like a denial, but his voice drifted off into a series of miserable sobs.

"It's hard for me to explain how badly I want to kill you right now. And I can assure you, no one in this room will tell anyone what happens in here." She stared at Ventnor with undisguised hatred. "Isn't that right, Captain Rogan?"

"Yes, Commander. I'm certain I wouldn't see anything."

"Captain Lafarge?"

"I just ask that you let me help, Commander." Lafarge's voice dripped with frozen venom.

"So, you see, Sp…Mr. Ventnor…" Travis almost choked on the word "Spacer." Even acknowledging the wretched traitor as a member of the navy sickened her. "…all you have left is what you can tell us. If that is nothing, I might as well throw you out the airlock now."

Oddly, while beating Ventnor was a violation of regulations, Travis knew she had every right as *Dauntless*'s acting commander to summarily execute him if she deemed him a danger to the ship.

"Please…" Ventnor whined pathetically. "I had no choice.

They would have killed me…"

"I suggest you tell me everything…or *I* will kill you." Travis sat for perhaps half a minute, but Ventnor was silent, save for the quiet sounds of his sobs. "Captain Rogan, take this man to launch bay alpha and throw him out of the airlock." She stared down at the prisoner. "Do you have any problem with that order, Captain?"

"None whatsoever, Commander." The Marine started moving toward the center of the room.

"No! Wait…"

Travis held up her hand, gesturing for Rogan to stop. "Are you going to tell me everything? I'm not going to ask again."

"Yes, yes…I had no choice. They threatened to kill me… my family."

"How did you get involved with them in the first place?"

Ventnor fell silent again. This time, Lafarge acted before Travis, lunging forward and slamming her fist into the side of his head so hard the chair he was shackled to fell onto its side. "I've had it with you," she said, clearly barely hanging onto whatever shreds of her self-control remained. She pulled out a small knife and held it to Ventnor's throat. "I'm not one of those honorable officers back there…I've been called a pirate more times that you can count, and by the Eleven Hells, that's exactly how I'm going to act here. Now you tell us everything, and the next time you whine about anything or stop talking, I will slit your fucking throat. You won't live to see any airlock."

Ventnor was lying on the ground, tears streaming down his face. "Please don't kill me…I don't want to die."

Lafarge straightened up and kicked him in the stomach. "I'm sure you don't…but you were willing to kill Captain Barron and Spacer Cole. Do you think Cole wanted to die? Do you think Barron does?" She kicked him again.

"They paid me. I had debts…gambling debts. I owed some dangerous people. They didn't tell me what they wanted me to do, not at first. They gave me the money…and then they started threatening me…"

"You pathetic worm…you think the gangsters in the Dannith Spacer's District are dangerous people?" Lafarge's voice was like death.

"What can you tell us about the poison you used?"

"Nothing." He looked up as Lafarge leaned forward toward him. "Nothing...I swear. They just gave it to me and told me to get it in his food."

Travis reached out and put her hand on Lafarge's shoulder. *Pegasus*'s captain was quivering with rage. "I'm not going to kill you now," Travis said, her voice somber, disappointment clear in her voice. She glanced over at Lafarge, and then back at Ventnor. "That is for one reason only...because I know Confederation Intelligence will want to...discuss...all of this with you in much greater detail." She crouched down, putting her face close to his. "But I want you to know, after they're done, and when you're tried for treason, and for the murder of Spacer Cole and the attempted murder of Captain Barron...." *Please...let it only be attempted murder...* "I will be there to watch you mount the scaffold, you miserable traitor." She looked back at Lafarge again. "And I am certain Captain Lafarge will also attend."

"Count on it," she said grimly.

"Captain Rogan," Travis said, her voice thick with contempt. "Put this man in the brig. I want four guards on duty outside his cell at all times...and I want your people to remain on alert." She didn't think it was likely there were any more double agents on *Dauntless*...but she wasn't taking any chances either. Not deep in Alliance space with Barron still in cryo-stasis.

"Yes, Commander." Rogan turned and hit the control to open the door, calling for two of his people as soon as the hatch slid to the side. The Marines moved to the center of the room and reached down, grabbing the prisoner.

Travis watched as the sobbing man was half-dragged out the door. Then she turned back to Lafarge.

"Let's get back to sickbay, Andi. Maybe Doc has gotten somewhere with his analysis."

*　　　*　　　*

"Commander, the transiting ship is *Vindictus*. Commander Tropus is on the line."

Vennius winced. *Vindictus* was a new battleship, launched less than a year earlier. That was good news, but the name jabbed at him. She was named for the vessel Kat had commanded before her ill-fated mission aboard *Invictus*.

He looked across the control room, past Cassius to the aide. He wasn't sure whether "commander" referred to him or to Cassius, but Sentinel-2's commanding officer remained silent, deferring to him. "On my line, Optiomagis."

"Yes, sir."

"Commander Tropus? This is Commander-Maximus Tarkus Vennius." He'd tended to let his formality lapse in recent years, and especially in the weeks since the coup, but somehow, welcoming a new battleship joining the beleaguered resistance seemed like an occasion worthy of a touch of ceremony. "Welcome to Sentinel-2, and to the true Alliance fleet. You and those who serve you display the honor you live by." It all seemed a little silly, but he knew many things played into the morale of subordinates. He hadn't seen Tropus in several years, but he remembered the officer as one of considerable talent, but also a bit of a stiff.

"Commander-Maximus, I am pleased to find you well. We feared the worst when we realized what had happened." A pause. Then: "Commander, I bring grim news. The usurper and his Union minions have rallied much of the fleet to their side, and they have hunted down many ships that would not join them. *Lanceae* and *Pugnator* have been destroyed."

"I thank you for the information, Commander. It confirms some other reports we have received."

"It is of no consequence, Commander-Maximus, save respect for the honorable dead. Calavius cannot win. The true Palatian warrior will always prevail. The traitors have no chance, regardless of the numbers they deploy."

Vennius wondered how much Tropus was putting the best face on things and how much he was performing for his crew. *Or does he really believe that nonsense...there are those in Alliance service who do...*

Vennius knew very well the commanders and crews of many ships had done what they had, not because they were traitors, but because they had believed Calavius's lies. When he'd lost Palatia, Vennius had lost the ability to reach most of the fleet in an effective way, to state his case alongside the usurpers'. It was easy to fault the officers going over to Calavius, but he reminded himself how convincing an argument can be when there is no opposition.

"We shall fight, Commander Tropus, that much I can assure you. We will never yield."

"Never," *Vindictus*'s commander repeated. Then: "Where do you want us, Commander?"

"On the left, Commander Tropus. *Aquila* was positioned there, before..."

"There is no victory without cost, Commander-Maximus. I am certain *Aquila* and her crew fought with great honor and distinction."

You have no idea how they fought...you weren't here. Vennius shook his head. He'd lived most of his life repeating pointless platitudes like that. *Aquila*, outclassed by the newer and larger ships she'd faced, *had* fought bravely, but she'd still been destroyed, her crew as dead as the would have been if their vessel had been blown apart as they fled from the fight. Vennius didn't believe there was no difference, that the manner of one's death didn't matter at all...but he no longer felt the comfort he once did from easy reference to honor and courage.

"Again, Commander Tropus, you have my personal gratitude for joining us. We speak too often of honor and duty as amorphous concepts, without taking the time to appreciate the courage of one's actions. Vennius out."

He cut the line and leaned back in his chair. Tropus's words, his reports about vessels flocking to Calavius's banner, none of it was unexpected. Yet, hearing it only increased the burden he felt, sitting there, waiting. He knew the next fight would make the previous ones look like skirmishes. Calavius had let his ego and ambitions get out of control, but the man wasn't a fool. He would know he had to destroy the resistance, that eventually the continued existence of his enemies would threaten the lies and propaganda he'd used to rally forces to his cause. If he had indeed gained more ships, he would launch an overwhelming assault…and soon.

Vennius tried to tell himself his people had a chance, but as before, he found it much more difficult to blindly believe in things. His forces would fight, certainly, but they would likely lose. The Confederation had been his best hope, but they had only sent one ship, not nearly enough to make a difference…not even a ship like *Dauntless*.

He took a deep breath. There was no point in such thoughts. All he could do was prepare, and be ready to fight to the end. The rest he would have to leave to fate.

Chapter Thirty-Five

"Your Supremacy, the fleet is underway." The officer stood in front of Calavius, at rigid attention.

"Very well, Commander-Altum. We will head directly for the transwarp link. It is past time to root out the last of the traitors, and restore honor and glory to the Alliance."

"Yes, Your Supremacy. It is our honor that you lead the fleet in person. Surely, our victory will be utterly complete."

"Indeed it shall, Commander. And it shall usher in a new period of greatness, one that sees our Alliance reach new heights of glory." He paused. "Go now, and take tactical command. Direct the units of the fleet and see our way forward."

The officer bowed deeply. "As you command, Your Supremacy." She rose and walked out of the room.

As soon as the hatch slid shut, Ricard Lille moved out from along the far wall. He and Calavius were alone in the room now, save for the two garishly-uniformed soldiers standing on either side of the new Imperator.

He's wasted no time on nonsense like that...imperial guards and custom uniforms. His mistress probably designed those...

Calavius actually had several mistresses, all of them beautiful Plebs, each seeking a route to wealth and social advancement in the bed of the Alliance's new ruler. Palatian women were unsuited to such roles, being as independent and warlike as the men. Most of the playthings of the powerful, whether men or women, kept by men or women, were offworlders.

Lille looked at Calavius. He was unsettled at how much time his new creature spent on self-aggrandizement…before he'd even secured his position and eliminated his still-dangerous rival. Lille maintained his outward displays of respect, but inside his usual disgust with people waxed. He had chosen Calavius carefully. The Palatian hadn't been his first choice, and perhaps not his second either, but he was sure the new Imperator was a capable warrior. Yet, he was surprised—and he scolded himself for allowing *that*—at just how quickly the veteran fighter had begun wasting his time and effort on foolishness.

"You have done well, Calavius. This fleet you have assembled…" *With more of my coin than I would have thought it possible to spend.* "…is indeed impressive. With your skill and your unyielding focus and determination, Vennius and his band of followers are surely doomed." Lille addressed the Imperator by his name, as he had throughout their period of plotting and working together. It would not serve to play at the role of subordination. He had invested an unimaginable fortune and months of his time aiding Calavius in seizing the Imperator's scepter. Their deal had been clear, and he had no intention of allowing his creature's ego to overwhelm his obligation.

"Tarkus Vennius was offered a chance for greatness, an opportunity to join me, to command my fleets and legions… yet he spurned me. Now, he will pay the price. And, when he is gone, the Confederation will know the bitter taste of conquest delayed. We shall right the wrong of my predecessor's timidity. We will come to the aid of your stalled fleets, and bring our mutual enemy to their knees."

Lille held back a sigh. He really did hate people. He had completed his mission so far with perfect success, but it was one to which he was ill-suited. Lille was a solitary man, one who preferred to keep his interactions with most people limited to killing them. Assassination was his specialty, his love. He was just as effective at manipulation and espionage, but he didn't derive the satisfaction from them he did from stalking and terminating a target. He'd agreed to this mission only as a favor to Villieneuve, one of his very few real friends…and even from his friend, he had extracted a tremendous price for his services.

"Tarkus Vennius will die, Calavius, at your hands. And when he is gone, along with the Imperatrix, you will have secured your control over all of the Alliance." Lille paused for a moment. "While I do not doubt your victory, I do feel we should discuss some tactics for the coming battle." Lille's eyes darted back and forth between the two guards. "Perhaps we should speak alone."

"I am Imperator of the Alliance, Ricard. My guards are with me at all times."

Lille suppressed another sigh. "Indeed, you are the Imperator…but there is one fight remaining to secure that scepter in your hand. For all of your abilities, and your undoubted courage, I would consider it a personal favor if you would indulge me. We are, after all, friends…and the idea that I could pose a threat to a warrior such as you is indeed laughable." Lille stared at the Alliance soldier turned monarch. Calavius was a veteran fighter, despite his current demeanor, but Lille didn't doubt he could drop the fool in an instant if he chose…and probably his two guards as well. "I urge you, my friend…take no chances now. Let us sit together and plan this final battle, as we did your entire ascent."

Calavius sat quietly for a moment, but Lille could tell his manipulation had worked. "Go," Calavius said, gesturing toward the guards. "Wait outside. I will call you when I need you."

The two soldiers snapped to even more rigid attention than that at which they had been standing. Then they marched toward the door, and out into the corridor.

"We are alone, Ricard. What would you discuss about the impending battle? Surely, we have assembled enough force to overwhelm Vennius."

"Perhaps I am a superstitious man, Calavius, but I go into every situation expecting the unexpected. Sentinel-2 is a powerful base, one with the firepower of several battleships. Destroying it will not be easy, nor cheap. But perhaps there is a way to augment our attack."

"I am listening, Ricard."

"I propose we prepare one of your frigates for an alternate use...ramming. The base is a stationary target. A ship that accelerates toward it can cut off its engines and shut down its reactor as it enters close weapons range. The station's weapons will cause massive damage, but with no reactor to breach, the bombardment will not stop the vessel. It will shoot systems to rubble, but the station will still be hit by a large mass traveling at very high velocity. The kinetic energy of the impact will vaporize the fortress...and since Vennius and the Imperatrix are almost certainly aboard, it will kill them both at a stroke."

"You propose a suicide attack?"

"Yes. Surely, among your thousands of enthusiastic followers, there are some few in whom dreams of glory and honor exceed intelligence. Only a skeleton crew will be needed, and I can promise you the funds to reward the families of the brave warriors. No doubt, you too, may be inspired to create some honor for their descendants, some meaningful inducement that costs nothing."

"That is definitely a possibility." Calavius thought for a moment. "Heroes of the Alliance...and a grant of Citizenship to the children of every Prob who volunteers for this sacred mission. A display for all to see...that Alliance warriors do not fear death in battle. In victory."

Lille nodded. "Very good." He paused. "I have one other concern. Reports from the survivors of the last battle state that there was a Confederation battleship present. It suggests that Vennius was able to request Confederation aid and that he received it. I had not anticipated that the Confeds would be able to respond so quickly, even if Vennius reached out to them. I urge you to prioritize the destruction of the Confederation vessel."

"One Confederation battleship? A weak and pointless display, and certainly not a match for even one of my capital ships."

Lille resisted the urge to shake his head. Calavius knew what had happened at Santis, he was well aware that a Confederation battleship, a fairly old one even, had defeated the Alliance's flagship. And yet, he was utterly convinced of Alliance superiority.

"Calavius, I do not dispute the skill and courage of your warriors." Lille was speaking carefully. Leading his creature to the decision he wanted would take some skill and care. "But the Confederation is not a society of warriors. They are schemers, capitalist exploiters who enslave their scientists, pushing them to produce ever-deadlier weapons. Your spacers and soldiers can easily defeat their Confederation opposites…" Lille knew the Alliance warriors were good, but he had serious doubts they were truly the superiors of the Confeds. "However, when you face the Confederation, you also face their technology. Their ships have weapons that outrange yours. Their fighters are faster, and they carry heavier laser cannons." A pause. "Please, my friend…do not underestimate them. Dispatch several of your ships to destroy the Confederation vessel. Once that is done, and the fortress, along with Vennius and the Imperator, is destroyed, your victory will be assured. You can return to Palatia in glorious triumph…and dispatch your fleets to punish the Confederation for aiding your enemy."

Lille always believed in making use of whatever opportunities presented themselves. He was concerned about the Confederation already having forces at Sentinel-2, even one vessel. But he also saw the use of it in fanning Calavius's hatred of the Confeds. A bit of insurance that the new Imperator would keep his promises and invade the Confederation as soon as Vennius and his followers were eliminated.

"Yes," Calavius said, his arrogance again seeping into his tone. "When Vennius has been destroyed, we will take our vengeance on the Confederation, for now they have twice offended us. First, at Santis…and now by their support of the traitors at Sentinel-2."

"Your words are indeed worthy of the Imperator of the Alli-

ance. I know now, even more than before, that our support of
you was not in vain. You are the leader your people deserve."
Lille spoke loudly, the sound of utter sincerity in all he said. It
was a skill, one he had honed over many years of plying his
trade. But his thoughts were far different from his words.

*Yes, Calavius. Secure your control, and throw your forces against the
Confederation. Learn how well they fight, how little your vaunted warrior
ethos will achieve against their primaries and their disciplined and well-led
navy. Throw your fleets into the cauldron, weaken the Confederation so that
we may conquer…first them, then you. You, for all your talk of honor and
courage…no doubt you will whimper like a child when the Foudre Rouge
soldiers burst into your chambers and drag you from your throne…*

"So it shall be, Ricard. I shall take your counsel. I shall order
the Confederation vessel destroyed at all costs…and, once it is
gone, we shall crush the rest of the traitorous fleet. And then
none shall question my rule."

Chapter Thirty-Six

CFS Dauntless
Cilian System
Deep in the Alliance
Year 310 AC

"Another two liters of blood substitute. And increase blood oxygenation levels twenty percent." Doc Weldon was dressed from head to toe in the pale gray garb of the operating room. His hands, slick with a bright sheen of blood, hovered over the almost-entirely covered body of Tyler Barron. The surgery had been going on for hours, as Weldon slowly, steadily repaired the massive damage that had been done to Barron's heart. "Now!" he snapped. "Move it with that blood substitute."

Atara Travis stood behind the clear plastic of the wall that closed off the operating theater from the non-sterile environment outside. Andi Lafarge was next to her, *Pegasus*'s captain looking very much like a stone statue, cold, emotionless...save for the single tear Travis had seen slide down her face. They both loved Barron, though in different ways. There was no jealousy, no bad feeling between the two. Travis's relationship with Barron was more that of a sister and brother, feelings he had returned over their years working side by side.

Travis had been surprised in some ways—and not in others—when Weldon had announced that he had developed an

289

antidote of sorts for the deadly poison that had put Barron near death. Not an antidote, precisely, but a variation on the genetically-engineered substance, one that functioned in the same way, but in reverse, its modifications taking the subject's DNA back to a normal condition.

It had taken him days to design the chemical structure, and more time to synthesize enough to administer to Barron. There had been no time for testing…Barron was almost past the point from which he could be revived. Not that there would have been any way to test the drug anyway, not without first infecting a subject with the deadly poison. Weldon had admitted to Travis that he wasn't even sure his concoction would work, that he might as easily kill Barron as restore his DNA. But it had worked, perfectly it seemed. And now, if Weldon's considerable skills as a surgeon were up to the task at hand, the captain might live after all.

"Everything will be okay," Travis said softly. Despite Lafarge's iron self-control, Travis knew *Pegasus*'s captain was in pain, watching the operation, waiting to see if Tyler Barron lived or died. She also knew it was a feeling of helplessness as much as anything else tearing away at her. Andi Lafarge had come from nothing, almost less than nothing, and she'd clawed her way to everything she had. Travis understood that very well. She and Lafarge were very similar in many ways. Both had come from the streets of industrial hell worlds, and both had taken dark roads to escape. Lafarge had continued on the road she'd taken out of the gutter, rebelled against all control, her mistrust of authority driving her to the dark fringes of Confederation society. Travis had sought instead to turn authority to serve her needs. They had reached very different places, but they were far more of a kind than was obvious at first glance. Travis knew the helplessness was eating away at Lafarge for a simple reason. It was doing the same to her.

"He looked so weak in that capsule before they took him to surgery. He seemed dead already, as though he was lying in a coffin." Lafarge's voice was monotone, almost without detectable emotion.

"Doc Weldon is the best surgeon in the fleet, Andi. If anyone can save Tyler, it's him." She was no better at fooling herself than Lafarge was, and her doubts came out in that last sentence. She knew Doc was brilliant—deciphering the genetic formula of the toxin, and crafting a way to reverse the chromosomal effects, was an extraordinary achievement. One, she suspected, that was even more evident to one who truly understood the science involved. But she'd seen Doc's face as he'd walked toward the operating theater. She knew doubt when she saw it. Doc Weldon was far from sure he could save Barron...and the worry she'd seen in his eyes preyed upon her as she stood and watched the procedure.

She felt the urge to do something, to help somehow, intervene and save the captain. But all she could do was stand where she was and watch. And wait. While the helplessness devoured her.

*   *   *

Jake Stockton sat on the bunk in his small quarters, staring at the wall. It was almost covered with decorations and awards he had received for his many desperate and dangerous missions. His eyes were on one in the center, a large platinum star that signified he was the top ace in the fleet. He had earned it, one fight after another, one kill at a time. He had deserved it when he'd won it, and for all the many months he'd kept it, but now it mocked him.

His past skill and dominance had been so great that nine months later, after his injury and surgeries and long convalescence, it was still his. No other pilot had yet passed his total kills, despite his failure to add to the tally since he'd been back in action.

If Dauntless hadn't been in spacedock all that time, Warrior would have passed you by now. He would have taken that blasted thing...and removed the burden from you. Dirk "Warrior" Timmons had long been Stockton's rival, and for years the two men had nursed mostly pointless and baseless grudges against each other. Timmons's transfer to *Dauntless*, and the need to serve together, had brought the two men closer, at least as effective partners, if not friends. They had learned to focus on the respect they each had for each other. Though it had long been no secret to those around them, it took a surprising amount of time for Timmons and Stockton to acknowledge that each one viewed the other as his only true rival. Though that had been at the core of their animosity, it was a respect that also served as a basis for a more productive relationship.

Until you became worthless...

Stockton's entire adult life had been centered on the sleek fighters the Confederation battleships carried. He'd loved flying, enjoyed the feel of the throttle in his hand, the sounds of his engines roaring, even the crushing pressure of full thrust maneuvers. Being the best had been a huge part of him...how much he hadn't realized until it was gone.

You should resign. Quit. Before you get your pilots killed.

Of course, with the Confederation at war, all enlistments were frozen. Still, after his service, after what he'd been through... he was sure they would grant him an exemption, let him go. Captain Barron would use his influence, after, of course, he did his best to convince him to stay. Stockton dreaded that, perhaps more than anything. He might work himself up to ask to be released, but could he stand his ground, look the captain in the eye and deflect the inevitable efforts to get him to remain, to fight his way back to what he had been?

What about Stara?

He had real feelings for Stara Sinclair. He loved her. But she deserved better than what he had become. He could barely look her in the eye when he saw her. Just like his pilots, she would be better off if he left.

He was almost there, ready to hang up his wings, to leave behind everyone who mattered to him. To descend into a pit of wallowing despair, somewhere no one could watch his self-destructive decline. Almost. But there was something there, the smallest remnant of what he once had been, screaming at him from the deepest recesses of his mind. Pushing him, standing up to the fear, to the memories of what he'd been through. It was distant, buried under the confusion and aimlessness that had dominated him. But it was just strong enough to stop him from quitting. He had lost what he was, what he had been. He didn't know if he could every get it back, but that fading light still flickered, and he realized it would deny him an easy exit. It would drive him forward...though whether to redemption or death he didn't know.

*   *   *

Andromeda Lafarge had been solid throughout the crisis, silent and stony as she'd watched Barron fighting for his life on the operating room table. She had shown almost no sign of the pain and fear she felt, no hint of the emotions roiling inside her. Until now. Tears were streaming down her face in a torrent.

She'd steeled herself to endure the uncertainty of Barron's struggle. She'd even, to the extent it was possible, prepared herself for the worst, for his death. But she found herself utterly incapable of holding back the raw emotion she felt standing there, looking across the room at Tyler Barron, on his feet two meters away, looking back at her.

"Tyler," she said, no other words coming to her. She moved forward, stopping as she saw Barron taking his own steps forward. He was slow, shaky...she could see the weakness in his movements. But he was there, his eyes wide open, and something very much like a smile on his face.

"I missed you. This was all a plot to get you here." The grin on his face widened, and he put his arms out, wrapping them around her. She could feel the lack of strength, the sharp contrast to memories of his powerful arms grasping her tightly. But he was alive, and that was all she cared about.

"I think there might have been an easier way, don't you? Maybe just ask, next time." She returned his smile.

"Doc told me what you did," he said, his voice still weak, but his tone more serious than before. "Thank you, Andi. The fact that you were able to get to the admiral, and find us all the way out here…it's nothing less than amazing. I knew how capable you were before, but this…"

"I had strong incentive. You, my dear Captain Tyler Barron, are not fated to die by some assassin's poison. It wasn't something I could allow to happen." She stopped and frowned slightly. "Should you be out of bed?"

"If that's an attempted seduction, you have a curious choice of timing." He paused. "I'm a little tired, but I could give it a try if you…"

"Enough of that," she said, partially holding back a small laugh. "But, now I'm convinced you're truly on the mend."

"I feel great," he said unconvincingly. Then: "Well, great is a stretch, but I feel alive, and right now I'll take that." He turned and walked back toward the bed and sat down. "Doc fused all the incisions. I'm actually at one hundred percent…or maybe ninety. It's just the fatigue that's left. And the soreness. A few days of rest, and I'll be good as new."

"I'm so glad to hear that, Ty." She walked over and put her hand on his face.

He looked up at her, suddenly wearing an uncomfortable expression. "I'm grateful for what you've done, and I can't tell you how happy it makes me to see you." He hesitated. "But you have to go now."

She stood where she was, slamming down her emotionless mask again.

"I want you to stay…but you just can't. This situation with the Alliance is very volatile. I've read Atara's notes on her meeting with Vennius. The new Imperator will attack here, as soon as he can…and with everything he can muster."

"I'm not afraid of a fight."

"No, you aren't. As far as I can see, you're not afraid of anything."

She just stood there. *I was afraid of watching you die…*

"It's not about courage. *Pegasus* is an amazing ship, but she has no place in a battle like this. You know that. And docked to *Dauntless*, she'd just be exposed to incoming fire, and she'll affect our maneuvering."

She wanted to argue, but she knew he was right. Her ship was her pride and joy, and she was well aware *Pegasus* was vastly more capable than any other ships of its class. But even a small escort could blast her vessel to slag. A fighter or two could even finish her. For all she wanted to argue, to give in to the urge to dispute what he had said, she remained silent.

"I also need you to do something for me." He looked up at her. "I need you to go back to Grimaldi, to deliver a message to Admiral Striker. I already sent word, but the situation is even more desperate now. I don't know how he'll do it, but he has to find reinforcements to send out here. If Commander Vennius is defeated, we will have the entire Alliance fleet invading the Confederation."

She stood there, still wanting to argue, but she found herself nodding slightly. She didn't want to leave, and she hated the idea of *Dauntless* being out here, facing whatever massive attack might be coming. But Tyler was trusting her with an important mission. It was a long way to Grimaldi, and a long way back. If she was able to get word to Striker, if the admiral could find some forces to send…it might make a difference.

"I'd also like you to take Ventnor and Shugart to Grimaldi and turn them over to the admiral. I suspect between the two of you, you and Atara got pretty much everything out of them, but I'm sure Confederation Intelligence would still like to have a go at it."

She nodded. "I'll do what you ask, Ty." Her voice was soft, the guard that was almost always evident in her words clearly down. "But I have one thing to ask of you. I know you have a fight coming here, and I know it will be a hard one." She paused. "Get through it. Don't die here. Please." It was irrational. She was asking for something he couldn't possibly promise, and she despised herself for her weakness.

"I'm not going to die here, Andi." Now Barron paused, looking up at her, his eyes locked on hers. "I promise."

She smiled. It was a level of foolishness she rarely tolerated in herself, but she nodded back at his words. She knew his promise was an empty one, a momentary triumph of emotion over rationality, but she believed it anyway.

She believed it because she had to believe it.

*   *   *

"Commander Fritz reports all systems green. She requested a few items from Commander Vennius, spare parts generic enough to be of use, and he complied. The shuttle arrived a few hours ago, and is being unloaded now."

Barron nodded, but his expression was distracted. He knew Travis was going over such mundane details for his benefit. She was perfectly capable of handling all of that on her own, and probably better than he would if he'd been up on the bridge or in his office.

"I appreciate the effort, Atara. Everybody knows you're the best first officer in the fleet, but you're a damned good friend too." He knew Travis understood how difficult it had been for him to send Lafarge away.

"Thank you, Tyler. But I just want to keep you in the loop. Doc says you can return to duty in a few days, and I want you to be ready. I'm tired of handling all this stuff by myself." She grinned.

"Did she go yet?" he asked.

Travis paused. "They're prepping now. They should push off in a little under an hour." She hesitated again. "She was going to come down and see you one last time, but…"

Barron nodded. "I understand."

The two were silent for a long time, Barron deep in thought but grateful for his friend's presence. Recent days had been very unsettling, not just his near-death ordeal, but the idea that an assassin had gotten aboard *Dauntless*. He'd always shared a closeness, a trust, with his crew. Whatever danger he had led them through, he'd always felt the confines of his ship were safe…a place he and his people could call home. It was too early to tell if what had happened would change that, but if it did, he knew that would be a painful loss.

"I wrote a note to Spacer Cole's family. Can you see that it gets into the comm traffic we're sending back with *Pegasus*?" He had survived the assassination attempt, but his longtime steward had not been so fortunate. Cole had been a good man, loyal to a fault, and Barron would miss him.

"Of course, Captain." Travis nodded, her sympathy for Cole's loss written on her face.

She stood up. "I think I should get back to work, Captain… and I think you should get some rest. "Doc says everything is fused and put back together perfectly, but you'll still have some soreness and fatigue. So, get some sleep, and we can put this whole thing behind us."

He nodded. "I will try to get some sleep. Maybe just a couple hours…"

"Commander Travis…"

It was Darrow's voice on the comm, and the instant Barron heard it, he knew something was wrong.

He and Travis exchanged quick glances, and she pulled the comm from her belt, holding it between the two of them so they could both hear clearly. "Yes, Lieutenant?"

"Commander, we're picking up fresh activity at the transwarp point…the same one the other attack originated from."

Travis looked back at Barron.

"Go, Atara. Get up to the bridge. Bring us to battlestations and get the fighters ready for launch. Power the reactors up to full, and get Fritzie and her people ready." He got up, wincing slightly at the soreness, but otherwise looking just a little tired. "I'll be right behind you."

"Yes, Captain." She paused perhaps a second or two, looking Barron over. He figured she was debating whether to argue for him to stay in sickbay. But whatever thoughts had drifted through her mind, she just nodded and headed toward the door, pulling the comm unit to her face and snapping out a series of sharp orders as she disappeared into the corridor. "Lieutenant, bring us to red alert. Scramble all squadrons. Bring reactor output to full power…"

Chapter Thirty-Seven

Fortress Sentinel-2
Orbiting Planet Varena, Cilian System
Year 61 (310 AC)

Vennius sat at the edge of the bed, looking down at the frail, emaciated form lying there. The Imperatrix had been a tall woman in her day, muscular, in every essence an image of the Palatian warrior. But age and wounds and despair had worn her down to almost nothing. Vennius had been hounding the medical staff for weeks, driving them to do all they could. They had healed her wounds, though it was clear now to Vennius, watching as she drifted in and out of an unsettled sleep, that the strength that had driven her for so long was almost gone. For the first time, he began to fear that his quest to save the Alliance's rightful ruler were for naught, that she was too weak. That he would watch her die in this bed.

What would he do if that happened? He had lost friends and loved ones before...he would endure the personal pain. But she was the Alliance's legitimate leader. What would his resistance be without her?

It will be exactly what it is now. You fight for her, but also much, much more. The Alliance is not the Imperatrix. It is not you, nor Calavius, nor any thousand of its warriors. It must endure, and you cannot allow it to become the possession of a man driven mad by ego and ambition, or, worse even, the puppet of a regime as contemptible as the Union.

Still, despite the thoughts, he felt lost, alone. He had many fine officers who had rallied to him, but without the Imperatrix taking command, so much of the responsibility had fallen to him. He had done what he could, but he was uncertain he was strong enough. They were all looking to him to lead them, to find a way to win. To save the Alliance. And he knew he was far likelier to lead them to death than an honorable victory.

His mind wrestled with dark thoughts. It was unthinkable that the Alliance he knew should die, that the span of its existence could be shorter than a man's life. Calavius would continue to call the domains he led the Alliance, of course, but in every way that mattered, the nation Vennius loved, and had served his whole life, would be dead.

He looked back at the Imperatrix. Perhaps it would be merciful if she died. What could it serve for her, who fought for her peoples' freedom, who saw her nation rise from subjugation to power and domination, to watch all she had fought and bled for destroyed? *I will do all I can, Flavia, my dear friend…I will fight to the last of my strength.* He shook his head slowly. *But I don't think it will be enough…*

The klaxons sounded. He turned with a start, reaching for his comm unit even as Cassius's voice blared through. "Commander Vennius, Commander Egilius reports vessels emerging from tranwarp point one. Unidentified, but presumed hostile."

"I'm on my way, Commander. All stations are to prepare for battle. Commander Egilius is to scout the incoming force and report back as quickly as possible."

"Yes, Commander."

Vennius stood where he was, feeling as though he should do more. But there was nothing else to do, not yet. Egilius commanded the fleet, and the last thing he needed was Vennius meddling in petty tactical decisions. The base crew was well-trained, and he knew Commander Cassius was more than capable of running his station.

Despite the almost unbearable weight on his shoulders, Vennius felt almost like an ornament, an officer of lofty rank with nothing much to do except watch...watch to see if his cause survived, or if it died under the guns of his enemy.

*   *   *

"It is time." Calavius sat in the conference space that had been transformed into a makeshift throne room as he addressed the fleet he had led to the Cilian system. It was the first time in half a century that an Imperator of the Alliance commanded his fleet into battle, since the earliest days of Palatia's wave of conquest. For all the desperate battles, and the thousands dead on so many worlds, the Alliance had never faced total war before.

After its warriors had poured forth from their newly-freed homeworld to take vengeance on their former masters, none had been able to match them. A warrior's struggle on an enemy planet, the trials of a ship or even a fleet fighting a capable foe... it was upon those things the Alliance's warrior culture was built, and none doubted the pain and suffering endured by its fighters. But as a nation, once established, it had never faced a war that truly challenged it, where defeat was a real fear.

But now Calavius, Imperator to some, black traitor to others, knew defeat *was* a possibility. He had the advantage, certainly, and his ego was largely in control now. But in the recesses of his mind, he knew the stuff from which Vennius was made, and for all he now hated and despised his former friend, there was realization, at least some portion that remained, that it would be a titanic struggle to destroy his enemy. That numbers alone would not be enough. That was why he was there, on *Perigrinus*, leading his fleet...because he knew, through all the self-aggrandizement and the fealty he had accepted from so many hundreds of officers, that he could still lose this war.

He waved his hand to the officer standing alongside the communications panel, and a moment later, the technician said, "You are live, Your Supremacy."

Calavius looked straight ahead. He was clad in a full-dress uniform, hastily modified to create the grand look he felt befitted him in his new rank.

"My warriors, I speak to you now as we move forward, into battle. This struggle is different from those we have endured over the years. We fight fellow Palatians, this time—traitors, warriors we once held as our brothers and sisters, who have lost their honor and loyalty. Who have made themselves our enemies."

Lille stood quietly against the far wall, watching as Calavius addressed the fleet. Ideally, Lille would have found a more grounded officer, but there were unfortunate tendencies among those susceptible to such persuasion, and any who were likely to accept his aid suffered from the same flaws as Calavius. Lille used their egos to gain their cooperation, but then he had to endure them during the actual operations…and do what he could to ensure megalomania didn't derail success.

"I urge you all to put aside any remembrance of those who have turned traitor. The warrior who fought at your side years ago but now stands with the vile Vennius is your enemy. Do not doubt that, not for an instant. Strike him down, as you would any foe. Nothing is so detestable as a traitor. Go forward, win the victory…and secure the Alliance for centuries to come."

Lille nodded, to himself as much as anything. He'd offered to help Calavius write his address, but the Imperator had said he would do it himself. And he'd done a respectable job. Enough to lift the morale of those following him, to help divert any hesitancy they had about fighting old friends.

Probably, at least. That is always difficult.

Lille had always felt different than most people, even from the days when he was pulling himself from the streets and beginning his rise to wealth and comfort. He didn't crave political power, like most of his peers in the Union, at least no more than was necessary to ensure his personal comfort and protect himself. He had an ego, he supposed, but not one that got out of control. Indeed, his mind was typically far more often focused on ways he could fail than on confidence of success.

He lacked the sense of camaraderie people seemed to feel so strongly. He enjoyed being alone. He had minions to support his efforts, but that was their sole purpose to him. He did not begrudge them their own rewards for service well done, but neither did he unduly mourn them when they were killed. His servants existed to do his menial chores, his lovers for sex, his contacts among the powerful to secure his position.

Gaston…he is a friend. Villieneuve was one of the few people for whom he had genuine emotion. But even that only went so far. The two were friends, of a sort at least, but they were also an excellent team. Lille wondered what would remain if he stripped away the patronage, the desire to perform a job well, the mutual protection the two men offered each other. *Is there something else there? Or is that just more of the foolishness people heap upon things?*

He looked up at Calavius, sitting on his—*why not call it what it is…a throne?* There was no feeling there, at least, no loyalty, and, indeed, very little basic respect. The new ruler of the Alliance was a tool, one he would dispose of if it became useless. *But you are not useless, not yet. Win this battle now, Calavius…crush Vennius so that we may rally the rest of the fleet and invade the Confederation.*

As soon as the main comm line was shut down, he moved to the center of the room, looking right at the man he'd maneuvered to within a hair's breadth of total control of the Alliance. Calavius had rallied his troops, and now Lille would do the same.

"Well said, Calavius. You have come far and struggled hard. Let this be the last battle, the first glorious victory of your reign. With one blow here, you can secure your rule." A short pause. "Lead your fleet…lead it to victory."

*   *   *

"The line will advance." Brutus Egilius sat in his command chair on *Bellator*'s bridge, looking forward, his face cold, almost like his visage had been chiseled from marble. The enemy ships had stopped coming through the transwarp point. Fourteen battleships. It was a large force, a powerful one, and it was supported by more than forty smaller vessels. It was enough to crush his fleet, to sweep forward and blast Sentinel-2 to atoms.

He had analyzed the tactical situation, reviewed an endless

series of possible battle plans...but in the end, he knew. His forces would lose. He could give speeches, rally his warriors, as he already had, but he couldn't fool himself. The battle was virtually hopeless.

Not that it matters...

Egilius was a Palatian warrior in every way. He would find victory if it was possible, make any sacrifice to attain it. But even in the face of certain defeat, he would fight to the end. There was nowhere for his fleet to retreat, no option to fall back and regroup. Commander Vennius had understood that from the beginning, and he'd made it clear to his fleet commander. Left with no option save certain death in battle or surrendering, calling upon the mercy of the enemy, Egilius's choice was made. It was no choice at all. If he could not have victory, he would have an honorable death...and he would kill as many of his enemies as possible before they took him down.

"Interceptor squadrons about to engage approaching enemy fighters, sir. Bomber squadrons are ten thousand kilometers behind."

"Very well. The bombers are to remain back until the interceptors are fully engaged." Egilius was taking a chance. He'd had a much higher percentage of his fighters equipped for anti-shipping strikes than normal. It would make the fight that much tougher on his interceptor squadrons, but there was no way around that. Something had to give. His battleships couldn't win a fight outnumbered more than two to one by vessels of the same types, crewed by men and women with identical training. If his bombers could get through in enough force to cut those odds, it just might make a difference. Even one worth the hell into which he was casting his massively outnumbered interceptors.

"All squadrons confirm, Commander. Lead interceptor squadrons now engaging."

Egilius flashed a glance at his aide. Metus was as much a warrior as he, but here was a difference. It was far easier, Egilius found, to commit to a fight to the death for oneself, and much more difficult to lead others there. Especially those like Metus, loyal, steadfast, admirable. *Bellator*'s executive officer deserved better than to die in a lost effort, blasted to bits by those who had once served alongside him. But that was likely the fate that awaited him. That awaited both of them.

He wondered if Vennius felt the same way, if he was on Sentinel-2 now, resigned to his own fight to the finish while feeling the weight of leading so many there with him. *Perhaps this is part of command, something thousands who came before me felt.* Regardless, he found it the most difficult part of the desperate fight, one that dug at him more, even, than the fear.

He stared up at the screen, watching as the fighters engaged. His interceptors were outnumbered four to one right now, and they would have to hold, somehow…at least until the squadrons from the base arrived. Sentinel-2's wings wouldn't even the score, not even close, but they would help.

His eyes moved to the side, to the cloud representing *Dauntless*'s fighters. His Alliance warrior's pride made it difficult for him to admit that the Confederation wings were superior to his own. He tried to write it off to better technology, which was certainly true, though he knew there was more at play. *Dauntless* was the most famous ship in the Confederation navy, and her squadrons boasted not just the top ace in their fleet, five of the top ten. Captain Barron's squadrons were an elite tool, a killing machine on par with the reaper's sickle. Egilius resented the thought that his allies were more capable than his own people in any way…but he was damned glad the Confeds were on his side.

He watched as the dogfight increased in size and ferocity. His people were holding out, somehow, taking down as many of the enemy as they lost themselves. That was losing math for an outnumbered force, of course, but it was still an excellent performance for vastly outgunned squadrons.

"Optiomagis, the battle line is to extend itself. Move to forty thousand kilometer intervals between capital ships."

"Yes, Commander."

He didn't like spreading his forces so thin, but it was better than being outflanked on both sides. He had half his escorts ships deployed between the battleships, struggling to plug the great holes and prevent enemy forces from swarming his big ships. The other half were deployed to each end of the line, as badly outnumbered as the fighters in the center, and tasked with buying as much time as possible before the enemy's light forces broke through, and took the battle line from the flank and rear.

His eyes were on the display, fixed on the approaching enemy line, when four of the battleships on the extreme left began to move away from the main force. He was confused at first, concerned it might be some kind of flanking maneuver. But then he saw it. They were moving directly toward *Dauntless*. The Confederation battleship had drawn more than its share of attention.

His first instinct was to divert a portion of his own line, to match the enemy maneuver...but he remained silent. The diversion of almost thirty percent of the enemy's heavy vessels created an opportunity to meet the others with less onerous odds than he'd faced moments before. He'd sent his own interceptors against a similar ratio, for comparable purposes. *Dauntless* would have a difficult time facing four battleships, but perhaps she could buy the time he needed. His ships would still be outnumbered, but it was the best chance they were likely to get.

"The line will accelerate forward, Optiomagis. Acceleration at 5g. All gunnery stations ready to engage as soon as we enter range."

"Yes, Commander."

Egilius looked back at the small blue circle representing *Dauntless*. The Confeds had answered Vennius's call and sent their famous battleship to his aid. *Dauntless*'s reputation alone was proving useful, provoking an overreaction from Calavius's fleet. Egilius had been doubtful that one Confederation ship—any ship—could alter the situation appreciably, but now he wondered if he'd been wrong.

Perhaps they can make a difference, after all. Though they may pay dearly in doing so...

Chapter Thirty-Eight

CFS Dauntless
Cilian System
Deep in the Alliance
Year 310 AC

"Enemy battleships closing rapidly, Captain. Primaries charged and ready to fire as they enter range." Travis was staring across the bridge at Barron as he exited the lift and strode to his chair. The bridge crew was at full alert, but seasoned veterans that they were, every eye was on the captain. They'd all been told he was okay, that he'd be reporting to the bridge shortly, but Barron suspected that was the kind of thing most of them had to see to truly believe.

"Very well, Commander." Barron slid his chair around and sat down, his eyes moving to the main display. *Still four ships heading our way. I guess we do have a reputation in the Alliance.*

Barron knew the attention the enemy was paying to his ship was helping to give Vennius's people a chance, but it put a lot of pressure on his crew. They had bested this many capital ships at Chrysallis, but there had been considerable luck at play there as well as skill…and those had been Union vessels. These were Alliance ships, and though they were supporting Vennius's rival, they were still from the same service that had produced Katrine Rigellus and her crew.

He hoped his people wouldn't draw false confidence from their engagement out in the Badlands. Memories of the titanic struggle with *Invictus* should temper any cockiness, but only half his crew had been there for that vicious battle. The others were replacements, some filling in for those who had been transferred, but mostly, for those who had died or been seriously wounded in combat.

Travis had commed him while he was on his way to the bridge to tell him what *Dauntless* faced. But even for him, it hadn't seemed real, not until now, sitting on his bridge, staring at the display.

"We will maintain fire with primaries until the enemy is in range of secondaries…then we will switch to laser fire." *Dauntless*'s particle accelerator primaries were deadly weapons, and even more so at short range, but they were very slow firing, taking over two minutes to charge compared to fifteen to twenty seconds for the laser batteries. The newer units had proven to be more durable than the old ones, but the charging time was a function of the vast amount of power required, and had not improved much. The upgrades had shaved perhaps ten seconds, but the primaries soaked up virtually every watt of power available, effectively shutting down the secondaries. And there was no way *Dauntless* could fight four Alliance battleships by shooting once every two minutes.

"Yes, Commander. Gunnery crews are ready at all weapons stations." A short pause. "Commander Jamison reports all squadrons are moving to engage."

"Very well." The enemy had overreacted to *Dauntless*…but they had underestimated her fighters. The approaching vessels had a screen of interceptors out in front, perhaps eighty fighters in total. That outnumbered the interceptors *Dauntless* had been able to launch, especially since Barron had ordered Green squadron outfitted for bombing runs. But he knew just what his pilots could achieve. They had fought well three years before, facing off against *Invictus*'s veteran squadrons. But then they were only a seed of what they were now. They had become a blade, honed by combat to a razor's edge.

"Commander Jamison reports his fighters have entered range. They are launching missiles now."

Barron had enormous faith in Kyle Jamison. The officer was a gifted pilot himself, an ace ranking in the top one percent of the Alliance's fighter jocks, but he was an even better commander. Barron had never met an officer more knowledgeable about mass fighter tactics, or more able to direct the operations of multiple squadrons. And those squadrons had some of the best pilots ever to climb into a fighter's cockpit. Dirk Timmons, Corinne Steele, Olya Federov…he was proud to command them all.

Jake Stockton…the best of them. If he can find himself. Barron had been worried about Stockton since the horrifying crash that had almost killed him. The pilot, once so unflappable, had lost something of himself, and Barron didn't know if he'd ever get it back…if he'd get it back before some enemy pilot put him down for good.

Jake, where are you…the real you. We've never needed you more than right now.

*   *   *

"Raptor, you've got a squadron coming in from the flank. You've got to bring your Blues around, now." There was urgency in Jamison's voice as it blared through the comm. Stockton had seen the enemy coming already, and he was thinking about how to respond.

No, that's not you. You are better than this. Your instincts have served you well, yet now you ignore them, hesitate. Why can't you trust yourself anymore?

"I'm on it, Thunder."

Kill yourself. Turn the squadron over to Talon, and do everyone a favor. He could hear the words coming from deep within himself, from the part of him that was disgusted with what he had become.

"Blues, I want odds to come about to face this squadron we've got coming on the flank. Evens hold off the fighters to the front."

His comm crackled with acknowledgements, his pilots responding with far sharper reactions than those he'd displayed recently.

His eyes moved to his scanner. There were two enemy fighters coming at him. He felt a wave of fear, and he hated himself for it.

Just fly straight ahead…you're a useless piece of garbage. They're all better without you. The Blues, the captain, Thunder…Stara. All of them.

He hesitated, thinking for a passing instant that he would give in to the voice tormenting him. But there was something else there too.

No…I do not quit. I do not yield…

Then act like it. Be what you are, what you were…or be nothing. It's time. Do you have the strength to overcome this? If the answer is no, let this be your last battle…

Images floated in his mind, past battles, sitting in the wardroom with Jamison, in his quarters with Stara…

No!

His hand jerked hard to the right. For an instant, he didn't even know what he was doing. It was an odd feeling, but familiar too. Pure instinct.

He angled his positioning jets and flipped his ship around, opening fire as he did. The range was long, but he kept shooting…and one of the fighters heading his way vanished from his screen. He didn't stop to think about it. His hand was already pushing hard in the other direction, blasting at full to alter his vector toward the other fighter.

The Alliance bird was coming on hard, and he could tell from its reactions to his moves, the pilot was highly skilled. He felt a touch of the fear, the hesitation that had plagued him, but he quickly shoved it aside. He changed his thrust angle again, gaining a jump on his enemy. The Alliance fighter matched his move, but not quickly enough. Stockton had altered his course yet again. His hand moved back and forth, adjusting his vector more quickly than conscious thought could follow. He felt an energy inside him, one that had been too long absent. One he had thought was gone forever.

He pulled back hard on the throttle, and then to the right. His eyes were fixed on the screen, watching as his adversary reacted to his every move…expertly, but just a little bit too slowly.

He wondered if the Alliance pilot was afraid, if his neck was wet with sweat as he tried to match the sudden maneuvers of the fighter he'd chosen as his prey. Was his mind racing, trying to understand what was happening, how the sluggish fighter he'd targeted was suddenly anticipating his every move?

Stockton had felt that fear, too many times since he'd returned to duty. He had forgotten how to trust himself, to surrender his reasoned judgment to the wild beast that lived inside him, the essence that made him the deadly pilot he was.

That's right…be afraid. You picked the wrong fighter, my friend. I am Raptor, and now you'll learn what that means.

He gripped the throttle hard, his finger moving slowly, steadily to the firing stud. He had worked his way almost behind his enemy, gained enough of an edge to close, to finish this. He blasted his ship forward, feeling the engines straining as he maintained full thrust. His finger tightened, and he heard the sound of the laser cannons firing. His enemy evaded his first shots, but Stockton's focus was unbroken. He angled his thrust again, even as the Alliance pilot struggled to escape. He could feel his enemy's moves, and he countered them immediately.

He fired again, barely missing this time. He stayed on his target, once again the predator, denying his victim's every attempt at escape. He could tell this pilot was a veteran. No doubt he had fought many battles, destroyed the adversaries he'd faced. Until now.

Stockton felt the pride, the controlled arrogance he knew was at the heart of every great fighter pilot. He'd lost it, almost forgotten what it felt like, but now it was flooding back. He fired again, a miss, and then one more time. A direct hit. The circle on the scanner stayed there for a few seconds, and then it vanished.

Stockton howled madly, the sound of his voice echoing

through his cockpit. His hands clamped together in triumphant fists, for just a second or two. Then he gripped the throttle again, his eyes back on the scanner, checking the status of his Blues for an instant before he began the search for another target.

Raptor was back.

*   *   *

"Maintain fire. All ships." Egilius leaned forward, watching as his battle line poured everything it had into the enemy's heavy ships. His forces were fighting hard, performing as well as he could have expected, but they were still outnumbered, even after the four enemy ships detached from the main formation to attack *Dauntless*. For all the damage his people had inflicted, his own ships had taken at least as much…and that was a losing ratio.

The situation with the light ships was even worse. His frigates and escorts were outnumbered by a greater margin than his battleships. They were falling back, struggling to keep the enemy forces from outflanking the fleet, but it was only a matter of time before they would be wiped out. For all his pride in his warriors, Egilius couldn't escape one fact. His forces were losing the battle.

"Commander…*Impetus* reports status critical. Power output below twenty percent. Engines failing."

Egilius shook his head, his eyes on the display. He wanted to order the stricken vessel to fall back behind the line, to buy time for emergency repairs. But *Impetus* still had three operable laser batteries, and just enough reactor output to power them. He couldn't allow the beleaguered vessel to retreat, not now. *Impetus* was right in the center of his already stretched out line. Its retirement would open a hole large enough for the enemy's battleships to pour through.

"Understood, Optiomagis. Commander Kleavus is to hold his position and maintain maximum fire." He knew his words were a death sentence to Kleavus, and the nearly one thousand Alliance warriors he led, but there was no choice…and it looked

very much like none of them were going to survive the battle
anyway.

Not one thousand on Impetus. *Not anymore.* His best guess was,
Kleavus's ship had two to three hundred dead already. The rear
starboard of the ship was nothing but twisted wreckage, bleeding air into space. But he didn't have the slightest doubt Commander Kleavus and his doomed crew would follow his orders,
that they would fight to the death to buy time. He wondered if
they would resent him, blame him for issuing the command that
sent them to their deaths. Alliance doctrine said no, that they
would do as they were ordered, with no animosity, no question.
But Egilius was beginning to realize that even Alliance warriors
were just men and women. The Palatians had built a warrior
culture that produced excellent and disciplined fighters...but it
had also developed one hell of a propaganda operation, and
created the legend of invincible warriors who feared nothing.
That, Egilius knew, was a fiction.

Bellator shook hard, pulling Egilius from his thoughts. There
was no time for such philosophical meanderings. Perhaps later,
if through some miracle, he survived the battle. Now, his people needed him.

"Damage control parties, concentrate on the reactors and
the transmission lines. I want as many batteries as possible firing." His quick glance at the screen told him that last hit had
been close to reactor B. It didn't look like the power plant itself
had been seriously damaged, but there were all sorts of red indi-
cators on the lines leading out toward the rest of the ship...and
power wasn't worth anything if it couldn't get it to the weapons,
engines, and other systems.

"Yes, Commander."

Egilius looked back at the display, his eyes moving across the
rows of circles, tiny lights representing massive ships with crews
of one thousand warriors. He was still looking when *Bellator*
shook again, harder this time...and the bridge went dark.

*   *   *

"Fire!" Barron's voice was calm, clear. His body ached, especially his chest. But that was only from the residual effects of the surgery, and not any real physical problem. His mind was sharp and clear, nothing like it had been before. He was ready, strong enough for what was needed from him. To fight what was starting to look ominously like his ship's final battle.

Dauntless had been pounding one of the Alliance ships, hitting it three times with the primary batteries. The target vessel was large for an Alliance battleship, but still three hundred thousand tons lighter than *Dauntless*. It had taken significant punishment—enough, Barron figured, to stop most Union vessels—but the Alliance battleship was still moving forward.

Barron read the damage assessments scrolling down his screen. He knew the enemy ship was in trouble. *Dauntless*'s weapons had torn into its hull and shattered its systems. There were casualties too, he knew, probably a couple hundred, at least. Whole sections of that ship had been torn open, their compartments exposed to the vacuum of space. Though too small for his scanners to detect at this range, he suspected bodies had been blow out of those great rents in the hull. *And parts of bodies…*

Radiation had no doubt taken its toll as well, both directly from the particle accelerators and also the residual effects from destroyed equipment and blasted shielding. He knew what it was like to be in such a ship…*Dauntless* had *been* such a ship, at Santis certainly, and other battles too. So, he could truly appreciate what it took for that captain and crew to continue to close, their engines damaged, half their guns knocked out. He respected the courage, and it made him think back to Captain Rigellus and her crew, the relentlessness they had displayed in combat. He admired these opponents…but that wasn't going to stop him from killing them.

The small icon on the display sparkled again. Another hit. Barron watched as the enemy ship's detectable energy levels dropped yet again. Her engines were still engaged, but at less than twenty percent power. Now, however, they were entering the range of their own primaries, and battered though they were, they opened fire. Barron felt as though he understood the captain, his need to lash out, to repay some of what his people had suffered.

Dauntless shook, taking a hit from the enemy's first volley, despite Barron's evasive maneuvers. *No Union ship would have hit us from this far...*

"Alliance damage control teams are highly effective," he said, his voice grim, determined. "We don't lay off that ship until it's dead in space." He looked over at Travis. "Bring us forward, Commander, right between that vessel and the next one in line. Charge secondary batteries. Port broadside target one ship, starboard the other."

"Yes, Captain." He could hear the relief in Travis's voice, even in the stress of the battle. He knew she'd been worried about him, and he was just as sure she realized he was back.

For as long as that lasts...it will still be a miracle if we get through this fight...

Barron's eyes were fixed on the screen, watching as the other three ships moved into firing range. *Dauntless* had enjoyed the advantage in range to this point, but the ratio of incoming to outgoing firepower was about to swing heavily against her.

"We're coming into range of the other ships, Captain," Travis said, telling him what he already knew.

"Get me Commander Fritz."

"On your line, sir."

"Fritzie, I'm counting on you and your people. You remember the Alliance gunners at Santis. They're a damned sight better than their Union counterparts. I'll do everything I can to throw them off, but evasive maneuvers will only go so far. We're going to take hits."

"We're ready, Captain. I've got emergency teams deployed in every critical section." A short pause. "We'll keep her in the fight as long as possible, sir."

Barron could tell from his engineer's tone...she didn't expect *Dauntless* to survive the battle. He wasn't sure he did either.

"Godspeed, Fritzie."

"And to you, sir."

Barron cut the line and turned back to the display...just as *Dauntless* shook hard, twice in rapid succession. He could hear excited chatter across the bridge, and Travis on the line already with Fritz's people. His ship was in top condition, and he knew she could take a lot of damage and stay in the fight. He doubted those last two hits had hurt anything critical...but they had confirmed one thing for him, something he'd never doubted.

The Alliance gunners were good. Damned good.

Chapter Thirty-Nine

Cilian System
Deep in the Alliance
Year 310 AC

"Let's go, Blues...on me." Stockton brought his fighter around, pushing his engines to their limit to alter his vector. "*Dauntless* is taking a pounding, and we need to make sure the Greens get in for their bombing run."

Dauntless's squadrons had torn into the enemy fighter screen, and in the swirling melee that had followed, they had driven the Alliance wings back with heavy losses. But Alliance warriors weren't Union conscripts, and "driven back" wasn't the same thing as broken. The enemy's retreat brought them back toward *Dauntless*'s approaching bombers, with no one but Stockton's Blues close enough to intervene.

He was still a little shaky. His old strength had reemerged, but he hadn't entirely banished the new fears... the memories of the flames. He doubted that would ever leave him, and he knew it would always be more difficult, that he would never be able to rely on the easy confidence that had once driven him. But he was Raptor Stockton, and whatever it took, he was determined never to lose himself again.

His eyes darted around the screen, and he became more concerned as he did. The Alliance squadrons had left a rearguard to cover their retreat, and that had given them a head start...now they were about to run into the Greens. That was luck as much as anything, Stockton was sure, an unfortunate coincidence that brought the withdrawing wings back just as *Dauntless*'s bombers were coming through. But it didn't matter how it had happened. The enemy interceptors would obliterate the cumbersome bombers...unless his Blues could get there in time.

"Full thrust....everybody. We're just going to make it in time to cut these interceptors off and save the Greens." *Or we're just going to miss...I'm not sure yet...*

His people would be outnumbered, thirteen pilots against perhaps twice that number. He'd never let that trouble him before, but he reminded himself these weren't Union pilots out there. His Blues were the best...but they were going to pay a price for this one.

He sucked in a deep breath, his chest resisting under the heavy g forces. The steady acceleration was hard to take, but he didn't dare ease off, not even for a second. It looked like his people *would* get there in time, at least if the enemy turned to face them instead of continuing on toward the bombers.

He glanced down at his readouts. Fuel status was still good. Lasers were fully charged. His fighter was as ready as it could be. And so was he.

His eyes fixed on the tiny dots on the long-range display, tense, waiting to see if his rapidly-approaching force was enough to divert their attention, to give the bombers a chance. He was counting on his counterpart doing something he wouldn't have done. He'd have split his force, sent half after the bombers and faced off against the interceptors with the other half.

Then he saw. The Alliance fighters were engaging their thrusters, changing their vectors toward Blue squadron. All of them.

Yes!

Stockton felt relief, for an instant, before the stress of facing so many enemy ships hit him. Still, he'd accomplished what he'd set out to do. The Greens were saved, and they'd have an unimpeded...

No...wait...

He'd been wrong. *Most* of the interceptors were coming his way. But a single squadron continued on the original vector, toward the bombers.

Damn. These Alliance officers know what they're doing. One battered squadron wouldn't make much of a difference in the fighter battle, but they could wreak havoc on an unescorted force of bombers.

I have to do something...

"Vagabond, on me. We're going after that group heading for the bombers. Talon, you've got the squadron."

"Acknowledged. Raptor..." There was an edge in Talon's voice. "Yes, sir." Stockton understood what was troubling her. He knew his people were still worried about him, and he couldn't blame them. But there was nothing he could do about it now.

"I'm with you, Raptor." Doug "Vagabond" Torrance was another Blue squadron old timer, a veteran of the fight at Santis.

Stockton angled his throttle, driving his ship hard toward the ships heading at the bombers. His eyes moved around on the display, his mind shifting around, weighing possible courses. He edged the controls to the side, a maneuver half based on analysis and half on his gut.

A quick glance told him Vagabond was right behind him. They were rapidly approaching the enemy ships, but it was going to be close. No matter what he did, the Greens were going to take losses, probably heavy losses. But he was determined that they wouldn't be wiped out.

"We're going to have to open fire at long range, Vagabond... damned long. It's the only chance we've got. Maybe if we can score a hit or two, the others will turn to face us."

"Roger that, Raptor. I guess we'll just have to hit from out here."

Stockton smiled. It seemed misplaced, in the middle of a desperate chase during a hopeless battle, but he was proud of his people, and he couldn't hold it in. He'd been too deep in self-absorbed misery to truly appreciate them in recent weeks, but he saw it in the matter-of-fact way Vagabond had spoken.

That's damned right…we just have to hit.

His fixed his gaze intently at his screens, watching as enemy fighters moved from the long-range scanner to the tactical display. They were still far out. Even a direct hit might not completely destroy a target, but he had to try.

He pressed hard on the firing stud, the sound of the lasers reverberating in the confines of the tiny cockpit. Then again, and again. A hit from this range was highly improbable, but that didn't matter to him. He *needed* to hit…and so he would.

He was tight, focused, but now he relaxed just a bit, allowing instinct to take over. He needed more than scanners, than AI-assists. He had to anticipate his target's moves, guess just right…and fire.

He shot again, and again. He was coming close, but close wasn't going to get it done. He fired again.

He opened his mind to the feelings in his gut, the unidentified part of him that had made him such a gifted pilot. Such a cold killer.

His hand loosened, and he felt almost as though he was slipping into a trance. But his mind was still active, his eyes still locked on the target's maneuvers. He waited…waited…and then he squeezed his finger.

He was watching the display as it updated. A hit!

The fighter was still there, but he quickly realized it was moving along on an unchanging vector, its power readings close to zero. He let the AI run the calculations this time…hitting a ship on a fixed course was nothing more than a mathematical equation, a job for a machine. Then he fired again, and an instant later, the icon vanished from his screen.

One down out of eight. But will the others turned to face us? Or will they finish off the Greens?

The Alliance ships had already taken down two of the bombers. Stockton maintained full thrust, firing constantly as he moved closer, Vagabond just off to his side. They hadn't scored another hit yet, but they'd put a few shots close…close enough to get the attention of the Alliance pilots.

He winced as a third Green squadron bomber winked off

his screen, but then he could see the Alliance fighters firing their thrusters, bringing their vectors around to face him.

We did it!

Stockton felt a rush of satisfaction, followed by a sobering realization.

Now all we have to do is take out seven enemy fighters.

Just the two of us…

*   *   *

"Fritzie, I need that power. We've got to keep the secondaries firing full." *The batteries we've got left, at least.*

"I've got half my people working on it, Captain. But the bays were hit hard. Right now, we couldn't land a single fighter. We've got to…"

"The fighters won't have anywhere to land if *Dauntless* isn't here…and we're not going to be for long unless we can keep pounding these Alliance ships."

"I'll transfer more crews to the power lines and reactors, Captain, but the damage is heavy. It's not going to make that much difference." A pause. "I can get you more engine power, sir…the lines there are in better shape. But the cut-off batteries are going to take longer."

Barron's eyes were fixed on his screen. The duel with the enemy ships had been a brutal one. *Dauntless* was badly wounded, but she hadn't been idle herself. One enemy ship was gone, a lifeless hulk with no energy readings at all. The other three were badly damaged, but to one extent or another, they were all still in the fight.

"Get me that power, Fritzie. Now." He turned his head. "Commander Travis, plot a course to pull us back out of the enemy's range."

"Yes, Captain." The two responses came back in rapid successions, Fritz's over the comm and Travis's across the few meters between their stations.

Barron didn't like the idea of retreating, but it made sense here. One of the enemy ships, at least, had severe engine damage. Even if the other two could match *Dauntless*'s thrust, the maneuver would cut the enemy firepower by a third.

"Engines engaging, Captain." Travis's words reached his ears an instant before he felt the thrust, a good 8g. He was surprised. He hadn't expected so much power from *Dauntless*'s battered reactors.

The move caught the enemy by surprise, and a whole series of volleys missed cleanly. *Dauntless* had been almost at a dead halt, save for her evasive maneuvers, so even at 8g acceleration, it would take some time to get back out of range. Three minutes, twenty seconds, Barron calculated.

"Commander...maintain as much fire as possible." Much of *Dauntless*'s available power was going to the engines, and what was left was constrained by damaged lines and conduits. But every shot counted now.

"Yes, sir. The rear starboard batteries are operational, and I think Fritz's people have managed to reroute the lines."

"Very well, Commander." Barron was watching the display as he heard the distant sounds of the batteries firing. His eyes remained fixed, waiting for the scanner report. Two hits! Both on the lead enemy ship.

Barron shifted in his seat. The g forces were uncomfortable, particularly on his sore chest. He'd enjoyed the new force compensators, but right now they were shut down. They'd taken damage, and *Dauntless* didn't have a watt of power to waste on luxuries. She was in the fight of her life, outnumbered and battered. Barron had managed to avoid paying too much attention to casualty reports, but he knew they were bad.

His Alliance allies were in no better shape, he knew, but his ship needed him now, and that was where his attention was focused...as it would be to the end.

Which won't be long now. Even if he managed to defeat all four enemy battleships—and he knew that wasn't going to happen—it would only buy a few minutes. Vennius's forces were acquitting themselves well, but they, too, were outnumbered. And the Alliance spacers facing them weren't going to falter or make foolish errors. There would be no morale failures, not in this battle, and, notwithstanding the skills of the officers in command, that made the whole thing more or less a question of mathematics.

"It looks like we got a jump on them, Captain. They're accelerating now, but only two of them are matching our thrust."

Barron nodded. Just what he expected. If *Dauntless* could get through the next couple minutes, the odds would be two to one instead of three to one, at least for a while.

"Maintain thrust, Commander. And continue maximum…"

Barron was thrown forward, his already aching chest slamming hard into his harness. A shower of sparks flew across the bridge, and a section of the ceiling collapsed and fell to the deck. Barron knew the hit was bad before he even looked to his screen for a damage report. And when he did look, he realized it was even worse than he'd thought. His display was dark.

He looked up, staring around the bridge. All the screens were blank…and as he was looking, the main lights went out, the bridge lit only by the glow of the emergency lamps.

He reached down to the comm unit, hitting Fritz's channel. "Fritzie, I need a damage report…" He let his voice trail off. The comm was also dead, nothing but light background static.

The g forces were gone too, or at least lessened. We're not in free fall… it feels like maybe 0.75g. So, we're not completely dead in space.

He exchanged glances with his first officer. Travis nodded. Then she turned her head and said, "All right, you all know what to do. Emergency procedures. Lieutenant Darrow, break out the portable comm unit and see if you can get engineering. We need to know how bad this is. It could be just a line rupture."

Barron listened to Travis's words, the subtle encouragement she was giving the bridge crew. But he knew in his gut that last hit had done critical damage. *Dauntless* was in trouble.

As if to confirm his thought, the ship shook hard again, and he could hear the distant sounds of explosions from deep inside his vessel.

*　　　　*　　　　*

Damn!

Stockton had been excited, riding high just a second before. He and his lone wingman had managed to take out five of the Alliance fighters in a swirling dogfight that was as hard and brutal as any he'd seen. The Alliance pilots were highly skilled and brave, but Stockton and his partner had fought like men possessed. They'd both heard the chatter on the comm. *Dauntless* was in trouble, and it sounded bad. Very bad. It was about more than saving the bomber pilots now, it was about them getting through and hitting the ships that were killing *Dauntless.*

He'd just about let himself believe they were going to prevail, that they were going to take out all seven enemy fighters. Then Vagabond got hit.

The pilot had been on the comm, mid-sentence when he went silent. Stockton hadn't seen it coming either. One of the enemy survivors had spun his ship around and taken a shot. The Alliance fighter had been far away, and Stockton knew both he and Vagabond had underestimated their enemy. With disastrous results.

He checked his scans frantically, hoping for a few seconds that Vagabond had managed to eject from his stricken craft. But there was nothing.

His eyes moved back to his scanner, and his muscles tightened, gripped by the deadly rage that had taken him. There was no thought in his mind now, save killing these last two Alliance pilots. He swung his arm hard to the side, angling his ship. He wasn't even thinking now...he was operating on pure instinct. He pressed the firing stud...then again.

He watched as one of the enemy ships vanished from the scanner. Now, there was only one.

The one who killed Vagabond.

He came about again, altering his vector to bring him straight toward his foe. He knew this was a pilot to be respected, most likely an Alliance ace who had never met his match.

Until now...

The Alliance pilot was weaving hard, almost defying Stockton to score a hit. He was firing, too, and the shots were well-aimed, coming dangerously close, despite Stockton's own evasive maneuvers.

He knew the bombers were clear, that he had accomplished his mission. But that didn't matter now. Nothing did…save the death of this Alliance warrior who had killed Vagabond.

All kinds of thoughts drifted around Stockton's mind, the idea that his enemy was simply doing his own duty, that the destruction of Vagabond's ship had been no personal assault. Stockton had once nursed all sorts of romantic perceptions of war…honor among those who dueled in their fighters, for example. But after three years of war, he had lost too many friends, been too badly hurt himself. He had watched his nation come to the edge of disaster, and he had seen one deadly battle after another. There was nothing left of the chivalrous knight in his cockpit. Stockton hated his enemies, and all he wanted was to kill them. Before they did the same to him, or another of his comrades.

He fired. *Close!* The shot almost grazed the enemy's fighter, but the pilot had been just a little too fast.

His enemy came about and fired a series of shots his way. Stockton's instincts saved his life, and his fighter swung off to the side, just before the deadly blasts went by.

He stared ahead, his mind black, empty save for his hunt. *I ride a pale horse…I am here for you…*

His enemy was good, very good. He suspected the pilot was cocky, arrogant, that his belief in his own invincibility drove him, as Stockton's had driven *him*. But Stockton's memory of the flames, the nightmare that had tormented him before, now drove him. *You are not invincible, whatever your Alliance doctrine tells you…and your confidence will be your undoing.*

He swung around, firing his engines full, decelerating hard. It made no sense, not by any set of fighter tactics or doctrine. Save one unwritten one. It was unpredictable. It would take his enemy by surprise.

And so it did. Stockton spun his ship back around and opened fire, blast after blast directed toward his enemy's location…until one found its mark.

It wasn't a direct hit, but it had damaged the enemy fighter. Badly. Stockton knew he could stop, return to his squadron, rejoin their fight. His old codes told him to leave this enemy, his fighter too disabled to pursue or to pose a threat to his comrades. But those thoughts were pushed aside. He imagined how many of his allies and friends this pilot would kill in the future if he allowed him to escape. He imagined Vagabond, the pilot, but also the man... He felt raw hatred, a lust for vengeance.

And, finally, he felt the flames, all around him. The indescribable agony...the true essence of war.

His finger tightened on the firing stud.

Chapter Forty

"The battle goes well." Lille stood alongside Calavius, looking up at the series of large screens the Alliance's would-be Imperator had ordered installed.

"Indeed. Our victory is assured. The traitor Vennius will soon be dead, and my only regret is that it shall not be at my own hands." Lille held back a sigh. He despised arrogance. He'd seen it again and again, the lust for power, the wave of over-confidence that took people as soon as they tasted success. He did not suffer from that affliction. He was a man of action, one not afraid to pursue what he wanted...but he always respected his enemies' abilities, and he never took anything for granted. The battle was progressing well, but it wasn't over yet.

Vennius's line was falling back steadily, his ships all seriously damaged. Even as they pulled back deeper within the defensive zone around the station, Calavius's smaller vessels were finishing them off and beginning to move around the flank. The fortress was pouring out heavy fire, but it, too, would soon be silenced.

"I believe it is time to send the Ram forward." The name was an informal one, but it described the function of the modified frigate. The ship had one purpose—to accelerate

326

directly toward its target, building up a massive velocity before it impacted. It had been created for the express purpose of destroying the Sentinel-2 fortress, a stationary target unable to evade the incoming vessel.

"I concur. It is time. Issue the order."

The Ram had nothing volatile aboard, no substances that could cause further damage after a hit. Most of its compartments had been opened to the vacuum of space to minimize damage from decompression, its skeleton crew of volunteers operating in space suits. Everything dangerous that was not expressly necessary for operation had been removed as well. It had no weapons of any kind. It was essentially a massive chunk of metal, with nothing more aboard than reactors and engines. And even the reactors would shut down when the ship entered firing range of the fortress, a precaution to eliminate the possibility of a containment breach that would vaporize the ship before it had achieved its aim.

The fortress would fire at the Ram, of course, and as soon as its crew realized the intent of the approaching ship, they would direct their most powerful batteries to destroy it. But that would avail them nothing.

Their lasers would melt sections of the hull. They would slice off bits of the ship. They would bore deeply into its guts, turning once-vital systems into molten rubble. But by the time the Ram was in range of these weapons, it would need no systems. Its sole purpose would be as a massive chunk of dense metal, traveling at tremendous velocity, and carrying almost incalculable kinetic energy with it.

The fortress's weapons were enormously powerful, but their yield was far from enough to vaporize such a massive chunk of dense matter. They were designed to destroy vital systems, to rip open compartments and cause secondary damage by decompression...and by the spreading of internal fires. But there was nothing flammable on the Ram, and no oxygen to support fires. There would be no systems still functioning, no ongoing fusion reaction. The only way to destroy the Ram would be to blast it to atoms, one chunk at a time. And the lasers of Sentinel-2 had not been designed for that.

Calavius was looking down from his perch, toward Lille.
The Alliance spy wasn't particularly paying attention, though.
His eyes were mostly on the display, at the Confederation battleship being pounded by three Alliance vessels. She looked dead
in space, and as cold and businesslike as he was, Lille couldn't
help but smile. He hadn't believed it at first when the reports
came in, identifying the Confederation ship as *Dauntless*. His
success at bringing about a change in the Alliance government,
in securing an ally in the war against the Confederation…that
was gratifying enough. But the thought of also ridding the universe of that cursed ship, the one that had interfered so many
times in the plans he and Villieneuve had concocted, was an
added joy.

The war would be over by now…except for Dauntless. *I will savor
watching its destruction…*

"Ambassador Lille?" Calavius's tone was imperious. Lille
found it extremely annoying, but his professional control
slammed back into place.

"My apologies," he said, his voice giving no hint of his irrita-
tion. He moved to the comm panel and said, "The Imperator
orders the Ram to move forward at once."

Then he turned back to the display. He didn't want to miss
a second of *Dauntless*'s destruction.

*   *   *

"Talon…you've got one on your tail." Stockton was one his
way back toward the squadron. The Blues, along with the rest
of *Dauntless*'s interceptor squadrons, were finishing off the last
of the Alliance fighters. The battle hadn't been without cost,
and Stockton could see the blank spots on his readout, Blue
squadron pilots no longer in action. Casualties had been heavy,
and all he could do was hope most of them had ditched. *Not
that we'll be able to pick them up.* The fighters were winning their
fight, but every time he glanced at the long-range scanner, the
situation in the battle as a whole had gotten worse. Their side

was losing…there wasn't a doubt about that.

"I'm trying, Raptor…but this guy is good. He's hard to shake."

Stockton felt his stomach tighten. Talon was one of his best pilots, an ace and somewhat of a legend in her own right. But he'd heard the tension in her voice. The fear.

"Hold it together, Talon. I'm on my way." He kicked in his thrusters, blasting at full toward her positon. His eyes dropped down to the scanner. *Is anybody else closer? No, no one.* Timmons and his Eagles were on the far side of the engagement. Federov and the Reds had pushed too far forward. And the other Blues were scattered, off chasing individual targets. It would have to be him.

He pulled back even harder, as if more force on the stick would coax extra speed from his engines. His could see on the scanner that Talon's pursuer was firing at her now. Her ship was jumping all around, wild evasive maneuvers. She was trying to shake the fighter on her tail, to avoid his shots. But he was getting closer.

Stockton could see Talon had encountered another ace, her equal at least. He watched, hoping to see her break free. But he knew that wasn't going to happen. The enemy fighter had too much positional advantage…and Stockton could see the Alliance flyer was too good to be shaken.

He had to save her. She had saved him earlier, and now it was his turn. But he was too far out. He shouted, swore at his fighter, called upon every spacer's god to increase the thrust his engines were putting out, but nothing changed the inevitable fact. It would be two minutes before he was in even extreme firing range, and that was going to be too much. Unless his approach rattled the Alliance pilot enough to scare him off.

No chance of that. This guy is good.

He felt rage, fear, urgency…and worst of all, helplessness. He watched as Talon resorted to ever more desperate maneuvers, trying again and again, unsuccessfully, to break away. "Talon, you can do this," he said, not believing it as it came out of his mouth.

"I can't lose him, Raptor…" Her voice was heavy with fear. Corinne Steele was a stone cold pilot, a veteran of the Battle of Santis, and of every engagement *Dauntless*'s wings had fought since. She had two dozen kills, and every decoration a fighter pilot could earn. But now she had met her match. Stockton knew it…and it was clear she did too.

"Corinne…focus! You can do…" His words stopped abruptly. The icon representing her ship vanished from his screen. He frantically checked his scanners, looking, hoping for the beacon from her ejection pod. But there was nothing.

She was gone.

Stockton felt the rage again, the same feeling that had taken him when Vagabond had been killed. He'd lost two of his oldest pilots in less than fifteen minutes, and his mind tormented him with calculations, with the realization that, apart from him, Blue squadron now had only four veterans of Santis remaining. Unending war and combat had taken their toll, even on his elite warriors. He wondered if any of them would survive the war. But those thoughts were quickly shoved aside, leaving only one thing in his mind. Vengeance.

His eyes focused on the enemy fighter, changing course, accelerating hard. He angled his throttle to match. He couldn't save Talon, any more than he could've saved Vagabond. But he could avenge her.

He stared straight ahead, matching every course change of the enemy. *You're dead, and you don't even know it yet…*

He struggled to suck in a deep breath, aching from the g forces he was enduring. But he wouldn't ease up, not for a microsecond. There was only one thing in the universe right now. He was Death, and he vowed to himself Talon's killer would fall.

*   *   *

"Andi?" Merrick's voice echoed across *Pegasus*'s cramped bridge.

Pegasus was hovering in front of the transwarp point, as

she had been for more than ten minutes now. She'd still been docked to *Dauntless* when the enemy fleet began emerging. Barron had ordered her ship to depart immediately, and to get out of the system before they were trapped in the battle. She'd obeyed, though she didn't hadn't wanted to. Barron had filled her head with all kinds of reasons she needed to leave—to send back his report and request for aid, to bring the prisoners to Base Grimaldi. But it was all utter crap, she knew…Barron had already sent back word of the situation. *No, not utter crap, but certainly exaggerated in importance, his machinations to get me out of danger.*

He knew this was coming. He was worried he wouldn't survive the fight…and he wanted me gone when…

She sat still, silent, not even acknowledging Merrick. She had promised Barron she would go. *But you didn't even get to say goodbye…*

She'd planned to see him one last time, though she had no idea what she would have said. But there hadn't been time. Something the enemy had stolen from her.

"Andi," Merrick said again, louder but still with a softness. "I know this is difficult, but…"

"No. I can't."

Merrick didn't say anything else. He just sat and looked at her.

"I can't leave…he's losing the battle. They all are. You can see that."

"I can, Andi," Merrick said, somewhat reluctantly. "But it's not over yet. Captain Barron and *Dauntless* are not easily defeated."

"They're not invincible either, Vig…" She paused. "Why would Admiral Striker have sent them out here alone?"

"I can't say what the admiral was thinking, Andi…except that he didn't order them out here. He sent *Dauntless* to Archellia. It was Captain Barron who came this far."

Lafarge understood why Barron had done what he had. The future of the Confederation rode on what happened here. But still, she was angry that he had put himself in such terrible danger.

"I can't leave, Vig. Not while this is still going on."

Merrick nodded slowly. "We're all with you, Andi. You know that. Whatever you decide is fine with us." He paused. "But what can we do? What action can *Pegasus* take that will make the slightest difference in a battle like this?"

She looked back at her second and her friend. Finally, she said, "I don't know, Vig. But I can't leave. I just can't." Another pause. "Bring us back toward *Dauntless*. Full thrust."

Merrick took a deep breath. "Whatever you say, Andi." There was fear in his voice, but determination as well. "Engaging full thrust…now."

*   *   *

"Fritzie, we're sitting ducks here. You've got to get me some power. At less than 1g, these three ships are all over us." As if the emphasize his point, *Dauntless* shook hard again, and a small console broke loose on the opposite wall and crashed to the deck.

"We're doing everything we can, Captain. The damage is widespread." Her voice was distant, staticky. "The central power core has been breached. We've got a lot of functional systems that just aren't getting energy. And the reactors are both on the edge. One more bad hit near either of them, and they'll scrag…and before you tell me to cut the safeties, the only thing that will accomplish is to vaporize us instead of leaving us with no power."

Barron held the portable unit to his face. The main comm was still dead, but Fritz and her engineers had at least restored emergency power to the bridge workstations. "If those reactors go down, we're dead Fritzie."

"I'm doing everything possible, Captain…but it won't help anything if I blow the ship up." He could hear the strain in her normally calm voice.

"Just do what you can, Fritzie. If anybody can manage something, it's you." He lowered his arm, letting the comm unit drop into his lap. He felt helpless, cut off. He had no weapons online, nothing to even shoot back with. Nothing to do but wait until the ships out there blasted *Dauntless* to rubble. Fortunately, the engines were still operational. Barely. But enough, at least, for some evasive maneuvers. Otherwise, he knew, *Dauntless* would be gone already.

He turned and looked over at Travis. "Commander, see if you can get down to engineering. Fritzie will do her best, but she can only be in one place at a time." He didn't like the idea of Travis being off the bridge, and he especially didn't like sending her to find her way through the ship right now. The lifts were all out, and the route to engineering was likely to be a torturous journey down access ladders and around piles of wreckage. But he wasn't ready to give up yet, and Atara Travis was the next closest thing to his being there himself.

"Yes, Captain." She jumped up and moved swiftly across the bridge, grabbing one of the portable com units as she did. "I'll advise you of my progress." She glanced back at him once, one friend looking at another, almost as if for the last time. Then she grabbed the top rung and climbed down the ladder and out of sight.

Lieutenant Darrow jumped from his own seat and walked across the bridge, covering the station Travis had just left.

"Lieutenant, I want you to…"

The ship rocked hard—a hit, a bad one. Then, almost immediately, another one. The bridge went totally dark, and sparks flew from everywhere, one overload after another blowing out equipment all around.

Barron spun his head, reacting to a loud crash, followed by a short, pinched scream…just as the battery-powered lights snapped back on. A girder, one of the main structural supports, had collapsed, crushing Travis's station…and instantly killing Darrow.

Barron bit back against the pain he felt. Darrow had been unfairly implicated in his former CO's treason, and Barron had taken him on *Dauntless* when no other captain would have him. The officer had repaid Barron with unflinching loyalty and flawless service. Barron had come to rely on his chief communications officer. Now, he was dead. Just one more of *Dauntless*'s family sacrificed to the war.

He felt sorrow, loss…but it was strangely tempered. Darrow was dead, but Barron didn't see any way the rest of his people were going to make it out of this fight. He looked around the dimly-lit bridge, and took a deep, unfettered breath. Even the moderate pressure from the engines' thrust was gone, replaced by zero gravity. The loss of simulated gravity had come seconds too late to save Darrow.

The engines were completely offline. *Dauntless* was stuck on its fixed, unchanging course. He knew it wouldn't take the Alliance gunners long to realize they had his ship. One quick calculation, and every incoming shot would hit.

His mind raced, but he came up blank. His people were going to die…*Dauntless* was going to die. And he couldn't think of anything to do. Nothing at all.

*   *   *

"Andi, we should pull back. There's nothing we can do… and a single shot from one of those battleships will blast us to atoms." Merrick was staring at the same display Andi was. It was centered on *Dauntless*, and it showed the three enemy battleships coming at her. Barron's ship had stopped firing moments before, but now, even the meager thrust she'd maintained was gone. She was continuing on the same course, velocity and vector completely unchanged.

He's going to die. Now. And I will watch, unable to do anything…

She winced as two more hits slammed into *Dauntless*. She was shaking, angry, frustrated. But there was nothing she could do. Nothing but watch as Barron and his people died.

She shook her head, some part of her even then unwilling to give up. But there was no way her ship could intervene. Throwing away her crews' lives wouldn't buy *Dauntless* another second.

"Reverse thrust," she said, her voice cold, lifeless. She retained enough of herself not to risk her crew's lives for no reason.

"Andi...we've got activity at the transwarp point." Merrick turned and looked at her. "Something is coming through. Something big."

Lafarge felt cold inside. If the enemy had another force coming in right behind her, not only would Barron die, but she would have led her own people to their deaths...for nothing.

She stared at the screen, even as a new symbol appeared. It was *big*, almost certainly a huge battleship. Andi Lafarge never gave up...not until now. But the sight of a massive ship coming in from behind her was too much. All was lost.

The second icon only confirmed her misery, and she hardly reacted to the third. It was over. They would all die, and the attempt to support the pro-Confederation faction would fail. The Alliance would invade, their ship's pouring across the almost undefended Rim border. World after world would fall... millions would die.

"Andi, we're picking up something on the comm."

She almost told him to shut down communications. She might have to die, but she didn't have to listen to the enemy gloat about it. Still, it felt too much like hiding, like cowardice.

"On the main speaker, Vig."

Merrick turned and hit a button. Then he just nodded.

"This is acting-Commodore Sara Eaton, Confederation navy, aboard CFS *Repulse*. *Dauntless*...please respond. Repeat, this is acting-Commodore Sara Eaton, Confederation navy, aboard CFS *Repulse*. *Dauntless*, please respond..."

Chapter Forty-One

Free Trader Pegasus
Cilian System
Deep in the Alliance
Year 310 AC

Lafarge froze, staring at the speaker in stunned silence. She'd heard the words, but her first thought was that it was some kind of deception. She wasn't privy to Confederation military dispositions, but she couldn't believe Striker had been able to pull three ships off the front. He'd told her it was impossible when she'd met with him at Grimaldi, that *Dauntless* was all he was able to send until he got reinforcements.

"Get the scanners at full, Vig. Are those really Confederation battleships?" She felt a faint speck of hope, but she suppressed it. She couldn't bring herself to accept what she desperately wanted to believe.

"They're big, Andi. Larger than any Confed ship I've ever seen. But the beacons check out. The lead ship is transmitting CFS *Repulse*, just like she said."

Eaton...the name was familiar. *Yes, of course...*

Barron had mentioned a Captain Eaton to her, the officer that had fought with him when he'd destroyed the Union supply base, helping to halt the enemy's initial invasion. She still wasn't sure it wasn't some kind of trick, but she let that spark of hope reignite.

"*Dauntless*, please respond. Captain Barron?" The transmissions continued. "Tyler? This is Sara Eaton. Do you read?"

Lafarge's eyes darted back to the small oval on her screen, *Dauntless*, still moving at a fixed course. She was picking up no detectable energy readings.

She grabbed her headset, strapping it on. "Attention *Repulse*...Attention *Repulse*. This is Captain Lafarge of the Free Trader *Pegasus*. Commodore Eaton...*Dauntless* is heavily damaged and under attack by three hostile Alliance battleships."

She waited, wondering if this Commodore Eaton would listen to her.

Then: "Captain Lafarge, we read your message. Is it possible *Dauntless*'s communications are down?"

Lafarge swallowed hard. "Yes, Commodore, that is very possible." Other things were possible too, all far worse than comm failure. "*Dauntless* is under attack. Captain Barron and his people are in terrible trouble. They won't last long." She tried to stay as cool as she could, but she suspected a little of her fear slipping into her words would only add to the sense of urgency.

"We'll see about that, Captain. *Dauntless* isn't going down, not if I have anything to say about it."

The comm line went dead, and a few seconds later Merrick turned toward her. "Andi, the new battleships are firing their thrusters. They're accelerating at..." He paused for an instant, a stunned look on his face. "...just over 14g."

She turned back to the main screen, watching as the three ovals moved forward, directly toward the ships attacking *Dauntless*. She'd never seen that level of acceleration before, but they were still pretty far out. She was glad that help was on the way to Barron, but she still didn't know if it would be on time.

They'll have particle accelerators...the range on those is... She tried to remember. Data like that was classified, of course, but she'd seen *Dauntless*'s primaries in use at Chrysallis. Her best guess was, Eaton's ships were maybe sixty thousand kilometers out of range. But that distance was dropping with every second of massive thrust the vessels put out.

Fifty thousand…

She looked back at *Dauntless* on the display. The enemy ships had realized her engines were down, and they were pouring fire into her. She knew Barron's ship, tough as she was, couldn't take much more pounding. At first, she thought the Alliance ships were going to ignore the advancing Confederation vessels, but then she realized one of them was changing its vector, moving to intercept.

They're going to try to hold Eaton's ships back until the other two finish off Dauntless.

Still, one less ship blasting away has to help…

She watched as the remaining two ships continued to close on *Dauntless*, firing relentlessly as they did.

He can't last much longer.

Thirty thousand kilometers…

She was shaking her head. Eaton was going to be too late. The Alliance vessel advancing to meet her force was accelerating too, and the distance between them was closing faster. *Twenty thousand…fifteen…*

She waited and watched, knowing Eaton's people had to get past this first ship and close on the ones attacking *Dauntless. Ten thousand…*

Her screens went wild, energy readings soaring. She wasn't sure for a few seconds what had happened, but then the scanners told her. Eaton's flotilla had fired their primaries, from almost ten thousand kilometers outside what she had though was their maximum range. And each of the three ships had fired four guns, not two like *Dauntless* possessed.

Her eyes darted back to the Alliance ship. It looked like six of the weapons had hit, and from the data coming in, they had virtually gutted the vessel. *Dauntless* had already inflicted heavy damage on the Alliance ship, but now Lafarge was getting a steady stream of damage assessments, atmosphere leaking into space, internal explosions…and then, suddenly, her scanners reported a massive energy surge. The Alliance battleship was gone.

She looked on in stunned silence. She'd never seen a weapon as powerful as the ones Eaton's ships had just fired—except of course on the ancient planet-killer at Chrysallis. She didn't understand what she had just seen, but she realized it might have been the miracle that could save Barron and his people.

Her eyes went to the Alliance vessels, the two battleships that were killing *Dauntless*. The firing had stopped. It took a few seconds for her to realize what was happening, but then she saw that the enemy ships were blasting their thrusters. They were changing their course, moving toward Eaton's approaching vessels.

She couldn't help but be impressed with the courage of the Alliance spacers. They had just watched the newly arrived ships obliterate one of their vessels, but they weren't running. They were moving forward to engage. *Whatever they're doing, they aren't firing at* Dauntless *anymore.*

That still left one question unanswered though…had Eaton arrived in time to save Barron and his crew? Or was it too late already?

*   *   *

"All forces forward. Attack…fight until the enemy is destroyed."

Lille stood quietly, watching the reports and scans on the row of displays. Calavius was acting like a typical Palatian officer, ready to throw everything into the battle, fearing the brand of cowardice far more than defeat itself. But Lille's attention was on the Confederation ships that had just arrived. They had fallen on the vessels attacking *Dauntless*, the ones that had come so close to ridding him of that troublesome ship, and they had destroyed them all.

He hadn't expected substantial reinforcement from the Confeds, not so soon. It was clear these ships were new, just out of the shipyards. They were heavier, stronger than anything he'd seen the enemy deploy. But his contacts had suggested the Confederation was months away from deploying any new battleships.

He looked over toward the screen displaying the fighting around the fortress. Calavius's fleet had pushed Vennius's survivors back steadily, and now his light forces were enveloping the enemy. Total victory was within reach…but Lille realized that could be a short-lived win. Very short.

Calavius's fighters had been roughly handled, and the survivors were low on fuel. And the Confederation ships had just launched their squadrons, no less than ninety fighters each. That was two hundred seventy ships total, almost one hundred of them armed as bombers. They were moving toward Calavius's flank even now, followed closely by their awesome mother ships.

Lille shook his head. He wasn't an admiral…he didn't know whether Calavius's ships could finish off Vennius's fleet *and* defeat the new arrivals. He suspected it would be close, and he'd learned not to underestimate the Confederation navy.

"Calavius…" He'd waited until the Imperator had stopped snapping out orders.

"What is it?" He could hear the tension in Calavius's voice. *Good, at least he sees the threat.*

"I believe you should order a retreat. Now."

"What?" the Imperator roared. "On the brink of total victory, you would have me turn and flee?"

"These Confederation ships are dangerous. They're fresh… and they're new ships, stronger and heavier than any of yours. If you remain committed, they will get between us and our exit transwarp point. You will be irrevocably committed to fight to the end. Your damaged ships will face these fresh arrivals."

"Alliance warriors do not fear such things."

"No, certainly not. I speak not to fear, but rather to the tactical brilliance of the man who made himself Imperator." Lille sometimes wondered how he said the things he did without wretching.

"If you retire, you will remain Imperator, and you will still have a fleet. It will be a setback. But you will still possess Palatia, and the battle to secure your position will continue." He paused. "If you commit everything here, and the Confederation ships cut you off…the loss of most of your fleet will doom your cause. Even if you were to escape with a small handful of ships, you would not have the strength to continue the fight. I am not asking you to back down…but to fight with skill and wisdom as well as courage. Remaining here is a bad gamble, one with less chance of success than a more prolonged battle. My people have fought the Confeds for three years now. I urge you…do not underestimate these new ships."

Lille stood where he was, looking up at Calavius. He was usually sure what his creatures would do, and his persuasive abilities had a strong record of success. But here was a struggle between the mindless bravery so revered by the Palatians, and Calavius's ego, his burning lust to be acknowledged as Imperator by all his people. Lille honestly didn't know what was about to happen, and that made him very uncomfortable.

Calavius didn't respond, not right away. The Palatian leader stared at the displays, his eyes fixed on the approaching Confederation forces. Lille just waited. Nothing else he said would help now, and provoking an angry response wasn't likely to help. He need Calavius to come to his own conclusion, to realize all he had just been told was true.

"Very well, Ricard," the Alliance ruler said grimly. "We will withdraw. We will reorganize and rally more of the fleet. Then we will destroy Vennius…and his Confederation allies."

Lille felt a wave of relief. He knew this would lead to a protracted civil war, but that served his purposes, at least to a point. If the Alliance front absorbed the Confederation's newly-constructed warships, that would help the Union war effort. Not, perhaps, as much as a full-scale invasion of Confederation space, but maybe enough. The Union had its own new construction, and while its productivity didn't match the Confederation's, neither did it have a second front to divert its reinforcements.

"Commander Balventius…the fleet will disengage and move back toward the transwarp point. At once."

"Your Supremacy…we have the traitors. We can destroy them."

"You have your orders, Commander. I trust that is suf-

ficient." Calavius's tone was imperious, but Lille could hear
something else the Imperator was trying to hide. Anger, crushing disappointment. But he was relieved to see that Calavius
retained enough judgment to make the right call.

"Calavius?" Lille's eyes were on the small oval that represented *Dauntless*. The ship was moving on a fixed vector, with
no detectable power output. But Lille wasn't willing to make any
assumptions...not with *that* ship.

"Yes, Ricard. What do you want now?"

He'd known of Villieneuve's planned assassination of Barron. Indeed, if he hadn't been in the Alliance, he almost certainly would have been tasked with the assignment. He hadn't
been aware if the attempt had succeeded, but he'd heard Barron's name on the comm chatter during the battle. And that
was enough to convince him *Dauntless*'s captain had survived
whatever plot Villieneuve's assassin had conceived. Retreating
was the right move for the fleet...but if it was possible to do
away with Barron and his accursed ship once and for all, he had
to take it.

"I want to redirect the Ram."

"What? Are you mad? If we withdraw, the Ram is our last
chance to kill Vennius."

Lille looked up at Calavius. "We cannot kill Vennius, not
without the battle continuing. With no ability to target and
destroy his shuttles, there is nothing to prevent him from aban-
doning the fortress. He will have time to get off the station,
perhaps even to evacuate most of his people. You know this
is true. Destroying Sentinel-2 itself is no doubt a useful objec-
tive...but I have one far more important."

"That is?"

"Send the Ram after *Dauntless*. It appears her engines are
dead, so she will not be able to evade. None of the other ships
are near enough to intervene. The Ram's current course is close
enough to modify with maximum thrust...we can target *Dauntless*, and destroy her before the rest of the fleet can stop it."

Calavius sat still, silent. He wore a foul grimace on his face,
and he shook his head.

"I ask you, Calavius, with all respect. For all I have done, for the funding and assistance I have provided...as your ally, your friend, I request this one thing." His statement was carefully crafted, intended to draw upon the Palatian sense of obligation, of honor.

"Very well, Ricard. If you are so fearful of this Confederation vessel, you may use the Ram to destroy it."

"Thank you, Calavius." Lille bowed slightly. "I am grateful for your wisdom."

And if we can't achieve total victory today, the destruction of Dauntless *and its troublesome captain will be a win all on its own.*

Chapter Forty-Two

Lafarge watched on the display as the attacking Alliance ships pulled back. Eaton's ships had pushed forward, accelerating at full thrust toward the flank of the fleet attacking Vennius's forces and the base...and the enemy had blinked. She knew enough about the Alliance to realize it had not been fear nor a failure of morale at work. She had only the most basic idea of what was happening in the Alliance as a whole, but she suspected the overall advantage lay with those possessing Palatia. Risking everything on a single battle seemed like a bad idea, especially when they could likely rally more forces and return in greater strength.

She was somewhat relieved that the enemy ships attacking *Dauntless* had been destroyed, but she was still worried. Barron's ship was clearly crippled, with no thrust, no appreciable power generation, no communications. She told herself he was still alive, but she knew there had to be massive casualties. She'd tried to reach *Dauntless* a dozen times, and Eaton had done the same, but there hadn't been any response.

Her eyes caught something, a small dot on the scanner. Her

fingers moved across her workstation, feeding power into the scanner, directing the AI to enhance the raw data coming in.

It was a ship, but not a battleship. Mass suggested a frigate. She couldn't get much else, not at this range, but there was one other bit of data that was clear. It was accelerating at full...and it was on a course directly toward *Dauntless*.

She felt a tightness in her gut. Why would the enemy leave behind one ship to attack *Dauntless*? She knew there was danger. With *Dauntless* blind and without power, even a frigate could cause catastrophic damage and destroy the ship given enough time. But it didn't make sense. Why *Dauntless* and not any of Vennius's ships? And why just one attacking frigate? *Dauntless* was off on its own, that was true. Vennius's vessels were distant, and Eaton's ships were moving at high velocity on a vector almost directly away. Even *Dauntless*'s fighters were at extreme range. But still, if the Alliance usurpers felt it was worth a suicide attack to destroy *Dauntless*, why hadn't they sent more than one frigate? It would take the single escort a considerable time to destroy Barron's ship completely, and before then, Eaton's ships might manage to reverse course and intervene.

Her eyes were fixed on the small dot as her scanners steadily gleaned more information. The vessel was accelerating at almost 10g, and there was no doubt it was heading right at *Dauntless*. "Vig, I want full thrust. We're heading back to *Dauntless*'s position."

"Yes, Andi." Merrick's voice was tentative, but he didn't offer any argument. Lafarge knew her friend was as aware as she was that *Pegasus* was no match for a frigate. But she couldn't just sit there and watch it happen.

She looked back at the screen as she felt the engines kick in. The dot had moved a considerable distance. *That thing has an insane velocity. That doesn't make sense. They'll never slow down enough to engage* Dauntless. *They'll get at best a passing shot or two before they zip by. And it will take hours to decelerate and come back around.*

She stared at the display, her eyes darting back and forth between *Dauntless* and the enemy ship heading for her. *Straight for her...*

Suddenly, a cold feeling cut through her. *They're not going to attack...*

"Vig, get me on the long-range comm now, maximum power, wide broadcast." Her voice full of urgency.

"Yes, Andi..." Merrick seemed confused, but he did as she asked. "On your headset..."

"Attention all vessels. Attention all vessels. There is an enemy frigate moving toward CFS *Dauntless*. I believe it intends to ram. *Dauntless* is completely disabled and without communications. It is possible they have no scanners either, so they may not even be aware of the threat. Any ships within range to intervene, please do so. That enemy ship must be destroyed."

Lafarge sat, waiting while her message moved out at light-speed, and any responses came back.

"Captain Lafarge, this is Commodore Eaton. My vessels are at full thrust, altering our vectors to respond...but out velocity is too great. We won't be in range before that thing gets to *Dauntless*."

Lafarge could hear the frustration in Eaton's voice. She knew the officer would do everything possible, but none of it would make a difference. Physics was a cruel master, and Eaton's ships were a slave to their current courses and velocities.

We're not going to make it either...not that we could do anything anyway. She almost ordered Merrick to cut the engines, but she held the command back. She knew she couldn't achieve anything, but it would be worse to just sit there, not even making the futile effort.

"I've ordered all my closest ships to respond, Captain Lafarge...but I'm afraid they will arrive even later than Commodore Eaton's." It was a male voice, gruff, an older man she'd have guessed. Commander Vennius? Who else could it be? The fact that the officer hadn't identified himself suggested that he, too, was upset and distracted by *Dauntless*'s plight.

She stared at the display. There had to be some way. She couldn't just sit there and watch *Dauntless* destroyed...watch Barron die.

Assuming he's still alive...

He is.

She knew the danger, the chance that everyone on *Dauntless* was dead. But she didn't believe it. Somehow, she knew he was alive. And now she was going to see him die, along with everyone else on *Dauntless*.

*   *   *

Stockton sat in his ship. The thoughts in his head had been a war between satisfaction at finally running down and killing his prey…and the realization that no amount of vengeance would bring Vagabond and Talon back. Then he heard Lafarge's broadcast.

Dauntless was in peril. Captain Barron, Commander Travis. Stara…

He looked down at his scanners, and he knew in a minute. No one was close enough to respond. Not Vennius's forces, not Eaton's ships, not even the squadrons.

No one but him.

His mad chase had taken him almost directly back toward *Dauntless*. His gut told him he could intercept the enemy ship before it hit its target. It would take full thrust, and a precise course adjustment, but he could do it.

He ran the calculations, confirming what he already knew. Yes, it could work.

He took a deep breath. A fighter against a frigate. It was a difficult matchup. No, not difficult. Damned near impossible. But it was the only way to save *Dauntless*.

He flipped on his comm. "This is Raptor. I can intercept."

He ran the course calculations a second time, and he had the AI double check as well. There was no room for error. He didn't have the time or the fuel for mistakes.

"Raptor, you can't take on a frigate alone." It was Jamison.

"There's no other way, Thunder." A pause. "I'll figure something." He felt a moment of uncertainty, a taste of the fear that had plagued him in recent weeks. But he slammed down on it hard. *I will do whatever has to be done.*

"Raptor, even if you can catch that ship...you'll burn all your fuel, and you'll be blasting into space at an insane velocity."

"There's no other way, Thunder." He blasted his thrusters, feeling the force slam into him an instant later. "There's no choice."

*   *   *

"Fritzie?"

"I'm here, Captain." The sound was poor on the portable comm units, but it was a hell of a lot better than sending runners back and forth on a ship four kilometers long, especially in zero gravity.

Barron looked around the bridge as he spoke, at the smoke and wreckage...and Lieutenant Darrow's dead body, or at least the parts of it sticking out from the immense girder than had crushed him. *That would have been Atara.*

"Fritzie...any chance at getting the scanners back online?"

His ship was in critical condition, but one thing had changed. The pounding had stopped. It had been twenty minutes since the last laser blast had hit *Dauntless*. And this was the sixth time in that period he'd asked Fritz about the scanners.

"Captain, it's taking all we've got to keep life support going. Comm, scanners...it's all part of the same problem. We've got massive power transmission breaks all over the ship. The good news is, given some time, it's relatively easy to fix most of it. The bad news is, the only way to do it is one severed line at a time."

"I know, Fritzie, but we're totally blind. We need to see what's going on. Without scanners or communications, we're totally cut off."

"The enemy stopped shooting at us, sir. That's what's going on. I have no idea what caused that, but it's good, whatever it is. Because if those ships had kept up the pounding, we'd all be dead by now."

"I know, Fritzie...but sitting here not knowing what's happening..." He paused. "I'm grateful for whatever reprieve we got, but we were in the middle of a battle, one that wasn't going very well."

"Captain...even if I get you scanners, and I'm not saying I can, what difference would it make? We've got no engines, no weapons...and if one more thing goes wrong down here, we're going to have no life support either. We're down to battery power, and when that's gone we'll have none at all. So, my priority has to be getting one of the reactors at least partially operational."

"You're right, Fritzie," Barron said softly. "The reactor is the priority." He paused. "But try to get me some scanners too."

*   *   *

Stockton watched as the Alliance frigate grew larger on his screen. He couldn't have caught the thing from behind, but he was coming in at an angle, and his calculations had been true. He'd only have a few shots before he zipped by, and he had to make them count. Part of him understood the hopelessness of his mission...but he would never give up.

He glanced down at the screen, tapping at his controls. He was trying to find the best place to target his lasers...and then he realized his course was no longer true. He was going to go by before the frigate got there.

He didn't understand. He'd checked and rechecked the calculations. Unless the enemy had changed its thrust.

Yes. The frigate had cut its engines completely. *But why?*

He looked at the full scan. Not only were the engines shut down...there were no energy readings at all.

He rescanned. The same result. The frigate's reactor was on extremely low output...or it was shut down completely.

Then, suddenly, he understood. With the reactors down, there was no way for incoming fire to destroy the vessel. There would be no core breaches, no catastrophic releases of hot reaction mass. The only way to destroy the thing would be to blast it apart, piece by piece.

That would take a thousand hits from his fighter's small

lasers. Ten thousand.

Shit!

Stockton adjusted his course, cutting back slightly on his thrust and angling the engines to compensate for the enemy's engine shutdown. He would follow through, take his best shot...but he knew now it was totally hopeless. There was no way his lasers could obliterate the entire frigate, and anything less would still leave a two hundred-thousand-ton mass slamming into *Dauntless*.

Stockton remembered enough of his physics to have an idea of the kinetic energy that would be released on impact... and to realize it was many times what it would take to vaporize *Dauntless*.

*   *   *

"Captain, I think I can get you some partial scans. I've only got battery power to work with, so you won't get any long-range stuff, and I can't hold it for long. But maybe you can get a quick sense of what's going on out there."

Barron couldn't help but smile briefly, even amid the carnage and destruction. Fritz had practically lectured him about the scanners being a low priority...and then she'd managed to get them working anyway. He wondered how much having Travis down there, giving Fritzie a taste of the same merciless intensity the engineer used to drive her own people, had to do with it.

"You're a wizard, Fritzie."

"It's not much, sir...and I'll have to put it on your workstation screen. We can't waste power on the main display. I'm stretching it to the limit even now, just to get these scans."

"Understood, Fritzie. I just want to get a look."

"Okay, Captain...should be coming on any second."

Barron looked down at the small screen as it lit up, and fuzzy images started to appear. It took about twenty seconds for the display to stabilize, and then it was clear.

The enemy battleships were gone. There was nothing else within the shortened range of the makeshift scans...except...

Barron looked for a few seconds, an instant's confusion giving way to cold understanding.

"Fritzie, I need the engines!"

"The engines? That's impossible, Cap…"

"We need to change our course. Now!"

"Captain…"

"Fritzie…there's an enemy ship coming right at us. If we don't get our vector changed now, it looks like they're going to ram."

"How long?" the engineer snapped back, instantly understanding the gravity of the situation. "There's no chance with the engines. But maybe we can blow out a few compartments… enough to give us a push."

Barron looked back at the screen, his eyes zeroing in on the velocity of the enemy vessel…and in an instant, he knew they were dead.

"Eighty seconds, Fritzie…maybe ninety."

"There's no way…we need to get charges to the outer hull… the lifts are down, the ship's cars are down…"

"Do what you can, Fritzie," Barron said, his voice making it clear he knew there was nothing his engineer could do, not quickly enough.

Then his eyes caught the second symbol, a tiny dot. A fighter…and it was heading right toward the Alliance ship. There was a tiny ID number next to it, and some words. He couldn't read them on the small screen.

He reached out, moved his fingers on the screen, zooming in. Blue One. Raptor.

He'd been worried about Stockton, as a member of his crew, as a friend. And now, the troubled pilot was the only one in range. But even if the old Raptor was back…what could one fighter do?

*　　　　　*　　　　　*

"Raptor, with the reactor down, you don't have any chance at all, not even that million to one shot. You might as well decelerate as much as you can before your fuel supply is exhausted."

Stockton let a small smile slip onto his face as he listened to Jamison. *You're a true friend, Kyle…I hope I've appreciated that the way I should have.*

"Thunder, I'm still going in."

"A few laser blasts aren't going to do anything. With the reactor down, there's just no way to vaporize that thing."

"I don't need to vaporize it, Thunder." Stockton's voice was cool, calm…almost as though the two were sitting over beers in the wardroom. "I need to change its vector. Just a little." *A miniscule fraction of one degree…and the farther out I do it, the less of a change I need.*

"Your lasers don't have any appreciable impa…" Jamison's voice went silent for a few seconds. "Jake, no."

"I'm moving along here, Kyle…pretty close to one percent of lightspeed. My fighter isn't that big, but—well, calculations were never my strong suit, but I'm betting it's enough." That was a lie. Stockton was a bit of a math whiz, something no one on *Dauntless* knew. If he hadn't been such a natural in the cockpit, he might have ended up crunching numbers at some science institute. *Where no one would be shooting at me…note to self, if you ever get a chance to talk to the young Jake…*

"I don't need to take the thing out," he continued, "just nudge it a little. With the reactor down, they won't be able to readjust. Not in time."

"Jake…"

"Don't worry, old buddy. I'm not suicidal, at least not completely. I'll eject at the last minute. If I time it right, the push from the release mechanism should shove me clear of the frigate." *And, if I miscalculate…well, I'll get a close up idea of the energy released hitting something at a hundredth of the speed of light.*

More like one two-hundredth, actually. He wouldn't be hitting the frigate dead on…the ship's vector was partially in line with his fighter's, and that would reduce the effective relative impact velocity.

Still enough to turn you back into the atoms you're made of, though… so don't miscalculate.

"You're too far out and moving too fast. You'll run out of life support before anybody can get to you."

"One problem at a time, buddy. First things first. And number one on the list is saving *Dauntless*." He moved his hand over the comm unit, but he hesitated. "And, Jake...in case something goes wrong, I just wanted to say, thanks...for everything. I know I'm a pain in the ass sometimes." He shut down the unit. It was selfish, he knew, to cut off Jamison, but he had to focus...and his best friend's frantic pleas, or heartfelt goodbyes, weren't going to help with that. Too many lives depended on this. Including Stara's.

He adjusted his vector slightly, checking and rechecking. He was dead on. He'd hit the ship just right...and if he'd figured everything perfectly, the frigate would miss *Dauntless* and go flying off into deep space. It wouldn't miss by much...but he'd settle for ten meters right now.

He looked straight ahead, his fingers moving across the dashboard, flipping a series of controls, activating the escape pod. He tried not to think past bringing his ship in and pulling the eject lever. Worrying about life support, rescue, if the ejection would push him far enough to escape the heat generated when his fighter slammed home...none of it seemed worthwhile. He'd rediscovered his instincts, and he would go with them. He'd either live or he wouldn't, but he had to do this, and that was all that mattered now.

He counted down, watching the looming mass of the frigate grow on his scanners. He checked everything one last time... and then he pulled the escape lever.

Chapter Forty-Three

Barron watched on the tiny screen as Stockton's fighter smashed into the Alliance frigate. There was a strange symmetry to it all. Stockton had done to the Alliance ship what it had intended to do to *Dauntless*. Might still do to *Dauntless*. Barron was far from sure Stockton's reckless bravery would succeed.

He was relieved to see that the pilot had ejected, and again when it became clear that Stockton's pod had cleared the frigate and the roiling energy of his ship's impact.

The fighter wasn't massive enough to completely destroy the frigate, but all around where it impacted, the vessel's hull melted and twisted. The partially operable scanners proved inadequate to the job of measuring the energy released, but he was sure of one thing. Whatever crew had volunteered for this mission—or been press-ganged into it—they were dead now. There was still a massive chunk of metal streaming through space, but nothing human could have endured the impact of Stockton's ship.

Barron watched the remnants of the Alliance vessel ripping toward *Dauntless*. He could see almost at once that Stockton had managed to alter the frigate's vector...but the impact had also split the ship into several pieces. Barron didn't have the scanning power or the AI, and all he could do was guess if one of those chunks was still on a course to hit Dauntless. Guess, and then wait.

He watched, counting down in his head, as several large pieces streamed past, missing his ship by several kilometers. His eyes were fixed on the last chunk, the smallest—though one still massive enough to cause catastrophic damage. For a few seconds, his gut tightened, and he thought it might clip *Dauntless*'s bow, but it just missed, passing perhaps one hundred meters away.

He let out a long exhale, turning toward the bridge crew, most of whom had no line of sight to the small screen. "It missed us. He did it!" But even as the words escaped his lips, he looked back to the screen. There was only one symbol left…Stockton's escape pod, transmitting its distress beacon. It appeared to be intact…but it was also traveling at the last intrinsic velocity of the pilot's now-disintegrated fighter. That meant Stockton was moving away from every ship in the system…at 0.01c.

Barron turned, moved to pick up the portable comm unit. But he stopped. There was no way *Dauntless* could launch a rescue boat, not now. The fighter bays were badly damaged, of course, but he might have risked that. But without power, there was no way to get a ship into the launch track, no way even to open the outer doors.

Jake Stockton had saved *Dauntless*. He'd saved Barron and every member of the crew. But there was no way they could rescue him, nothing they could do but sit and watch him drift off into the depths of space. Watch him die.

Barron looked down at his headset connected to the ship's dead comm system. He couldn't even contact the pilot, couldn't thank him.

Couldn't say goodbye. All he could do was watch his friend disappear into the endless darkness.

*   *   *

"I've dispatched two escorts with instructions to proceed at full thrust. They are the only light ships undamaged in the battle…but I fear they will not reach your pilot in time." There was genuine sorrow in Vennius's voice. Lafarge was surprised as she listened to the broadcast, but then she realized she shouldn't be. Alliance warriors respected courage above all things…and what Jake Stockton had just done was as pure a display of raw bravery as she'd ever seen.

She was still shaking, still trying to convince herself that *Dauntless* had truly been saved. She couldn't be sure who was and was not alive inside the battered hull, but she felt certain Barron was okay. She couldn't explain why, but she didn't doubt her instinct.

She'd been listening to the back and forth comm chatter. Everyone in the system was trying to get to Stockton, to save the heroic pilot. But none of them could do it. All their efforts would be in vain.

It's a good thing we blasted this way at full thrust…

"Vig, set a course to go after Stockton. We're closest, and our velocity is already close to half his."

"Yes, Andi…I've got it ready now."

She just smiled. "Then, let's go." She flipped on her comm unit. "Attention all vessels, this the Free Trader *Pegasus*. We are close to Commander Stockton, and already traveling at 0.005c. We are moving to recover him, and expect to arrive in…" She glanced over at Merrick as he mouthed some words to her. "… one hundred seventeen minutes." She didn't know how much life support a fighter's escape pod carried, but she was pretty sure it was more than two hours. So, if nothing else went wrong, Commander Stockton wouldn't pay with his life for his heroics…and that seemed right to her. On many levels, not the least of which was, she owed him big. He had saved *Dauntless*… and that meant he had saved Tyler. Whatever else happened, she was going to give the wild pilot a big wet kiss…and then she'd drink him under the table, her treat.

"All right, Vig…let's go get him."

*   *   *

Barron gazed at the screen in astonishment, seeing the three ships but not quite believing it, even as he listened to the voice on the comm Fritz had just restored.

"Sara, what in the Eleven Hells are you doing out here? Not that I'm not glad to see you...or ungrateful that you saved our lives. But I'm shocked." Barron was leaning back in his chair. Fritzie had gotten reactor B started again...gingerly, she'd assured him. She'd used the resulting power to get a few things working, including the lifts, and the comm. The bridge was still a wreck, but some work had been done, including—*thank God*—the removal of Darrow's body. Barron mourned the officer's loss, as he did all those who'd been killed in the battle, but he'd been looking back at the dead man's still-open eyes for hours. Darrow deserved better, a more dignified resting place.

"Admiral Striker sent me. He figured you might need some help."

"He figured right. You got here just in time. I had no idea why the enemy ships stopped firing at us. I'd have never guessed." He paused. "But where did your ships come from? I've never even seen anything like those monsters."

"They're new...fresh out of the shipyard. Considering the urgency of the situation, Admiral Striker waived the normal testing and shakedown cruises. We've had to chase down a number of malfunctions and minor problems, but all things considered, the ships are in great shape."

"But I thought it would be four or five months at least before any new battleships were ready."

"Well, as it turns out, the admiral can be pretty persuasive when he's motivating civilians as well as military personnel. It seems like a shipyard owner on Thralia was trying to impress someone by driving his workers a bit harder than most of the other Iron Belt moguls. And it worked. Admiral Striker went there to give the man a commendation...and he offered him something—I have no idea what—if he could speed things up further. And so, here we are."

"That's amazing."

"I'm betting those Thralian workers would have a different opinion, but yes, it turned out to be vital. If the admiral hadn't dispatched us when he did, not only would *Dauntless* have been destroyed, Commander Vennius would have been defeated too."

"Well, once again, let me assure you how welcome you are." He paused. "But I should be speaking more formally to a superior officer. Congratulations on the promotion, *Commodore* Eaton."

She laughed softly. "No, sir...it is I who should be addressing the superior. I'm *acting* commodore. My orders were to bring these three ships after you...and to place them and myself under your command. I must say, it wasn't easy finding you. either. We knew you'd left Archellia, but we had no idea you'd be all the way out here, in the middle of the Alliance. At least I bring good news as well as reinforcements. I have your star, Commodore Barron, as well as the orders for your promotion... sir."

Barron couldn't believe what he was hearing. He tried to respond, but no words came.

"Your orders are to remain here, to command the entire flotilla and to operate as you see fit to support any Alliance faction opposing the Union or Union control."

"Very well," he said softly. It didn't seem adequate, but it was all he had. "Again, Sara, my thanks...for everything."

"You're welcome, sir. It will be a pleasure to serve with you again." A few seconds later: "Commodore, there's one other thing. If you would like to transfer your flag to *Repulse*...she's quite an upgrade from anything else in the fleet, except of course her two sisters here. She'd make a fine flagship."

Barron looked around at *Dauntless*'s shattered bridge, the acid sting of smoke in his eyes, the piles of burned out circuitry still lying on the deck. She'd been old when he'd stepped aboard to take command, and he'd taken her to hell and back more than once. *Repulse* was the obvious choice for flagship.

For anyone else.

"Thank you, Sara, but I think I'll decline. I'm honored to

have *Repulse* and her sister ships here, but I don't think *Dauntless* and I are through with each other. Not yet."

*   *   *

"I want to thank you again. For saving my life. And now for saving Jake as well. He's a handful sometimes, a real pain in the ass…but he's like a younger brother to me, and he did save *Dauntless*. I've never been happier when someone disobeyed my orders."

Andi Lafarge looked back at Barron. She was overcome with relief that he had survived, but she only intended to let him see a little slice of that. He was a vulnerability for her, and if she had to have a weakness, she was damned sure going to stay in control of it herself.

"I don't take *orders* from you, Captain…Commodore… whatever. I trust you'll remember that the next time you have a *request* for me to do something." She smiled. She wanted to jump into his arms, but she didn't. He would ask her to stay… or she'd turn around right now and blast off in *Pegasus*.

"Well then, I'm glad you ignored my request." He returned her smile. "You need to go back, Andi, before the next attack comes…"

She felt disappointment building up. She'd never show him, but…

"…but if I haven't used up my allotment of requests, I have one more. Stay a little while? Just for a few days?"

"Well, since I did blow off your last *request*, I guess I could give you this one." She knew Barron would try to send her back before the next fight. She didn't know what she would do then. She was sure of only two things.

One, she was beyond relieved to see him alive, well… and likely energetic enough for her to make good use of her extended time here.

And two, that whatever she did, however much Barron whispered in her ear in the dark, or put on his commodore's star and belted out commands…*she* would decide whether she would stay or go. Andromeda Lafarge didn't take orders. From anyone.

Epilogue

"Thank you for landing my fighters, Commander. My damage control teams should have our bays operational in two days." Barron walked next to Vennius, across Sentinel-2's cavernous launch bay two.

"Of course, Commodore. We are allies now, are we not?" Barron could hear a faint discomfort in his host's voice.

"Now that Captain Eaton has arrived with reinforcements, perhaps you should send out more of your light craft. Your enemies have been repulsed three times…that may open the door for you to persuade others to your side. Perhaps we should even consider operations outside this system…once our ships are repaired."

"I agree with your logic, Commodore. I will send out the light ships…to the border stations and other bases farthest from Calavius's reach. I know several of the commanders there. It is likely we will be able to secure the allegiance of at least some of them." He paused for a few seconds. "Still, there is little doubt that Calavius controls more forces than we, even if we are successful in rallying more. This war—and that's what it is, a civil war—will be a terrible conflict, one where we have no room for error. Calavius can recover from defeats like those he suffered here, yet one disaster would be enough to destroy our cause. We must always remember, our enemy controls most of the communications, the media. We will fight many traitors in this conflict…but we will also battle legions of warriors guilty of no more grievous a crime than believing what they were told. We must have the victory, at all costs. But killing such warriors will bring me no joy, no sense of honor."

Barron just nodded. He'd become somewhat of a student on the Alliance in the three years since he'd battled *Invictus*, but Vennius continued to surprise him. The Commander had a long service record, and by all accounts, he had been a ferocious warrior when he was younger. Barron didn't doubt his courage or skill now, but he sensed far more wisdom in the old man than he'd expected...and sadness as well.

"Commander..."

"Yes, Commodore Barron?"

"I want to ask you something...beyond our tactical and strategic discussions."

"What would you know, Commodore?"

"You knew Commander Rigellus, didn't you?"

Vennius paused, a strange look coming over his face. He looked as though he wasn't sure how to answer, what he wanted to say.

"I did, Commodore." His voice was harder-edged than it had been. "She was the daughter of my oldest friend, and after he was killed, I looked after her...almost as one of my own children."

Barron could hear the pain in Vennius's words, and now he understood just what it was costing the commander to work so closely with him.

"I offer my condolences, sir. I didn't know Commander Rigellus, and I was able to speak with her only once, for a brief time... at the end of our struggle. She struck me as an extraordinary woman, and a warrior of great courage and honor. I regret that I was compelled to meet her as an enemy."

"I hated you, Commodore, for a long time. Some part of me will always nurse anger toward you. But I have met you now, and you have come to my aid. You and your warriors have shed blood alongside mine. I owe you a debt." He looked right at Barron. "Your battle with *Invictus* was not of your making, and honor does not allow me to fault you for defending your worlds.

It is a comfort to me, such that it is, that Katrine faced a worthy opponent, that her last battle was against an honorable warrior. It is, perhaps, not much for one mourning as a father...but to my people, it is something."

The two men stood for a few moments, each silent, thoughtful. Finally, Barron said, "I would ask one more thing of you, Commander."

"Yes, Commodore Barron?"

"Is it possible for us to go somewhere, to sit quietly and talk? If you're willing, I would have you tell me more about Commander Rigellus, for I feel certain that if fate hadn't conspired to make us meet as enemies, I would have called her a friend."

Vennius turned and looked back at Barron, silent for a moment. Then he said, "Yes, Commodore, I would like that. Let us go and share a meal...and I will tell you of the woman you faced in battle at Santis."

                    *   *   *

Stockton walked down the corridor, Andi Lafarge at his side. "I don't know how I can thank you, Andi...but I'll try once more." He stopped and turned toward her. "I won't forget what you did. I'll probably die out there one day...but please, not gasping for air in an escape pod. What kind of an end would that be to the story of Raptor Stockton?"

Lafarge looked back at the pilot and laughed. "Well, we certainly couldn't let that happen, could we?"

Stockton shook his head. It felt a little strange to be back, almost like he'd been gone for months instead of hours...and, in a way, he realized he had been. He'd beaten the fear that had threatened to destroy him, but he knew he wasn't the same as he'd been, not entirely. That Raptor had been young, a cocky kid under the veteran's skill and veneer. The warrior, the ace pilot was back...but he wasn't young anymore. There were some things that could not be regained once lost, and that was one of them. He hoped he would add wisdom to his traits, that the change would be a good one...but he still missed what was gone.

"Jake!" Stara Sinclair turned the corner and raced down the hall. She ran up and threw her arms around him. He returned the hug warmly.

"Stara…I'm so sorry. I was…"

"None of that matters," she said softly. "You came back to me…and that's all I care about."

Lafarge smiled. "Well, I suspect the two of you don't need me hanging around…"

"Thanks again, Andi." Stockton reached out his hand.

"My pleasure, Jake." She took his hand and they shook. "I gave you a ride, but now that you're here, how you use your time is up to you." She looked at Sinclair and nodded. Then she started off down the corridor.

"Don't forget," Stockton said as she left. "Wardroom three, twenty hundred hours. You bring your best bottles, and I'll bring mine."

"Oh, don't you worry, Lieutenant. I'll be there. I'm dying to see if you fighter pilots can hold your liquor…or if all those stories are just so much bullshit."

*   *   *

Barron sat at his desk, a small tablet laying off to the side. He'd read Striker's communique—three times—and he couldn't argue with anything it said. But it troubled him nevertheless.

We cannot fight both the Union and the Alliance. It is essential that Commander Vennius's faction is successful. He had no issue with that, no argument to make. It was self-evident. Still, seeing it written out explicitly made him even more aware of the massive weight on his shoulders.

The middle of the communique was unimportant, congratulations on his promotion and assurances that Striker believed in him fully. It was all appropriate, and he appreciated it, but to a certain extent he viewed it as boilerplate.

Then, the final words, the ones that struck at Barron's honor, and his respect for fellow fighters. If *Commander Vennius does not prevail, you must do everything possible to ensure maximum possible losses in the fighting. If we cannot have an ally, if we must face a hostile Alliance, that Alliance must be as weak as possible. Whatever the cost.*

Whatever the cost…Barron had seen the cost of war, the thousands who had died already, several hundred of them under his direct command. He understood what Striker meant, and why the admiral had said what he had. He even agreed with the necessity. But he'd never before led his people with the idea of maximizing casualties, even among his enemies. That was the work of a butcher, not a warrior. It was cold, calculating, gruesome…but he knew he would do it.

He'd always considered himself a warrior, one who tried, at least, to maintain a reasonable code of honor. But he was a patriot too, and he was well aware of the threat the Confederation faced.

If the Confederation needed him to be a butcher, he knew that was what he would be. However much he despised himself for it.

*   *   *

"Tarkus…you have become the hope of our people, the sentinel who guards our honor." The voice was soft, barely audible. The Imperatrix was weak, fading. Vennius had struggled with all his skill and ability to save her, to get her out of the palace and bring her here. But now he knew…the Imperatrix was dying.

"Your words do me too much kindness, Your Supremacy." He was kneeling next to the bed, his face hard, as if carved from stone, even as the pain wracked him inside.

"I am glad you are here, Tarkus, as I prepare to leave this life. I have called you friend for many years. I still remember that young warrior, all enthusiasm and fire. You have done well, my old comrade, yet, like me, you had the misfortune to survive too long…to live to see your nation imperiled by traitors from within. It is a darkness I would rather have been spared."

"And I, Your Supremacy…yet we cannot think in such ways. If the Alliance is imperiled, there is all the more need for us to fight."

"Such will be the burden lain at your feet. Death shall spare me, and there is little I can leave to aid you save my best wishes."

"Your Supremacy…"

"Please Tarkus…I fear yours will be the last words I hear. Let them be those of a friend, not a subordinate. I set aside the scepter, for I no longer have the strength to wield it."

"Yes…Flavia. I have been your friend…always."

"I must ask one last thing of you, Tarkus, though I wish with all my heart I could spare you."

Vennius looked down at the old woman. His eyes displayed his sadness for a friend's passing, but his stomach was knotted, tight with the realization of what she was going to say, of the weight she was about to put on him.

"You must succeed me, Vennius. You must be Imperator."

He screamed to himself inside, every bit of what made him the man he was crying out for escape. But he knew there was none. He could not deny her final request…nor could he abandon his duty. If there was any chance to defeat Calavius, he had to take the scepter…he had to make it a contest between two equals.

"Yes, Flavia…I will accept the scepter. I will succeed you."

She looked up at him, a serenity he'd never seen in her before on her face now, almost like a mask…or perhaps a true face after a mask was removed. She smiled, weakly…then she closed her eyes, and she was gone.

Vennius rose to his feet, standing at attention, paying his own silent homage to the extraordinary woman who had just died. Then he took a deep breath. Once again, duty ruled his life, his actions.

He was Imperator of the Alliance. *The way is the way…*

*   *   *

Egilius had just gotten the word, and he'd announced it to the fleet. Tarkus Vennius was no longer Commander-Maximus…he was now Imperator of the Alliance. He couldn't think of any Palatian he considered more worthy, and yet, the joy at the news was tempered by the specter of war. Egilius feared no conflict, but he'd never imagined leading his warriors against his own people. The Alliance's culture had been shaped by Palatia's earlier servitude, and it was very much an "us versus them" philosophy.

Until now.

He was uncomfortable with the Confederation's involvement as well. He didn't dislike the Confeds. They had fought well, as hard as his own people. But he felt a vague hint of shame at needing an outside ally. He'd be dead now, he knew, without the Confeds. Vennius would be dead as well, the cause utterly lost. He was glad to have the allies his forces needed, but there was a taint to it.

The way is the way…and yet, is it? If we are to survive, if we are to defeat the traitors, the way must change. Even if we win, we will never be the same again.

He looked around the bridge. *Bellator* had been badly damaged in the fighting. If the enemy hadn't withdrawn…

But they had retreated, and the war he so dreaded would go on. Palatian would kill Palatian, and the bloodletting would continue. Until one side completely destroyed the other.

Then, what will be left?

There was noise all around. For as close as *Bellator* came to destruction, she was already under repair, the grit and fire of the last battle already giving way to preparations for the next.

He knew that battle would come, soon. And when it did, he would fight.

Long live the Imperator…

*   *   *

Lille stared through the clear panel along the outer wall of the station, to the blackness of space beyond. The fleet had returned to Palatia, and even now, the worst damaged ships were under repair in the vast orbital spacedocks. His cause was not lost—far from it, in fact. A quick, easy victory had eluded him, but there was little question that Calavius still had greater strength, even with the newly-arrived Confederation ships. The Imperator had raged wildly when the fleet had first retreated, but Lille had managed to calm him down, and to focus his thoughts on his continued strength in the contest.

The new Confederation ships were a concern, of course. Their existence had escaped his notice, the information gathering efforts in the Confederation shipyards apparently falling down on the job and failing to report ships so close to completion. Those operatives weren't his, of course...and that was reason for them to give thanks. His response to such failure would have been swift and decisive.

Still, he couldn't imagine the Confeds had any more ships they could spare, not for half a year, at least. *And they'll have to send some of it to the front, to offset our own new ships.*

He wasn't overly worried about the final outcome. Even if the Alliance's civil war left it weakened, its forces available to invade the Confederation reduced, it would have the desired effect. And in the meantime, even the civil war was drawing in Confederation ships.

What was bothering him was Tyler Barron...and *Dauntless*. His ship had transited before the Ram reached the Confederation battleship, but he'd been optimistic the suicide ship would rid him of his infuriating foe. It had been weeks before he'd gotten word...he had very limited assets in Sentinel-2, and what agents he did have found it difficult to get information out. When the report finally got to him, it had been far from satisfying. Tyler Barron and his ship had both survived. Even the grievous damage *Dauntless* had suffered was proving to be repairable.

Lille shook his head. He knew Villieneuve hadn't had a choice but to assign Barron's assassination to another agent. Lille had been in the Alliance, neck deep in the coup. But the botched job only reaffirmed his belief that if he wanted anything done right, he had to do it himself.

And that was exactly what he was going to do, orders from Villieneuve or not. Tyler Barron had to die...and Ricard Lille